Paradise of Fools
A NOVEL

Jane Rawlinson

Paradise of Fools

'. . . they close their eyes, those gates
by which reminders enter,
And in a Paradise of Fools contented live.'

Richard Dadd, 'Elimination of a Picture'

André Deutsch

The author wishes to acknowledge
with gratitude the award by
the Scottish Arts Council
of a grant towards travel and research

First published 1991 by
André Deutsch Limited
105–106 Great Russell Street, London WC1B 3LJ

British Library Cataloguing in Publication Data
Rawlinson, Jane
  Paradise of fools.
  I. Title
  823. 914 [F]

  ISBN 0–233–98641–3

Printed and bound by
St. Edmundsbury Press, Bury St Edmunds, Suffolk

To
David

Richard Dadd b. 1817, Chatham, Kent;
d. 1886, Broadmoor Hospital, Berkshire.
His best known painting
'The Fairy Feller's Master-Stroke'
hangs in the Tate Gallery.

Chapter One

ODAY, I found trapped in the leaves of a book, which have held it prisoner these past fifty years, the following letter:

Suffolk Street,
Haymarket.

April – 1843.

Dearest Elizabeth,
  Such excitement, can you imagine? Dear Richard is
home again . . .

Can I indeed!
And having once imagined, could I ever forget . . . ?
Forgive, dear Reader, the vagaries of an old lady for whom the sentiments aroused by this short extract echo in the memory with greater clarity than the faded ink of the letter. Nor, I pray you, dismiss my own manuscript as the mere rambling indulgence of senility. Appearances can be deceptive. Perception depends on so much more than the mere play of light and shade upon the retina of the physical eye, especially when that same eye is hampered by cataracts and failing vision. But the inward eye does not lose its powers so readily. It becomes, if anything, sharpened and more tightly focused.

Ah, Memory! If there is anyone responsible for this change in the inward eye which renders the past closer than the present, it is you. What tricks you play with the twin perspectives of time and experience as you wander not within the narrow path of reason and logic nor through the conventional avenues of historical and documentary accuracy, but quite at random

1

through the higgledy-piggledy and unashamedly personal channel of sentiment and feeling.

Not that I am, myself, an overtly sentimental being. You see before you on the occasion of our beloved Queen's Diamond Jubilee, this twenty-second day of June 1897, a lady who, despite sharing a similarity in age with her monarch, is vastly different from her in every other respect. Therefore, I do not find myself on this particular evening fêted by a whole nation, but on the contrary entirely alone, relishing the comfort of my own snug fireside. Beyond the drawn curtains of my parlour lies the thick silence of a Devon summer's night, heavy with the pollen from countless hedgerows and almost over-burdened with stars.

Do not, I beg you, draw from this information the inference that I am without family or friends, for I am blessed with both in abundance. To be alone is not necessarily to be lonely. To enjoy the indulgence of being solitary once in a while is, in my experience, one of the rewards of a long and eventful life.

On such occasions, memories proliferate like those same stars in the heavens above. Whole constellations appear, one upon the other to infinity. It is pleasant then to allow oneself the pleasure of turning perhaps one image, perhaps whole clusters of images, over and over like stones in the palm of one's hand; to polish them one against the other in the fine grist of imagination and recollection until they sparkle in the memory, and reveal, maybe, a certain truth at last.

Whatever that truth may be, it is the result of neither speculation nor conjecture. It may come with all the cataclysmic splendour of a shooting star which burns a groove across the heavens, or gleam more tremulously like a narrow shaft of sunlight through the aperture of a key-hole. It may illuminate past mysteries or reveal the significant in the insignificant, picking out some minute detail which has been hitherto overlooked. It may tell us more about ourselves than the subject or object of our scrutiny.

Unlike the Queen, who today celebrates sixty glorious years upon the throne of our beloved country, I cannot lay claim to any memories of particular significance to the common weal. Empires do not rise or fall at my command. No burden of State weighs upon my shoulders. My own reminiscences tend towards the personal, and are prompted by mere Chance – such as the discovery of this letter from a once dear friend.

The book which contained this precious note is one of those little 'treasuries', tightly packed with strict rhyming couplets which abound in roses and violets and sunlit woodland glades, circumscribed by the singsong chant of the verse. But though conventional in style and imagery, no such severity attaches to the loosely passionate sentiments expressed therein. Hence its appeal to my then youthful ardour – and there also, the reason it has lain unopened by me this past half-century since the rude awakening of my engagement and subsequent marriage.

The inscription on the inside cover of the book reads: *'To my dear friend, Elizabeth C from Maria Dadd. With affection. Christmas 18—.'* But it was not this brief message which captured my attention so much as the fateful square of yellowing parchment which fluttered on to my lap like the first swallow of Summer, and there determined to make its nest.

The simile is apt. For that harbinger, that first black arrowhead, seems to plummet from unfathomable heights with the warmth of the African sun still burnishing its glossy feathers. Reader, Cupid's dart could have caused no greater tumult in the breast of this beshawled and bespectacled septuagenarian! Over all the chasm of years which separate me from the girl I then was, the words still have the power to move me.

'Richard is home!' The joyous notes ring out like bells resounding in the feeble frame of my chest in ever wilder waves of sound. They echo in my ears in the sudden rush of blood from a quickened pulse. *'Richard is home!'* A new warmth flickers through the thick, grey crust of ash which has long damped it down. Those long forgotten emotions arise and take shape like a Phoenix, glorious in their ultimate triumph.

But who else would share the memories of those days now? Of all that happy crowd, who remains? Even Richard lies in a grave marked only by a numbered stone which I have never seen. My family protest that the journey would be too much for me, and to what end? Merely to disturb the sober regimentation of grass and stones and draw attention to its inhabitant, even in death? And I am too frail to go against their wishes now.

And what of the others? They are all inaccessible to me now. Mary Ann is gone to America with Arthur; Robert, Stephen, Sarah, George and John have all been scythed down by the old reaper Time. Which leaves only myself and Maria. Maria? Ah poor, dear friend, what could you now write or know of all this? What add to the poignant words 'Richard is home!' which ushered in every subsequent tragedy? His. Yours. And mine!

I have, over recent years, since age and infirmity reduced me to a more sedentary habit of life, pondered the matter with increasing urgency. And perhaps the re-discovery of this letter in Maria's handwriting is the sign for which I was waiting. Perhaps it is that little nudge by Chance or Fate which edges us in a certain direction whether we will or no. Reader, for lack of any other suitable candidate for the post of biographer of this same unhappy person, who is also a distant relative by marriage, I venture to put myself forward.

I have recently been angered by reading accounts written in the memoirs of so-called 'friends' which purport to be true reminiscences of Richard, but which amount to little more than libellous attacks upon his character by persons whose professed knowledge reveals only their own profound ignorance; whose insignificant anecdotes pay more tribute to their own superficiality than to the portrayal of one whose depth, knowledge and talent was to theirs as the mighty ocean is to a rain drop.

The closeness between our families, the Carters and the Dadds, is one which can be traced back over several generations, back indeed almost as far as the history of the Royal Chatham Dockyards themselves, with whose fortunes ours were so closely aligned. It was Richard's father Robert who first broke that long-standing association with the sea, by choosing for himself the career of apothecary. He distinguished himself within the town in several other fields besides, notably those of philanthropy, education and mathematics, and turned his back on the old tradition.

Only my family remained true to their roots, as solid and comfortable as those oak trees whose fortunes were the responsibility of my father. He watched over them from their arrival in the shipyards as mighty gnarled trunks to their transformation into vessels which were the pride of our country, and their dizzy departure down the slipway into the cold grey waters of the Medway.

It was amid the thrum and turmoil of this busy industry that we were born, – my two brothers, my sister, and I. And in a house not two hundred yards away, our dear friends the Dadds were launched into the world in apparently unending succession. For whereas my mother was content with producing two boys and two girls, Mrs Dadd attempted to double that number, and forfeited her life in the attempt.

Since our parents were the greatest of friends, we children saw much of one another, especially in those days when the first Mrs Dadd was ailing. Some portion of her numerous offspring was often to be found within our house or seated at our table. Indeed, my mother sought in no small measure to fill the space left in those young people's lives on the demise of their own dear Mama.

The advent of the second Mrs Dadd introduced a new degree of formality into the relationship between our families. My parents could on no account be on such easy terms with a lady not many years senior to their eldest daughter, and Mrs Sophia Dadd, fearing perhaps for her own dignity, held herself somewhat aloof. For my own part, I remember admiring her exceedingly, and on one occasion offending my mother by asking her why she was not as young and beautiful and why she did not dress as gaily as Richard and Maria's new mother.

Reader, I tell you these things merely to establish my credentials in your eyes. If greater recommendation than this intimacy is required, perhaps I should acquaint you with the fact that over the years my own personal commitments have removed me both physically and emotionally from those whom I once held so dear. For I believe it to be of the greatest advantage to the biographer to maintain a strong emotional attachment to his subject while at the same time establishing that certain distance which is conducive to objectivity. I believe that I qualify in both respects. But I must warn you that much that is painful awaits us here: more of Sorrow than of Joy; more of death than life, or death in life, than perhaps one might care to contemplate.

But all that comes later: let us for the moment concentrate only on Joy, – on the letter and on all those emotions of innocent first love and tremulous hope which it aroused in my girlish heart.

First, let us picture the letter writer herself. Richard produced a charming watercolour of that very scene: Maria, seated at the desk in the front parlour of the house in Suffolk Street, Pall Mall East, with a sheet of paper and a vase of flowers in front of her, and a pen clasped tightly in her hand.

Number 15 was a fine Georgian establishment, set in a mellow golden street whose gentility bore marked contrast to the often frenetic activity of the Haymarket against which it stood in such rude conjunction. One obvious advantage of the situation was its proximity to the Royal Academy of Art, which benefited the professions of both father and son; the former, with respect to his gilding business and his test-tube incursions into the technical world of the artist, and the latter, from the proximity to his studies and to the best that the metropolis could offer in the world of art.

Behold then my dearest friend, Maria, delicately chewing on the end of her pen while she decided how to proceed. Though some two days had elapsed since the occasion which she was describing, some trace of excitement lingered yet, betrayed by the slight flush on her cheek and by a certain tremulousness in the hand that guided the nib. Though Maria's hair is now as snowy as my own, she remains in my mind as her brother captured her — in that familiar, impatient gesture as she tossed back her fine, dark ringlets and wrinkled her brow in concentration as she continued.

In fact, Richard has now been home for two whole days, not to mention the time which it took him to travel up from Dover. You must forgive me for not having written immediately. I am well aware that you perhaps more than anyone must have been eagerly anticipating his return . . .

Of course I had to forgive Maria both this delay and that further one engendered by the new, and sometimes wayward Penny Post.

Our happiness amounted almost to delirium. It was such a surprise! He was a good two weeks ahead of schedule in his haste to see us all again . . .

I can now say with all the benefit of hindsight, would that it had been so straightforward! Though we all, family and friends alike, awaited his return with scarcely controllable impatience, we did not expect him for some time yet. It was only later that we discovered that he had eluded his patron's vigilance in Paris and hurried home alone. Simpleton that I was, at the time I even flattered myself that my own self had some small part to play in his early arrival. It was only as the days turned into weeks and his appearance in Chatham was still looked for, that my first breathless hope faded, and I gradually realised my error.

But for now, let only Joy be our concern, let us make the most of it while we may, and return to that happy day in April 1843, when, as Maria wrote, the Dadd family were seated around the breakfast table absorbed in Richard's latest letter, posted in Alexandria, from which his father was reading aloud . . .

' *"Prior to sailing up the Nile, we visited the Pyramids . . ."* ' Robert Dadd senior here paused to adjust his spectacles and to exclaim, 'To think of it! Dear Dickie has seen the Pyramids!' and to clear his throat since his voice had suddenly turned quite gruff with emotion.

'One of the wonders of the world,' piped in his youngest child John, only to be silenced with shushes of impatience by the rest of his brothers and sisters. So intent were they on every word that no one noticed the door open to allow a figure to slip silently into the room.

'Go on, Pa, please,' begged Maria.

Mr Dadd gave a final harrumph and straightened his cravat. ' *"I know not how many Arabs there were, but they made noise enough for eighty; scuffling and quarrelling with each other . . ."* It sounds to me,' he continued, folding the sheets of paper and peering over the top of his spectacles with mild rebuke at each of the excited faces in turn, 'very like the unedifying spectacle which I had the misfortune to witness on the landing this morning between a certain pair of young, I hesitate to use the word, gentlemen . . .'

'Pa,' shrieked Maria, 'we want to know what he says!'

'Very well, my dear.' The patriarch took a sip of coffee and smoothed out the letter, prior to continuing his recital.—

'I at length found myself inside a square shaft of rapid descent slippery enough and dirty enough, with a candle in one hand and an Arab in the other . . .' The voice, which came not from their father but from the opposite side of the room, over by the dresser, took everyone by surprise.

Maria was, as always, the first to react, – on her feet like quicksilver and hurling herself in the direction of the speaker.

'Richard!'

'Steady on!' The young man fended off the attacks from all sides until sufficient calm was restored for him to approach his father's chair, and taking his hand, to shake it heartily.

I must here, dear Reader, lest you become lost in the narrative, take the opportunity to offer a slight digression, and introduce Ellen. Ellen had served as nursemaid, cook, housekeeper, teacher and mother, as occasion demanded, for as long as any of the eight Dadd children could remember. She had in every way imaginable made them her life, having arrived with the first Mrs Dadd as a young country girl of fourteen, and remained at her post long after the fleeting and brilliant reign of the second Mrs Dadd. She thus enjoyed motherhood vicariously, not merely as a contented observer, but also as a participant in all the pleasures and dangers of married life and maternity.

At the time of Richard's return, Ellen, then in her mid-forties, was a handsome, rosy-faced woman, somewhat inclined to plumpness. Her figure was sufficiently well-covered to be pleasantly yielding and her face bore witness to a happy inward glow of good humour which was rarely absent. Long service and devotion had accorded her something of the status of a grandmother, and left her free to receive confidences and to indulge and pet and spoil; – indeed to smother rather than mother those whom she had once nursed and chivvied through all the attendant dangers which beset them from conception to young adulthood.

And now, her missing chick had returned to the nest! She seized on Richard's arrival with all the fussy extravagance of a farmyard hen. Had he not lost weight? Could she not detect a certain pallor beneath the sunburn? For no one, she knew with a quiet serenity, could ever look after him as well as she could herself.

'Dear, oh dear,' she protested as she set an extra place at the table, 'I never thought to see you alive again, Master Richard, indeed I didn't!' Ellen wrestled with the extra cutlery as if it were possessed by all those foreign devils which she so feared.

Richard gently relieved her of the offending articles. 'Why's that, Ellen?'

'Those foreigners, they might have boiled you and eaten you alive.' At the very thought, a cup and saucer rattled alarmingly in her hand.

'The Egyptians,' Richard commented, relieving her now of the precariously poised china, 'were civilised when you and I still lived in caves.' He took the spare chair which had been placed for him to the right of his father, and began ladling sugar into his coffee.

'I have never lived in a cave,' said Ellen, 'and I'm sure I never intend to!' Her bustle quivered with indignation at the thought.

'A figure of speech, Ellen,' said the master of the house irritably, 'the merest figure of speech. Now,' he continued, turning to his son, 'tell us all about your trip.'

'Well,' Richard began, then overcome by the immensity of all he had to relate and not knowing quite where to start, he remained silent.

Fortunately, his youngest brother John was not so inhibited. He launched into an account of the latest school intrigues, – of marbles leagues and an apparently unending string of related themes of which his audience had no conception, – until at last his father was driven to interrupt him with the familiar low growl, like that of a tiger preparing to pounce, which always produced an instantaneous response. The result was a concerted indrawn gasp, like the swish of a cane as it is raised and hovers in ghastly immobility prior to falling upon its victim. All the air seemed at once sucked out of the room, and into this vacuum the plate

9

of kidneys arrived, a vast heap still bubbling in their own juices and filling the room with their bitter smell.

Ellen took the plate from Cook and slammed it down on to the table in front of Mr Dadd with a triumphant 'There!' and suddenly everyone could breathe again.

'Of course . . .' Robert Dadd senior began, as he speared kidneys with his fork and heaped them on to Richard's plate.

'Father, I really don't want any,' his son protested weakly, forsaking the authority of a young man of twenty-five in favour of a childish whine. For all his experiences, nothing had changed. His sisters, Sarah and Maria, began to giggle.

But Robert Dadd pursued the action with mechanical intent, oblivious of everything but his own train of thought. 'Your friend Jock Phillip has been seeking to fill the gap left by your absence.' He pushed the mustard towards his son as he spoke. 'I fancy that his attentions, though correctly filial towards me, are something warmer than brotherly towards one of your sisters.'

Maria blushed furiously at this observation, which sent her youngest brothers Arthur and John into fits of mirth.

Richard sighed and held out his coffee cup for Ellen to fill.

'Are you quite better, Master Richard?' she asked, peering at him anxiously. 'Your poor father's been so worried about you.'

'Do I look as though he needs to worry about me?' the young man replied.

'You look just like a gypsy, Richard!' laughed Maria.

'I can play as well as one too,' her brother replied, 'if only I had my violin with me!' Seized with inspiration, he took up the carving knife and used it as an imaginary bow, holding up his left arm as the instrument. His father leant forward, his lips framing words which were inaudible above the din. Arthur and John stamped their feet and hummed a wild buzzing melody through the prongs of their forks while his sisters clapped and waved their arms in the air.

Richard rose to his feet, totally ignoring his father's attempts to attract his attention by plucking at his sleeve. Shaking himself free, he walked around the table, serenading his siblings with music which, as his bowing indicated, became ever wilder.

Reader, the first time I read Maria's letter, imagine my feelings! The Dadds were quite unlike any family I have ever known, before or since. Always, there was this same spirit of gaiety which was so lacking in my own family, a *joie de vivre* which was infectious, and which, during those early days in Chatham, I had once shared. In spite of the demise of the two Mrs Dadds, it seemed that their spirits were unconquerable. They defied death. They seemed to laugh in its teeth. They sang, they danced, they talked, – oh to hear them talk was like sitting on a mountain top at the centre of an electric storm with ideas crackling about you like lightning.

We were left behind in Chatham; – that is what it felt like. I sometimes thought that I might suffocate down there while Life itself passed us by altogether. I lived for Maria's letters which sparkled in the dull night of my own existence like a shooting star which illumines the heavens for an instant, and is gone. As I read about Richard's return, I too could hear that strange wild melody that he conjured out of the air as if Maria had made it audible for me too.

And yet, how envious are the Gods of our little human joys! How keen they are to prick even the smallest bubble of pleasure and return us to the grimmer realities of life. Seated by my cheerful fire, I polish my spectacles and turn the page, as I did so many years before. And now, as then, a chill runs through my soul which not even a bonfire of all the timber of Her Majesty's Royal Dockyards could thaw.

For then, wrote Maria, George came home, – George who had stayed out all night. He walked in, just like that, without a trace of embarrassment, and began dancing to the imaginary rhythm.

'George!' cried Richard, 'a regular dervish, aren't you?'

George's smile broadened and he whirled faster than ever as if he would drill a hole through the floor and disappear down it, which his sisters no doubt wished that he would – the whole company, save his prodigal music-playing brother, stunned into silence by the fact that he had entered a scene in which even

11

the table legs were discreetly veiled, without a stitch of clothing about his person.

'You never told me you were in Egypt,' Richard shrieked to George above the uproar.

'Nor was I,' bellowed George in return. 'I'm a natural.'

Then, Robert Dadd senior clapped his hands, – once; twice; three times. There arose an abrupt and terrible silence, a heavy oppressiveness in the air like that which precedes a thunder storm. Nine anxious faces turned towards their parent and waited for the storm to break. Nothing happened. Robert Dadd sat there as if carved from granite, immovable as a statue. The top of his balding head gleamed like polished stone. His eyes were closed.

Richard ceased his frantic bowing. George meekly accepted a dressing gown from Ellen, tied the cord around his waist and collapsed into an empty chair. Stephen, in obedience to his brother's hand on his shoulder, sank stiffly into his seat. Still nothing happened. Robert Dadd senior unaccountably did nothing. In that moment it was as if he had abdicated responsibility; as if God had forsaken the world. His children, even though most of them were quite grown up, were like shipwrecked mariners, cast upon uncharted waters, adrift and not knowing what to do nor where to turn in their bewilderment.

It was Richard who seized the rudder in an attempt to save them, but instead piloted the boat into the churning waters of anarchy and chaos. 'I hate kidneys,' he said, his attention at last focusing on the plate in front of him, on which the kidneys were stacked like some steaming heap of camel dung. His nose wrinkled with disgust. Making stabbing movements with the knife, he impaled the shiny crescents of offal one by one on the long blade. 'I have always hated kidneys,' he continued. 'For twenty-five years you have made me eat kidneys, but let me tell you something once and for all. I never want to see another kidney as long as I live.' And he held the full length of the knife against his father's throat like some grotesque necklace. 'Take it, take it,' he continued, now waggling the ghastly skewer under his father's nose. 'Eat the bloody things yourself!' The gravy ran down his wrist and dripped on to his thighs, – so much gravy! It trickled pleasantly on to his trousers, warm and thick. Raw blood almost. On the deep blue material it made softly spreading maroon patches.

Maria covered her face with her hands.

George looked up from his chair, saw the gory knife, and smiled. '*See how my sword weeps for the poor king's death!*' he quoted.

'*Henry VI*,' Richard responded.

George applauded. 'Your turn!'

Richard pondered for a moment. '*I shall see / The winged vengeance overtake such children*,' he said.

'Duke of Gloucester. *King Lear*. Act III, scene seven.' George crowed with delight and reached out for the coffee pot.

Robert Dadd senior, who during this interchange had gained possession of the knife, pushed back his chair and stood up. 'I will see you in my study, George,' he said as he left the room.

George's hand jerked away from the coffee pot as if it had been slapped. He shrank visibly inside the dressing gown. '*. . . their best conscience / Is not to leave undone but keep unknown*,' he said bravely, but his voice trembled.

No answer was forthcoming.

'Richard?' George appealed.

Richard ignored him. He was staring with increasing horror at the spreading stain in the crook of his elbow.

The clock struck nine.

'Goodness,' said Ellen, clapping her hands lightly, 'just look at the time!'

Arthur and John exchanged horrified glances, grabbed their school bags and fled. They were gone, out into the street with the door banging loudly behind them before anyone spoke again.

'Master Richard, come now, let me take a look at that arm.' Ellen materialised at Richard's shoulder with a bowl of water and a bright white cloth.

'Ellen?' Richard turned to embrace her, seeking comfort as he had done as a little boy.

'Now then, Master Richard, don't you mess up my clean dress with that nasty arm of yours.'

'I'm not nasty, am I, Ellen?' He looked at her pathetically.

'Now, I didn't say that, did I?' She dabbed away at his arm.

'It's funny, Ellen,' he said, looking down at the wound, 'I can't feel a thing.'

'That knife's very sharp. Your father sharpened it himself.'

13

'Father sharpened it?' asked Richard, getting to his feet.

Ellen clung to his sleeve. 'Dicky . . . Dicky, stay a few days. Let Ellen look after you and make you better.

But with a napkin clutched as a makeshift bandage to the gash in his arm, Richard rushed out into the street.

Since, as I have explained earlier, the Dadd family was well known to the inhabitants of Chatham in general, and to ourselves in particular, it will come as no surprise to you to learn that it was here that Mr Dadd first turned in his adversity. Thus it was that my parents learned from Richard's parent the stark facts which I had concealed from them in Maria's letter.

Mr Dadd came to Chatham, ostensibly to consult the family practitioner, a person whom I shall, for reasons of professional etiquette, call Dr Smith. Once he had seen the doctor, he came to call on my parents. It required only the merest prompting from my mother, before the unhappy man spilled out his sorry tale.

My parents listened to him in stony silence, scarcely able to grasp what he was telling them. They sat there, one either side of our elegant fireplace, their features frozen in mirror-images of horror. Their appearance at the time was much as it has been preserved in those twin portraits which now hang on my dining room wall. For Richard himself once flattered them into sitting for him, and they had presented the dear artist with expressions born of a mixture of disapproval, vanity and apprehension.

I have hung them in the dining room rather than in here, since a certain formality and stiffness in the composition makes them too austere for my cluttered and comfortable little living room. They are far better suited to the chill northern light and the dark mahogany furniture, the little used china and the polished silver plate. They look out sombrely, one from either side of the tea urn which, though regularly polished, is now so seldom used, but which once graced our own busy living room in Chatham.

My parents were, you must understand, like Mr Dadd himself, upright and respected persons who were totally without hypocrisy and who spared not themselves that same rigorous degree of scrutiny to which they subjected the behaviour and character of

14

others. Perhaps that is why I have banished them to a little used room, for I still experience from their unmoving lips the silent rebuke which attaches to my own fond and admittedly lackadaisical ways. I do not say that they lacked affection; only that they expressed that love in the fulfilment of their God-given duty to drive out the devil from the souls entrusted to their possession, and to nurture in his place all that was good. To be a recipient of such love was often uncomfortable. At that time in particular, my life seemed to stretch out before me like a perilous tightrope slung over the abyss of hell. On that silken cord, the sun of their approval and love shone like God's own grace, but one slip, one second of wilful rebellion, and it was as if clouds had fallen like shutters over the light and warmth of their affection, leaving me alone and cold. Then my step faltered and became unsure, as I felt all about me the echoing void of eternal darkness.

I was weak: I confess it. Because I feared to hear them condemn him, I preferred to avoid the topic. Because I saw them pale at the very mention of Richard's name, but could not ask the reason why, my own imaginings painted to me a quite terrible picture. And yet, from all that I heard from Maria, Richard was well.

Richard looks quite wonderful, Elizabeth, Maria wrote. Father had been quite concerned by previous reports from Sir Thomas that Richard had been out of sorts since a bout of sunstroke. You certainly wouldn't think it to see him now – you would be quite bowled over, I assure you.

And I was quite ready to be bowled over. I yearned for the experience. To me, the only evidence of Richard's strangeness was the fact that since his return from Egypt, the days had matured into weeks and still he did not come to see me. I heard regularly from Maria and lived for her every word, first frantically skimming the closely written pages for some personal message, some indication that he still thought of me, and only when that feverish scanning was done and my disappointment subdued, was I able to treasure each gem which her friendship communicated to me.

On opening one such communication, a pressed violet fell from the envelope and fluttered like a dying moth on to the floor. I groped at my feet for this fragile harbinger of I knew not what, while that nonsensical childish rhyme, *Roses are red, Violets are blue*, piped as pure as the notes from a flute in my brain. Alas! The explanation for the presence of that evocative little flower was more prosaic. Maria had found it lodged between the pages of an encyclopaedia, where it had lain since one of our spring walks together over the chalk cliffs. This poignant reminder which transported me into those days gone by, when I loved Richard with a purer and more sisterly affection, was a cruel blow indeed. My love had grown more demanding, less innocent.

The awareness of this fact made me conceal it. I hid it away like some cancerous growth, some evil, for I knew that my parents would not approve. And their disapproval made it more sinful by degrees. I lost my appetite and I grew pale. I passed more and more time before the mirror, not consumed by vanity, but in the fruitless quest for some sign of those charms which might have recalled me to his attention. I studied my nose, my mouth, the shape of my eyebrows a thousand times a day. I held strands of my hair before my eyes in sunshine and in shade to try if it should be categorised as chestnut or auburn, amber, gold or mud brown, and it appeared to me as all of these in turn. My eyes proved similarly elusive, violet or azure, blue or turquoise, as changing as the depths of the sea, as sparkling as the surface reflection of a windswept lake or as dull as the stagnant waters of a farmyard pond. And did this phenomenon make me into a creature of mystery, a woman whose enigmatic properties would draw like a magnet? Not a bit of it! I saw only that he might judge such physical inconstancy to be indicative of a similar failing in character; a sign that I was not to be relied upon.

As a final arbiter of my personal appearance of fifty years ago let us appeal to Richard himself. For my own young face, as he defined it, still smiles out of its frame on my parlour wall with all the serene confidence of a sheltered childhood. It is distinguished by youth, rather than by beauty, nicely rounded, fresh-skinned, clear-eyed, and set about with rather ordinary brown hair screwed uncomfortably into a profusion of those corkscrew curls which were then so fashionable. But if I see nothing to excite repugnance, neither do I detect, alas, – if I am to judge myself strictly, — anything which would conjure up a grand passion. Such is revealed not only in the features but in the style of the portraiture, — in the approach of the artist to his subject, which in this case is one of unremitting diligence rather than of inspiration. But in 1843, I was young; and the eye of youth, though keener for physical details, lacks the intuitions attendant upon age. I saw neither so far, nor as deep as I do now.

At that time, Robert, Richard's eldest brother, was a frequent visitor to our household, since he was engaged to be married to my dear sister Catherine. How their transparent happiness stung my own bruised feelings! How often would I turn away from their joy to contemplate the depths of my own longing and misery! For with Robert came news of Richard: how busy he was working up the sketches from his travels and entering competitions and exhibitions and far outshining any of his contemporaries. On hearing such reports I experienced a glow of pleasure and found consolation in dreaming up for myself the role of some medieval maiden who waits in her tower secure in the knowledge that her knight will return at last to lay his triumphs at her feet.

And when Robert was with us, so was his brother George. For George occupied lodgings in Chatham where he worked as a carpenter in the dockyards. Robert sometimes delivered a letter from Richard to his brother, and as the same was drawn from his coat pocket, I feared I might faint with the intensity of the hope that there might be something for me too; that a second package might appear, — a second name, my own, written in that beloved hand.

I was doomed to disappointment, and to depending on George for those few snippets of masculine affairs which Richard saw fit to relate to his brother, and which amused him enormously. George found in me a ready listener and an enthusiast for anything to do with his adored elder brother. I absorbed every barbed piece of information much as a martyr receives the arrows that bring him nearer to his God. I say barbed, because all this came to me at second hand, and though my parched heart sucked in every drop of news, as a man stranded in the desert might be driven to lick the very dew from his boots, these letters only conspired towards a similar end — to whet the appetite for more of that same fare.

The threads that there were to be picked up after a long absence! The changes to be commented upon, and the delight to be taken in all that was familiar and unchanged! So Richard seemed to have returned to a busy life in which, quite apart from his work, he enjoyed many an evening among his friends, revisiting his favourite haunts, where the story of the dramatic events at his father's house soon became quite celebrated. And I learned from George himself that, possessed of the courage afforded by a few drinks, Richard's re-enactment of George's brazen entrance into his father's respectable, middle-class drawing room became quite celebrated.

You can imagine the embarrassment which this in particular caused to my tender ears. Nor, had I been George, would I have taken much pride in the widespread broadcasting of such exploits. But George was entirely immune from any shame on that score, and entirely wanting the delicacy of feeling which had restrained his sister from labouring the ultimate truth of his state of dress, or lack thereof. It was left to Richard, via George, to enlighten me, and to regale me with endless recitations of the reaction of his friends to the event.

'Must've given the old gaffer quite a turn,' observed Billy Frith, chuckling into his frothing tankard of ale.

'I'm not used to this,' protested Richard, as the pints lined up before him, 'and I'm starving. Order me some bread and cheese before I pass out.'

'Too strong for you, is it?' Billy stretched out his lanky legs and laughed. 'Or is it just too deadly dull and boring? Would you prefer a hubble-bubble and a Turkish coffee served by a maiden in a yashmak?' Here Richard's friend got to his feet and wove his body in an impoverished imitation of a belly dancer.

'I have seen,' said Richard, somewhat the worse for liquor, 'belly dancing that would make your hair curl with pleasure, indeed it would, Billy.' His eyes gleamed at the memory.

'And what was your old pater's comment on that score, I wonder?'

Billy and Richard, knowing that in neither of their respective

18

and respectable households would such a subject ever be mentioned, caught each other's eye and laughed.

'Poor old Pater,' said Richard at last. 'Do you know, I do believe he's aged in the nine months that I've been away.'

'Haven't we all, dear boy!'

'No, seriously, Billy, I think he's losing his grip.'

'In what way?' Billy tackled a passing waitress and pulled her down on his lap. 'Here's something else that's changed since you've been away!'

'New, ain't she?' Richard peered at the girl.

'My new model,' said Billy proudly. 'Dolly.'

'Looks like one too,' observed Richard.

'Won't you introduce me to your friend?' Dolly patted her hair and pouted in Richard's direction.

'Mr Richard Dadd, RA,' announced Billy loudly.

'Steady on,' murmured Richard blushing, 'not yet.'

'Any minute now,' continued Billy. 'I'm merely anticipating. Mr Dadd is, my dear,' he buried his whiskers in the girl's ear, 'and I quote one of our most learned and distinguished critics, "one of those shining lights which brighten Art. No living artist possesses a more vivid or delicate imagination." '

'Oh shut up, Billy,' said Richard, squirming with embarrassment, 'people are listening, you know.'

'And so they should, dear boy, so they should!' Billy levered the girl off his knee, manoeuvred himself upright and bowed in the direction of the curious faces. 'Gentlemen,' he called, 'a toast to the safe return of my friend. The greatest happening in the world of art since Michael Angelo!'

At this point, Dolly extricated herself from Billy's embrace and moved off, looking back over her shoulder as she went to give Richard a huge wink.

Richard did not respond.

Billy looked at him in surprise. 'I say,' he asked after a pause, alarmed by his sudden change of humour. 'You haven't gone all religious on me, have you? I mean, you haven't been converted or anything like that?'

'It's not that,' said Richard dully. 'I was thinking about George again. Poor George was naked!'

'But you were laughing about it just now,' said Augustus Egg

19

as he slid into the empty chair between his friends. 'But what I don't understand is, where had George been, and what had he been doing?'

Richard shrugged. 'I left before we found out.'

'It gives new meaning to the term, stripped of all I possess,' chuckled Billy. 'How did your Pa cope with that one?'

'He just sat there. Struck dumb as it were. Then he said, "Who saw you?" as if that were the only concern.'

'He'd been all through the Haymarket and up Suffolk Street, at that hour of the day, without a stitch?' Billy whistled with admiration.

'It would make quite a good picture, wouldn't it?' commented Richard. 'I mean, George there, totally exposed amid all the fine flummery of the theatre-going crowds. It would serve as an excellent example of hypocrisy and the fact that the passions – the base ones, I mean – are constantly asserting their superiority over the intellectual and noble ones.'

'Er, quite.' After two hours' steady drinking, Billy for one was not prepared to dispute the point.

With hindsight, how easy it is to say that these sudden changes of mood were indicators or signs of this or that. With foresight, how differently might we have acted! But we are not Gods. We can only act to the best of our ability and in accordance with a judgement based on a conscience well-grounded in principle. At the time, we all, family and friends alike, saw only a friend who was subject to sudden and unaccountable fits of depression and moodiness which we sought to alleviate. Everything that we did for him was done for the best of all possible motives; that of love.

Richard's friends thus refused at first to abandon him to the blackness of his vision. That evening, they escorted him from the public house to the door of his residence to an accompaniment of backslapping tomfoolery and general hilarity which would have melted the most frostbitten of humours. Friendship was even carried to the extent of braving that old dragon, Richard's landlady, and proceeding into her very lair.

At which point they were discovered. Four pairs of drunken feet, though inaudible to their tiptoeing owners, were sufficient to cause Mrs Jenkins' coffee to slop into its saucer and send her parrot clinging to a perch which swung as wildly as a palm tree before a hurricane. Not that the paragon made any comment. She simply stood there at the foot of the stairs, tall and gaunt as a giant exclamation mark of rebuke, and watched their progress until the door of Richard's room closed silently behind them.

'I say, Humby old chap,' chortled Richard, from the safety of his den, 'there'd be a fortune in it for the bootmaker who could make silent soles!'

The last member of the quartet, Humby, was no artist but a bootmaker by trade. He laughed in appreciation of Richard's suggestion. 'Soles or souls?' he asked. 'Is the question intended to be metaphysical or metatarsal?'

Richard's expression changed abruptly. He sank on to the settee and after removing one of his boots, he gazed at it anxiously. 'If one kept one's soul in one's boots,' he observed, 'it would be a sorry thing to see it trampled underfoot at every step.'

'Indeed it would, Dicky, you're right there,' replied Billy heartily, 'only you've got the wrong sole,' and he slapped him on the back. 'I prefer mine fried in butter and parsley!'

Richard flinched from the blow as if he had been attacked.

'You go,' Billy said to the others, who were looking exceedingly anxious. 'I'll stay with him. Cheer him up a bit.'

Egg and Humby put on their hats. 'Are you sure?' they whispered, their enthusiasm to be gone competing with shame at that very desire.

'Quite sure.' Billy ushered them firmly outside. 'What about a nice tune?' he suggested by way of distraction. He took Richard's violin from its case and blew off the dust.

Richard drew his fingers listlessly across the strings. 'Out of tune,' he commented sadly.

'That's easily put right,' said Billy.

'It's not just this,' said Richard, waving the instrument, 'it's my whole life.'

'All artists feel like that at times,' said Billy comfortably, stretching out his legs. 'It passes.'

'Does it?' Richard turned the pegs which shrieked in protest

21

as the strings tautened. 'I'm not so sure.' He placed the violin against his shoulder and drew the bow across the strings.

'Something not too hectic,' suggested Billy, remembering the tale of the family party.

'Worried, are you?' Richard smiled at his friend's discomfiture.

There was something threatening about that smile, in the dim candle-light, which had Billy on his feet and out of the door in an instant.

Behind him crazy chords broke out. As he reached the safety of the downstairs hallway, it occurred to him that he had forgotten his hat, but nothing on earth would induce him to return for it. As he opened the front door, he could hear Mrs Jenkins already thumping the living room ceiling with her broom handle and wailing plaintively, 'Mr Dadd! This is a respectable neighbourhood!'

Mrs Jenkins' version of the incident, which in other, less accurate accounts accords more glory and heroism to the narrators and more wildness to the subject, represents, in my opinion, the nearest we shall get to the truth about Richard's behaviour at that time.

Mrs Jenkins' intimacy with the conversation was ensured by the frugality which she observed in furnishing her lodger's rooms. This fulfilled two functions. Firstly, it ensured that every word carried clearly through the floorboards. Secondly, it saved considerable expense to herself. I am tempted to add a third, which was the retailing of considerable quantities of coal at inflated prices to counteract the draughts. But there will be occasion to learn more of Mrs Jenkins later.

At the time, the state of Richard's mind was one of furious debate among us all. It totally eclipsed any concern over George's extraordinary behaviour, Stephen's increasingly rigid correctness or Maria's repeated attacks of hysteria. Richard monopolised everyone's attention. How much might have been avoided if we had not been so blind; if we had listened to one another like different members of the orchestra who play their parts in harmony and so construct together one glorious, symphonic

22

whole! Instead, we all pursued our own pet theories and so failed to notice that not one, but several among us had already lost our parts and were badly out of tune.

How often do we discount the evidence of our own eyes and ears; how often turn our backs on that darker side of human nature which it pleases us to ignore! In this I was as guilty as everybody else. I closed my eyes to the unpalatable truth that Richard had changed as far as it was possible for a human being to change and still retain human form; to the fact that the person who was the object of my affections, that charming and thoughtful companion, was only fleetingly and at increasingly rare intervals to be found inside that shell.

For Kindness itself would not have been too strong a metaphor to describe the Richard of old. He was never happier than when helping somebody. Indeed, this instinct prompted him to introduce Jock into the family, – in 1836 was it, or 1837? – soon after his arrival as a stowaway on a ship from Aberdeen to the Port of London. Richard met Jock at the Royal Academy, where they were both enrolled for sketching classes, and at once took this friendless young man under his wing. By virtue of his early circumstances, Jock lacked the advantages of Richard's wide acquaintance in artistic circles, – or indeed, in any circles at all. For he had started life as the son of a country shoemaker, and had risen via the trade of house painter to become an artist's assistant in his native city.

Such different backgrounds made not the slightest difference to their friendship; Humby, after all, had a similar background. Richard did his best to make his intense and often awkward new friend feel more at ease in the world, by introducing him to his family. The Dadd family did not take to Jock at once. His manners were unpolished and his lack of social grace embarrassed both himself and his hosts. Indeed, I recollect one little incident over the dinner table, on the occasion of his first visit, when Mr Dadd inquired rather formally, whether Mr Phillip 'would partake of a little white wine or red?'

Poor Jock, who had never partaken of either in his life, found himself placed in a quandary. Then Richard, perhaps sensing something of his friend's predicament, said encouragingly, 'Father's white is generally considered of a high standard.'

However Mr Dadd, who always took his guests' best interests very much to heart, countered Richard's recommendation by saying, 'The red of that year is generally considered the superior of the two.'

This did not help poor Jock at all. He looked down at the fragile long-stemmed glass alongside his plate as if regretting that he had ever set eyes on it. Then in a mood of desperate compromise, he responded politely by saying, 'I'll take a little of both, if you please, sir.'

This answer quite broke the icy formality which had so far characterised his visit. Mr Dadd obliged by filling the guest's glass with a mixture, and we all looked on helplessly as Jock sipped at the cloudy fluid with the utmost composure.

Thereafter, the whole family took Jock to their hearts, so that he found in their company all the benefits of domesticity, including those good square meals which it gave Ellen so much pleasure to devise for him. Jock's confidence and social accomplishment increased with every visit, and it is no small credit to Richard that this dark, uncouth, provincial character could, in no time at all, pass himself off as quite a man about town.

Nor did Richard neglect his friend's professional development. He promoted it with as much zeal as his own. He was always ready to recognise and applaud another artist's talents, and to celebrate their successes. Recognising Jock's abilities, Richard at once introduced the young Scot into his sketching group, where, in company with those other burgeoning young artists, they would illustrate scenes from Byron and Shakespeare in an ambience of good-humoured rivalry and beer.

But as time passed, Richard's 'friends' fell away one by one. Not one remained to help him. Nor was my behaviour any the less worthy of blame, for I confess that I paid less heed to his sufferings than to my own. Reader, I wallowed in them! I did nothing to alleviate their pangs, but revelled in the gentle melancholy into which I fell that summer. I even went so far as to encourage it. I trod those same familiar paths which we had once trodden together as children, and there indulged in luxurious bouts of sighing and tears.

I could, of course, have gone to London and stayed with Maria as she pressed me frequently to do. One postscript in his hand, one message from his lips, just the utterance of that one word 'Come!' and I would have been in Suffolk Street faster than words can express the thought.

But no such summons came. And I remained obdurate.

O my wicked vanity!

Chapter Two

HE did not come as Spring blossomed into Summer. On my solitary walks, I watched the corn grow, then flower and seed, and then the first tinge of gold touched its delicate bell-like fruit. Swallows darted like tiny arrowheads low over the sparkling surface of the River Medway. The parents were now rearing their second brood. They swooped and rose over the water, their beaks crammed with insects for those clamorous fledglings in the nest under the eaves above my bedroom window. And still he did not come.

My love which, like those nestlings, cried out for nourishment, received no such gratification, though it would have been satisfied with less than a full crop. It did not demand the total self-sacrifice of those weary parents who were busy the live-long day. One word, one gesture would have sufficed. For one glance from those deep blue eyes I would have sacrificed a whole summer of unclouded skies.

As my sister's wedding day approached, the work of preparation absorbed all our time. The house was scrubbed from top to bottom, from beneath the roof tiles to the flagstones on the cellar floor. Nothing less would satisfy my mother, who demanded as much perfection in those nooks and crannies upon which no guest would ever cast his eye, as she did in the parlour and the hall. As for the outside, an extra gardener was taken on so that the choicest blooms might be cultivated in the hothouse and herbaceous borders to provide for vases, bouquets, buttonholes and Grecian urns, indoors and out, as fitting floral tribute to the innocence and beauty of the bride.

As for my sister and myself, though we were spared the more arduous of household duties, do not imagine that one second of that summer found us idle, for never was such a stitching and carrying on! Quite apart from the wedding dresses, there was

26

my sister's trousseau to prepare. The nightdresses and chemises, undergarments and over, left our fingers as sore as if stung by a thousand bees, and our eyes dry and pricking with the effort of concentration by daylight and lamplight.

Reader, you must ask yourself whether I felt no pang of envy at my sister's happiness, no regret that her union with her beloved was not my own? There were times when envy filled my heart with a bitter blackness, when I could scarcely see the fine material and my stitching went sadly awry; when every garment completed seemed a shroud for my own joy. But the mechanical nature of the task worked its own anaesthesia upon my feelings and at last I suffered no more than a piece of material suffers at each piercing of the needle.

Even the sight of Catherine and Robert burned itself into my mind with all the dullness of familiarity, much as a new carpet soon ceases to impress or a new wallpaper to startle the eye. Robert resembled his younger brother Richard neither in appearance nor in personality. He was, instead, remarkably like his father, with the same abundance of deep brown hair which curled delicately over an elfin face. But in character there was nothing elfin or ethereal about my future brother-in-law. His was a prosaic, practical, steady nature, much suited to my sister's own. Though I often took the liberty of observing him, – and for this ample opportunity was afforded by reason of his total absorption in my sister, – I saw nothing of those flashes of brilliance and imagination with which his younger brother was so richly endowed. Indeed, unable quite to comprehend my sister's infatuation with so eminently worthy a being, such feelings of envy that did tear loose from their moorings were directed simply towards her state, rather than towards herself. From the bottom of my heart, I wished her well.

As August the tenth dawned, did I then feel nothing? Ah yes! The feelings in my breast were in such a tumult that I was almost beside myself with nervous agitation. I would at last see Richard! But do not be too hard on me, Reader, if I now tell you that the prospect did not thrill me. Such is the contrariness of human nature that I would even have welcomed his refusal of the invitation. His position in regard to myself would then have been abundantly clear.

For Richard was coming with his family, to celebrate the marriage of his older brother. It was an invitation he could hardly refuse. Which left me where, if anywhere, in his affections? How should I meet him? What should I say? I was resolved to be as cold towards him as possible, to punish him for the anguish he had caused me. But such a resolution is more easily taken in the privacy of one's room, than executed to the hurt of the dearest and kindest person in the world when he stands before you so trustingly.

As it was, the great day arrived, and I shivered my way into the primrose silk and struggled with the buttons on my new white gloves as if smitten with an ague. To tame my own nervousness required such effort of mind that I had scarcely the energy left over to consider my sister at all. Her constant queries about her own dress, her veil, her flowers, almost drove me to distraction.

Maria was to be my twin for the occasion. After her arrival and the joy of seeing her again, we were soon dressed alike, with our hair arranged in identical manner and every aspect of our garlands, bouquets and silks complementing the other. And somehow we found ourselves walking into the church, two trembling seraphs, in the footsteps of the bride.

In the front row, to the left of the aisle of the little country church, which was on that day illuminated by pillars of sunshine as solid with dust as those carved stone columns which supported the roof, stood the Dadd family – or as many as could comfortably fit into such a confined space, for they overflowed into the second row, and the third and so forth, like the waves of the incoming tide.

Richard stood to attention on his father's left. I could see him the instant I entered the church. Though he was but of average height and build, I could have picked him out in a crowd of thousands. Beyond Richard was Stephen, then George – on this occasion clad like his brothers in a suit of conventional sobriety. Finally, the two youngest sons, Arthur and John, were forced to sit with their sisters Mary Ann and Sarah who had expressed their desire to be escorted on this happy occasion by the faithful Ellen. In this matter they had been over-ruled, and found themselves placed instead next to the less comfortable presence of their senior aunt.

Aunt Smith was a small rubber ball of a woman. Her general build, combined with a complexion which glowed like the smouldering embers of a log fire, seemed to indicate a correspondingly jovial temperament. Closer acquaintance, however, revealed beneath the soft and frilly caps which she favoured, a nose like a ferret and a flush which was the product of high blood pressure and a choleric disposition.

Set against the Dadd family was my own. The Carters, though not as numerous, contrived to fill the same number of pews partly because of a more extravagant and fashionable use of material on the part of the ladies and partly by virtue of the incessant energy of the junior members of the clan. The latter migrated from pew to pew with alarming frequency, diving under the benches and bobbing up unexpectedly hither and thither so that a casual observer might be forgiven for thinking that at least a score of children were present, rather than a mere handful.

As the organ bellows wheezed and groaned, manoeuvred by two stout lads up in the gallery with such enthusiasm that the music itself was scarcely louder than their laboured breathing, the groom, with a nervous last-minute adjustment to his cravat, stepped forward into the aisle and prepared to bestow upon my sister, Catherine, the honour, as it then was, of his name.

Relieved momentarily of our official duties, Maria and I sat at the side of the altar, leaving the bride and groom for the time being the focus of attention, and I had ample time to study the congregation in greater detail.

So it was that I noticed Mary Ann Dadd smooth out some minute crease in her black silk with a certain self-satisfaction. Black silk for her brother's wedding! Even disregarding the pagan elements of the union, which must have been painful indeed to one of her gloomy disposition, surely on this occasion the joyousness of the sacrament might have afforded her a dispensation from her nun's weeds.

Though maturity has enabled me to admire in her the single-mindedness with which she has always pursued her charitable works, I have never felt warmed by that spontaneous affection which causes us to overlook many a minor failing in lesser mortals. She has always nourished an absolute belief in self-sacrifice as the highest ideal, and been sufficiently confident of

29

God's love and approval to forgo present happiness in the knowledge that her reward would be the greater in heaven.

I knew that the match between my sister and her brother did not entirely please her. Though it was the culmination of a lifetime's friendship, she would have preferred to see Robert united with someone of a more serious nature; – someone, in fact, rather like herself. If ever she were to have been in the position of choosing a bride for her brother, she would not have chosen Catherine. For Mary Ann, the only true marriage was one made in heaven, a union of soul and intellect. With such stringent demands, it is perhaps not surprising that she never met anyone who lived up to them.

Mary Ann was ever fearful of strong emotion and passion. That men's passions could be easily aroused was an observation she frequently made, and she often quoted the unhappy outcome of her siblings' lives as an example of its evil effects. Richard, George, Stephen and Maria, – she traced the fate of each one back to her dear Papa's impetuous second marriage, for which she laid the blame squarely on the seductive wiles of a step-mother scarcely older than herself.

Mary Ann's present uneasiness was betrayed by her surreptitious glances here and there, as she observed the effect of her sister Maria upon the many men in the congregation. Her own sombre attire deflected any such attention, as black rejects the light, but Maria in her dress of burning gold attracted admiration as a candle flame attracts the moth. And I read in Mary Ann's proud look the bitter triumph that she, at least, would never have the fate of a man's soul upon her conscience.

I sat next to Maria like a brazen Jezebel, in my youthful pride glorying in the spectacle we presented. The yellow satin of our dresses snatched at the sunlight, which trembled and shimmered in their folds as if the sunbeams themselves were imprisoned there. Conscious of our attractions, I wondered for how long I could remain invisible to the one whose gaze I most earnestly sought. While I dreamed of Richard, Maria – as she told me later – dreamed of the day when she would be the bride, and she mentally deposed her brother and invested the dark suit with the darker, finer features of John Phillip.

Was the poor bride, then, invisible to all? Was she simply the projected image of innumerable hopes and dreams? Even Mother afterwards confessed that through the refracted vision of each tear drop, she saw not my poor sister, but herself as she had been on her own wedding day; and had wondered at the metamorphosis of feelings over the years, from love to fear on her side, and from adulation to a continuous, censorious disapproval on his.

You might wonder at the tactlessness of my mother's remarks, made as they later were to me on the eve of my own wedding, as she sat on my bed watching me carefully tie up my hair for the night. Reader, though Richard's name was never mentioned between us, my mother was not blind. She knew full well that I was entering the state of matrimony with a mind unclouded by passion. And if there are no veils across one's eyes, there are none to be cruelly drawn aside. If there are no hopes, there are none to be dashed. I had agreed to marry a good, honest man from whom I expected nothing except companionship and all that the term implies of mutual respect and a certain conjunction of interests. In that expectation, I was never disappointed. Expecting nothing, everything was a gain. There could be no disillusion but only the gradual unveiling of qualities of character and depths of feeling which were a constant revelation and delight. Reader, my husband brought me far more than I deserved, and I trust I repaid him in like kind.

But I digress; this is the story of my sister Catherine's wedding and not my own.

'Say after me,' the Vicar intoned, stooping slightly towards the happy couple to beam his approval. 'I, Catherine Carter, take thee Robert Dadd to my wedded husband . . .'

As if there was not enough of delight in the words, those which followed, – 'to have and to hold', – were sufficient to send tremors of ecstasy down my spine. For at that moment I knew that Richard had noticed me. I could feel his glance burn like fire along the length of my spine. I did not need to turn to know that this was so.

And at that exact moment, as if confirmation were needed, he dropped his hymn book with a resounding clatter and I cast a sidelong glance in his direction. His eye caught mine, and he winked so that I blushed and trembled until I feared that I might faint right there on the altar steps.

Richard told me later, during the reception, that the way his eye had caught mine was sheer coincidence. His thoughts were far from embracing me. Resentful of the enforced day of leisure when he would rather have been working on his pictures for Sir Thomas Phillips, his mind was filled, not with the soft, drifting colour schemes of rural England, but with the harsher, more vibrant colours of a brighter, harsher world.

He had looked briefly around the assembled congregation, from whose expressions and comportment he would have been hard put to tell that he was not at a funeral, and thought back to other festivals of music and dancing, – to the drum's beat and the whirling, brightly coloured clothes; the dignity of happy people celebrating an event which ensures the survival of the human race; people not afraid to demonstrate exactly how they felt, for whom feeling and expression were one.

To his right, his father's black sleeve intruded on his vision as stiff and straight as an artificial limb. Richard's eyes wandered upwards to the high white collar, starched and ironed until it gleamed. And he remembered then those pathetic trains of prisoners he had seen, mere walking skeletons in the iron collars which bound them one to the other as they were goaded along the banks of the Nile to certain torture and death. For those unhappy victims there was no choice; they were simply the playthings of the Pasha, living and dying at his will. Surely his father could hope for more from life than that?

At this point in a reverie which made him totally deaf to the exchange of vows between the happy couple, Richard reached up to loosen his father's collar, and so to liberate him from all that ensnared him. In the course of a short and silent struggle during which Robert Dadd senior fought to free himself from Richard's grasp, the hymn book clattered to the ground. The clack-clack-clack, sharp as castanets, with which it bounced from pew to shelf to kneeler and finally on to the stone floor was sufficient to distract Richard from his endeavour. In stooping to retrieve the fluttering manual, he caught my eye.

I turned back to the altar with a serene smile, as illumined by transfiguring joy as a stained glass window is by the sun.

And so it was that I was totally unaware of the strange scene which now took place behind me. For Richard, hearing the introductory chords of the organ, and glancing at his newly retrieved hymnal, which had fallen open at a hymn well known to us all from childhood, ignored the number posted on the hymn board above our heads, and began to sing, '*Have you not heard what dreadful plagues / Are threatened by the Lord . . .*'

Lost in my little world of illusion, I saw only the words on the page of my own hymnal; heard only my own voice, soaring as it were above the whole congregation. '*Love Divine, all loves excelling . . .*' I sang with all my heart, treasuring that moment when Richard had looked at me. I gave the words a profanity which was never intended, relating every syllable to that one exchange of glances which meant so much to me, but nothing, alas, to him.

And then at last we were all outside in the sunshine, with the bells chiming in great peals which broke about our ears so that everyone laughed and clasped their hands to their heads and all was merriment and light. The carriages seemed to fly along to the accompaniment of the sharp clop of hooves and the jingle of harness buckles, and the ribbons in the horses' manes fluttered in the wind.

There in the carriage I sat, next to Maria so that our dresses rippled together like golden waterfalls until it was impossible to tell where one ended and the other began.

'My dear twin sisters! Alike as peas in a pod,' observed Richard fondly. The appellation did not entirely please me, for I yearned to be something more than a sister to him. But the starving man does not complain at being thrown crusts of dry bread. He takes what is offered, and derives therefrom such comfort as he is able. So too did I abstract and distill from that less than pleasing observation a fondness of tone and expression which afforded me some degree of comfort.

Richard was sitting opposite me, so close that at the least jolt his knees brushed against mine and we were forced constantly to apologise and disclaim and smile at one another. Beside Richard sat his brother Stephen, a stiff dark figure who seemed altogether ill assorted to the mood of the occasion.

If only, I wished, this little journey could last for ever!

'Could you not paint this moment so that it will never fade in the memory?' Maria cried out to her brother, expressing that self-same delight which I did not dare to express.

Richard laughed and said that he couldn't imagine a nicer picture but perhaps the subject was better suited to his friend O'Neil than himself. He looked so much his usual self that I found myself watching him closely, searching for some sign of that strangeness of which I had been warned. Finding none only caused me to look more closely still, until I could see that he was at last becoming irritated by my attention.

Too soon we arrived back at our house, where, the weather being so beautiful, the guests were at once ushered out again into the large, walled garden. Seated on a white-painted, wrought-iron bench under the spreading boughs of a horse chestnut tree, and attended by their bridesmaids, the bride and groom received their well-wishers with every appearance of joy and modesty.

Already the servants were at work, rearranging the seating and the food so that not a minute of sunshine would be lost. Richard and Stephen, George and Arthur were enlisted at Ellen's behest to carry outside the heavy oak dining table with its precarious load of cold meats and salads. My mother meanwhile was anxiously overseeing the spreading of rugs and blankets to protect the ladies' dresses from the grass.

All was laughter and brightness when lo! Mr Carter and Mr Dadd were seen in close conference shaking their heads sadly over the unexpected degeneration of the party. What about the more senior guests? Had the danger from wasps and bees been considered? the possibility of sunstroke (a subject upon which Mr Dadd was still extremely sensitive)? the deleterious effect on the jellies, creams and blancmanges?

All at once it was apparent that this impromptu arrangement simply would not do. Mr Dadd and Mr Carter clapped their hands and instantly everything was set in reverse motion, though the younger guests persisted in wandering along the herbaceous borders or pausing to sit on the rockery wall, heedless of the admonitions of their elders.

From the darkness of the dining room, as Ellen related, we could be seen as if on an illuminated stage. Every action, every word, every gesture was digested and pronounced upon without right of appeal by the senior relatives, who did not stir from their posts by the food, awaiting only the given signal to fill those empty plates which glowed on their laps like so many moons.

'Did you see that?' Aunt Smith had begun the conversation, as Richard stood unwittingly beside me on the lawn, centre stage.

He had waylaid me with a request for a rose, – or for as many roses as I could spare. I offered him one which he pinned to his lapel. He asked for another, and I refused. He slipped his arm through mine and led me away to a shaded bench where he would, he said, explain the reason for his request.

Reader, I was aware of all those disapproving eyes on us, but how could I refuse? And were we not now brother and sister, almost?

We sat there under the tree, with the sky above us as serene and blue, he declared, as any he had seen on his travels, and he began to explain the reason for his strange request for my basket of flowers . . .

Nothing in Victorian England, he vowed, could have prepared him for his first sight of that legendary land of Egypt. He was there on deck as the Citadel of Alexandria rose up on the horizon and the setting sun glanced off the golden dome of the central mosque, burning its image into a brain already tuned to fever pitch by anticipation, – Iskandria, one-time capital of Alexander, attacked and pillaged and fought over for centuries by Romans and Arabs, by Moslems and Christians; trading centre of the Mediterranean and guardian of the Nile Delta and of all the fabulous wealth of the African hinterland.

Well before the boat drew into harbour, the city was plunged into the inky colourlessness of twilight, a darkened procession of silhouettes set against a sky so pure that it made the senses ache. All the while the cries of the muezzins, 'Allah-o-Akbar', echoed again and again, harsh and discordant, twanging at the heart-strings, one voice vying with another to call the faithful to prayer.

'What does it mean?' Richard asked his Greek guide. 'What are they saying?'

'God is great,' Constantine replied carelessly as he accepted a fat cigar from his employer, Sir Thomas Phillips.

'Only,' Sir Thomas added with a superior smile, 'as you and I know, Richard, it is the wrong God.' And he exhaled a cloud of smoke with the same complacency and ease with which he would repel all heresy and idolatry.

Richard drew away from the pair to absorb on his own the essence of the city. For darkness fell swiftly after the merest brushstroke of twilight, and already the whole vast continent lay shrouded in a heavy silken blackness broken only by that precious symbol of the Infidel, the silver sliver of a crescent moon.

But this did not mean that the city now slept. The dockside was crowded with porters and street vendors and officials jockeying for position. In the flickering pools of light from a thousand torches glistened a hotchpotch of faces of every colour, race and creed, jostling side by side with horses and mules, donkeys and camels.

Richard clung to the rail and thought he might faint with the wonder of it all. His attention was drawn now here, now there, leaving each half-absorbed impression superimposed on its predecessor in a dizzying whirl of shape and colour. He inhaled deeply to steady himself, but his lungs only filled with a headier tang of cinnamon and cardamom, unwashed bodies and cheap, sweet perfumes, mingled with the cloying stink of human and animal excrement, and the rottenness that came in a poisonous cloud from the direction of the fish market.

Then the gangplank was lowered, and those on shore immediately tried to storm aboard, only to be repulsed by the crew striking out with their oars. Such ferocity served not to deter, but rather to invite further invasion.

Richard watched as the trunk containing all his painting equipment descended on the shoulders of a burly sailor, to be at once swallowed up in the crowd. Convinced that he would never see it again, but still too dazed by circumstances to suffer much concern on its behalf, Richard then struck out for the shore himself. With a brace of Turkish soldiers fore and aft who laid about them with their rifle butts, forging a way forward inch by inch, he set first one foot and then the other on African soil.

Never before had he been so beset by people. They clutched at his hair, his collar, his hands, his arms as he strove to keep up with his companions. Had it not been for the soldiers who followed, he feared that he would have been irrevocably lost. In a state of complete bewilderment, he ran the gauntlet to an ancient horse-drawn cab, which stood huge and black and solid as a rock in this sea of shifting humanity. Sir Thomas and Constantine were already seated inside. Sir Thomas was mopping his face with a large handkerchief. Richard ignored the invitation of the two men to join them under the protective covering of the hood and swung himself instead up at the front of the calèche alongside the driver. At once they were off at a gallop. Those beggars who still clung to the sides and back of the vehicle, were shaken off and the cries of 'Bakhsheesh!' died away to a confused and inconsolable murmur, like that of a child crying itself to sleep.

The driver then leaned forward. His whip crackled like lightning against the surface of the road, the lash snaking in and out of the legs of the stampeding horse. As they drove he clanged a large brass bell which was suspended from the side of his seat, and children and old men, cats and dogs, mothers and babies, costers and priests, threw themselves into the overflowing gutters for safety. The tail of the driver's white turban worked loose and streamed out behind him, and his eyes gleamed with excitement. When Richard looked behind, he saw that they were being pursued by an equally reckless coachman, driving a second wildly swaying calèche which contained the luggage.

The horse's shoulders and haunches darkened with sweat. Richard, clinging to the precarious seat with both hands, felt the hot air stream over his face and the dust thrown up by the horse's hooves sear his eyeballs.

'The hotel,' he gasped, turning to the driver, 'is it far?'

The man nodded. 'Oh yes, effendi. Is too far.' And he abruptly pulled on the reins and announced, 'We arrive.'

'Are you sure this is the Hotel Majestic?' asked Sir Thomas, since the name above the door clearly indicated that it was not. Already eager hands were hauling at him.

'Hotel Majestic,' he repeated very slowly and loudly, batting off the offers of assistance right and left with his cane as if he were swatting flies.

'Yes, effendi. This is hotel.' The driver jumped down eagerly and stood there, beaming in anticipation of a good tip at the end of a job well done.

'But not the Hotel Majestic,' Sir Thomas persisted.

'Why you want that hotel, effendi? This very good hotel.'

'I want to go to the Hotel Majestic!' roared Sir Thomas. 'I have a reservation.'

The driver stood there sulkily. 'Hotel is hotel. Bed. Eat.' Lest there be any misunderstanding, he acted out each word as he pronounced it. 'Women. You want. They have.' His gestures outlining the attractions of the latter left Sir Thomas's eyes bulging and Richard convulsed with laughter.

Here Constantine intervened, and in not more than an hour the baggage was ransomed from the hotel porters, carefully counted and re-stowed and the cab moved sedately out of the hotel fore-court towards its rightful destination; – and to the first of many nights which Richard was to spend lying sleepless and tormented by images more gripping than the bite of any flea or bed bug. They exploded like fireworks across his brain, each one more brilliant than the last.

'Dear Billy,' he wrote, 'Dear Maria,' 'Dear Egg,' 'Dear Humby,' in an attempt to disburden his mind of these feverish impressions. But Egypt was not to be shaken off so lightly. It was as if, from the first moment, the country and its people had captured his very soul — a circumstance of which he was later to be given incontrovertible proof.

From the rose red city of Alexander, Richard then related how they had journeyed to Cairo. The voyage was haunted by the singing of the oarsmen as they strained upriver through the swamps and fertile plains of the Nile Delta. While Sir Thomas amused himself by taking potshots at crocodiles, Richard sat and absorbed everything about him until he felt himself drawn inexorably backwards in time. He saw blind oxen turning the water wheels alongside the river to irrigate the crops. He saw a thousand Ruths carrying away water jars on their heads and holding his heart captive with a look, the merest glance, before the boat passed on and they were gone, — a pair of dark eyes, a brilliant veil and the glint of a bronze ornament before all faded to become no more than the glimpse of a hibiscus flower against the greenery.

On the river banks squatted villages whose houses were scarcely distinguishable from the mud on which they stood. Never far from these pitiful dwellings, crouched at the water's edge, groups of women slapped their river-coloured rags against outcrops of sandstone, or scoured huge pans with handfuls of coarse sand until they gleamed dully on the mud flats like so many beached suns. And as they worked, the women sang. The boat drifted in and out of their strange chants as through a dream, on and on until there were no more villages, no houses, and only the endless company of kingfishers and herons and nervous flocks of duck who scurried into the papyrus at their approach. And then he saw at last the sacred ibis, floating down the river on rafts of lotus leaves in the everlasting sun which rebounded with double brilliance off the sparkling surface of the water.

So at last they came to Cairo, where he saw the Nile in all its glory: one mighty river before its fragmented meanderings to the sea; a vast swollen body of water, the artery of Egypt. He saw the cellar in which Mary and Joseph with the infant Jesus had sought refuge from the excesses of King Herod and then passed on, leaving scarcely a trace on the history of this ancient civilisation. He met the Pasha Suleiman, an ageing tyrant who devoured his people like a vengeful god, and dutifully admired (for who would dare do otherwise?) the childish hand in which he penned his fateful edicts. For this was a skill the monarch had but recently acquired, at an age when he might have been more profitably employed in making peace with his Creator.

Not that Suleiman in His Magnificence had neglected this duty. Richard worshipped with his eyes the tremulous beauty of the mosque which was to be his boast and his tomb; a dazzling confection of marble and precious stones thrusting arrogantly heavenwards. And he looked at the slender minarets and thought of the savage cruelty of the man who, when his ostler asked for shoes, had him shod in iron and then laughed until the gold crowns of his teeth danced as much as the crown upon his head.

He was glad to shake the dust of Cairo from his heels and turn towards a more ancient civilisation, one in which there was balance and principle and harmony. So Richard, on horseback, approached the Pyramids.

He outstripped Sir Thomas with the greatest of ease, his ignorance of the art of riding being here a considerable advantage. While Sir Thomas confounded his poor horse with a tight rein and a pincer-like grip of the legs, which the poor beast took as a signal to halt, Richard simply copied the native guides, and letting go the reins, clung to the pommel of his saddle and yelled 'Y'Allah!' with the best of them.

He thundered over the desert floor, the horse picking its way nimbly among the razor-sharp boulders. The hot wind seared his cheeks and the Pyramids reared out of the desert sand before his eyes; — Cheops, then Cephren, then Mycerinus, mightier by far than the Pharaohs who built them and yet as insubstantial as a sorcerer's illusion.

Richard arrived on the Giza Plateau in as much of a lather of sweat as his steed, with his clothes clinging to him and his legs still trembling violently from the speed and exertion of his journey. But up he went without hesitation, and the Arab children swarmed after him, eager to be his guide, though there was no other way but upwards to that magnificent pinnacle which pointed the way to infinity; up and up from block to block, scrabbling for a footing, pushed and pulled, levered and hauled on all sides and by every limb and article of clothing. And at last, he stood there, where Cheops met the sky, with the desert haze stretching endlessly one way, in such an expanse of nothing as can scarcely be imagined. In the other direction was the green snake of the Nile and the jumble of dusty streets that was Cairo.

All the while, the children and guides clustered about him and stroked his knees and thighs and kissed his hands and begged for bakhsheesh as he stood there feeling like a god. And like a god, he dispensed his favours liberally and carelessly, and laughed to see how greedily they fell upon the riches, scrambling after the coins with total disregard for life and safety and then gambling with them right there as close to heaven as it was possible to be.

When the money was gone they closed in on him again. Like Gulliver among the Lilliputians, rendered helpless by the sheer number of them, Richard laughingly surrendered. And so they dragged him down to earth again and into the tiny passage which led to the very heart of the Pyramid. Somewhere ahead of him in the darkness was the torch for which he had foolishly paid in advance, but wherever it had got to, no light reached him in that nightmare of jostling bodies. His shoulders and elbows grazed against the walls, and avalanches of dust fell in response to the shouting and cursing of his companions.

Half choking, half crouching to protect his head from what he could not see, Richard only knew that the path was ascending and that the heat was becoming more intolerable by the minute. His shirt still clung to his back from the exertions of his gallop followed by the fury of the climb, and his face burned as if he had been shovelling coal into a furnace. Perspiration trickled in acid streams down his scarlet cheeks, as if he were approaching the very centre of a volcano.

At last he could stand upright, and when his eyes had adjusted sufficiently to the smoky torchlight, Richard found himself within a narrow stone chamber at the centre of which stood an empty sarcophagus. Even the cries of his numerous tormentors were suddenly silenced. He put out his hand to touch the coffin. The rough stone was deliciously cool and he felt momentarily tempted to lie down and let that deep pool of darkness close over his head; it was almost as if it were waiting for him, calling to him. He had known at once that he was standing in the miraculous room where a calf's brain might be perfectly preserved forever; where a dull razor blade left overnight would recover its edge. To prove the point, one of the Arab boys picked up a blade from the rim of the sarcophagus and drew it across his finger. The frenzy which broke loose as the dark blood welled to the surface echoed and re-echoed in horrifying clamour from the surrounding walls and off the granite roof.

Richard looked up bewildered, his attention drawn away from the coffin as he tried to follow the wild waves of sound.

'Bakhsheesh, effendi!' prompted the boy, holding out his hand and allowing the blood to trickle into a sticky black pool in his upturned palm. 'Bakhsheesh!'

At once everyone fell to fighting to get hold of the razor blade, so that each might give proof to the Milord of the power of the Pyramid and of their devotion to duty.

Richard, seeing where this was leading, stood with his hands to his ears and his eyes shut tight to fend off the nauseating spectacle of self-mutilation. 'No!' he roared. 'No!' his voice reverberating round the tiny chamber like the roar of a mountain lion, so that the guides were at last terrified into silence.

Hurriedly they led him away from that place, down towards the daylight. He felt their sticky palms all about him. Blood or sweat? – it was impossible to tell. Like a sleepwalker, he let them guide him down towards the light.

Down towards light? Did not even the tiniest seed in the earth strive upwards, he asked me, towards light and warmth? Did not the drowning man strike out for the surface above his head? the mole thrust his snout towards the freedom of the sky above his head? But powerless and bereft of will, Richard felt himself dragged down and down by his guides. It was the first intimation that everything in his world had suffered a reversal; that nothing was any longer what it seemed.

Richard was strangely impassioned by this recollection. He gripped my hands tightly and looked into my eyes with a frightening intensity.

'Yes, Richard,' I said to him, trying to calm him. 'I can see how confusing it must have been, with the heat and the dust . . .'

But he gave no indication that he had even heard me, and proceeded once again with his reminiscences.

There was, he insisted, too little time for reflection; no space in which each experience could be assimilated before they moved on. For Sir Thomas adhered strictly to the itinerary. In that country where time seemed to have moved backwards since its glorious zenith some five thousand years before, where minutes and hours had no significance, Sir Thomas clung to the virtue of punctuality which served him about as well as a straw to a drowning man. He tried to impose seconds on a calendar lived by the seasons, to implant a sense of urgency in a fatalistic people who knew that all human effort was useless; for whom things happened when they happened as part of an implacable chain of events – or not at all. And much frustration he experienced because of it. The boat was not ready on the appointed day; the crew did not materialise; the provisions did not come when they were promised. He became apoplectic in his rages.

But at last the expedition was ready. They were off, up the Nile. The river, a satin ribbon set in green borders, twined through endless yellow tresses of desert. Here the temples began, each paying tribute to Osiris the Sun God, whose seed is the Nile, that fecund flood which impregnates his eternal bride, Isis, who is Egypt, causing her to multiply and bring forth fruit. The evidence was everywhere: in the date palms whose fruit nestled densely in a crown of leaves; in the maize which grew golden and tall; in the plump and luscious melons and grapes beloved of Cleopatra and centuries of Pharaohs besides; in the tales told in the hieroglyphs of a thousand temples.

And the temples themselves! Worlds of stone. Unfathomable exercises in geometry and perspective. Rectangles and squares, light and dark, sun and shade, perfect in their frozen harmony. A symphony of dark pillars set against blinding light. Gleaming gold pillars against a terrible blackness. The spaces which are pillars and the pillars which are spaces. Only the touch could tell, for the eye was ever deceived, ever drawn onward against its will.

43

On and on, the river free-flowing and seductive, – as silken to the touch as the waters of the womb; as soft as night when the boat was tied up and countless stars gleamed in a velvet sky; when the Captain put a light to the pile of brushwood and the flames leapt up, and the crew relaxed from their labours and huddled around its warmth, the light flickering off their *gellabiyahs* as they warmed the skins of their drums and tambourines.

And then such music from the smoke-blackened, tautened instruments! The sinuous rhythms and the nasal choruses. Sitting cross-legged in a wider circle just beyond the fire's glow, the older crew members watched as the young oarsmen seemed to grow as tall and bronzed as gods, as slender and graceful as women as they twined and stamped, treading carelessly barefoot among the glowing embers. The hems of their white garments drifted in and out of the flames like surges of foam on the seashore. As they moved, the eyes of the dancers became gentle and vague, focused on the magic of some inner opiate world, while those of the onlookers took on a new and predatory aspect. Glittering dangerously beyond the shrinking circle of charmed light, those pairs of reddened eyes encircled the dancers like a pack of desert wolves.

The miracle lasted only as long as the meagre supply of firewood. As the flames died down, the crew, old and young alike, became ordinary men again, – dark, coarse and ruffian-like. Richard could not understand the metamorphosis, could not grasp the moment of transformation or regression when these wonderful creatures slipped back into mortal guise.

'Sir Thomas,' he inquired of his robust and industrious patron, who even at that hour of the night was poring over his endless maps and diaries, making notes and calculations and timetables that would never be followed, 'have you ever seen such a thing?'

'Savages!' said the gentleman stoutly as he folded away his spectacles. 'I pray God to spare me from being witness to such obscenity ever again.'

With this reply Richard had to be content, for none other was forthcoming. Nor did he have the opportunity to test his observations further on his own account, for on Sir Thomas's orders, no further bonfire was kindled. From then onwards, the

44

voyage continued on a quieter note – on the surface at least – as far as Thebes.

Thus far Richard's narrative had proceeded normally enough. I revelled in his descriptions of foreign climes, and told him how I, had I been a man, could have imagined no more wonderful thing than to pass my life in experiencing the wonders of distant places at first hand. Nor was I alone in experiencing the frustration that attaches to my sex. Maria, too, had often spoken to me on the same score, and I wonder whether Mary Ann might not have proved a formidable missionary and derived considerably more satisfaction from life as a worker in the field rather than from knitting woollen squares in the missionary headquarters in Shoreditch.

But then Richard told me how he had arrived by river at Thebes. Thebes! Just imagine it – city of a thousand gates!

City of extortion and bribery, said Richard, where beggars swarmed like flies on the top of the temple walls and lowered containers on lengths of string to outwit the vigilance of the guardians. There was no escaping the whines for bakhsheesh which nagged the eardrums. Yet there was a beauty which even they could not desecrate, a timelessness which they could not disturb; – avenues of sphinxes with that half-smile born of an inner contentment, a secret power.

When Richard sat and sketched among the obelisks beside the sacred pool, he was surrounded by soldiers who kept the populace at bay. Established on a canvas folding stool with his sketchpad on his knee, he traced the famous Hypostyle Hall whose pillars soared ever upwards into a burnished sky. So absorbed was he that the hours passed, and he became aware only gradually of the intense heat slowly penetrating his turban, his hat, his skull, and now boring down through his brain, travelling ever deeper until the whole of his body glowed from this delicious inner core of fire. For a moment he experienced a freedom of soul which enabled him to see into the very heart of those lotus columns, or to soar upwards to perch on the very top of Queen Hatshepsut's obelisk and take in at a glance the whole of the ancient city and every one of its thousand gates. It was as if the spirit of creation had breathed upon him, creating him anew.

He finished his sketch in a fever of excitement and saw that it was good. By then, the sun was setting and he was suddenly beset by anxiety. Rebirth involved death, whether physical or spiritual. Looking at his body he could detect no change, but perhaps it was still too early to detect any signs of putrefaction. There was no time to lose. He scrambled his belongings together and returned to the *Golden Moon* which was anchored nearby, in a lather of sweat and almost choked by dust and fear.

Sir Thomas was annoyed at the lateness of his return. That a native should be unpunctual was only to be expected, but a true-born Englishman . . . ?

His disapproval was of less significance to Richard than the uncertainty as to whether he now belonged on the East Bank of the living, or the West Bank of the dead. It all depended on whether his body had died or not. But how was he to find out? He noticed the twitch of Sir Thomas's nostrils, and the fact that he was keeping his distance. He had to admit to himself that there was an unpleasant smell, which, after checking his shoes for dirt, he traced to his own armpits. The odour was reassuringly that of a man in a healthy sweat, for he doubted that a corpse was capable of being anything other than cold. On the other hand he was no stranger to the expression 'breaking out in a cold sweat'. A question of semantics, surely? He chuckled and sniffed again. What did a rotting corpse smell like? Not the putrid, blackened remains of long dead dogs which he had observed about the streets, but the recently dead, the decently, recently human dead?

He was still asking himself this question when Sir Thomas gave the order to cast off.

'Where to, effendi?' asked the Captain.

'The West Bank, of course,' snapped Sir Thomas.

His instruction, combined with a significant look, was sufficient to send an icy wave the length of Richard's spine. He had to clench his jaw to prevent his teeth chattering with fear. The full implications of his situation suddenly came before him with nightmarish clarity. He was bound for the West Bank, where the sun and light and life sink to rest. He was bound for the Gate of the Western Horizon and the long dark night of the soul. He would have to take on, single-handed, the many-headed serpent Apopis, destroyer of light and goodness before the judgement which would decide whether he was worthy to become a son of Osiris.

He cast longing glances back towards the east bank, reluctant to leave it now, but the black space of water between the barque and the landing stage widened, and the cries of bakhsheesh became muffled by distance. There could be no going back, – not for him. He set his face resolutely towards the West.

'Tomorrow the funerary temples,' announced Sir Thomas.

Richard nodded dumbly. What objection could he possibly make?

'Queen Hatshepsut's first, I think,' said his noble patron.

Now this did sting Richard to object. Even the most ignorant of tourists knew that this temple had been for the mummification rites of women only. 'I would prefer the Ramessarium,' he said stiffly.

Sir Thomas chewed the corner of his moustache and flushed more pink than the sunset. 'Queen Hatshepsut's!' he growled.

Richard resigned himself to the inevitable. What, after all, was gender? He had seen with his own eyes the metamorphosis of the boatmen into beautiful young girls. He had seen the lust on the faces of the older men. If those boys could change so easily, then why not he? Let them unman him if they would, what difference did it make after all to one who was now dead?

'And after that, the City of the Dead,' Sir Thomas continued with relentless logic. Then he stalked off and began his customary pacing of the small deck, – a habit Richard found peculiarly irritating since he completed each length in thirteen paces and was forced to add a curious half step somewhere between a skip and a hop, which destroyed any regularity of rhythm his movement might have had.

To distract himself, Richard turned his attention to Ahmed, the young boatman who, now that they were safely away from the shore, shinned up the mast to unfurl the sail. He had often drawn him doing this, the hem of his sky-blue *gellabiyah* gripped between his teeth. Now came the glorious moment when the expanse of white canvas shook free and plummeted heavily downwards until the wind took up the slack and ballooned it out and the ship bounded forward in response. At this, the crew shipped oars, the helmsman pulled against the rudder and the boat swung round with the sail leaning dizzily outwards, carving a great arc in the evening sky.

The sun was sinking rapidly westwards, and the palm trees were ragged against the fading light. A flock of Egyptian geese passed like hieroglyphs over the face of the sun, and Richard stared after them, despising his own ignorance at being unable to read their message. They were approaching the middle of the river at a fine speed, that mid-point between the two worlds of the living and the dead, and he watched with increasing apprehension the pitiless driving force of that full-bellied sail.

Suddenly, as if in response to his feelings, the canvas slackened then sagged in huge folds. The boat faltered and was momentarily still until the current took over from the wind and carried it gently downstream.

'Oars!' roared Sir Thomas.

The Captain was cringing obsequiously as he came up on deck. 'The men say, effendi,' he bowed until his nose all but rested on his knee, 'that the hour is now sunset. First they must wash, then pray.'

Sir Thomas's anger bubbled in his throat, while from the eastern bank the call to prayer coiled in a whiplash of exhortations about the boat, ending with the exultant cry, 'God is Great!'

Richard hoped that it was so. For there in the blush of sky before him, he saw sinking, even as the sun sank, the crescent moon and its message of hope. The night before him would be doubly dark.

'Then the men must eat,' – the Captain was already halfway down the hatch as Sir Thomas's book thudded against the upraised cover, – 'and after that they will row.' At which he quickly disappeared below deck.

With the disappearance of the sun the light failed fast. The evening was unusually chilly. Sir Thomas re-appeared from his cabin in a vast black cloak which Richard had not seen before, and stood there, silhouetted against the fading peach of sunset like some ancient figure of evil, while the boat lay stranded in the middle of the Nile, drifting in endless lazy circles.

Ahmed descended from tying up the sail and began to peel potatoes by the light of an oil lamp. Richard took out his sketchbook. It was not a picture which would appeal to Sir Thomas, – the boy peeling potatoes and chuckling, his big square toes splayed out on the planks to support him as he squatted there.

Ali was sent to help him. Ali was always sent to do the jobs nobody else wanted to do, like emptying the commodes or swabbing down the decks, – or peeling potatoes. Though a friendly enough lad, he stank in his layer upon layer of filthy rags, and tonight he was wrapped up like a mummy. Richard looked at him suspiciously.

Also in the circle of light, Richard could see the cook stooped over a charcoal burner frying onions in coconut oil, – a smell soon pungent enough to banish even that of Ali. His own smell, Richard was pleased to notice, seemed to have vanished as well. He was pleased too with his sketch, which would work up very nicely in oils in the manner of one of the Dutch masters, with the three faces in the warm circle of lamplight while their bodies faded away into darkness. The thought brought him sharply back to the present. Fading into darkness was not a pleasant prospect.

He set off for a turn about the deck to steady his nerves, and also to test his legs, and as he walked, he passed by the little window of Sir Thomas's cabin. This aperture was at about knee height, but angled so that the merest glance downwards was sufficient to give a clear view of the lighted interior.

Sir Thomas and the Captain sat at a small table with a bottle of brandy between them. Sir Thomas was dealing cards. Richard hesitated a moment, fascinated by the expressions on the faces of the two men, and stepped back slightly so that they should not see him if they chanced to look up.

The face of Sir Thomas remained impassive although the faint flush on his cheeks and the way his moustache gave the occasional twitch indicated that he was under pressure. As Richard watched, Sir Thomas arranged his hand, placed one gold piece from the pile by his left elbow at the centre of the table, poured himself a small tot of brandy, then pushed the bottle towards his opponent.

The Captain, who was notoriously fond of both cards and alcohol, raised the bottle straight to his lips. His hair was dishevelled and the buttons of his shirt undone. He was perspiring freely. He stared at his cards until his eyes bulged, then carefully turned them upside down and studied them again.

'Well,' said Sir Thomas, 'do you admit defeat?'

The Captain took another swig and giggled feebly.

Sir Thomas flung his hand face downwards on the table and drummed his fingers impatiently.

The Captain stood up, rummaged in his pockets, and finally, by dint of turning the lining inside out, produced fifty piastres.

Sir Thomas, with an unkind laugh, upped his stake to five gold pieces.

The Captain's eyes bulged. He slipped the gold ring off his finger and added that to the pile. Sir Thomas picked it up and studied it intently.

'Very old,' chuckled the Captain, 'very, very old. Very valuable.'

Sir Thomas held it up to the lamplight, went over to his desk and took out a magnifying glass. 'What's this curious figure?' he asked at last.

The Captain took another long drink. Then he shook his head to clear it and announced with great dignity, 'That is the sign of the god Osiris, King of the Underworld, Judge of the Dead, whose right eye is the sun and whose left eye is the moon.'

All at once the significance of the name of the boat struck Richard. The *Golden Moon*; — this was surely more than coincidence. This was no mere boat, but a solar barque transferring the dead to their final resting place under the all-seeing eye of—

'Osiris!' sneered Sir Thomas.

The Captain, with considerable difficulty, drew himself up to his full height. 'Sir Thomas,' he said, 'I will wager my god against yours!'

'The devil you will,' replied Sir Thomas.

The kitchen staff chose, or were directed to choose this moment to empty overboard the scrap bucket. There was a loud clatter as the pail struck the edge of the boat, and turning round, Richard saw that what he had taken for waves sparkling in the starlight, were none other than the heads of countless crocodiles.

'Sobek,' said Ali cheerfully, referring to the crocodile god who devoured the souls of the unworthy.

Richard nodded and smiled.

'Meat,' said Ali. 'How it stinks!' He tipped up the bucket. The water churned momentarily with the lashing of tails and then was still again.

But Richard knew the beasts were still there. He could see the dark hollow of an eye beneath the glint of each rippling scale. Apprehension gripped him. He was decomposing, he knew he was. His whole body broke out into a cold and clammy sweat. And beneath him the battle of the cards continued. He knew now that he had stumbled upon something of far greater significance than a mere game: this was a contest of supernatural proportions, – the God who was now his God against the God of Sir Thomas.

Sir Thomas was first to lay down his hand, and Richard saw the triumph on his face as he reached out to take the ring.

'Not so fast, my friend!' The Captain quietly laid down his cards to show a royal flush.

At that moment, there was a strong gust of wind. The sail billowed and spread. Richard breathed deeply. The gods of ancient Egypt were victorious. He felt the wind on his face and heard the soft hiss of water sliding like silk beneath the keel of the boat as they flew on into the West.

Richard remembered nothing more until he awoke in a cave, halfway up a cliff face. It must have been facing east, for the rising sun streamed into the dark interior and groping fingers of light crept into the darkest corners where they illuminated ancient graffiti similar in style to the temple paintings, but in content quite obscene. At the sight of one man in the act of penetrating another, Richard covered his face with his hands and groaned aloud.

Instantly, Sir Thomas was by his side. 'Welcome back to the land of the living, my boy!' He placed his arm about Richard's shoulders and attempted to lift him to a sitting position.

Weak though he was, Richard pushed him away angrily, and proceeded to crawl towards the mouth of the cavern. There, in the entrance, he found various pots and pans containing what he at once perceived to be funeral meats. Though Sir Thomas protested, he devoured them greedily as was his right, for their

51

purpose was to nourish the body while the spirit was in the under-world. And his body was pitifully wasted; his legs had dwindled to little more than skin and bone.

'Enough, Richard, enough now!' Sir Thomas tried to drag him away. 'Don't overdo it, you'll make yourself sick.'

He was too late, for Richard's shrunken stomach, protesting at the sudden intrusion of the rancid leftovers of the previous night's meal, reacted predictably by disgorging its contents.

Sir Thomas explained to Richard that it was ten days since he had opened his eyes. 'I was quite worried about you, m'boy,' he insisted, and was forced to stop and clean his spectacles after this emotional outburst.

'Is that the mortuary temple?' inquired Richard, looking tact-fully away into the valley beyond.

'It is,' said Sir Thomas, quite his usual self again. 'And we've been there, only you won't remember. All according to the itin-erary, you know.'

Richard knew as well as if the perfume of those precious herbs and ointments still lingered in his nostrils. And yet ten days in the mortuary temple was, he knew, not sufficient to preserve the body. It was a fear which was to remain with Richard for the rest of his life, if such a living death could be called life; – that his body would decompose before his spirit had the chance to work out its salvation. And for that reason, he told me as we sat together on that bench while the older guests sipped their sherry and watched us through the windows, he had to seek out the Arch-fiend, the many-headed serpent Apopis, and destroy him. Only in this way could he prove himself a true and worthy son of Osiris.

Chapter Three

'RICHARD!' I admonished him, 'all this gloom and talk of death on a day like today!' I raised my hands in a gesture which embraced the sun, the sky, the garden, and the charming sight over by the herbaceous border, where Catherine, as dazzlingly white as an angel, was showing off her wedding ring to Ellen.

'Mother,' he replied, 'died on a day like today.'

Reader, I remembered that day as if it had been yesterday, though I was only five at the time. Mrs Dadd had died during the night. My parents called round the following morning to offer their condolences and to bring the children back to our house. On this account, we went with them, Catherine, my brothers and I, though we were not allowed into the house.

It was a glorious morning. Dewdrops sparkled like diamonds, rocked in their cradles of lupin leaves, and a thrush too full to hunt for another worm preened itself on the lawn in the sunshine. The seven children were huddled together under the tree by the gate watching all the comings and goings. We joined them, not quite knowing what to say. Then Mary Ann suggested we should pick flowers for her mother.

'Why?' asked Sarah. 'She can't see them anyway.'

'It's what you do,' her elder sister explained, 'when people die.' And Mary Ann bent over the nearest flowerbed to hide her tears as she grasped sightlessly at the misty blue love-in-a-mist, marigolds and cornflowers.

George copied her as always, snatching at daisies with his dimpled, toddler's fingers. Round and roly-poly, often toppling over, he frowned with concentration as he grubbed up grass and roots as well as flowers, then laid the whole muddy mess in his elder sister's lap.

I followed Maria, who was attracted like a butterfly to the

brightest of colours, the brilliant, trailing clumps of nasturtiums that licked like flames over the edges of the lawn.

Eight-year-old Richard stood over us scornfully. 'That's silly,' he said, looking at our cheerful posies. 'Nasturtiums don't have any perfume, and you have to pick flowers with a perfume otherwise everyone will notice how Mother smells.'

He trampled angrily over the lovely drifting plants with their water-lily leaves to get at the roses which lay beyond. They were at their peak; fat and full blown. Already, in spite of the dew which still lay on them, they were surrounded by heavy bees, drunk on nectar. We looked at him with horror, for that was Mr Dadd's special rosebed, his pride and joy, recently re-stocked with a selection of the newest varieties.

'Remember the rat!' he admonished us as he started to pick.

We looked at one another and gaped with horror. How could we ever forget the rat? Stephen had found it only weeks before, stinking and covered with flies. Richard had poked its stomach with a sharp stick, whereupon it had exploded in a stench of gas and a mass of green entrails which had made us all retch.

Richard picked more and more roses. He gathered them until his arms were full and his hands were scratched and bleeding. I thought that he was terribly brave because he did not cry, – not then, or even when his father came outside and scolded him for damaging the rosebed.

When we got home, back to that very garden in which we now sat, Mother rubbed a salve into Richard's wounds for fear that they might fester, and bound them up with clean white strips of linen. Watching Mother reminded me of the story of Lazarus in the tomb . . .

'But you're not dead, Richard!' I said brightly, returning to the present.

'Can you prove to me that I am alive?' was his next question.

Reader, at that stage, I got up and left him. What further proof could I give him than the evidence of my own love, which at that moment shone quite naked in my eyes, or the compromising proximity of our sun-drenched bodies on that narrow bench? If more was needed, it was all about us, in the fragrance from my roses which enveloped us in a cloud of burning incense, in the liquid sheen of my rippling gold silk or the cascading trill of a blackbird which fell like a waterfall about our ears. What more did he want? But even distancing myself from Richard brought me no relief. For I only returned to the party in the house, and to the first of many hurtful comments which I was to endure that day.

'Throwing herself at him,' snorted Aunt Smith, before she was aware of my presence. 'A yellow rose!'

'So long as it's only roses!'

'What's he done with the red one he had before?'

'He put it in his pocket.'

'A rose? In his pocket?'

Nor did my harmless action go unnoticed in the sitting room where the intermediate generation were sipping glasses of that sweet sherry, which no one had thought to offer to the elderly aunts to sweeten their tongues.

Mother admonished me later for my very public act. In vain did I protest that Richard had begged a rose from me, wishing thus to proclaim his kinship with myself and Maria in a harmony of colour to which the red rose at present on his lapel offered too great a contrast. That was the last time that Richard's name ever passed between us. I never distressed her by mentioning him again, not even through all the dreadful events which took place barely two weeks later. From the day of my sister's wedding, Mother closed her mind to him as if he had simply ceased to exist. And perhaps he had – in the form which she had known and loved. For in childhood and youth he had ever been a petted and cherished visitor to her house and table, delighting her with his constant good humour and never-failing consideration.

Mr Dadd, in conversation with his old friend the doctor, appeared to be in a state of almost unbearable agitation at the sight of Richard, on the lawn, in full sunlight.

'Do you not think,' he was asking, 'that he should be advised to stay out of the sun entirely?'

'My dear Mr Dadd,' replied the other, 'I do not fancy that much harm can come to him from the few minutes he has been standing out there.'

Mr Dadd's attention was next distracted, it seemed, by the sight of George standing in the rockery surrounded by catmint, in the process of removing his jacket and hanging it over a branch. His father held his breath, as did everyone else who had heard tell of George's past extravagances. Not here, we all prayed inwardly! Not now!

As for poor Mr Dadd, his glass of sherry shook so violently in his hand that my mother was forced to step forward and relieve him of it, out of concern for the recently cleaned rug. She also took the opportunity to distract him from George by drawing his attention to Stephen sitting now on the garden swing on which he had spent so many happy hours as a child. But Stephen also appeared to be watching George, for all at once he got up, buttoned up his own jacket which was previously undone, and tightened his necktie until his eyes bulged in their sockets.

When it appeared that George was content with merely removing his jacket and rolling up his sleeves on account of the heat, everyone relaxed. Conversation resumed. Father moved among his guests offering more sherry and receiving compliments on the quality of his cellar. And while his fellow guests sipped at their drinks, Mr Dadd returned to his previous, nagging worry like a terrier to a bone.

'Do you not think, my dear doctor,' he persisted, 'that it is deucedly hot and that I had better call him in? See, even Elizabeth is quite flushed with the heat!'

'Mr Dadd, pray calm yourself,' advised the doctor.

As I passed among the guests, it seemed that the other main topic of the day was Richard's behaviour in church. If I moved to escape one interpretation, another was upon me. And if I sought solitude away from this idle chatter and speculation, it still pursued me in snatches borne upon those little gusts of wind which played among the table cloths and shook the petals from the dying roses.

How we all sought some rational explanation for his behaviour! George was convinced that Richard had been attempting to strangle his father right there in the church, but then George always had a vivid imagination. Stephen was of the opinion that a bee had somehow become entangled in his father's cravat, and vowed that he had heard it buzzing quite loudly. Mary Ann sharply rebuked her father for having dressed with less care than the occasion demanded, as if he had deliberately provoked Richard. Sarah had no opinion on the matter, she vowed she hadn't noticed the incident at all. She was a poor, spiritless creature whose habits of observation were made duller by an unhealthy degree of introspection. It is quite possible that she saw and heard nothing. Arthur and John simply giggled and thought it all a huge joke. Life had never been livelier, they agreed, than it had been since Richard's return.

In the course of these exchanges, Mr Dadd uttered not one word of censure against his son Richard. Indeed, he dismissed the incident as being of little or no significance. He could not see what all the fuss was about, he said. He accepted whole-heartedly Mary Ann's rebuke and confessed to a nervousness which had led him to rush his usually punctilious toilette. From this observation, he went on to suggest to anyone who happened to listen, the possibility that his collar had been so crooked that it could not fail to attract the attention of his son, who acted only with the commendable intention of protecting his father from ridicule.

At the thought of this, his son's solicitude, Mr Dadd could apparently restrain himself no longer. Forging a track through the other guests with scant regard for good manners, he leant through the open casement and bellowed a summons to his son. 'I say, sir, come here, if you please!'

Richard detached himself from his companions and approached his parent with such prompt obedience and good grace that he quite won over every heart. In the eyes of the company assembled over lunch, it was the father and not the son who evinced every sign of madness.

At last the food had been served and eaten and the last jellies, overcome by heat and exhaustion, had subsided into amorphous islands set in watery pink pools. The aunts were similarly slumped in their chairs, in a state of dozy shapelessness. But scarcely had the last plate been cleared away than the young people were outside and active again, amazing everyone with their energy and high spirits.

Even before a gentle snoring had replaced the buzz of conversation in the shuttered rooms, and as the maids bent their perspiring brows over vast tubs of tepid greasy water, there came the clock-clock of croquet mallet on ball. The hoops were set out and the teams chosen, and Maria and I had tucked up our yellow silk skirts in a way calculated to cause the utmost consternation to Mary Ann.

Poor Mary Ann sat in silent disapproval on the shaded steps of the conservatory, too young to join the elderly relatives, and far too old to mingle with the young people of her own age. From the small reticule which she carried wherever she went, Maria and I observed her to take out first her sewing, and then a pair of eye-glasses. The stitchwork was exquisitely fine, the colours tastefully chosen, a subtle blend which, though surprisingly sober for someone whose face still showed traces of that youthfulness which so acutely afflicted her brothers and sisters, was admirably suited to its purpose. For if Mary Ann was guilty of any secret ambition, it was this: to complete a set of church kneelers one for each member of the family, and the whole consecrated to the memory of her dead mother.

'Do you want your sewing?' we heard her inquire of her sister Sarah, who sat, as always, at her feet.

Sarah shook her head. She rested her head on her knees, and idly traced patterns in the dust with a twig.

Maria and I were at that moment gaily clumping about in the flowerbed among the dahlias, pursuing our search for a missing ball.

'Sarah?' we heard Mary Ann inquire sternly, 'Have you been drinking?'

'The merest sip,' the poor creature replied.

'Your deportment,' commented her sister, 'implies a greater indulgence.'

Maria and I crouched down behind the michaelmas daisies and shook with laughter. Oh I know, Reader, that you will think us heartless and perhaps be of the opinion that we should have hastened to extricate Sarah from the jaws of the dragon. But she sat at the feet of her elder sister out of her own choice. She had always scorned our lesser amusements, though I sometimes detected a gleam of longing in her eye as she turned down our many invitations. If she wanted to be dreary, that was up to her. We crouched down in the undergrowth and felt our way among the dense greenery for the hard globe of the wooden ball.

Sarah sat there before us, as straight as a ramrod, then idly picked a strand of variegated ivy and twined it round her fingers. 'The devil finds work for idle hands.' Mary Ann looked at her reproachfully before threading her needle.

'Do you not feel tempted to join in yourself?' asked Sarah wistfully as our ears were assailed by another outburst of laughter and shouts of encouragement from the lawn.

'Never!' came the prompt answer.

And that I could well believe. To my knowledge, Mary Ann had not played a game since the age of ten: since the time that her mother had fallen ill after George's birth, and she had taken her mother's place in the house – a position confirmed two years later when Mrs Dadd died.

'Playing indeed!' She stabbed her needle into her embroidery.

I am not sure how the conversation proceeded, for at that moment Richard came to aid us in our search. In the cool moist greenery which was as dense as any jungle, our hands met frequently as they groped among the leaves and flowers. But at last, – though too soon for my taste which this gentle dalliance suited admirably, – the ball was found, and with a cry of triumph, Richard tossed the scarlet ball out into the open, where it rolled down the sloping path and right up to Sarah's feet.

'You two not playing?' he asked, leaping out into the open and pulling me after him by the hand.

Mary Ann treated the question with the contempt it deserved, but Sarah half rose. 'May I?' she asked her sister timidly.

'Of course!' Richard took her fingers in his. 'Why do you ask?'

We returned to the game with my own feelings raging sadly in my breast. To take me by the hand was the gesture of a lover. But to take his sister by the other at the same time?

When the game of croquet was ended and the sun had slipped behind the topmost branches of the chestnut tree, Mother asked me to help dispense tea to our guests.

'In church – thank you, dear,' Aunt Smith was saying as I handed her her cup and saucer, 'he was singing the wrong hymn. I've never heard anything like it. A regular caterwauling. Wrong words . . .'

'Wrong words?'

Aunt Smith nodded with satisfaction. Flushed even beyond normal and emboldened by the unusually large intake of rich food and drink, she shimmered like a beacon in the gloomy room.

'Which words?' Though another cup was taken from my hand, it was taken thoughtlessly, for all attention was on that terrible old lady. For terrible she appeared to me at that moment, as she launched herself like a gladiator on to the attack.

'I wouldn't like to say, really I wouldn't!' Aunt Smith would not tell, – not for the reason imagined by the assembled company with mingled horror and anticipation, but because the truth was not shocking enough. 'No!' she exclaimed resolutely. 'I am not to be persuaded.'

'But Aunt Smith,' I ventured timidly, anxious to defend my love in an atmosphere which had become thick with ghastly conjecture, 'merely to mistake a hymn? What harm is there in that?'

'It was,' she said heavily, letting each word fall into the silence like a millstone into a pond, 'a children's hymn!'

'A children's hymn!' I laughed out loud with the relief.

But even here, Aunt Smith outmanoeuvred me. 'Exactly!' she said in a tone which now condemned the action itself rather than the content as her audience had hitherto supposed.

'Which one?' I ventured.

Aunt Smith, still somewhat the worse for liquor, here burst into song.

> *'Have you not heard what dreadful plagues*
> *Are threatened by the Lord,*
> *To him that breaks his father's laws*
> *Or mocks his mother's word?'*

At this point, several of the other assembled dowagers took up the ghastly, creaking chant.

> *'What heavy guilt upon him lies!*
> *How cursed is his name!*
> *The ravens shall pick out his eyes*
> *And eagles eat the same!'*

An abrupt silence followed this recital. I saw at once that I had played right into her hands. Before, all minds had been concentrated on possible blasphemy. Now the word 'insanity' trembled in the steam that rose from the hissing urn. If Aunt Smith held the trident, I unwittingly held the net, and any further protestations would only serve to enmesh Richard more securely.

Feeling like Judas, I held my peace, and the old people here let the matter drop and raised their blurred eyes to the outside world where the young people whirled past at dizzying speed like so many butterflies. One alone paused to acknowledge their stares. Richard, his fading colour now retouched by the day's exposure to the sun, stood briefly before them like a young god and saluted the Emperor's box.

'*And eagles eat the same!*' he echoed in that light baritone which I knew so well from those evenings we had spent around the pianoforte.

For whom he intended this tribute, I shall never know. Surely from his sunlit stance his eyes could have made little of the gloomy interior and its still more sombre inhabitants. Could it have been my own pale silk which glimmered soft as a moth amid the twilight?

'Poor dear boy,' murmured Aunt Smith, and with this expression ringing in my ears I took up my teapot and stepped outside.

'But my dear Robert,' the doctor was saying from the bench under the horse chestnut tree, 'I fear you are giving yourself all this upset for nothing. I see no signs of this insanity which so haunts you.'

I poured the tea with a hand rendered unsteady by relief.

'Did you not see how long he took to pass the salt at table?' asked his distracted parent.

'A momentary abstraction, quite common in company. I am often taken that way myself. Especially with a good plate of cold roast beef in front of me!' The doctor patted his ample stomach and laughed heartily.

I handed him his cup, but would far rather have flung my arms about his neck and kissed him gratefully.

'Twice during the meal he had to absent himself.' The good father had been nearly distraught with worry during those two short intervals.

'The call of nature,' said his good friend. 'You are worrying too much.'

'But twice?' Robert shuffled in his chair at the intimate turn the conversation had taken. 'A kidney infection perhaps?' he suggested hopefully. 'Something he picked up abroad?'

'Alcohol,' said the doctor easily. 'Goes straight to the bladder.'

This information caused me to blush, and I prepared to leave them to their intimate discussion. But I could not attract Mr Dadd's attention, nor by any means induce him to take the cup and saucer in his hand, so I sought about the grass for a flat place on which to leave it.

'In church,' Mr Dadd began, wondering that the bruising on his neck had not already provoked comment since it was severe enough to give him the utmost discomfort when swallowing.

'My dear Robert,' said the doctor firmly, 'you are making yourself ill! I must beg you, get a grip on your imagination. It is running wild. Look at that young man . . .'

Richard at that moment executed a brilliant sequence of shots on the croquet pitch which had the doctor on his feet, clapping his approval.

Richard turned and acknowledged the applause with a little bow before handing the mallet to his partner.

It was sometime later that Papa concluded a long speech in the centre of the lawn, gratifyingly surrounded by his guests.

'The happy couple!' he said, reaching the point at last and raising his glass. 'May God bless them now and always!'

The company followed suit with promptitude. Glasses were downed and Ellen and Mother were obliged to administer replenishments before the bridesmaids could be similarly honoured.

It was by then late afternoon and the garden was plunged into that heavy golden shade which is the precursor of Autumn. As if that were not sufficient reminder of the maturing of the season, the horse chestnut tree which dominated the setting already bore its spiked fruit like so many brilliant green miniature hedgehogs. In these picturesque surroundings, the party was assembled round a table on which stood the cake, tier upon tier, magnificently crowned with snowy crests of icing in which nestled sugar flowers, marzipan birds and looped satin ribbons.

The toasts over, weary and somewhat flushed from their exertions, the young people sank thankfully back on to the grass. Benches and chairs were now brought outside for the older generation. The air of exhaustion which hung over the gathering might well have been taken as an indication that there had already been quite enough excitement. But there was more to come. At a signal from Mother, Father clapped his hands briskly, and George and Stephen emerged from the house carrying an artist's easel, complete with a picture draped in a length of white linen.

'Ladies and gentlemen,' Father began, and the atmosphere changed instantaneously. At once everyone was all attention. Even Ellen, who had been solicitously handing out shawls to the young ladies, – smoothing out a damp ringlet here and tut-tutting over a fevered brow there, – ceased her ministrations.

Mary Ann set aside her sewing and removed her spectacles, for it was only with near work that she had trouble, her far sight was formidably accurate. Next to her crouched the contrite figure of Sarah, her breathing still somewhat hectic following her exertions with the croquet mallet.

'Richard! You never told us!' said Maria. She was at once on her feet with excitement, while Ellen's lovingly placed shawl straggled unheeded from her shoulders.

The eyes of Mr Dadd filled with tears of pride. He caught sight of Richard looking at him as if to say 'There! You see!', which he acknowledged with a little bow, and a raising of his glass. All his dreams for his son were in that moment writ plain upon his face: Richard Dadd, RA, ARA, – the honours stretched out endlessly before him and he saw himself already standing deferentially in the background insisting modestly that genius would out and that he could claim no part at all in his son's success . . .

'I hope it's not another of those fairy paintings,' muttered Aunt Smith quietly, but not quietly enough. 'I never held much with fairies and nonsense like that.'

These were sentiments which my own parents shared whole-heartedly, but the shushes and laughter which greeted Aunt Smith's pronouncement, not to mention simple good manners, forbade any overt agreement. Everyone maintained a stony silence, as if at any moment those buxom, naked beauties so much feared, might leap from the canvas and cavort openly before them on the grass. Father stood tight-lipped, Mother toyed with her handkerchief.

'Fairies, Aunt Smith?' called out Richard. 'No, no. I have done with fairies.' He seemed strangely agitated, a condition which met with the approval of all assembled as a sign of becoming modesty. I would have moved to his side to lend him the encouragement of my support, but in the general stillness which now prevailed, such an action would have attracted unwelcome attention.

On either side of the easel stood the bride and groom. Robert then indicated that his new wife should have the honour of removing the cover. Catherine blushed and drew back as far as she was able within the compass of her husband's restraining arm. At last, urged on by the impatience of the company, Robert pulled his arm even more tightly around his bride's waist, kissed her gently on the cheek to the cheers of all, and they then acted as they had promised to do for the rest of their married lives — as one. And they drew aside the cover together.

The revelation met with a stunned silence.

'What is it?' Aunt Smith at last ventured where no one else dared to tread.

'A dead camel,' said Richard.

'Dead?' asked Aunt Smith.

'Almost,' replied Richard. 'Well, it depends on what you mean by alive.'

And he went on to tell us all about the camel.

He had been walking down a palm-lined track away from the Nile, with Sir Thomas and Constantine, the Captain and their escort of Turkish soldiers, towards a dusty village whose mud houses were decorated in perfect pastels of yellow and turquoise. They were following a crowd of people in what they presumed was the direction of some festival. When further movement became impossible, Richard peered over the heads of the people in front of him, expecting to see a display of horsemanship or perhaps some strolling players or a snake charmer.

Instead there was merely a camel lying on its side with its long legs entirely blocking the thoroughfare. A few brave souls up at the front made a show of clambering over these obstacles. The camel kicked feebly and the crowd screamed with laughter as one old woman was pitched suddenly forward, the tomatoes from the basket on her head flying in every direction.

'Make way there,' called out Sir Thomas in tones which assumed instant obedience; but of course no one had taken the slightest notice.

Richard tapped the shoulder of a man in front of him. '*Il gamil da*,' he asked. 'What is wrong?'

He shrugged. 'Is too sick,' he said.

Some fifty men were trying vainly to right the poor beast, some pushing, some pulling, some belabouring it with sticks. One man even lit a small fire under its tail. When this entertainment palled, the crowd began to grow restive.

'Why don't they go round the back way if they're in a hurry?' Richard asked Sir Thomas. The village consisted of a single row of dusty houses on either side of a dirt track, which was little better than the desert beyond.

The grunt with which Sir Thomas answered was the nearest they ever came to conversation in those days. But Richard was familiar enough with his patron by now to know it as expressive of his usual low opinion of the fellahin.

Since they were likely to be detained for some time, Richard took out his sketchpad and began to draw some of the faces in the crowd around him. Mistaking the focus of his interest his immediate neighbours at once jostled him to the front of the crowd where he would have a better view of the camel. Here he started transposing on to paper, not the camel, – a dusty-coloured hump of no particular interest, – but the houses and the people beyond, which made a pleasant enough composition.

It was then that several men, bearing axes, came running on to the scene. They made a splendid sight, like ancient warriors storming on to the field of battle; only there was no battle, but merely a sick camel in its death throes.

'What are they going to do?' Richard asked the man next to him. His neighbour made chopping motions with his arms, whose meaning soon became clear to him. For the men gestured to the people nearest to them to stand back, and swinging their axes wildly over their shoulders they began hacking at the camel's legs.

Richard turned and forced his way back through the grinning people to Sir Thomas's side. 'Stop them,' he begged. 'Send in the soldiers!' For the soldiers, being Turkish, were universally feared.

Sir Thomas grunted.

'It's inhuman,' Richard protested.

As the men went on with their grisly task, the camel made no sound. It simply raised its neck and looked at the men in mild surprise, then pillowed its head on the dirt again. At this point Richard was violently sick. Sir Thomas looked away disapprovingly, while the people nearest to him laughed and pointed, their amusement spreading until everyone was laughing and even the men who were wielding the axes were forced to lay down their tools and roar at the sight of the thin-blooded foreigner.

There were flies too. They swarmed in the rivers of blood until they flowed as black as trails of molasses. They buzzed in the onlookers' eyes and ears, their feet still sticky from their ghastly repast.

When all four legs were off and a sufficient margin of street clear, the people began to push past. But the children were reluctant to leave, and one mother, gripping her veil between her teeth, seized her two small children, one in each hand, and dragged them away. Sir Thomas and Richard were swept along in the general confusion. The ribs of the camel moved regularly up and down while, with that same look of pained surprise, its eyes watched the scene that was now taking place beside its head.

With the still warm legs stacked like the tapered trunks of saplings right by the camel's nose, its owner set up an impromptu meat stall. The housewives fought and screeched over this unexpected offer, as the owner hacked off pieces to order. Sir Thomas despatched the Captain forward to choose a choice cut of the thigh joint for his dinner. The women at once covered their faces and made way for him.

'I for one shall decline to eat it,' said Richard.

Sir Thomas looked surprised. 'When in Rome . . .' he mumbled, evincing a complete change of attitude which was yet further proof of how susceptible were his standards to expediency.

'For God's sake,' Richard protested. 'It's still alive!'

Someone had placed pans beneath the stumps of the camel's legs to catch the blood. Though the pans were full, the raw ends of flesh and bone were no longer bleeding, but dark with flies. The stench was abominable, though why, Richard could not tell, for the camel was still breathing feebly, and surely it could not rot while life yet remained? The question had, he said, haunted him ever since.

After this little narrative, all eyes turned to Robert Dadd senior, who slumped forward in his seat with a loud groan.

'Richard,' protested Maria, laughing, 'you could at least have given them a live camel for their wedding present! A live camel is much more use.'

Richard looked at her curiously. Her lips were parted and the sound straggled coarsely out of her throat. 'From the moment of our birth,' he said, 'we all carry the seeds of decay within us.'

'It's got no legs!' Aunt Smith objected.

'That's why it is dying,' commented the artist impatiently.

Catherine buried her face in Robert's shoulder. 'It's horrible,' she sobbed, and Robert patted her soothingly on the back as if she were a child.

'Look at the flies!' said George, licking his lips. 'I never knew you could paint flies like that, Dicky.'

Richard inclined his head in receipt of the compliment.

His younger brothers, Arthur and John, together with the Carter grandchildren, pored over every detail.

'Look, you can see right inside its legs. Do our legs look like that inside, Uncle Richard?'

The forthright comments of the children were enough to bring the adults to their senses. Father stepped forward.

'Come along,' he said, flinging the cloth back over the easel and shooing the children back to their seats. 'Let us now carry on with the, um, – entertainment.'

There was still a distinct air of unease among the guests, a restlessness which had not been evident before.

'I think,' said Maria loudly, 'that someone ought first to thank Richard for all the time and trouble he has put into preparing this present for Robert and Catherine. For I am sure that it is very cleverly done even though we are not all sufficiently well educated in the field of art to appreciate it fully.'

How I loved Maria for that speech, and how I wished that it could have proceeded from my own lips and heart! For I saw the look of love and gratitude which Richard gave his sister, which might otherwise have fallen on me.

'Quite right,' agreed Papa, rubbing his hands together. 'Who, er, would like to propose a vote of thanks to our, er, young artist friend?'

In the silence that followed, everyone became aware that the unthinkable was taking place. After a mere three hours of marriage, the happy couple were already quarrelling. To be sure it was a disagreement of most discreet proportions, consisting of muted squeaks on the part of the bride, and deep reassuring assertions from the groom.

'Say what you like, Robert, it isn't coming to Poplar.'

'But Richard has taken such a lot of trouble.'

'That's not the point. If that picture goes to Poplar, I will not.'

All about me, my Carter relatives twitched nervously in their seats, while Richard's father, poor man, sank down in his chair and buried his face in his hands. And no one rose to give Richard thanks for the gory little masterpiece he had created. Maria attempted to salvage the occasion to some extent, by offering not words, but a burst of applause in which she was joined by George and then by Arthur and John.

So ended my sister's wedding party, – on a note of scandal and horror which soured everything that had gone before. As for me, I was left, if anything, more confused than ever. For how was a young girl to separate the tangled skeins of love and hatred, the tender touch from the hand that held the knife, the actor from his part, when such problems are not to be solved even by an old woman who has weathered nigh on eighty years?

Chapter Four

I had only to endure my present anguish and uncertainty about Richard's state of mind for another two weeks, before a sequence of events was set in motion which unfolded itself with a ghastly inevitability. Perhaps the blame should be laid squarely at the door of Fate. For disaster could only have been prevented by denying that strongest of ties; those mutual bonds of love and responsibility which exert their hold from the cradle to beyond the grave, and form the very basis of all civilisation. Reader, I refer to the relationship which exists between father and son.

If I have omitted any mention of the bond between mother and child, this is not to imply that I consider it of little value. Indeed, it is perhaps the vital factor missing from our equation. But in this present case there was no mother, and all led to ruin and abomination and the denial of the very existence of filial devotion. There were of course further relationships to be considered, those between sister and brother and between brother and brother, but all proved equally frail and as easily broken. At one stroke, and with no apparent thought for the consequences, he reduced them all to that pitiful category of orphan.

In the final analysis, it is vain to seek to apportion guilt; we must all shoulder the burden equally. Our love was weak where it should have been strong; misguided, when that lost soul was crying for direction. We feared to be cruel to be kind. It is a dilemma which faces every parent, brother, sister, lover, friend or teacher who is in danger of being beguiled by affection into losing sight of the need for restraint. Reader, I would counsel you: ever be strong, do not flinch from your duty to God and to your fellow man lest similar tragic consequences be laid upon your shoulders.

We did nothing. We sat back and prayed only that the decision be taken from our hands; and taken from our hands it was. It was as if we delivered up the victim, bound and helpless, to an all-devouring Fate. And Fate leapt at the invitation. She took the bit between her teeth and bolted, dragging us after, so firmly were we entangled in the bridle we had fitted with such loving hands. We could no more have escaped than one can seek safety by throwing oneself from a fast-moving train which is doomed to crash.

After the wedding, my parents would no longer entertain the thought of my spending so much as one minute in the Dadd household. I am therefore unable to provide you with my own account of what happened on that later, fateful weekend but two weeks thence. For such accurate information as I can provide, I am indebted to the police, the Coroner's Court, the evidence at the trial, the tireless investigations of journalists, medical reports, first-hand information from family and friends, and lastly to the written evidence of Richard himself; furnishing any deficiency therein with an imaginative reconstruction of my own devising.

Reader, let me return you to London, to a time which is exactly a fortnight removed from my sister's wedding. If that earlier time had seen the mere sliver of a new moon, it was now approaching the full. It drew the tides of the oceans to new heights, and threw them down upon the sea shores with a crushing vengeance. And beneath the surface of those swelling waters, the currents ran as swift and treacherous as those hidden in the human mind, which break upon uncharted reefs and signal disaster to many an unwary navigator.

It is to Newman Street that we must go for this next chapter of events, – to Richard's lodgings. How I came to have such an intimate knowledge of his domestic arrangements, will be revealed at a later date. Accept for now that our relationship was entirely innocent. I never at that time visited his lodgings either in company or alone, though I must confess that this was due less to regard for propriety than to lack of opportunity. My parents conspired to keep me away from London.

The scene is the doorstep which marks the entrance to the property of the redoubtable Mrs Jenkins, – a doorstep distinguished throughout the entire length of the street by its gleaming state of sterility and the presence of identical geraniums in identical twin pots (which Richard termed 'the guardian angels' of the property) and whose presence or absence delineated the divisions of day and night more purposefully than sunrise or sunset. Every night without fail, in went the geraniums and out went the cat. Throughout the summer months the procedure never varied. And in the morning, the inverse was set in motion – in the course of which we discover Mrs Jenkins arranging the tubs with mathematical precision, and straightening up from her task to find herself surrounded by a trio of handsome, artistic young gentlemen: Billy Frith, Augustus Egg and Henry O'Neil.

'Go in, my dears, go in!' Mrs Jenkins hustled these members of the Clique indoors and up the stairs to Richard's studio, – not out of a desire to be kind but fearful that such a gathering of young gentlemen might draw undue attention to her doorstep. It didn't look good. Nor did the good landlady want them cluttering up her hall.

'He's gone shopping. Won't be long though. More eggs,' she explained, proud to show off the extent of her knowledge of the techniques of painting. Her sister Doris could never have remarked with such nonchalance that a lodger of hers had gone out for more eggs when she knew quite well that there were a hundred or more already stacked away upstairs. But then Doris did not get such a class of lodger as she did herself. What could you expect down in Poplar?

'He's doing an awful lot of painting,' added Mrs Jenkins, piqued that none of the gentlemen expressed the least degree of surprise at her erudition. 'Morning, noon and night . . .' she continued, waving them on in direct contravention of Richard's instructions to allow no one into his studio while he was out. She then stood at the bottom of the stairs marking who took the trouble to wipe his feet or offer her a good morning, who trailed his fingers up the wallpaper or left sweaty prints on the banisters or took the stairs two at a time.

'You know the way?' she called after them, as if anyone could get lost on the one flight which led to the small landing.

'Yes, thank you, Mrs J.,' Billy Frith called down.

71

Mrs Jenkins waited until the last young man was out of sight before she entered her living room and closed the door firmly behind her. A brightly coloured parrot squawked briefly at her entrance, fluttered to the full extent of his chain, then settled back on his perch.

'Well, Pieces, my love,' said the good lady, — Pieces of Eight being the bird's name, — 'did you ever see such an invasion at this hour of the morning?'

The parrot cocked his head and fixed one bright eye upon her, drinking in every word of her report.

'I don't understand it, indeed I don't. Visiting at this hour of the day. Orgies and whatnot, I shouldn't wonder!' And Mrs J. took up her post by the lace curtains and scanned the street avidly for her young lodger's return. 'More eggs indeed!' She clucked her tongue in disapproval, a sentiment which was echoed to perfection by the bird.

'Well I never!' it ventured.

'And neither did I!' the lady exclaimed. 'That makes the third basketful this week.'

Upstairs in Richard's room, Frith, Egg and O'Neil, far from indulging in any of the vices which haunted Mrs Jenkins' lurid imagination, were standing mutely around an easel in the centre of the studio. On the easel was a cartoon showing St George and the Dragon, with a maiden clinging to her protector's shoulder.

'Nice looking girl,' said O'Neil.

'His sister,' Billy Frith explained. 'Maria. The others wouldn't sit for him, not in costume.'

'Why ever not?'

Billy laughed. 'God would not permit.'

'I came to see him last week,' remarked Egg nervously. He was looking through the window into the street in a state of considerable agitation.

'Why didn't you say so before?'

'It wasn't the sort of thing I wanted to get around.'

'We're his friends,' objected Billy. 'We have a right to know.'

Egg hesitated before he went on. 'He wouldn't let me in.'

'Well!' chortled O'Neil. 'You were snubbed, weren't you?'

'I wish it were that simple. He's coming now,' warned Egg. He had turned quite pale.

'Sit down, old chap, get a grip on yourself,' murmured Billy.

Downstairs the net curtains twitched back into place. 'He's coming, Pieces m'boy.' Mrs Jenkins retreated hastily, sat herself on the sofa and took up her Bible.

'Well I never!' squawked the bird.

'With a whole basket of eggs over his arm,' continued his mistress with a significant glance.

'The door was locked,' Egg was saying. 'He thrust a knife under it and yelled, "Go away, you devil." '

'And you just went away?'

'Come on, Billy, what would you have done in my place?'

The three looked at each other. What indeed could have been done? Break the door down? Send for a doctor or policeman? Richard had a perfect right to be alone if he so wished.

The front door slammed and they heard the hum of voices downstairs.

'Mr Dadd,' called out Mrs Jenkins. 'Is that you?'

'Since you were spying on me not five seconds past, I think you can assume that it is.'

'Me?' protested the lady. 'Looking at you? You flatter yourself, Mr Dadd! I only feared for the weather and the washing.'

'Well, well.' She heard his foot on the stairs.

'Mr Dadd, in here if you please!' She recovered quickly from her embarrassment and resumed her usual, hectoring tone.

Richard descended the stairs, and stuck his head round the door.

'Mr Dadd,' she remonstrated, indicating the basket over his arm, 'this is not a hatchery.'

'Well I never!' The parrot scuttled along its perch towards the visitor and glared at him malevolently.

'You dare!' said Richard, seeing its eye on his cuff buttons.

'The eggs, Mr Dadd,' pursued the landlady.

'Mrs J.,' he said patiently, turning the full power of his blue eyes upon her. 'How many times must I explain to you that they are necessary in the mixing of paint?'

'But so much paint!' She set aside all pretence of reading, removed her spectacles which were in any case too askew for accurate vision, and slammed the good book shut.

'I have whole sketchbooks which must be transposed into compositions illustrating my travels. For Sir Thomas,' he added knowing that the mention of that titled gentleman would mollify her somewhat.

'Such a dear brave gentleman!' Mrs Jenkins' eyes grew misty. 'To face an unruly mob of revolutionaries alone; without fear!'

'Some say he got in the way quite by accident,' said Richard irreverently. 'By the way, he's coming this morning, at eleven o'clock.'

'Here?' gasped Mrs J. There was just time, – yes just, if she could bring herself to pay a whole penny rather than the usual half, – to get a message to Doris. 'Sir Thomas, coming here?' she repeated.

'Well I never!' shrieked the bird.

Richard, in a moment's inattention, moved too close to the perch and a sharp beak fastened on his ear lobe. 'Damn you!' he exclaimed.

'Mr Dadd; I will not tolerate such language, really I won't.' The poor lady sank back on to the cushions, quite breathless.

Richard backed towards the door, apologising profusely.

'And another thing,' Mrs Jenkins called after him, 'not too much of this painting, young man. I don't want to come upstairs and find my dear husband's bedroom has been turned into a regular Sistine Chapel.' And she shrieked with laughter at this display of wit, in which she was joined by the raucous, uncomprehending screams of the parrot.

'Well, to what do I owe this honour?' Richard halted on the threshold of his room. His voice was far from welcoming and his three friends backed away against the far wall.

'We were just passing, Dicky,' said Billy. 'Called in to see how the cartoon was going.'

'Well, you've probably already had a good look, haven't you?' Richard put the basket of eggs down behind the settee.

'We haven't seen you lately.' O'Neil took his courage in both hands and stepped forward to take another look at the easel.

'No, I've been busy.' Richard indicated the pictures around the walls. 'Working up things from my sketchbooks.'

'Maria, isn't it?' said Billy, pointing to the female figure again.

'Billy!' said Richard. 'That common observation is not worthy of you. Comment if you like upon the draughtsmanship of the whole or on aspects of the composition, but to single out the model is something I would only expect of a layman.'

Blushing furiously at this rebuke, Billy broke out into nervous laughter. 'Truth is,' he confessed, 'I'd heard you weren't quite yourself lately. So I came to see for myself.'

Richard threw himself down into a chair and smiled charmingly up at his friend. 'Oh? And who told you that?'

'I forget,' said Billy airily, dismissing the question and returning to stand thoughtfully in front of the easel. 'Truth is I don't quite know what to say.'

'Meaning,' said Richard, stroking his chin, 'that you don't think much of my entry for the competition?'

'No,' said Billy bluntly, 'if you put it like that. In execution, yes. Indeed, I wish I had your skills.'

'The subject then?'

'Is one that I do not care for, but every competition sets its own, so you haven't much choice, have you?'

'We are getting somewhere at last.' Richard leant forward as he spoke. 'The composition bothers you then, – the interpretation?'

'If you insist,' Billy burst out. 'It's the dragon. It won't do at all, you know.'

'The dragon?' Richard looked from face to face and saw in each the same disapproval. 'Well then,' he said, 'we've always been quite honest with each other, so tell me.'

'If you must know,' stammered Billy, 'it's the tail.'

Richard burst into laughter. 'Is that all?'

'It's too long.' Billy spoke sulkily, unused to being laughed at.

'I would not like,' spluttered Richard, 'to lose my friends because of a tail.'

Egg and O'Neil had become as stony-faced as Billy.

'It is quite mad,' Billy observed stiffly.

'Mad, eh?' Richard looked thoughtful, then he laughed again. 'And which of you has ever seen a dragon to know whether my idea of one is "mad" or not?'

The others shuffled uneasily on their feet.

'Don't take it personally, Richard,' O'Neil began.

'How else can I take it?' Richard got to his feet angrily.

'The appearance of even a mythical creature is bound by certain conventions,' observed Billy.

'How stuffy you all are.' Richard strode up and down the room. 'How boring! If we listened to people like you we'd still be drawing buffalo on cave walls with charred sticks.'

'People won't like it, Richard,' Egg warned.

'People won't like it!' Richard mimicked him angrily. 'What do I care if they like it or not?' For a few minutes he walked to and fro, considerably agitated. Then he stopped beside his picture. His voice quietened and he spoke with immense dignity and authority. 'I am an artist. I follow my imagination. If I am not true to its dictates, then life has nothing further to offer me.'

At this speech, there was a ripple of applause from the doorway and a feminine voice said with enthusiasm, 'Well said, Richard!'

They all turned to see Maria, quite charming in her light summer muslin and sun bonnet. Richard greeted her warmly, hardly noticing as his friends took their leave, though there was something final about the way they disappeared with scarcely a backward glance. He was too absorbed in the magical presence of his sister, whom he took by the hand and led into the room.

'What do you think of it?' he asked.

'Wonderful,' she replied. 'You're better than ever, Dicky.' She pointed to the figure of the woman and asked, 'or is it just vanity?'

Mrs Jenkins' living room was rendered quite dark by the three gentlemen who gathered on the pavement immediately outside, there to discuss their friend Richard with much shaking of heads and the exchanging of sorrowful glances.

Mrs J. had, fortunately, propped open the lower half of the sash window with one of those bits of old stone which her late husband used to bring back from his visits to the South Coast. Fossils he called them. She had given them many a worse name, but had to admit that they did come in handy from time to time. Now they proved the point by making her party to a description of every deviation of her lodger's behaviour. Knives, and heaven only knew what sort of carry on besides. It was enough to make Mrs J. uneasy in her bed at night in spite of the stout lock which she had recently seen fit to attach to her bedroom door. She wondered whether she would not be wise to insist on the immediate departure of her lodger, and resolved to speak to him on that very matter at the next available opportunity. Until then, she would endeavour to persuade her sister Doris to stay with her; she would feel safe with Doris around.

Her servant girl stood in the doorway, waiting to take the note. Mrs Jenkins urged upon her all possible speed, so that her sister might catch sight of her famous visitor. The child vowed to do her best. She was quite trembling with excitement at the thought of the time it would take to get to Poplar and back. Though Mrs Jenkins was happy to provide a cab fare in the outward direction, it would be up to her to walk the distance back. The day stretched before the little waif, as good as a holiday.

Reader, there now occurs an episode concerning myself, which I would in all honesty have preferred to conceal. Even after so many years, it has the power to wound my very soul. The charge is both personal and impersonal and I know not how to answer it. Were it levelled at a specific defect of character, I would have laboured to put it right; and I would have done so not merely out of love, and the wish to please my beloved, but out of the desire to work towards that increasing state of perfection which must be our goal here on earth.

In autobiography, one might well be excused for drawing a discreet veil of silence over affairs which are not particularly flattering to oneself. One can select only those incidents which present one's self in the best possible light, and edit the rest in a manner which, if not exactly prejudicial to the truth, could certainly have the effect of offering a different perspective upon it. With regard to someone else's character, one can take no such liberties. If, as biographer, I choose to present to you a certain character, the truth of my portrait of this individual must take precedence over my own sensibilities as author.

Do not, therefore, judge me too harshly. It is not easy to expose oneself to possible censure, even upon the altar of Verity. I offer myself from the highest motives, for against the following allegations I have no defence. To correct such faults, if correction is deemed necessary, would have been beyond the wit of any young girl. I appeal to your better reason: could it have been expected of someone of my youth to go against everything that had been instilled in her from her tenderest years? To turn her back on family and home? In short, to reject the form and the comfort of a whole way of life? I could not do it. Mine was no reformer's zeal, no heroic temperament which could drive all else before it in passionate commitment to an ideal.

Not that the 'crime' for which I was so harshly judged is indicative of any viciousness of character. I was not prone to that affectation and pride which afflict so many well-bred young ladies. Mine was essentially a homely nature. I was no more nor less than the child of a very ordinary family, and well schooled in the niceties of principle and society alike. If such be a crime, then I bow to your judgement. It might have been different if I knew then what I know now. Reader, if that young girl had possessed this old woman's mind, she might have responded to the call.

But she was so very ordinary, so very conventional!

For your further understanding in this sad matter, let us return to the dialogue between Richard and his sister Maria. The subject, as you will not be long in divining is, of course, myself.

'I had a letter from Elizabeth today,' Maria was saying, in the room over Mrs Jenkins' head.

'Oh?' Richard removed the pencilled dragon from the easel and replaced it with a watercolour of a mosque.

'She says how dull Chatham is since our family left. She is all alone now that Catherine has gone as well.'

Richard moved the easel so that the light from the window fell full on it. Then he stood back and considered the effect.

'You're not even listening,' Maria accused him.

'Chatter away,' he said, 'it doesn't bother me.'

'Then it should!' retorted his sister. 'They want her to marry J.L.'

Maria watched Richard closely. Even this remark did not seem to cause him any concern.

'But I saw you, Richard . . .' Maria could not quite understand his complacency.

'Doing what?' he asked pleasantly.

Maria shrugged and her brother put his arm around her. 'What do you think of that one?' he asked, pulling her close to him.

Maria rested her head on his shoulder but refused to be distracted. 'Holding hands in the shrubbery, selecting a yellow rose from Elizabeth's basket.'

'So what?' he laughed. 'Is there anything so significant in that?'

'It depends,' Maria said carefully, 'on the motive behind your action.'

'Motive?' Richard looked at her closely. 'Why do you talk of motives? I wished merely to adopt a colour more in harmony with that of your pale yellow silks than the rather vulgar red I was wearing.'

'That is not how Elizabeth saw it.'

'Oh Elizabeth!' said Richard impatiently. 'Why all this talk of Elizabeth?'

'And I saw you looking at her in church.'

'I looked at many people in church,' he responded lightly. 'I even looked at Aunt Smith. Would you like me to propose to her?'

'Richard,' Maria reproached him, 'don't you like her just one little bit?'

'Can't you be satisfied with one marriage between the Carters and Dadds?' Richard withdrew his arm from Maria's shoulders and stepped away angrily.

'Before your journey—' Maria began.

'Things are different now. A journey like that changes a person. When you come back, it is as if you see things through new eyes.'

'What has that to do with Elizabeth?'

Richard sighed and took one of Maria's hands in his. 'Maria, how can I put this without hurting you?' He paused to stroke her hand gently. 'I have seen women such as Raffaello and Michael Angelo painted, and as free from affectation. You should see them as they go to fetch water or to help in the fields. They carry themselves upright and walk with such a gait as a rational creature should use.'

Maria snatched her hand away from him. 'They were probably women of low origin and no morals or education whatsoever!'

Richard sighed. 'Perhaps. But to me, everything about them conveyed a truthfulness of character, a thing to be more prized than all the boarding-school accomplishments.'

'Is Elizabeth then to be slighted because she is too refined for your tastes?'

'I knew you wouldn't understand.' Richard moved away from her and stood with his back to the window so that his face was hidden in its own shadow.

'Oh Richard,' she appealed. 'I'm sorry. Don't let Elizabeth spoil things between us. Show me some of these wonderful women.'

'I haven't time,' he answered shortly. 'Did you bring everything I need for my entertaining?'

'Shortbread, with Ellen's love,' replied Maria lightly. 'Fit, she insists, even for the refined palate of a gentleman such as Sir Thomas, who has sat at the Queen's table.'

'And the sherry?'

'Father's best, he assures you. And sends his love and hopes you will come to dinner tonight.' Maria unpacked her basket as she spoke and arranged the two glasses on a silver tray on the sideboard. 'And he says you may return the glasses at the same time.'

Richard busied himself about the room setting out pictures here and there, continually dissatisfied with the arrangement and shuffling them around.

'Shall I go, Richard?' asked Maria.

'Please yourself.' Richard finally decided on the painting to be set in pride of place on the easel; – only it wasn't quite finished. He removed his jacket and took up his brush and palette.

'There's something else I wanted to ask you, Dicky,' Maria said hesitantly.

Richard grunted with impatience.

'It's about Jock.'

Richard seemed not to hear her. He was mixing a curious purple-pink colour.

'I want to be able to meet him somewhere.'

'You have a home,' Richard remarked amiably enough. 'A most comfortable home comprising drawing room, parlour, library, hall. A most desirable residence with ample space for receiving guests.'

'It's not that, if you must know. It's Father. He doesn't give us a moment's peace together.'

Richard paused over his collection of brushes. Picked one up then put it down again muttering angrily. 'Did you have anywhere in mind?' he growled.

Maria disregarded the warning tone. 'Don't be so obtuse,' she said, now as angry as her brother. 'As a matter of fact I did.'

Brother and sister momentarily glared at one another, each daring the other to say more.

'Here of course,' said Maria defiantly.

'It is not a relationship I care to encourage,' Richard observed. 'He has no talent and no future.'

'How can you say that!' Maria stamped her foot. 'People speak very highly of him.' She leant against the table, gripping the edge tightly behind her.

'Besides, I do have your reputation to consider.' Richard rinsed his brush very carefully, without looking at her.

'You sound just like Father.'

'Oh do I indeed?' That really put Richard in a temper. 'Imagine,' he roared, 'how it feels to come home and find your sister hanging round artists like some cheap model.'

'I love him, Richard.' Maria spoke with tears in her eyes.

'I dare say young Dolly tells Jock exactly the same thing after she has said it to Frith and to Egg and to—'

'That's not fair!' Maria fumbled together her bonnet and shawl, anxious only to be gone. 'You've no right . . .' she sobbed, making for the door.

Richard smeared paint on to his palette and stirred it round and round with his knife into a thick soupy mess.

'And,' continued Maria, with the door partly closed between her and her brother, 'if it is cheapening myself to act as an artist's model you needn't think that you can use my services any longer either. You can find someone else and pay her. Just like a whore!'

Richard flung the knife. It rebounded harmlessly off the door which Maria slammed behind her.

'Good morning, Miss Dadd,' remarked Mrs Jenkins pleasantly to the flushed and weeping figure who half ran, half fell down the staircase into her hall. 'Lovely morning!'

Maria hastened past without acknowledgement.

'Such manners,' observed the good lady to her faithful parrot as Maria sped along the pavement outside at such a pace that the lace curtains were set aquiver. Then she heard Richard's footsteps thunder across the room over her head and the next minute he flung open the sash window.

Anxious not to miss one second of the drama, Mrs Jenkins was instantly out on the front doorstep, polishing away at the already clean brass bell as if her life depended on it.

Above her, Richard stuck his head out of the window and opened his mouth to yell after his sister.

'I'll trouble you to remember, Mr Dadd,' called out Mrs Jenkins' sharp voice with the vowels grating one against the other like the teeth of a saw, 'that this is a respectable neighbourhood!'

Richard, rather disappointingly, banged the window down, leaving Mrs Jenkins to her solitary and now unrewarding task. She was somewhat surprised. Mr Dadd usually gave as good as he got. What could be the matter with him? Perhaps there was something to the rumours, after all.

I think it highly likely that far from wishing to cause another scene in the street, Richard had hastened to his window with the intention of calling back his sister and making up their quarrel. For Richard was deeply attached to Maria and it was most unlike him to wish to cause her hurt. He would have sooner wounded himself for he was the kindest creature imaginable.

It behoves me here to explain the somewhat enigmatic reference to a Mr J.L., whose name Maria mentioned in connection with my own. Mr L. had for some time been a business acquaintance of my father, though considerably his junior in years. Of late, affairs relating to the shipyard, and then the pleasure of companionship, had made him a frequent visitor to our house. My mother, as was her habit, now that I was the only remaining child of the family, and a girl at that, often teased me about his visits and his attentions to myself. Such an agreeable man would not, she vowed, be drawn to such frequent attendance on an old lady like herself.

About J.'s behaviour, I had remarked nothing which could be attributed to more than a polite regard for my welfare. But despite every denial on my part, Mama would have it that his presence depended entirely upon my own, and she must have broadcast this ridiculous notion widely enough for it to have reached the ears of Maria. Certainly at that time I had never spoken to her about it.

Ah Maria! You did your best to press my suit. What sort of lover was he that did not even respond to the threat of a rival? Alas, the answer was only too clear. It was unfair to goad him and expect a response from that tortured mind. It only heaped coals upon the smouldering embers and drove him ever deeper into the arms of Distraction.

But his attempt to extricate himself, to call back the sister he so loved, was thwarted by his interfering busybody of a landlady. In what different frame of mind, then, might he have received his other visitors that day. Might there not have been a more cordial welcome perhaps for Jock? A kind word for his father and for Sir Thomas Phillips?

But no, her meddling, which could at times be comical, was in this instance tragic. Richard retreated behind his closed window, and Mrs Jenkins, cheated of her prey, retired to her parlour to lick her wounds.

Had she remained a moment longer at her unnecessary work, Mrs Jenkins would have been fortunate enough to have witnessed the arrival of another visitor. That she missed his arrival was a pity, for the person who was then walking up the street, in a manner surprisingly vigorous for such a warm day, ranked high in her estimation; – she considered him to be a regular gentleman. As it was, the first notice she had of his visit, was a respectful knock on her living room door.

'Come in,' she called, the Bible once more open on her knee.

'Am I disturbing you?' came the soft Aberdeenshire voice.

'Blessed are the meek,' Mrs Jenkins intoned, having chanced upon that very page.

'For they shall inherit the earth.'

'Mr Phillip,' exclaimed the landlady with delight as she closed the good book with a resounding smack.

Jock Phillip held out a small posy of flowers. He had not enjoyed the status of gentleman for so long that he had forgotten the delights which privilege can so easily bestow.

Mrs Jenkins plunged her long thin nose into the proffered blooms and inhaled deeply. There was no need for words, for a deep blush expressed her delight.

'Your poor friend is upstairs,' she said, mouthing the words for fear that Richard might hear.

'Poooor?' inquired Jock, lingering over the word as only one of his extraction is capable.

'He is not quite himself this morning, poor lamb.'

Jock looked seriously upset by this news. Indeed he might have been quite happy to leave his compliments with the good lady and make a hasty exit, had she not ushered him firmly towards the stairs.

'I am sure,' she continued, 'that the sight of a good friend like yourself is all that is needed to restore his humour. Those others, they always go upsetting him.'

'Which others?' said Jock, finding himself edged slowly but inexorably across the hall, with Mrs Jenkins firmly planted between himself and the street door.

'It was his sister,' she continued, 'who seemed to upset him so.'

'Maria?' asked Jock apprehensively as the street door and all chance of escape shrank ever further from view. 'Was Maria here?'

'You just missed her.' Mrs Jenkins advanced, forcing the young man to retreat, step by step, up the stairs; until at last, straightening his jacket, Jock knocked timidly on his friend's door.

'Don't just stand there, laddie, come in!' Richard was all affability.

Jock, far from being reassured, entered nervously, leaving the door wide open behind him.

'Well?' said Richard, scarcely looking up from his work.

'Just called round, old man,' stammered Jock, 'I'd heard . . .'

'Never listen to gossip,' said Richard lightly.

Jock approached the easel. 'Interesting, Richard.'

'Just an old tomb. They're two a penny, you know.'

'A lot of purple, ain't there?' Jock commented, his confidence increasing by the minute since Richard sounded quite his usual self.

'Have you ever been in the desert at dawn?' he now asked his visitor.

'Well no, actually,' Jock was forced to admit. 'No deserts in Scotland, you know.'

'Well,' said Richard in pleasant tones, 'I'll thank you to keep your ignorance to yourself.'

Thoroughly snubbed, but trying to hide his hurt, Jock strolled nonchalantly over to the window.

Richard, by now enjoying himself, took up a thicker brush and added more purple.

'Purple sand?' inquired his poor friend, at last goaded into speech.

'Purple everything,' Richard assured him. The more Jock's eyes bulged, the thicker he laid it on.

'Even, er, camels?'

Richard nodded vigorously.

'Um, that was quite a nice little picture when I came in.' Jock stood cautiously behind Richard, peering round him on tiptoe, for he was considerably the shorter of the two.

Richard splashed an outrageously purple minaret on to a purple mosque.

'It might have fetched ten guineas,' observed Jock, cut to the core by this waste of potential earnings.

'I am concerned,' said Richard, 'with art, not prostitution.'

'You never worried about earning an honest penny before.'

Richard daubed in a purple sunrise. 'I am not averse to prostitution, as you very well know,' he said as he worked away, 'but when it comes to my sister . . .'

'I fail to see the connection . . .' Poor Jock was quite bewildered at the turn the conversation had taken.

'Oh come on, Jock. No doubt Mrs Jenkins has already told you she was here this morning.' Richard turned round suddenly and painted a thin purple streak the length of Jock's nose.

'You're making me out to be a villain then?' A scarlet flush crept up from Jock's collar and spread slowly over his neck.

'I say,' said Richard admiringly, 'what a colour!'

But Jock did not stay to be admired. He stormed out of the room with all the dignity which he could muster and stalked off down the stairs.

'Mr Phillip,' called Mrs Jenkins in alluring tones from the parlour.

Jock's footsteps did not falter.

Mrs Jenkins, with the nosegay of flowers pinned to her flat and tightly corseted bosom, which called to mind nothing so much as a recently decorated tombstone, closed the living room door and threw her Bible at the cackling parrot.

Friends, they called themselves! Was it friendship to run like startled rabbits at the first approach of the hunter's gun? Fine friends they were who wanted only the glory of a few memories with which to bejewel their own lack-lustre autobiographies! Had he been sick in body, they might have sat by his couch day and night in tender solicitude. But of spiritual nourishment, they offered none, for they had none to give.

Reader, perhaps you have never known what it is to be kept at a distance by virtue of one's sex. To be immured, ensnared in the straitjacket of womanly passivity. Now more than ever I longed to go to him, not from any interested motive which desired a return of that passion which haunted me; I should have died sooner than let one murmur, one plea, escape my lips. I wanted only to be his nurse, his guardian, his angel. I yearned simply to prove my friendship by remaining at his side when all the world was against him.

But I could not.

Downstairs, Mrs Jenkins got to her feet in alarm, as a peal of laughter broke about her ears. She wasn't against people enjoying themselves in her house. She even found it possible on occasion to overlook that which exceeded the bounds of polite amusement, like when the young gentlemen got together for a bit of a drink and some fun. After all, she had once been young herself. She and Mr Jenkins had enjoyed a party from time to time; – or rather, Mr Jenkins had. But to hear a young gentleman, whom she knew to be entirely on his own, bellowing with laughter – it positively made her blood run cold.

Purposefully seizing her feather duster, Mrs Jenkins upended it, perched on the arm of the settee, and rapped severely on the ceiling. This had the opposite effect to that intended. The laughter upstairs became nothing short of demoniacal, and to make matters worse the parrot echoed it with glee.

'Pieces!' she roared. 'Pull yourself together!'

What with shouting and banging and trying to block her ears all at the same time, poor Mrs Jenkins quite failed to hear the ring at the door bell. It was only when her sister Doris, driven to the extremity of letting herself into the house, had entered the room and attracted her sister's attention by tugging at her skirt, that Mrs Jenkins came to her senses.

'Upon my word, Ethel!' came her sister's voice.

Mrs Jenkins lowered herself to the ground where she paused to straighten her dress, exclaiming all the time, 'I won't stand for it, indeed I won't!' until she was at last recovered sufficiently to peck her sister on the cheek.

'Have I come into a madhouse or what?' inquired Doris, as her sister resettled her corsage and Pieces smoothed his ruffled plumage.

Her question met with complete silence, as if the pandemonium of the last few minutes existed only in her mind. But Mrs Jenkins' ears still rang with the chaos, which had set up an unpleasant buzzing in her head.

Richard, who was sensible of the fact that the door bell was ringing, had stopped at once in mid-cackle. Could it be that Sir Thomas had arrived early? The thought was sufficient to bring him instantly to his senses. He shoved the remains of the canvas picture, through which he had thrust his foot, under the sofa and scraped the dollops of purple paint off his palette and into one of Mrs Jenkins' precious vases. Then he scurried around collecting dirty socks and shirts off the floor and stuffing them out of sight wherever he could, – behind the cupboard and into the large brass pot under the aspidistra, snatching by the way at a handful of its leaves with which to polish his shoes. By the time he realised that this visitor was not for him, the room was well on the way towards looking respectable.

Maria arrived back in Suffolk Street flushed and faint with exhaustion. Her condition was such as to cause the greatest anxiety.

'You shouldn't have walked all this way, Miss Maria. Not in this heat, you shouldn't,' reproved Ellen, as she removed Maria's bonnet.

For Maria was beyond doing even such a simple thing for herself. She lay on her bed on the deliciously cool linen while Ellen drew the curtains and applied a cold wet cloth to her scorched brow.

But the reaction of her father to her state was the very opposite of that calm reassurance of which she stood in such dire need.

'What was Richard thinking of,' he raged, 'to send you home like this!' He was pacing up and down the tiny room, up and down, with his hands clasped behind his back.

'It wasn't Richard,' said Maria weakly, trying to defend her brother.

'What did he say to you?' Robert Dadd paused briefly at the end of her bed to glare down at her.

Maria closed her eyes. 'Nothing, it was nothing,' she moaned.

'You don't come home in this state for nothing!' Mr Dadd ran his hands through his hair, quite distracted.

'I ran and I became over-heated, that is all,' said the poor girl.

'Hush,' said Ellen, 'you're home now. Everything is all right.' And she again wrung out her cloth in the icy water.

Maria felt herself sink into the soft bed. It was a pleasant sensation, like drowning. 'Sing to me, Ellen,' she whispered.

And Ellen dismissed her employer with a wave of her hand, and began softly, 'Rock-a-bye baby . . .'

'Father!' called Stephen, as his parent sped through the hall.

'Can't stop.'

'But Father,' Stephen protested, standing there stiffly in his black jacket, indistinguishable from the shadows behind him. 'There's someone to see you in the shop.'

'Tell them to call back later. I must see Richard.' Mr Dadd wrenched blindly at the front door catch.

'Your hat, Father.' Mary Ann hurried out of the dining room. 'Remember the sun.'

'I must,' he stammered, 'I must go to Richard. Sir Thomas is to visit him this morning and I fear . . .' In his agitation he grabbed at the nearest headgear.

'A deerstalker in mid-summer, Papa!' Mary Ann gently replaced it with something more fitting and kissed him. 'Take care, Papa,' she said. 'It won't do for you to arrive in a lather, you know.'

Robert Dadd was fortunate in obtaining a cab almost as soon as he turned into the Haymarket. Indeed, the distance to his son's flat was covered so fast that he had scarcely time to compose himself. He therefore dismissed his conveyance at the end of Newman Street and proceeded on foot, to give himself time to collect his thoughts. As he advanced along the street, he was somewhat dismayed to see Sir Thomas already approaching Richard's front door from the opposite direction. For an instant, Mr Dadd was tempted to break into an undignified sprint in an effort to reach his son's house first. Then realising that he could in no way effect an entry unobserved, he reconciled himself to the fact that there would be no opportunity of seeing his son alone, to ascertain whether he was indeed fit to receive his distinguished patron.

From the cordial manner with which the father greeted Sir Thomas, no one could have guessed at the apprehension which tightened its steel bands about his chest.

'My dear Sir Thomas!' Robert Dadd advanced with arm outstretched.

'Mr Dadd, I had not thought, indeed I had not anticipated the pleasure of seeing you this morning.' Sir Thomas's handshake was warm and hearty. Though he had not liked to bring an escort, he was relieved that he would not have to face Richard alone.

'How is the dear boy?' he inquired.

'Quite well, I thank you,' said the father with an unusual and not entirely heartfelt degree of optimism. 'Quite recovered. Back to his work, you know.' As he spoke he removed his hat and passed the brim between his fingers twirling it faster and faster. 'In fact,' he lowered his voice, and leant confidentially towards the knight, 'you would never know . . .'

Upstairs, crouched down behind the sill at the open window, Richard strained to hear what was being said. His father's voice had become so quiet that from this height it was inaudible.

'Come on up, won't you?' he shouted down.

The two men looked up and then waved with tremendous enthusiasm.

'Richard, dear boy!'

Richard slammed the window shut.

Mrs Jenkins flung wide the portal. 'Sir Thomas,' she exclaimed with a deep flush and a low curtsey from which she had to be rescued by Doris. 'Mr Dadd.' To the latter, she gave merely a bow, gracious but not servile. He had, after all, no title and distinctions had to be observed or else where would we all be?

The two gentlemen stood on the steps, locked in one of those contests of civility.

'After you.'

'No, I insist.'

Mrs Jenkins was entirely enraptured by the lovely display of manners. 'May I present my sister, Doris?' she inquired after they had sorted themselves out. 'From Poplar,' she added. 'Indeed, Mr Dadd, practically a neighbour of your eldest son and his bride.'

Mr Dadd failed to acknowledge the relationship with whole-hearted enthusiasm, but Doris blushed and curtsied while protesting, 'Really, Ethel!'

At last the two gentlemen negotiated the two Sirens and found themselves on the top landing.

After a suitably dramatic pause, Richard flung open the door and welcomed his visitors with a smile. His appearance was somewhat dishevelled and there was an unaccountably large quantity of purple paint on his right toe, but Robert was relieved that, in all other respects, his son presented every appearance of normality.

'A glass of sherry, gentlemen?' he inquired. 'Did you bring another glass?' he hissed at his father under his breath.

The latter shook his head, embarrassed at his lack of forethought. Richard was immediately through the door and on to the landing, where he discovered his landlady busily dusting the dustless banisters, aided by her sister.

'A sherry glass, Mrs Jenkins, if you please,' said Richard, and the good lady scampered off, delighted to be of service.

Sir Thomas, meanwhile, was wandering from picture to picture. 'Most impressive, my dear boy. I would never have believed it,' he murmured.

'Were you afraid,' inquired Richard, handing him a glass of sherry, 'that I might be too mad to paint?'

His father cleared his throat nervously. 'Of course not, my boy! We have never lacked faith in your abilities. And I, for one, shall carry that confidence with me as far as . . . um . . . the grave.'

'Let's have no talk of graves and suchlike on a lovely day like to-day, Mr Dadd,' shrilled Mrs Jenkins, bustling in with one glass on a tray emblazoned with a picture of Brighton Pavilion. 'Mr Jenkins was partial to a glass of sherry,' she told them. 'His very glass.' Tears stood out in her eyes at the thought, though she noted with slight disappointment that Sir Thomas was already served.

'I'm honoured, Mrs J.,' said Richard. 'Very honoured.' He turned upon her the full strength of his blue eyes and smiled warmly.

'A pleasure, I'm sure,' the good lady replied, blushing and backing towards the door.

Richard poured sherry for himself. 'Cheers!'

'Your very good health,' responded Sir Thomas.

'Why are you always mentioning my health?' asked Richard with some irritation. 'From Cairo to Vienna to Paris, – always my health.'

'I meant nothing by it.' Sir Thomas gulped at his drink.

'A mere figure of speech.' Mr Dadd attempted to step into the breach. 'A convention.'

'I am very well aware of what he means,' said Richard; 'behind the convention. For if he meant nothing, why would he say it at all?'

His visitors shuffled nervously from foot to foot.

'Those,' said Richard, indicating the pictures on the walls, 'are mere trifles. If you would care to face this way . . .' He set a canvas on the easel. ' "Halt in the Desert". You might recall, Sir Thomas . . . ?'

'Can't say I do, m'boy. Syria? Egypt?'

Richard looked at him with disgust. 'Those nights around the camp fire . . .'

'Ah! Turkey . . . or was it Palestine?'

Robert Dadd put down his glass so violently that the sherry slopped over on to the table cloth. 'But it's preposterous. It looks as though the moon is impaled on the sentry's spear.'

'Which is impossible,' said Richard blandly, 'as anyone in their right senses will tell you. That is merely how it looked.'

'It's ludicrous.'

'Maybe; – but true. The visual impression is of course corrected by the brain's interpretation.' Richard calmly poured himself another sherry.

'Haven't you had enough?' asked his father.

'That is for me to decide.'

'You know it makes you over-excited.'

Sir Thomas, who had become more and more embarrassed during this exchange, wandered over to the mantelpiece and became immediately absorbed in a sketch of himself in Arab costume.

'I am an artist,' Richard said angrily. 'If nothing ever excited me I would be a carpenter like George. Or, God help me, a chemist like you!' Richard wrenched the picture off the stand and replaced it with another.

Sir Thomas returned, looking at this one with interest. He took out his opera glasses and peered at it closely. 'Now who, I wonder, is that delightful little boy?'

'You wouldn't remember,' Richard said sarcastically. 'The son of our Captain. He was on our boat for a month.'

'That dirty little beggar!'

'Dirt is only skin deep, as they say. Ahmed, his name was.'

'Curious name,' interrupted his father.

'They were all like that,' chuckled Sir Thomas. 'Quite barbaric.'

'To them no doubt,' said Richard, 'Thomas or Robert must sound equally strange.'

'What nonsense you talk sometimes, Richard,' reproved his father. 'Good Christian names like that!'

Richard went across to the window and opened it wide to let in some fresh air.

Downstairs, Mrs Jenkins, hearing the noise, raised her eyebrows. 'It makes my head ache, Doris, really it does,' she protested as she sipped at her tea in the parlour. 'All day long, up down up down up down like a yo-yo until I can't keep track of whether it's open or shut.'

'If I were you, dear,' advised her sister, 'I'd give the gentleman his notice.'

'But he pays up good and proper, Doris. There's the problem.' Mrs Jenkins put her cup down with a clink. 'And on the whole he's no trouble. It's just the window. It's not good for my nerves.'

The parrot broke into raucous laughter and Mrs Jenkins threw her teaspoon at it. It missed the bird and went straight through the front of her china cabinet with a noise like the tinkling of bells. Mrs Jenkins burst into tears. 'My nerves is all in rags and tatters,' she protested as her sister set about clearing up the damage while batting about her with a cushion to keep the parrot at bay.

'Could have been worse,' observed Doris gloomily. 'Six penn'orth of glass should see you all ship-shape again.'

'Six penn'orth!' Mrs Jenkins rolled her eyes to heaven, where they appeared to become fixed in their orbit. For at that moment she heard Sir Thomas cross the room above and step outside on to the landing. 'He's coming,' she gasped, searching for her reflection vainly in the missing pane of the china cabinet. And both ladies were within the instant wedged tight in the living room door shrieking their farewells to the good knight.

While Maria slept away the afternoon in a leaden, drug-induced sleep, Ellen sat beside her in a rocking chair creaking back and forth, back and forth, until her gentle snores were indistinguishable from the distant steady rumble of carriage wheels over the cobblestones of the Haymarket.

Elsewhere, Mary Ann and Sarah had shed their domestic preoccupations for the afternoon and were knitting squares for blankets in the dingy premises of the local Missionary Society. The weather was hot and heavy. The needles protested like so many mewling kittens. From time to time, Mary Ann, seeing her sister's longing glances out at the sunlit street, led a hymn or a prayer to recall Sarah's attention to their task.

'If it is hot here,' said Sarah at last, 'imagine how much hotter it must be in the jungle' (for Africa being hot was of necessity jungly and frequented by tigers), and she imagined with dismay rows and rows of tiny black children fretting against the clinging, scratchy wool. 'Richard says,' she remarked, 'that in Africa, only cotton is bearable next to the skin.'

'Oh Richard . . .' sighed Mary Ann.

Oh Richard, thought Robert Dadd senior in his laboratory, end-lessly weighing and measuring ingredients to obtain the perfect varnish.

'Why don't you have a rest, Father?' inquired Stephen gently, standing like a shadow behind his parent and watching with deep misgivings every error in his calculations, every slip and slop of his unsteady hand.

'I must,' said his poor distracted father, 'get it right.' For if Richard became famous as an artist, he, Robert Dadd, could lay some small claim to immortality in the perfection of a protective coating which would ensure the preservation of his son's works for posterity.

'Try this,' he cried to Stephen, as he shook up a muddy looking sludge in a bottle.

'Father,' objected Stephen, holding it up to the light. 'It is quite opaque.'

'No matter, no matter. It will dry clear, I assure you. And then Richard . . .'

Richard, far from concerning himself with the techniques of his profession, was fast asleep on his studio couch, having finished off the bottle of sherry.

It was some hours later that he awoke, as a slight chill to the air announced that the sun had set and evening was fast approaching. He sat up, physically refreshed, though with a head befuddled from the alcohol and a terrible dryness in the throat.

He staggered to the door and bellowed for a pot of tea, which was delivered by the little servant girl whose complexion that day bore witness to an unusual degree of exposure to sunshine and fresh air.

'Don't tell me,' he remarked drily, 'that the lovely weather has induced Mrs Jenkins to let you out of doors!'

'No indeed, sir. I was sent to Poplar with a message.' She put the tray on the table.

'A message, eh?'

'For her sister, sir. So that she could come and see Sir Thomas. I had to go fast so that she would arrive in time.'

Her words recalled the events of the day and Richard remembered his promise to dine at his father's house. Realising the lateness of the hour, he told the girl to drink the tea and eat the madeira cake herself, and grabbing the basket with the now empty decanter and sherry glasses, he set off at a gallop into the darkening streets.

The summer's evening had brought most of the London populace out of doors, and he found himself impeded at every step. To begin with, he apologised frequently both for his own inattention and for that of others, then seeing that the frequency with which he was forced to raise his hat was becoming ridiculous – a regular little puppet show, he abandoned this display of manners and proceeded along the pavements much as everyone else did, – as if only he had a right to be there.

By the time he reached the Haymarket, he was forced to leave the footpath altogether and take to the gutter. Hemmed in by pedestrians on one side and the theatre carriages arriving on the other, he nevertheless made better progress, though at some danger to his person. All the time he was conscious that hurry as he might, he was going to be late. This fact, combined with his awareness that his dishevelled appearance was sure to provoke outspoken disapproval, caused him acute distress. A momentary inattention to his surroundings was his undoing. A speeding carriage caught him a passing blow on the head, and Richard toppled heavily to the ground.

Richard fell. It is a wonder he was not killed by the throng of vehicles and pedestrians, or that having once been discovered to be still alive, he survived the application of all those conflicting remedies which were visited upon his person. For who was to know that he lay unconscious not above a hundred yards from the very refuge to which he was bound, where loving arms would have received him and protected him from the furies of the storm which beset his mind?

His fall was, you see, not merely on to the cobblestones, but through the very surface of life and into a swirling confusion more dense than any London fog. How often, over that weekend was he observed like a drowning man to rise and sink and rise again. But no lifeboat came to his rescue, none dared venture to his side over those murky waters. Family and friends teetered alike on the brink. Oh, they wailed and shrieked and wrung their hands and called on God to help them. But God did not come to their aid, and poor weak human beings that they were, they stood rebuffed by the ferocity of the same waves which battered him. So they relinquished him to the waters which closed for the third time over his head; – and swallowed him up.

Chapter Five

I have often considered whether physical death might not have been preferable to what now lay in store for Richard; whether it might not have proved kinder if that blow on the head had proved fatal. Destiny thought otherwise. So it was that somewhere after midnight, Richard was awakened by a shriek which tore at the lining of his skull as if it would scour the very membranes from the bone. The sound rose and fell like the scream of a saw blade and Richard clasped his hands to his ears and rocked his head to and fro, pressing one ear and then the other against the harsh upholstery on which he lay.

When he ventured to open his eyes, he saw that the sound proceeded from a pair of female gullets which gaped voraciously to emit these breathless, mirthless gasps which bordered on hysteria. The owners of these gullets, two ladies on the far side of the room, were dressed from head to toe in tight scarlet satin which heaved and pumped as vigorously as blacksmiths' bellows so that the passage of air, constricted by the narrowness of their throats, found expression in that terrible series of tortured sounds. And around each blaring trumpet bowl frothed a torrent of hair of exaggerated profusion. Each curl and ringlet writhed and squirmed with every gasp, as if it had a life of its own.

Beyond these twin Medusas, Richard gradually made out other still more sinister figures; – a whole panoply of kings and queens and fairies, wizards, whores and brides, all grouped together in silent and faceless battalions and as still as corpses.

With some effort he turned to face the light, which burned through his eye sockets and into his skull like catherine wheels, in whirling crimson flashes. Gradually, Richard was able to discern a third figure seated at the very heart of these fireworks. This young lady, identical to, and equally loathsome as her sisters, was applying a prodigious amount of scarlet to her lips and cheeks.

This action was evidently the source of the merriment, for the thicker and brighter the colour became, the shriller was the piercing, glass-shattering, response.

Richard groaned and buried himself further under the rug which had so far rendered him invisible.

'Oh my Gawd!' shrieked one of the maidens. 'There's someone here spying on our toilette!' For Richard had been unceremoniously deposited upon a couch in the dressing room of a Haymarket theatre and promptly forgotten in all the excitement which preceded the show, and the flowers and champagne which followed it.

'Not louder shrieks to pitying heav'n are cast, / When husbands, or when lap-dogs breathe their last,' quoth the beauty at the mirror in a curiously gruff voice.

'George!' said Richard, suddenly sitting bolt upright and clutching at the arms of the sofa to steady himself as his whole world spun around. 'What are you doing here?'

George, rather shame-faced now that his disguise had been seen through, removed his wig. 'Just having a bit of fun, Dicky,' he said, standing there like a sulky schoolboy.

'Bit of fun?' Richard asked.

George wrung the wig between his hands and framed his scarlet mouth in a pout.

'You do make a lovely girl though,' Richard observed.

The girls clung to one another and bellowed with laughter.

Richard turned on them frostily. 'Won't you introduce me, George?' he said. 'Where are your manners?'

'Tina and Franny,' he said.

The girls shrieked. 'Wrong again, George.'

'Oh hell,' said George, 'does it really matter?' He looked helplessly at his brother. 'Anyway,' he asked slyly, 'what are you doing here? I thought you were just a bundle of old clothes.'

Explanations were offered with which I will not trouble you, since a more lucid account has already been furnished. George, as might have been surmised from his general condition, had already drunk deep. Nor was he disinclined to continue his imbibing. For he now plumped himself down on the sofa, rudely jolting the poor befuddled invalid, and proceeded to add to his torment by slamming a jug of porter on to the table alongside.

'Want some?' he asked, not very graciously.

'Porter?' asked Richard with disgust. 'Do me a favour, Georgy!'

So the nightwatchman was once more despatched to the tavern, this time for a pint of best Bordeaux.

'And what do you do for a living, my dears?' asked Richard.

'We sing,' replied one of the ladies, airily. 'And we do a bit of dancing.'

'Solo?' he inquired.

They looked at each other and giggled.

'Chorus,' hissed George. 'Back row.'

The two harpies closed in. They perched, one on each arm of the sofa, clinging to the sofa back with their scarlet claws to maintain their balance.

'I ought to take you home, Georgy,' said Richard.

'I can take care of myself,' George replied and poured himself another mug of porter. One of the girls slithered heavily down the incline of the arm and spreadeagled herself on his lap. George wrapped his arms round her and imprinted a huge pair of scarlet lips on her forehead.

'He won't come now, Father,' Mary Ann was saying gently, just round the corner in Suffolk Street. 'It's past midnight.'

'He said he would come.' Mr Dadd gestured helplessly towards the platter of cold food which had been set out on the sideboard, dinner having been dispensed with hours ago.

'Why not eat something yourself?' suggested his daughter. She helped him to a slice of roast beef, just as he liked it, still delicately pink in the middle.

He did not seem to notice when she placed the plate on his knee.

'Father,' she chided him. 'You must eat now.'

Stephen and Sarah sat at the table by the window, playing chess. Every time a cab was heard in the street, Stephen lifted up a corner of the curtain to look outside, and each time he was disappointed.

'There,' said Sarah triumphantly, taking advantage of his inattention. 'Now I've taken your knight.'

Stephen brushed all the pieces off the board angrily.

'Just because you were losing!' laughed Sarah.

'Some of us,' said Stephen sharply, 'have to work tomorrow. We're not all artists who can stay up all night and sleep all day as the mood takes us.'

'Oh, I couldn't sleep anyway,' said his parent from deep in his favourite chair. 'You all go off to bed, I'll just doze quietly here.'

Mary Ann obediently tucked her needle safely into her embroidery and folded her work carefully away in her mother's sewing box. Then, after extinguishing all the lamps save one, she bade her father good night and ushered her brother and sister out of the room.

If Richard's absence was the cause for much anguish in one household, in another, it afforded an opportunity for some amusement.

'Tell you what, Doris,' Mrs Jenkins was saying to her sister over their third jug of ale, 'why don't we just go upstairs and you can have a look at his pictures for yourself.'

'What if he comes in, Ethel?' Doris was seriously alarmed at the prospect.

'We could tell him we're just cleaning.'

'At this time of night?'

'We could take a few things with us. You know, like stage props.'

The two ladies moved somewhat unsteadily into the kitchen which soon rang with their efforts to collect the tools necessary for their disguise. The tin bucket chimed against the iron fender, the mop and the broom became entangled in the table legs, the dustpan sang out against the sink, until at last the little servant girl, awoken from her exhausted slumbers, stumbled from her cubby-hole under the stairs.

'More ale, ma'am?' she asked, holding her hand out for the jug with her eyes still tight shut.

'Don't be so impertinent,' snapped Doris. 'Go back to your room.'

Though 'room' was an exaggeration for the airless closet, the little servant girl reeled sleepily back into the darkness and collapsed upon her bed of rags, while Mrs Jenkins and her sister staggered up the stairs armed with their brushes and mops until they at last reached the landing whose floorboards, to their drunken feet, seemed as mysteriously precipitous as the stairs.

'You should get in a carpenter,' sniffed Doris, as they picked themselves up off the floor. 'It's probably death watch beetle.'

'You only get that in churches, Doris,' protested her sister.

'I must warn you,' Mrs Jenkins continued as she groped for the door handle, 'that Mr Dadd is a thoroughly modern painter. Don't expect anything, well, edifying. He is thoroughly "modern" in his ideas.' She spoke the word uncertainly, not sure in her own mind whether it implied compliment or censure. 'What I mean is, Doris, you won't find any heroes or saints or things like that.' She was about to go on when a deep voice from down below made them stop dead in their tracks.

'. . . notice the merits of a pencil,' it said.

'Oh my Gawd,' breathed Doris, holding the mop before her like a lance. 'He's back.'

'. . . to which we owe a graceful compliment,' came the voice again.

Mrs Jenkins let out a sigh of relief. 'It's all right, Doris,' she said. 'It's only Pieces.'

'Pieces?'

'Oh yes. He enjoys all Mr Dadd's reviews.'

Richard was awoken very early the following morning, by the sensation of drowning in a sea of taffeta. He struck out boldly for the surface to find the gas lights still burning brightly in that subterranean chamber, echoed and re-echoed in the glare of the angled mirrors.

Leaving the others still asleep, he made his way unsteadily over to the stool in front of the mirror on which he had first observed his brother, and sat down heavily. The sight that he beheld was not pleasing. Puffy grey pouches bulged under his eyes, and the lower part of his face was covered with an evil-looking black fuzz like the spread of a ghastly fungus. He was about to turn away in disgust, when his attention was caught by an ugly black mark smeared across his right cheekbone, like a coal smut.

He ran his fingers over the lump, then scratched at it with his nails. It did not shift. He got to his feet now, and leant close to the mirror to get a better look. The mark became more and more obvious, reflected a thousand times over from every angle, hideously plump and casting its shadow on the skin around it.

His first thought was one of total amazement that no one had ever pointed out this monstrous deformity before. The only logical conclusion was that it had not been there before. Perhaps it had drawn its terrible sustenance from this night of debauchery. His hand crept up again to his face. There were now black hairs like spider's legs sprouting from the tip. He had to act quickly.

In his pocket, for such had been his habit of late, he was carrying a razor. He now took it in his hand and with careful precision, sliced the top off the horrible protrusion. Even before the flow of blood obscured his vision, he saw from the dark ring at the base that he had not gone deep enough.

Going through his pockets for the second time, Richard found his knife, – a rigger's knife, which he used for trimming canvas. It had a strong black handle and a four-inch retractable blade. As he pressed the switch, the blade sprang out with a satisfying snick. Blood was now flowing so fast that he had to work by touch. He gritted his teeth as the blade struck deep and glanced off his cheekbone. He uttered a howl of pain and fell across the dressing table in a dead faint.

When a sharp ring at the door bell roused the whole household in Suffolk Street, Mary Ann Dadd opened the door herself.

'Mrs Jenkins' compliments, ma'am,' said the untidy chit who stood there. 'Mrs Jenkins sent to say that young Mr Dadd has not been home all night and she thought you might like to know.'

'Thank you,' said Mary Ann, smiling to hide her distress while she felt in her pockets for a penny. At all costs she had to keep the news from Papa.

It was too late. He was standing just behind her. 'We must send for the police,' he said; 'they must find him.'

103

'Come, Father.' Mary Ann closed the door on the girl and led her parent back into the living room. 'Richard is young. There are a thousand places he could be . . .'

'A thousand?' Robert Dadd searched his exhausted mind for just one.

'Billy Frith's, Augustus Egg's, Henry's . . . Papa, need I go on?'

Mr Dadd's spirits had risen as each name was mentioned. 'Of course, of course,' he nodded eagerly, repeating each name after her. 'I was once young myself,' he chuckled. 'Dear, oh dear!'

'He could be at Jock's lodgings,' continued Mary Ann, delighted by the effect of her suggestions.

'Yes, yes!'

'Or Humby's, you know how he likes an evening with Humby. Singing and games. Perhaps a little bit of gambling.' Though they both disapproved heartily of this vice, it became, even as she mentioned it, a symbol of harmless normality.

'Gambling, oh my word, gambling. Boys will be boys.' Her father seemed to relish the thought, quite forgetting his former edicts on the subject.

However, all attempts at cheerfulness and enthusiasm were soon dispelled by the arrival of Humby. He too was looking for Richard.

Richard came round for the second time in the space of a few hours, to find himself lying on another sofa, though to be sure this one was considerably more comfortable than the last, being covered in the softest velvet in a restful shade of deep, bottle green.

'Good God, not on my death-bed, am I?' he inquired. For there they all were, his whole family – Father, Stephen, Mary Ann, Sarah, Maria, Ellen, George, and even his old friend Humby, – gathered about him with pious expressions of tender concern.

'George,' he said, catching sight of the scarlet dress, whereupon he burst out laughing. And seeing that he was going to be all right, everyone else laughed too at the spectacle of George leaning against his father's sober mahogany desk, clad in scarlet satin.

'Just you lie still, Master Richard, there's a good boy,' advised

Ellen, who was trying to apply pressure to Richard's cheek to staunch the flow of blood.

'What is it, Ellen?' he asked.

'Just a cut, dear,' she rumbled reassuringly.

'Must have cut myself shaving,' Richard mumbled.

'You never came home last night, Dicky.' His father's pale face loomed up close. 'I was worried.'

'Oh, last night . . .' Richard now remembered. The shame of it, when he should have been at home at his father's side! He flung his arms round his dear parent and begged his forgiveness.

When the two at last drew away from each other, and Mr Dadd had recovered his composure, he blew his nose loudly and said he would be much obliged if Richard would accompany him to a doctor.

Seeing the sorry condition of his parent, Richard at once agreed and after a hearty breakfast, during which his father was quite overjoyed by his healthy appetite, they set off on foot for Dr Sutherland's consulting rooms. On this outing, to Richard's great relief, they were accompanied by his friend Humby, for he sincerely doubted whether he could handle his father on his own.

'Ah yes. Sunstroke,' said Dr Sutherland.

Richard watched his father. A rich purple pink colour had crept up his neck and over his face and was now breaking in warm waves against the snowy crests of his eyebrows. Then the flush ebbed, sucking the wash down inside his collar. Richard bent down and peered underneath the desk to see whether it hadn't flowed right down and out of his trouser leg to form a rosy pool on the carpet.

'Ahem!' The doctor cleared his throat loudly. 'Richard,' he tried again, referring back to the letter from Dr Smith, 'you suffered, I believe, a *coup de soleil* while in Egypt.'

Mr Dadd, unable to bear his son's silence, answered for him. 'Yes, yes. He was sketching in the sun.' This time the magenta wave rose and did not recede.

Richard leant forward and touched his parent gently on the

arm. 'Steady on, Father. You're going to burst a blood vessel.' He watched his father dab at the corner of his mouth with a handkerchief, but there was no hiding the flecks of foam that kept gathering there. Any minute now, he feared that the doctor might summon help and that he would see his parent bundled up in canvas and whipped off to Bedlam.

'When was that?' the doctor persisted.

'What?' asked Richard loudly.

'The *coup de soleil*,' prompted Humby.

'Let me see . . .' said Mr Dadd.

'Mr Dadd, please,' the doctor was clearly becoming exasperated with the poor old gentleman, 'let your son answer for himself.'

'Sunstroke! Yes.' Richard stepped in to rescue his foundering parent. His father was indeed highly coloured, – unduly so, since the day, though hot, was nothing by Egyptian standards. 'The Egyptian fellah toils all day in a sun which is far hotter than ours. I suppose it all depends what you are used to,' he observed.

'Yes. Quite so.' The doctor began to write furiously.

'Did you have your hat on, Father?' asked Richard, quite unable to remember whether his parent was bare-headed or not during their walk.

'But what about you, Richard?' his parent countered irritably. 'Did you always keep your hat on?'

'Yes, oh yes,' Richard replied earnestly. 'I always wore my vest too.' He here got up and paced up and down the room. 'And I had a red fez, with a wet cloth wrapped around it.' He paused as a worrying thought occurred to him. 'But I had no spirit to protect me from the rays.'

'No spirit, eh?' The doctor threw down his pen. Some things were too ridiculous to be worth recording.

Richard, meanwhile, was examining a picture over the mantel-piece – a tasteful watercolour of the sea spangled with the exploding lights of an electric storm.

'Turner, ain't it?'

'Quite a nice little picture,' responded the medical man.

Richard looked at him in surprise. 'Quite nice? My dear doctor, how can you dismiss—'

'Richard, we are not here to discuss painting,' his father inter-rupted.

'I have been told,' said the doctor quickly, 'that you have been employing an extraordinary and unnatural range of colours.'

'Purple camels,' chortled Humby.

Richard slapped his thighs and roared with laughter. 'Did Jock tell you that?' he asked when he could speak.

Humby nodded.

The doctor was clearly not amused. 'I believe it would be true to say that even a three-year-old knows that a camel is not purple but beige.'

'Beige?' Richard exclaimed. 'Bayje! My dear doctor! Even a three-year-old can perceive that under certain conditions an object takes on the prevailing colour which surrounds it, whether it be the glow of dawn or the sunset. Look at Turner — do you criticise him for making the sea orange and yellow?'

Mr Dadd twisted uneasily in his chair. 'You see, he gets excited and then his ideas run away with him,' he said.

Richard turned his back on the other three. He placed himself in between the marble nymphs who supported the mantelshelf and left the others to their ridiculous deliberations. He resolved to allow himself to be no more drawn into the conversation than his marble companions.

Meanwhile, at home in Chatham, quite unaware at the time that there was any cause for concern in Richard's behaviour, nor that the recommendation of the eminent physician would be one of constant supervision, I was preparing happily for the arrival of my dearest friend, Maria.

Her visit had been arranged during the wedding, when Maria and Stephen, George and I had formed the plan of attending the forthcoming military manoeuvres together.

My mother constantly reminded me that nothing I did would bring forward their arrival by so much as one second, but I paid her no attention. I could settle to nothing. Every cab which turned into our street had me running to the nearest window. Every ring at the door and I was down the stairs and into the hall like an arrow. For besides my eager anticipation of Maria's company, my parents were insistent that I should not venture into the crowded streets unaccompanied – and how I longed to be there!

You might wonder how three of Mr Dadd's children could have brought themselves to abandon their parent at a time of such distress. It was Richard himself who brought this about, by sending a note via Mrs Jenkins' little servant to say that he would welcome a trip into the country with his parent, there to unburden his mind to him. The place he selected was Cobham; – dear, green, leafy, secluded Cobham. Indeed, could there be any pleasanter refuge from London on a sweltering summer's weekend? Except of course, my own, dear Chatham, which lies but five miles due east across the River Medway.

Mr Dadd was apparently a different man as he raised his head from the brief note which he had read avidly while standing on the doorstep. If there was anything about it (such as the spelling and the indecipherable hieroglyphs about the edge of the notepaper which caused Mary Ann to raise her eyebrows), her father overlooked such small considerations. He was transformed by the invitation. He returned indoors with a spring in his step and a watery gleam to his eye.

Richard loved him. Richard needed him. His beloved son would only have to speak, there among the rich tired greenery of late summer, beneath the trees he loved so well, for everything to be made clear. And once everything was made clear, his father knew that it was as good as put right.

He scarcely had time to put pen to paper and address a quick note to his son Robert to advise him of his great joy, before Richard himself arrived and the plan was put into effect.

The departure of Richard and his father into the country for the weekend was not, I believe, viewed everywhere with the same enthusiasm.

'Gone?' asked Doris. 'Gone where, Ethel?'

'Gone off for a weekend in the country with his Pa,' said Mrs Jenkins as if nothing could be more natural for a young gentleman.

'I hope his father knows what he's doing,' sniffed Doris.

'Heads he do, tails he don't,' squawked the parrot.

'No one asked your opinion.' Doris spoke sharply to the bird. 'I wouldn't go away with him myself. Not after all the carryings on.'

'You don't understand, Doris,' said her sister, thinking of the parties she too enjoyed in her youth, 'what it is to be young, and an artist. Personally, I like to hear the violin, — and the dancing and sounds of merry-making.'

'Not until three in the morning,' Doris frowned, 'and not when I know that he's all alone up there, yet making enough noise for thirty.'

'When all's said and done, Doris,' Ethel Jenkins was determined to defend her young gentleman to the last, 'there has to be a bit of give and take where Art is concerned. Young Mr Dadd is a bit eccentric, that's all.' Mrs Jenkins, feeling exceptionally broad-minded this morning, chose to ignore the dents in the ceiling made by her broom handle.

Her sister remained sceptical. 'Eccentric . . .' She lingered over the word, which was not one in everyday use in Poplar. 'I'd say just plain mad.'

'Surely not,' protested her sister. 'You saw Sir Thomas with your own eyes. Genius, I'd call it.'

The parrot cackled his agreement.

'Personally, I wouldn't be surprised if he's demolished the whole of the upstairs from the noise he was making.'

Mrs Jenkins turned quite pale at Doris's suggestion.

'He's probably chopped up all those nice chairs into firewood,' she continued, rather enjoying the effect of her words on her poor sister, who here uttered a strangled cry and leapt to her feet. 'And as for Mother's aspidistra . . .'

Before she could finish, Mrs Jenkins was out of the door and up the stairs. Once again she was thwarted. The door was locked.

Mr Dadd and Richard, on the steamer to Gravesend, stood on the deck enjoying the wind and the sunshine.

'Not too hot are you, Dicky?' his father inquired.

'It's perfect,' smiled Richard, closing his eyes the better to enjoy

the sensations of warmth and light, his nose sifting the salty air.
'Just perfect.'

'You don't know how much this means to me,' said Mr Dadd,
relishing his son's enjoyment even more than his own. 'Cobham!'
he continued. 'It will be good to see the place again.'

'Scene of my very first paintings,' murmured Richard. 'All those
boring green landscapes! Those endless avenues of trees!'

'You had to start somewhere,' said his father, thinking back to
those happy times. 'Your mother was so proud of you.'

'Step-mother,' Richard corrected him.

Mr Dadd shrugged and let even this observation pass. He would
gladly swallow any personal hurt to preserve the happy mood
of intimacy even though, for him, the sun momentarily lost its
power. He laughed off his qualms and tried instead to concentrate
on less troubled matters. 'Those wonderful oaks!' he remarked.

'Beeches,' said Richard.

His father shrugged again. If Richard said they were beeches,
then let them be beeches. He wanted nothing to sour his present
mood.

'Sour!', however, was the comment made by Mrs Jenkins as the
locksmith forced open Richard's studio door.

'Bad eggs,' said Doris complacently.

Even the locksmith recoiled from the stench. Mrs Jenkins
hastily paid and dismissed him. She had her pride. She didn't
want any stories getting about.

Doris had the presence of mind to fling open the window whose
welcome draughts of fresh air both ladies inhaled greedily before
turning back into the room, their handkerchiefs clutched to their
noses.

'My God, Ethel!' objected the stouter sister.

'An artist,' said Mrs Jenkins, 'uses eggs to mix his paints.'

'But not bad eggs,' objected the other.

The eggs were everywhere – so thick that they had had to
tread on them to reach the window, crunching the shells into
the floorboards as they went. As the fresh air gradually dissipated
the fumes, the two ladies took stock of their surroundings. The

tables and chairs, though somewhat awry, were undamaged. The aspidistra, whose brass container was discovered to hold at least three dozen raw, scrambled eggs, was found to be unharmed, though a trifle dry, standing in Richard's top hat on the dressing table.

'I wouldn't put up with it myself,' commented Doris. 'It's disrespectful in my opinion. Mother wouldn't like to see her precious plant—'

She was interrupted by a squawk from Ethel. 'Look at these, Doris!'

Mrs Jenkins' eyes were wide with horror as she leafed through a bundle of papers. The two women spread them out on the dining table: – Sir Thomas, Billy Frith, Jock Phillip, Humby, Egg, O'Neil, the Pope, the Emperor of Prussia, Mr Dadd, they were all there.

'He does get a good likeness,' said Mrs J. approvingly. 'Very like, I must say.'

'What's this then?' asked Doris, pointing to the red line across the neck of Richard's parent.

Mrs Jenkins balanced her spectacles carefully on her nose and peered closely at each portrait in turn. When she came to that of Mr Dadd, the scarlet gash across the throat was no longer mistakable, and before Doris could catch her, Ethel Jenkins turned a terrible shade of grey and crumpled up at the foot of the table.

Barely half an hour later, the door bell clanged violently over the door of the chemist's shop in Poplar High Street and Doris, twice her usual size, being strung about with bags and baggages, – having declared that she wouldn't stay another minute in a madhouse, – eased herself through the doorway and into the perilously narrow space before the counter.

'Mr Dadd himself, if you please,' Doris insisted, instantly dismissing the young person who professed to be at her service. Though the physical energy required to cover the distance from Newman Street in record time had been expended by a series of unfortunate horse teams, Doris's head had been going over like the clappers ever since she bade farewell to her sister. Fuelled by a lurid imagination, countless horrors coursed through her mind at breakneck speed, while her pounding heart pumped blood through her veins at an equal rate. Hot from her exertions, she therefore presented a truly awesome appearance from which the apprentice was only too happy to make his escape.

Robert Dadd junior issued forth from his laboratory to be met with a voluble outburst from a total stranger concerning rotten eggs and cut throats.

Mary Ann Dadd, meanwhile, was offering Doris's equally distraught sister, Mrs Jenkins, a cooling drink. The poor lady alternately gulped at it and then laid the glass down on the table, while her hand slid nervously up and down her throat as she exclaimed how lucky she was not to have been murdered in her bed.

'I'm sure,' Mary Ann murmured soothingly, 'that Richard never intended you any harm, Mrs Jenkins. Indeed he always spoke very fondly of you.' Her voice was like the gentle murmur of a river, which foundered and broke on the unheeding boulders of Mrs Jenkins' agitation.

'Very fond?' said the poor lady, looking anxiously at her fingertips for any trace of blood. 'Oh dear me, yes, very fond!'

'I can see,' continued Mary Ann, 'that the whole episode of my brother's illness has been very distressing for you. Rest assured, it is now over. He will not trouble you any more.'

'Why's that then?' Worse still than the prospect of the mess to be tackled was that of no more rent coming in. 'Not done away with hisself, has he?'

Mary Ann laughed easily. 'Oh dear no! Nothing like that, Mrs Jenkins.' And she poured some more raspberry vinegar into Mrs Jenkins' glass. 'Today he has gone away with his father for a quiet weekend in the country, during which he has expressed the wish to settle his mind about those matters that have been tormenting him. He seemed,' she said quite calmly as she passed the glass to her visitor, 'quite his usual self when they set off together.'

To Mrs Jenkins' eye, the deep purplish tinge of her drink had the most unpleasant connotations. 'The eggs, Miss Dadd,' she said severely, for she felt how close she had come to letting her own disquiet be lulled by Mary Ann's composure. It was all very well to dismiss her fears in a sunny drawing room in the fashionable West End. It was quite another to lie in bed fearing for her life. 'The eggs,' she insisted, 'are not the least of it. Oh dear me no!'

Mary Ann leant forward pleasantly. 'Mrs Jenkins, what else has Richard done?'

With great relish, Mrs Jenkins produced from her bag the bundle of drawings. She laid them on the table one by one, reserving Mr Dadd until last.

Even then tragedy might have been averted. From the privileged position accorded by distance in time, one may now look down upon that night much as an eagle in his mountaintop eyrie may look down and see the world spread out like a map below him. His eye can see all roads at once. He can take in at a glance the roughness of each track, the steepness of its incline, the dangers and obstacles which lurk just beyond every turn. But he inhabits a different world; his is the freedom of the skies and winds, the high isolated peaks. He scorns to intervene in the petty world of mortals far beneath him.

Nor can we alter by one jot what has gone before, for all our fine perspective. Like the eagle, we can see the pattern, we can see the folly of mankind as it pursues its inevitable course towards chaos. But we can see it only with hindsight.

At this moment of crisis, the miner or the sailor, the farm labourer or the factory hand would have taken some practical step, reached for his coat and made all possible speed, – by train, coach or boat, on four legs or on two, – towards the place where danger threatened.

But that dear, unhappy family responded in the only way it knew, which was so sadly unsuited to the present need. It is a fault to which many highly educated individuals are subject. For action they substitute thought. For intervention they employ the pen. So all at once, letters began flying in every direction, time-consuming and time-wasting, and causing confusion and panic wherever they were delivered.

Thus, Robert Dadd junior wrote from Poplar:

Dear Mary Ann,

I have just received what can only be described as an hysterical visit from a large lady who turns out to be the sister of Richard's Mrs Jenkins. I could scarcely make head nor tail of her story, except that it contains bad eggs and cut throats!

I know, dear Mary, how very busy you are, but would be grateful if you could spare the time to look into these extraordinary tales and see what dear Richard has been up to. Whatever silly jokes he may have perpetrated, he seems to have frightened these good ladies half out of their wits. I am writing to you rather than Father, as I know how much this sort of business upsets him. If I could spare the time, I would be only too happy to come up to town myself, but alas business does not permit.

Catherine joins me in sending her best love and kisses . . .

The writing here became scarcely legible, since Robert's bride of two weeks at that moment implanted on his bent neck a series of kisses enough to distract any man from his duty.

His reply, however, slowly traversed the distance from Poplar to the Haymarket, to reach its recipient who, after a quick perusal of the contents, paced up and down the empty dining room with a display of restless energy of which few would have credited her capable.

'What shall I do, Ellen?' Mary Ann asked her trusted nurse, who was at that moment studying the sketches brought by Mrs Jenkins.

'Well, dearie,' said Ellen reasonably, 'you saw him more recently than they did, and you weren't in the least bit worried.'

'I hadn't seen all these, then.'

Ellen tidied the sketches into a neat pile and tapped them briskly on the table. 'Perhaps it was just a little joke.' She laughed uneasily.

'A joke, Ellen? Oh no. That's not Richard's sort of a joke. It's too macabre.'

'What did the doctor say?'

'That he shouldn't be left alone.'

'That's all right then. He's got his father with him.' She smiled as if that settled the whole problem.

'That's just it,' said Mary Ann. 'Father's not as young as he used to be and—'

'He's quite capable of looking after himself,' replied Ellen firmly.

'Is he, Ellen? If only I could be sure . . .' Mary Ann took up a pen and began to write.

Dear Stephen, she began, *forgive me for troubling you on your weekend expedition, but I am increasingly uneasy in my mind about Richard and Papa. You know, of course, of Dr Sutherland's advice that Richard should be under constant supervision, and of all the reasons we have had of late to be concerned about him. Today, when Richard and Papa set off to spend the weekend in Cobham together it seemed such a hopeful sign! We watched them depart with such confidence in our hearts that dear Richard was entirely himself again. All that joy was soon dispelled by a visit from Mrs Jenkins. What she found was, I am sure you will agree, sufficiently alarming in itself.*

Mary Ann wrote fast and carelessly, recounting all the details of the visit, Robert's response, and her own fears.

Stephen, she continued, *I pray you, do not dismiss my misgivings as the mere product of an over-active imagination, for you know me better than that. I beg of you, please, to be so good as to go over to Cobham and see how they fare,*

115

and so set my mind at rest. I cannot get out of my mind that horrible, grisly picture of Papa with his throat cut, nor the thought that Papa is even now alone with Richard and possibly at his mercy. They are staying at the Ship Inn. Please Stephen! I implore you!

Having despatched a messenger with directions to find Stephen with the greatest possible haste and to deliver the letter into no hands but his own, Mary Ann took a second sheet of paper, which she addressed to her brother Robert.

In ignorance of the unfolding drama, Maria, Stephen, George and I had climbed to the top of the cliffs to the west of the town which commanded a fine view over Chatham. From there, the dockyards and the fortress were spread out like children's toys among which we could pick out the red coats of the soldiers.

As the first cannon fire announced the start of the manoeuvres, we settled ourselves to enjoy the spectacle along with an excellent hamper of food provided by my mother.

'This is bliss,' said Maria, lying flat on the grass and staring up at the sky, heedless of the excellent display of military tactics.

Stephen and George ate fast and gradually edged away from us girls to draw nearer to the scene of action. They drank in every shot and feasted their eyes on the outpourings of smoke which erupted here and there like an enormous firework display. They were both as excited as schoolboys, which prompted Maria and myself to reminisce about our childhood in Chatham when the Dadds and the Carters were so close.

'Why didn't Richard come?' I now asked my friend. 'He would have enjoyed it so much.'

Maria closed her eyes and avoided my look. 'Oh Richard,' she said, dismissing him. 'He's not interested in anything these days except his silly old paintings.' And she went on to tell me about the quarrel over Jock. 'He doesn't seem to understand,' she said, 'that other people have feelings.'

I busied myself threading daisies together in a chain, with my head bowed over the little flowers so that Maria could not see my face, for I was deeply hurt by this intelligence.

'Anyway,' continued Maria carelessly, 'he's gone to Cobham for the weekend with Father.'

'Oh?' Though I feigned indifference by concentrating on driving my thumbnail through a daisy stalk, my mind was singularly active. Richard could take a weekend off to spend it in the country with his father, but he was too busy to travel those extra few miles to Chatham!

I knew Cobham well. At that time, it held many pleasant associations for me which have since been overlaid by darker memories. As children we often wandered through the grounds of the park and enjoyed the shelter and peace of the vast old trees, which had been there from time immemorial. Richard enjoyed going into the great house itself whose many paintings provided his first taste of the excellence of art. He once took me round himself. I was quite overawed by the grandeur of the house, and by the ghostly dust covers which shrouded the many rooms, but Richard was kindness itself. He took me by the hand to encourage my faltering steps and spoke of the paintings in such a way that they came alive for me too, until I hastened from one to the other as eagerly as he did himself. What an excellent teacher he would have made! What a kind and loving father to his children!

In later years, there were more summer excursions to Lord Darnley's estate and to the fine mansion house which had become a popular and fashionable venue for sketching parties. While Richard, and sometimes his friends, worked at their easels, Maria and I explored the surroundings.

I almost blush, even now, to think of the two of us, dressed in our prettiest and most fashionable garments, posing self-consciously in front of the most picturesque aspects of house and grounds, – peeping fearfully from between the stone arms of some leering, weather-beaten satyr, or gazing mistily into the slug-filled depths of a mouldering Grecian urn, the garden all the time ringing with our cries of 'Richard, will you paint us like this?'

Richard accepted all our posturing with his usual good humour, sometimes replying that he had no intention of being turned into a society artist. We were, in our turn, careful never to go beyond the bounds of light-hearted teasing, for we knew how he despised those painters who struck extravagant attitudes, or who followed only fashionable themes.

I loved to be near him while he worked, to watch the patient transposition of the scene before us on to his canvas. Distilled through his vision, the image seemed to me more real than the original, illuminated by something peculiar to his own vision. He never drove me away. If the process went well he might turn to me with a smile of pure pleasure. Yet if such satisfaction was denied him, he accepted this too with patient resignation and a smile which was no less warm. And when his day's work was completed, our party repaired to the Ship Inn, where we sat in the front parlour over some refreshments while we awaited the arrival of our conveyance back to Chatham.

The Ship Inn was a pleasant old public house which had drowsed in Cobham High Street for many centuries. It was the sort of place into which one might ease oneself with the same feeling of belonging as a foot slipping into a well-worn shoe. Reader, until that terrible day, my memories of it were never anything but pleasant and slightly hazy, glossed over as they were with that lassitude which comes from an early start and a day in the fresh air with the most convivial of company. And when I picked up the newspaper in those dark days which followed, the name of John Adams was instantly familiar. For John Adams had often ministered to our needs. Then suddenly, he was famous. He was sought out by policemen and newspaper reporters, and his observations about my dear friends became all at once the focus of national interest.

It was said that when Mr Dadd and Richard arrived at the Inn in the late afternoon of the twenty-eighth of August 1843, they found him behind the bar, polishing glasses in preparation for a busy evening.

The day had been hot and the roads were dusty. The threshing machines were gradually ceasing their roar and rattle, and many a load of grain was carried proudly homeward, glinting like golden mountains in the rich tones of the late afternoon sun.

'What a journey!' As he spoke, Mr Dadd, with a carelessness born of familiarity, slung his hat on to a stand where it quivered momentarily, then roosted.

'Trouble with the ferry, sir?' inquired John Adams.

'John! It's good to see you again.'

The bartender shook his old acquaintance heartily by the hand. As the two conversed quietly, Richard, who was uninterested in such social pleasantries as the bounty of the harvest, the continued clemency of the weather and the consequent excellence of business, took a seat by the window from which he commanded a good view of the street.

The two had advanced as far as reciprocal enquiries concerning the health of Mr Dadd's fourth and John Adams's fifth child, when Richard startled them by abruptly slamming shut the window.

'I'd thank you to leave that open, sir,' said the publican pleasantly. 'It gets uncommon hot in here.'

Richard turned up his coat collar and exclaimed petulantly, 'I'm feeling the draught.'

John Adams accepted the explanation with a slight bow. This reminder that a customer is always right recalled him abruptly to his role; – which distinction had been set aside by the pleasantness of Mr Dadd's manner. 'Can I get you gentlemen anything?' he now asked, somewhat formally.

Mr Dadd eased his jacket cuffs comfortably over his shirt and flicked imaginary specks of fluff off his sleeves. 'I'll take tea if you please, John,' he said heartily, anxious to make up for his son's sharpness.

John looked expectantly towards Richard.

'What about you, eh?' Mr Dadd prompted his son.

Richard twisted his head and peered over his shoulder. 'Who?' he demanded angrily.

At this stage, the entrance of some farm labourers caused a diversion. John Adams ushered them speedily out of the saloon and into the public bar and then returned fanning the air with his napkin and apologising for the unwholesome farmyard taint to the atmosphere. 'If the young gentleman will permit,' he said, moving to open the window.

Richard at once objected, pulling his jacket collar even higher so that his face was almost completely concealed, and his eyes glittered strangely over the top.

His father was forced now to take John aside and explain in a whisper which carried clearly to Richard's ears, 'He's not been well, you know.'

John Adams looked curiously at Richard, who sank even deeper down inside his jacket, while his hands batted about his head as if he were warding off a swarm of bees.

The labourers, impatient for their drink, now re-appeared at the door, protesting about the lack of service and inquiring why they were suddenly not good enough to be admitted to the inner sanctum where they had sat in the same seats these past twenty years during the harvest season.

At last, on Richard's entreaties, the gentlemen were admitted. His father turned his back on them in disapproving silence, but Richard sought to make up for his rudeness by casting conspiratorial winks and grimaces over the shoulder of his parent to reassure them of their welcome.

'Here you are, sir.' John returned and placed the tray of tea on the table. 'Will that be all, sir?'

The question roused Mr Dadd from his state of distraction. 'We'd like beds, please,' he said stiffly.

'We're full up tonight, I'm afraid, sir. It's the lovely weather. Half London seems to be in Cobham these weekends. I can get you beds in the village, though – one, or is it two, sir?'

Mr Dadd, mindful of Dr Sutherland's instructions, answered, 'One will do; this is my son, you know.'

'Get two if you can.' Richard's brusque contradiction of his father's order caused John Adams to pause and look from one to the other in bewilderment.

In the ensuing silence, Richard raised his cup to his lips, took one sip and then spat it out.

'Is there something wrong with it, sir?' their host inquired.

'Why?' Richard asked in return. 'Should there be?'

'No, no,' John Adams hastened to reassure him. 'It's just the way you, er, looked at it.'

120

'Well, you can't be too careful, can you?' Richard broke off a corner of toasted bread and raised it to his mouth. Then he sniffed at it suspiciously and put it down again.

'Don't fancy that either, eh?' said his father jovially. 'Well, what would tempt you, Dicky, eh?'

'The Scourge of the Pharaohs, they called it,' his son replied.

'What?'

John Adams stood there, uncertain whether to go or stay. 'No one's ever complained before,' he observed.

'And spend the day with a bare bum hanging over the side of the boat,' said Richard loudly. Then oblivious of the stir this comment provoked, he sat there humming quietly to himself.

Mr Dadd dismissed their host and poured another cup of tea. His hand was shaking.

'Care for a walk, Father?' Richard asked casually.

'No. No thank you. I'm too tired.' His parent sagged in his chair as if even the effort of sitting upright was difficult to sustain.

'Pity. It's a lovely evening.' Richard drummed on the table top with his fingers and hummed more loudly.

'Don't let me stop you from going.'

'No. Well, you couldn't, could you? Not if I wanted to, that is.'

'No, I suppose not. What about our little chat though?' Mr Dadd raised a forced laugh. 'I've been looking forward to it.'

'A little time, that's what I need first. To think. Just a little . . . time!' With this observation, Richard clasped his hands to his ears and suddenly got up and rushed from the room.

His father, delayed momentarily by the necessity of righting the cups overturned by his son's flight, was at once after him. But by the time he reached the door, Richard was out of sight.

What happened between now and the fall of darkness, – that fall of darkness which brought more than night with it, – is not entirely clear. It is conjectured that Richard spent the intervening hours in the park familiarising himself with its geography, while his father searched for him in vain in the town and its environs. And how could we, at such a little distance removed, have remained totally impervious to the drama which now entered its final act? Reader, I do not know the answer. It is almost as if each event is encapsulated in its own time and space, – otherwise how could we have interpreted the shuddering of the earth beneath our feet as something so trivial as the mere setting of touch paper to gunpowder? For we were about to live through, not merely an earth tremor, but the opening up of fissures and chasms which threatened to suck us down into the bowels of Hell.

Heedless, thoughtless girls that we were, caring only for the moment and a passing tremor of excitement, Maria Dadd and I covered our ears with our hands to shut out the cannon's boom and hurried down into the town whose narrow streets were dense with people. We had long since lost Stephen and George, but that didn't trouble us in the slightest. Holding hands tightly, lest we should also be separated in the throng, we made our way as best we could among the excited crowds.

The atmosphere was quite unlike that of our usual, dear old Chatham. It was as if the town had thrown off its overcoat of staid respectability to reveal an inner self which was all exhilaration – trumpets and drums and violent explosion, enjoyed all the more for knowing that no real danger threatened. We absorbed the excitement until our cheeks glowed and our feet ached from the pavements we had tramped. We paused from time to time to buy sugared plums or gingerbread from little huddled stalls where the scene was more carnival-like than military. And when we were too weary to take another step, we returned home to be met by the usual complaints.

'The sooner everything settles down to normal the better,' my father, Thomas Carter, opined. Then, determined not to let the events of the day get him down, he helped himself to a large plateful of roast chicken.

'I fear the boys' meal will be quite ruined,' said my mother mournfully, looking at the two empty places.

'Please Mrs Carter, don't trouble yourself on their account,' Maria said to her. 'Papa would certainly insist that they went without.'

'And how is your dear Papa?' inquired Mother. A shred of cabbage had somehow become detached from her previous mouthful and now trembled on her bosom.

Maria caught my eye and stifled a giggle. 'He's very . . . um, not very well, Mrs Carter.'

'Indeed?' A spot of gravy now landed neatly on top of the stray cabbage.

Strange it is that even in the face of tragedy, the minutiae of life have a capacity to implant themselves upon the memory with as much tenacity as affairs of cataclysmic importance. For I remember as clearly as if it were yesterday, how Papa here imperiously tapped his own breast on the exact spot where the offending relic lay; and while Mama scrubbed fretfully at her bodice with a table napkin, he inquired whether Mr Dadd's ill-health could possibly be the occasion of such mirth?

Of course Maria and I shook our heads and denied the accusation vehemently.

'It is Richard,' said Maria very soberly, 'that causes him such distress.'

At the mention of his name at my parents' dining table, I became quite breathless.

'Ah yes, Richard,' mused Mama, as she picked up her knife and fork again. Whether she would have said anything further is doubtful, but at this point there came a ring at the door which quite distracted us all.

'Can that be J.?' she asked, looking at me. 'If so, the dear boy is uncommonly early.'

However, it was not J. L., but a courier with a letter for Stephen Dadd, bearing with it the strictest instructions to put it into no other hand but his own, and that with the utmost expediency. Since we had at that time no knowledge of its contents, the messenger was merely directed into town, to the place where we had last seen Stephen and George, – and that, some hours earlier.

The letter despatched to Robert Dadd junior met with no such delay. It was in his hand within the hour, though he did not act upon it immediately. Instead, he allowed the contents to simmer in his mind along with the last rays of the setting sun as he sat in his garden in Poplar. My sister Catherine, his bride, wandered among the flowerbeds with a basket over her arm, selecting the choicest roses to adorn her dressing table. She made a charming sight. Whenever she looked up, she caught her husband's eye upon her and smiled warmly. Forgetting his problems for a moment, Robert sighed with content and, having lit his cigar, replaced the matches in his breast pocket. At once his fingers encountered the piece of paper which was Mary Ann's letter.

The thought at once dispelled his happy mood. How he wished they would just leave him in peace and not trouble him over every trifle! Richard had been the cause of so much dissension over the years with his refusal to settle down and learn a good steady trade like everybody else. If only his father had been a little firmer, less easily led on by Richard's insistence on 'imagination' and 'broadening one's outlook' − and all that arty claptrap which was, as far as Robert could make out, merely an excuse for idleness.

Nor had he forgotten the fact that Richard was the cause of the first disagreement between him and his wife, − and over a dead camel, of all things! Damn Richard! My brother-in-law here got to his feet and paced impatiently between the herbaceous borders, displacing a smell of catmint and lavender as he walked carelessly between their ranks.

'Robert,' called Catherine, 'what is troubling you?'

'Richard,' he answered abruptly.

'Is there something wrong?' Catherine put down her basket and slipped her hand through her husband's arm.

'I didn't want you to be worried,' he confessed.

'I have a right to worry,' she insisted, quietly approaching and taking his hand, 'and to share your worries.'

Robert squeezed her hand in gratitude and silently gave her the letter.

'Of course,' was her immediate comment, 'if Mary Ann is so concerned, you have a duty to go.'

Within the half hour, his small bag was packed and she stood bravely at the garden gate, waving her husband good-bye. It was their first parting since their marriage.

By the time Richard returned to the Ship Inn, it was mid-evening and almost dark. The bar was crowded. At the cottage piano an old man quavered softly the words of a popular song.

'Ring the bell softly
There's crêpe on the door.'

Richard, much affected by the words, dropped a guinea into the old man's mug which stood on top of the piano.

'John Adams?' Richard inquired at the bar.

The young woman paused in her drawing of pints to answer, 'I'm sorry, he's off duty, sir.'

Richard stared at her suspiciously. 'You're John Adams in disguise, aren't you?'

In spite of his expression which had nothing of humour in it, the woman laughed good-naturedly. 'Can I get you anything, sir?'

Richard looked at the plant into which he had earlier emptied his cup of tea. It looked suspiciously limp. Dragging at his collar, for suddenly the heat and the smoke were too much for him, he set off to find his father.

He found him in the hotel lounge. The only other occupants of the room were a pair of foreign-looking working men playing poker. They glanced briefly at Richard, then returned their attention to the game in hand.

Richard crept up behind his father. 'They are playing for the Captain's soul,' he whispered.

'What's that, eh?' The poor man was quite startled. 'Oh it's you, Richard m'boy. Nice walk, eh?'

Richard flung himself into the armchair at the other side of the fireplace, where he sat sullenly kicking at the stack of logs on the hearth.

'What's all this about the Captain's soul?' inquired his parent.

'Heaven or Hell,' replied Richard.

Mr Dadd waited for a more comprehensive explanation but none was forthcoming. Mesmerised by the game, Richard was growing increasingly unsettled.

'Shouldn't be allowed,' said his father stoutly. 'In a public place.'

'Better where it can be seen. When it's all hidden, – that's much worse.'

The men, aware of his close scrutiny and lured on perhaps by the prospect that this well-heeled young gentleman might be drawn into the game, placed their bids in an ever wilder fashion.

Richard's agitation became intense.

'What would you like to do?' asked his father, casting about for ways to distract him. 'What about another nice walk, how would you like that, eh?' And he at last prevailed upon Richard to accompany him.

Back in London, at the house in Suffolk Street, Mary Ann, Ellen and Sarah, whose shared apprehensions had reached a state little short of hysteria, had dismissed their supper tray almost untouched. Nor were they able to set about their sewing with much more attention.

'I blame myself, Miss Mary,' said Ellen. 'I tried to tell Mr Dadd but I fear that I was not sufficiently forceful in my opinions.'

'I'm sure you did what you could, Ellen dear.' Mary Ann's hands were trembling so much that she could not thread her needle. 'Father can be so obstinate at times.'

'Stephen is the nearest,' Sarah pointed out reasonably. 'It is not far from Chatham. He will have received your letter and set out at once. I know it.'

Unfortunately, the letter on which they now pinned all their hopes still lay in the pocket of that messenger boy, whose small fortune, so liberally dispensed by Mary Ann in the hope of procuring his unswerving devotion to duty, was being rapidly converted into a more liquid form of reward. Scarcely able to stand, he now lolled against the counter of a public house in Chatham High Street while he scrabbled in his pockets for his last few coins.

Had he but remembered the purpose of his visit, which was to seek out a certain Mr Stephen Dadd, he had merely to raise his eyes to discover him. For George Dadd, having divested a certain itinerant musician of his piano accordion, was now playing it on the opposite side of the same bar with more enthusiasm than skill. He was accompanying his elder brother in a brisk sea shanty, while the latter, his voice having long since succumbed to the dense fumes of tobacco in the ill-aired room, had had recourse instead to executing a series of dance steps of quite dazzling bravado considering the size of the table top on which he was standing.

But alas, the messenger had no eyes for any of this. He was fast discovering that his new-found popularity was in danger of lasting no longer than his little stock of gold. He watched hungrily as the glances of the ladies were drawn towards the scarlet coats and gold braid of the off-duty soldiers like magnetic particles to the North Pole. And at last, he threw down his empty glass in disgust and groped his way towards the door.

Meanwhile, Richard and his father walked briskly down Cobham High Street. As they reached the last gas lamp of the village, Mr Dadd hesitated, ready now to turn back. Richard however strode on and was soon lost in the darkness. His father, though fearful, was ever mindful of Dr Sutherland's advice. Besides, what was there to be afraid of? Was not Richard his son? So reasoning, he stepped out of the charmed circle of that last lamp and plunged into the darkness of the road leading to Cobham Park.

Richard arrived at the park some distance ahead of his father, and after listening intently for the echo of his footsteps along the road, hopped nimbly over the stile and slipped off among the trees.

'Richard, are you there?'

Richard could just make out his parent, lingering by the stile.

'Tu-whit to-whoo,' he called, just to let him know that he was on the right track.

'I'm going back,' called his father. 'I've had enough of this silly game. You can catch me up.'

But he didn't move. Richard knew he wouldn't go. His father wouldn't leave him alone in the dark.

'To-whit to-whooo!' he called again, and had the satisfaction of seeing his father climb over the stile and follow him into the trees.

At about the same time, my sister's husband, Robert Dadd junior, having succeeded in catching the last ferry of the day to Gravesend, was having considerable difficulty in obtaining transport to Cobham. Most cabbies insisted that their horses were quite foundered since they had spent the best part of the day taxiing people to and from the manoeuvres in Chatham, from which public service it seemed no reasonable sum would divert them. Robert, though by nature prudent to the point of frugality, was at last driven to offer an amount which would under normal circumstances have been considered outrageous.

Even this extravagance told against him, for the drivers were convinced that only a madman would offer so much cash merely to drive to Cobham and were fearful of accepting. However, one was found who vowed he was willing to risk giving the devil himself a ride for such a king's ransom. And so my brother-in-law at last found himself seated on an uncomfortable bench, whose seat contained more of horsehair and considerably less of leather covering, rattling along behind a lumbering, knock-kneed nag at a rate of some four miles an hour to the belated rescue of his parent.

Maria and I, still in a state of blissful ignorance, were by then squeezed side by side into my own narrow bed, each holding in our hands a slim bundle of letters variously secured by scarlet ribbon (Maria's) and pink ribbon (mine).

'I'll show you mine,' I promised my friend, 'if you will be sure to show me yours afterwards.'

After much giggling, and many protestations of embarrassment and expressions of undying trust, the two respective ribbons were untied and the contents almost torn apart in our haste to communicate the contents.

'*My darling Elizabeth*,' Maria read aloud, though in a subdued voice for fear of anyone overhearing, '*you cannot but be aware for how long I have cherished the thought of you in my bosom . . .*'

Maria here stopped abruptly. 'Elizabeth,' she said, 'if this is the most passionate J. can get, there is no way that I can ever show you my letters from Jock. They are positively red-hot by comparison!'

'Let me see,' I gasped, almost wrenching them from under my dear friend's elbow. I opened the first and began reading. '*My life, how I long to crush . . .*' My eyes widened. I refolded the paper abruptly. 'I can't, Maria, really I can't. It doesn't seem right.'

'Elizabeth,' said Maria. 'You're blushing!'

'If J. said such things to me . . .' I said indignantly.

'But he wouldn't, would he?' Maria pointed out. 'I mean he's not artistic.'

'Do you think,' I now took the liberty to inquire, 'that Richard would write such letters?'

'He feels things very deeply,' replied his sister.

'What does your father say about you receiving such letters?' I then asked her.

She shrugged. 'You don't think I'd show them to him, do you?'

'Doesn't he ask to see them?' I was amazed at some of the liberties allowed by so stern a parent as Mr Dadd.

'Jock writes to me, not to my father. It's not Father he's in love with.' Maria giggled.

'Father opens all the post,' I confessed sadly. 'If a letter like that came to me, he'd probably burn it.' A new possibility occurred to me. 'You don't think Richard has written to me, do you, and that Papa—'

'No.' Maria interrupted me too quickly.

'Do you think I should marry J. then?' I asked her.

Maria occupied herself with binding up her letters and did not answer.

'Does he never mention me?' I persisted.

I received no answer to my question, for there then occurred such a hammering at the front door that we looked at one another in consternation.

'What if it's George or Stephen coming home drunk?' asked Maria in alarm. 'What will your father think?'

In the event it was neither, but the messenger boy with his pennies exhausted, who had somehow managed to stagger the distance from the pub and thunder with his fists upon our door before he quite lost the use of his legs. As Father opened the door, he feebly flapped the letter above his head and muttered the words 'For Mr Stephen Dadd', before falling in a heap on the doorstep.

Huddled on the landing in our nightgowns, Maria and I watched as Father turned the envelope over and over between his hands. He was shortly joined by Mother, who repeated the operation.

'I think, my dear,' said Papa, 'that if the letter is as truly urgent as it purports to be, then perhaps the sister of the said gentleman should be asked to peruse it.'

'You mean,' inquired Mama, 'that Maria should read the letter?'

'Is that not what I have just said?' Father regarded her long-sufferingly.

We only just had time to leap back into bed, hide the letters and extinguish the candle, before Mama entered my room.

'Maria,' she called softly, apparently deaf to the stifled laughter. 'Maria, my dear, are you awake?'

At last it seemed that all thoughts and energies were to be focused upon that one spot in the universe, and upon the two people who most required our consideration.

But by then it was too late. There was nothing anyone could do, for no one could reach them in time.

I must warn you, Reader, that the following scenes are not for the squeamish. In spite of my own repugnance at drawing such matters to your attention, I follow my calling faithfully. These details were available the length and breadth of our island in the daily press. They were, I am reliably informed, even used by Mr C. D., one of our most eminent authors, whose custom it was to depart sufficiently far from the outpourings of his own lurid imagination, as to entertain his house guests with walks through what came to be known as 'Dadd's Hole', there to enact these grisly moments for their edification.

Robert Dadd junior still sat in the ancient carriage, shuddering along the Kent by-ways in the moonlight, and was at last obliged to lower the window and stick out his head to urge the driver to go faster.

'You see, zir,' came the slow reply, 'this be night-time and it's dark, see. There's no knowing if the horse might stumble and do hisself an injury in the darkness.'

And with this answer, Robert had to be content. He flung himself back on the scratchy upholstery and bit nervously at his nails as he willed the miles away.

'I've had enough of this,' Mr Dadd was saying, quite breathless from following his son's erratic progress among the beech trunks.

'Spoilsport!' called Richard from somewhere tantalisingly nearby.

Mr Dadd struggled grimly on until his hat was lifted clean off his head by a low hanging branch. 'You'll be the death of me!' he snapped angrily.

'Death, death!' crooned Richard, drawing out his razor blade and closing in.

'Well?' Mama put her candle down on the bedside table and seating herself on the end of the bed, she watched Maria closely.

Maria looked at me and giggled. We both knew just how boring Mary Ann's letters could be – full of exhortations to goodness and obedience and containing nothing more exciting than the day's recipes or the latest news from the Missionary Society. My friend therefore slid her thumbnail somewhat less than enthusiastically under the seal and prised it loose.

The author of the letter was at that moment kneeling by her bedside and saying over and over to herself, 'Blessed are those who trust in the Lord, for they shall be comforted.' Yet the prayer brought little comfort; rather it troubled her even further with her lack of faith. If she could only believe sufficiently, all would yet be well. 'Blessed are those . . .' She knelt there until her knees ached and her shoulders were stiff with the cold. 'Blessed are those . . .'

The first slice of the razor blade slid harmlessly through the collar of Mr Dadd's coat. At first, he was not even aware of what was happening. Then as Richard raised the weapon again, its blade glinted in the moonlight.

'What on earth is that?' said Stephen, as he fell over the prone form of the messenger on the doorstep. His voice was muffled because George at once fell heavily on top of him. 'George, just prop yourself up for a bit, will you?' he asked irritably, trying to feel for the door key in his pocket.

A ghastly scream echoed from the window over their heads.

'What is it?' George started shivering violently.

'It's only Maria,' said Stephen, well used though not entirely inured to the sound. Before he could find his key, he was greeted in the doorway by my father, bearing Mary Ann's letter.

'Why did no one come and look for me?' he protested, glancing in alarm at the contents.

George slumped against the house wall, quite forgotten by everybody, while Stephen rushed here and there, trying to calm

Maria and to allay the fears of my mother and myself, while Father scoured the streets in search of a cab.

'Richard,' said his father, very quietly and calmly, 'give that to me, there's a good boy.' He held out his hand for the razor.

Richard looked quietly down at the razor in his hand and began to weep.

Mr Dadd pocketed the weapon, and satisfied that all danger was passed, he took his son in his arms.

'How many miles to Cobham?' Robert junior bellowed out of the coach window.

The carriage, which had been moving more and more slowly, finally ground to a halt. Robert could hear the horse's teeth tearing at the grass on the roadside. He leapt angrily from the cab, seized the whip from the sleeping driver and gave the horse a thwack which had the poor tired creature rearing between the shafts like a circus animal, and then setting off at a gallop in quite the wrong direction.

Richard, with his face pressed against the soft velvet waistcoat, felt the heavy stuff of his father's overcoat close around his back.

'Dicky,' his father murmured, as if he were a child, 'there there, Dicky.' His arms clasped his son firmly to him. Richard struggled to free himself, and his fingers closed on the handle of the rigger's knife. The blade sprang out with a snick that was inaudible among the rustling of the leaves.

My father, who could find vehicles in plenty but none to drive them, at last repaired to an inn where he was successful in hiring a horse. Stephen leapt upon its back and set off at a gallop in the direction of Cobham village.

Father returned to find George comfortably asleep on the door-step alongside the messenger lad.

'Come along now, my boy,' he said, all joviality. For he too, in his youth, and his sons after him, were wont to celebrate the manoeuvres to excess. 'Let's get you into a nice comfy bed, eh?'

But George refused to be helped up and declined the offer of a comfy bed. 'It's on fire,' he said by way of explanation.

Father summoned Mother, who obligingly tripped up the stairs to the guest room and returned with the reassuring news that the bed was just as she had made it up herself that morning. 'Cool clean sheets, Georgy,' she told him.

'Flames,' insisted George. 'Fire and sodomy.'

Mama turned pale, and Papa sent her off to bed.

'Come now, George,' Father then thundered, 'that's quite enough of that. Bed!' He roared the last word as if he were in charge of the manoeuvres themselves.

But George huddled on the ground, gibbering with fear.

His two brothers, still posting towards Cobham, were, as we all feared, too late. Richard had already arrived back at the wooden stile, leaving his father dead, or dying on the grass. He was badly out of breath and somewhat bruised. Instead of leaping over easily, he hauled himself up with his hands, leaving his bloody fingerprints on the topmost plank, and after falling heavily down on the roadside, he set off at a brisk pace towards Dover, — and the Continent.

Chapter Six

WHAT can I say of the next twenty years? All that could be said about them could as well be contained in the history of the twenty days which succeeded upon the events of the last chapter and witnessed the sequestration of my hopes and dreams. For Reader, they did not die. They remained alive just as Richard did, though they too were never again at liberty to sweeten my days with their promised perfume and fan the air about my head with their gentle wings.

They did not take easily to imprisonment, but they feared exposure more. As my beloved fled to France, they too were driven into hiding. When he was dragged into the black abyss of mental distraction, they fought their impending doom by refusing to believe in what was happening, by denying reality. It was a hopeless struggle from the first. Outnumbered by the forces which massed against them, they at last held up the white flag of surrender and gave themselves into captivity.

As Richard stood motionless in the courtyard of the asylum in France, gazing blankly at the sun which he said was his father, my dreams were at last revealed for what they were by the bright light of Reason. I accepted the yoke of reality upon my shoulders and applied myself to its bitter service with all my strength. There was no other way. In short, even while Richard was still in hiding, I agreed to the announcement of my engagement to J. L.

My engagement was a desperate measure enforced upon me by the wishes of my parents. Just as the hunted deer will cross water to shake off the hounds which bay for his blood, in like manner did Richard cross the Channel. The trackers cast about and sniffed among the thickets and tangled undergrowth of his life, but their quarry was fled. Deprived of their prey, yet driven onwards by an insatiable bloodlust, everything was game. I was like a poor, trembling hare which had stumbled unwittingly across their path.

I had neither strength to brave the current nor a deep dark hole in which to hide myself away. Their fetid breath stank in my nostrils and their teeth were already at my throat. 'I Elizabeth Carter, take thee . . .'

I did not falter as I recited the words. I said them willingly enough, but without expression or emotion. They arose from the grey monotone of a soul that was sick almost to death. I did not care what happened to me. But Reader, do not pity me! If anyone was to be pitied, it was that good and kind man who led me to the altar. He deserved something better than this poor numb creature who delivered herself up to him like an empty husk.

Yet he never knew what a poor bargain he was getting, of that I am sure. In spite of the chaos into which we were all thrown by virtue of our close association with the Dadd family, we Carters kept our heads. Of course, we grieved with and for our dear friends. The inquest was held; a warrant issued for Richard's arrest. Mr Dadd was buried; George sent to an asylum. Maria remained with us for many days before she was fit to return to the sad remnants of her family. Stephen, Robert and Catherine were frequent visitors to our house and table. We all suffered together, and it was not necessary for any outsider to seek for a deeper cause for my own distress than all that had gone before and which still beset us on every side. I disciplined myself to be ever more discreet, to keep a strict guard on my tongue and on my actions, so that J. at least was spared the knowledge of my attachment to Richard.

My wedding was a quiet affair, taking place in that brief interval between Richard's extradition from the Continent and his trial. I was on my honeymoon when he stood in the dock in the dark blue cloak which matched his eyes. But Reader, no cloak could have concealed the chink of iron manacles beneath its ample folds! Though the courtroom lay a hundred miles away, nothing could escape the dry and burning eye of my imagination. They exposed him, body and soul, bruised and bleeding, to the rudeness of the scoffing multitudes who packed the courtroom and lined the streets for one glimpse of the infamous parricide.

J. was infinitely kind. His patience never failed, though I fear there were times when I must have tried it sorely. For though we were travelling in the remotest country regions, yet there was no escape. Ever more sensational stories of the murder and the trial pursued us wherever we went. There was one evening when we were sitting in the dining room of an hotel in the small, secluded town of S——, when a ballad-monger in the street outside saw fit to entertain us with the bloodthirsty doings of Charles Dodds, that unnatural being, that aberration of nature. Popular culture, with little heed to accuracy or truth, may have bestowed the wrong name, but there was no mistaking to whom they referred.

J. at once asked our host to move the fellow on, and although the deed was accomplished with alacrity, the damage was already done. The strains of his song so echoed in my brain that I was quite unable to finish an excellent repast. My appetite was fled. Unnatural? Aberration? How could such terms be applied to the dearest, kindest being that ever lived? To one whose nature was so sensitive that the sight of an injured bird could move him to tears? And yet he was guilty – no, not guilty, that is impossible, though it cannot be disputed that it was his hand that held the knife. Let us rather think that his light, which was made to shine so brightly, had been eclipsed by some darker power which henceforth used him for its own evil purposes.

For at the last, the mob was cheated of its hanging; the hounds of their prey; the moralists of the satisfaction of a lurid example of good triumphant over evil. For Richard was never convicted. The mercy of our laws is such that he was detained during Her Majesty's pleasure, and conveyed to the same Institution which contained his poor brother George. Rather than hang him, they buried him alive, along with my hopes. I did not see him again for forty years, until the grass grew green on the grave of my own dear husband.

Do not imagine that those intervening decades found me anything but happy. If my spirits never attained the heights of ecstasy nor did they plumb the depths of sorrow. Reader, a deep content gradually cast its mantle about my shoulders as softly as the first, plump flakes of snow which fall silently from a sky that is heavy and grey. Nothing occurred to disturb the even tenor of my days. The seasons passed, each bringing their own quiet happiness from the pine-scented fires of a winter's evening to the gentle summer breeze which drifted down from the high moors and filled the house with the perfume of gorse and heather.

I first became conscious of how deep an impression my gratitude towards my husband had made on me, – how it had cast aside the shadow which so blighted it, and was ready to burst into the full flower of devotion, – when I saw J. hold our firstborn child in his arms, and beheld the look of adoration on his face: a warmth of feeling which encompassed us both. At that moment, I felt deeply ashamed for withholding a love which was his by right. As for those secret yearnings which I still harboured in my soul, I bade them be gone. They left, taking with them their frost, and like those deep peaty pools on the high moor on which the ice cracks and thaws in ever-widening circles, my heart opened to give and to receive in equal measure all the rich joys of a happy family life.

Over the years, I did not lose touch with the Dadd family, though of necessity our intercourse was less frequent. The journey to London was long and arduous and not to be undertaken lightly. Nor did I like to leave the delights of rural Devon and my own growing family for the bustle of a metropolis which I now found disconcerting. We had cut ourselves off from the rest of the world. I had spun a warm, silk-lined cocoon about our charmed circle; within it we were safe and warm. But Reader, how fragile was that little universe, how vulnerable to the trials and tribulations of neighbouring constellations!

There were times when travel was forced upon me, when the needs of my own sister Catherine in London seemed greater than my own. Such excursions were like great rents torn in the fabric of my peaceful existence. I felt myself exposed to every whim of the elements, – battered and buffeted, pushed and pulled in every direction whether I would or no.

Such was the peril in which I felt myself on every expedition that I vowed that each trip would be my last. For, as I walked the London streets, the shadow of the great walls of Bedlam seemed to haunt me. As I sat with Maria in that atmosphere of paint and turpentine, there opened before me dangerous vistas of 'What Might Have Been'.

For Maria married her Jock, the little Aberdonian who had been

Richard's close friend at the Academy. Mother and I were in Suffolk Street, soon after Mr Dadd's funeral, helping with the packing when the marriage was arranged. Sarah had already departed for Billy Frith's, where she took up the post of governess to his children. Mary Ann was to go and live with my sister Catherine and Robert, in Poplar. And Maria?

Jock found her, seated on her trunk in a house whose memories echoed with an ever greater resonance as the quantity of furniture decreased.

'Richard is found,' she announced as Jock came into the room, though she had scarcely seemed aware of his approach.

'I saw it in the papers.'

'So did everyone else,' observed Maria wryly, indicating with a gesture the crowd outside. 'He was discovered in a coach in Fontainebleau, attempting to cut the throat of a fellow passenger.'

'Maria,' said Jock, attempting to put an arm round her to comfort her, 'it makes no difference, you know.'

'It makes a world of difference.' Maria walked over to the window and looked down into the street. Immediately, excited cries could be heard. 'The sister of a murderer,' she continued, 'do you really want to live with that?'

'They will soon forget,' insisted Jock.

'If Richard were dead, perhaps.' Maria retreated from the window and stood leaning on the mantelpiece over the cold grate. 'Or even if he stayed in France. But they insist on bringing him back to stand trial, you know.'

'That doesn't bother me,' said Jock carelessly. 'Besides, if you take my name— '

'Are you implying that I should marry you simply to escape the infamy of my own?'

'Maria, I love you!'

'Besides, Father would not have approved.'

'It is your own wishes you must consult, not those of the dead.' The boy who had once stowed away on a ship to come to London and realise his ambitions as a painter, was not to be shaken off so easily.

When at last she walked down the aisle beside him, it was as if the intervening years were trodden into dust. Present to watch her triumphal progress were all Richard's old Academy friends and acquaintances. In cafés and restaurants, in studios, parlours, public houses, art galleries, and even in the hallowed precincts of the Royal Academy itself, Maria lived again through all the successes and failures we both remembered so well from our younger years. A whole world was restored to her and she found herself adored and deliriously happy in return.

'Come in, come in! Jock is expecting you.' Maria would open the door of the little apartment herself, for they could not afford a servant, and be at once submerged under a heap of capes and top hats, walking canes, gloves and scarves, with which she staggered through to the bedroom – the hall being far too narrow to admit of a coatstand.

'Maria, what do you think of this?'

'Maria, would you use oils or . . .'

'Is not this composition a little heavy? If I were to move . . .'

'Mrs Phillip, what do you think of this Rossetti fellow?'

She hardly had time to put down their outdoor garments and enter the studio with the glasses and ale before the questions broke in a storm about her ears, at times quite bewildering in their range and intensity.

'Give me a minute to think, don't rush me!' she cried, bustling among them with refreshments, while Jock turned his most recent failure to the wall with an exclamation of disgust.

Amid the happy chaos of these bohemian surroundings, Maria became young and light of foot. Her eyes sparkled and her cheeks burned as she found her opinion most flatteringly sought after.

'I really couldn't say. You presume upon my opinion too much.' She would often protest her unworthiness and beg to be excused from giving any opinion at all, for she doubted her own judgement on such matters. 'Richard,' she then added tentatively, 'would probably have said . . .' and she strained to hear his voice from the past, while her audience listened with bated breath.

Jock was less happy. 'Why – ' I once heard him yell, as he closed the doors on the last guest – 'why did you tell them all that?'

'They asked me, Jock, and I told them,' faltered Maria.

'Then tell me,' he said, 'tell me what is wrong with this.'

Maria looked at the painting and hung her head. Richard's contempt for her husband's talents was too loud in her ears. 'It is past midnight, Jock,' she protested. 'I am too tired, I cannot think straight.'

It seemed to me then that not one among Maria's newly resurrected friends valued her for herself; perhaps not even her husband. It was as if she had, after a brief flowering, become invisible again. But still I envied her. At such times, it was not my dreams which seemed unreal, but my life with J. and the children which hovered on the horizon like a mirage, shimmering and distant and inaccessible.

How could I relate all this to my husband, and by exposing what was a false dream to me, shatter what was reality for him? Whenever the summons from the family came, I obeyed solely at his behest. 'Go!' he would say, interpreting my reluctance in the manner most flattering to himself. He was a man not given to introspection nor greatly endowed with imagination. His eye was caught only by the glint of sunshine on the water and he never sought to look below its surface to where the tangled weeds snatched at the unsuspecting fish and the jagged teeth of barely concealed rocks lay in wait for the unwary mariner.

The year 1860 saw me on one of these infrequent trips away from home, when we all gathered together for the first time since Mr Dadd's funeral. Although this occasion too was the consequence of a bereavement, it lacked the numbing sense of shock which so overshadowed that previous interment. I saw too why previous family gatherings had not been attempted during the intervening years, – not even for Maria's marriage. On the seemingly endless journey from London to Manchester on which we now embarked, – with all the Dadds (for they would not be split up) crammed into the space of one small carriage, – no amount of crush, no numbers of jam-packed bodies could have made up for the absence of those members who were not with us. Two there were, whose names wove freely through the tapestry of conversation: dear, kind Mr Dadd, whose fondness was perhaps his undoing, and Arthur, who was gone to seek his fortune in America, and apparently doing very well there. But there were two other ghosts among us, whose presence was palpable though their names were never spoken aloud. Richard and George, Richard and George, Richard and George, – the very wheels seemed to sing out the rhythm of their names.

141

At last, weary from the arduous train journey, yet still exhilarated from the rattling pace of the iron monster, we found ourselves, – together with all our bags and baggage, – deposited by a cheerful cab driver in a quiet residential street in Manchester: Robert and his wife Catherine, his sisters Mary Ann, Sarah and Maria and their half-brother John, and myself. Also of our company were Maria's two young children, Amy and Colin, together with their adored nanny Ellen, who was then rising seventy and who huffed and puffed continually as if the task of overseeing that lively pair was altogether too much for her.

While the older generation of Dadds – now considerably altered by that solidity which so often characterises middle age – stood in silent contemplation of their brother Stephen's house, poor Ellen chided the children in a rumbling undercurrent of admonition. One might have thought that she had acquired it only recently from the incessant rhythm of the train had the rest of us not been accustomed to the sound for the past thirty-five years, – certainly for much longer than the existence of the London to Manchester railway.

'Stephen looks respectably settled,' observed Robert at last. The house was solid and double-fronted, the brass knocker well polished, the window panes pleasantly clean and shiny in spite of the heavily industrial surroundings. Everything about it spoke of a quiet air of prosperity.

The expression used by Stephen's elder brother was perhaps unfortunate. For it was not long before we found ourselves escorted directly to the front parlour where the dear man was indeed settled, never to rise again in this mortal life. He lay before us in a modest but nicely-appointed coffin lined in gleaming white silk, quite unable to fulfil the part of host though it was one which would once have given him untold pleasure. In contemplation of the departed, the maid then left us, closing the door and stalking off without a word.

'Well,' said Maria, laughing nervously. 'There's a strange welcome!' After a quick glance at Stephen she paced restlessly about the room.

'Who is it?' asked Colin, staring impassively at the body from the safety of Ellen's arms.

'Your Uncle Stephen, God rest his soul,' explained Mary Ann.

'I want to see. Let me see!' Amy clung with her small hands to the side of the coffin, and jumped up and down so that she might see over the edge.

Sarah lifted her up for a better look. 'Uncle Stephen?' asked the child. 'Who's Uncle Stephen?' She leant forward to touch him, but Sarah snatched her away and put her down.

'He hasn't changed at all,' said Maria. 'Not really. A bit greyer perhaps over the last twenty years, but then aren't we all? I mean, look at you, Robert!'

Robert stiffened and Catherine jumped to his defence. 'I think he looks even nicer,' she said; 'so much more distinguished.'

'Jock hasn't got one single grey hair,' Maria told us all. 'Not one!'

'That probably comes,' replied Mary Ann, 'of never shouldering his responsibilities.'

'Responsibilities?' Maria asked incredulously. 'What do you mean by that?'

This argument among the siblings was dissipated by the entry of Stephen's widow, Marianne.

Marianne we found to be a small, plump woman, homely of face and figure. We all stood there on the other side of her husband's body, looking at her – I fear – curiously.

'What did you pay?' asked Maria bluntly, examining the wood and the workmanship of the casket with equal care. 'George would have done better, you know, and for free.'

The others looked at her, tight-lipped with embarrassment.

'You're right there, my pet,' Ellen said to break the silence. 'A lovely little worker he was.'

'Is,' corrected Maria. 'Say is, Ellen, there's a dear. They make him work so hard, you know.'

'Whatever you say, my love.'

Maria's face was quite puckered with anguish on her youngest brother's account. 'He's like a great furry bumble bee,' she said. 'He'd never hurt a soul, our George.'

'He's a lovely lad,' affirmed Ellen pleasantly, and Maria's expression cleared, a smile breaking out on her face like the sun from behind a storm cloud. The little moment of awkwardness was over. The rest of us breathed a sigh of relief.

'Who's that?' asked young Colin, tugging at Ellen's hand

and pointing at the lady who had entered. Ellen hushed him anxiously.

'Marianne,' said Maria warmly, stepping across the empty space between them and holding out both her hands. She was as tall and slender as her sister-in-law was short and stout. She hovered over her momentarily and then drew her hands up to her lips and kissed each in turn. 'It must be very hard for you,' she observed. 'Indeed, I don't know how I could bear it.'

'Sometimes,' replied her sister-in-law calmly, 'we have to accept that God knows what is best.'

Mary Ann nodded her head violently in agreement with these sentiments.

'To me,' the widow continued, 'it is a relief to know that at last he is at rest.'

'How can you say that?' sobbed Maria (and here I stepped forward to take her in my arms and comfort her), 'when you have lost a husband, and we have lost a brother?'

'His life has been for several years a living death,' said the widow calmly. 'As you see he is now at peace.' She smiled fondly down on her husband as she spoke. 'And so am I,' she said simply.

It was a brave speech by one whose life, for many years, had been shadowed by insanity; for though Maria was unaware of it, the rest of us knew only too well the many tribulations she had lived through.

The truth had been deliberately withheld from Maria. It was not my decision to keep her in ignorance of it, but one made by her elder brother and sister, whose wishes I felt bound to respect. Blood-ties are held to be stronger than those of friendship alone, though it is a belief which I hold in some doubt in the light of my own experiences. Be that as it may, Maria's nerves had been sadly awry since the birth of her children. She had at times the air of a wren, who peeps shyly out at the world and who is startled unbearably by the least sound, the least threat of danger. It was feared that any shock might drive her febrile constitution to the point of collapse.

I still think that the decision made by Robert and Mary Ann was not wise. The death of an otherwise healthy young man in a family in which longevity was the norm, could not but give rise to anxiety. I have always been of the opinion that the truth can never harm when administered with an appropriate dose of affectionate and judicious support. Its concealment, though, is dangerous, weaving a web of deceit which in the end traps creator and victim alike.

Ever since she had heard the news of Stephen's death, Maria must have suspected that we were keeping something from her. The silences in the train which met her endless questions had become so oppressive that even the children's heedless chatter and demands to be entertained, provided welcome diversion. It was as if everyone was avoiding the topic which should have been on all our lips; brother Stephen, his life and his death.

When Robert assumed the role of patriarch after his father's untimely demise, he became the centre for family communications. He wrote and received letters regularly both from Manchester, and from Milwaukee. Thus he also assumed the role of family censor, passing on what pleased him while suppressing the less palatable facts which he deemed unsuitable for general circulation. None of us was aware of the full horror of Stephen's last years, except Robert. It was only gradually that the true meaning of 'Stephen's illness' became apparent even to me, and I considered myself one of the best informed members of the family since my relationship with Catherine had ever been close.

I now found myself looking on helplessly as Maria found all her efforts to extract information from her brother entirely frustrated. He sat there, larger and more pompous than ever his father had been, − bloated, it seemed to me then, on those confidences which he had never divulged. I watched as Maria became more and more bewildered by the situation. For her own grief at the loss of a much-loved brother was quite unreflected in the faces of the rest of the family. How could death bring nothing but relief, − even to a widow, whose love for her spouse she had read in her eyes?

'He has been ill for a long time then?' she asked as we sat waiting for the funeral cortège to arrive. Her perseverance as she tried to find her way through the maze of deception could only be admired; and her bewilderment must have been compounded by the glances and evasions which met her query. For Marianne looked at Catherine, Catherine looked at Robert, and Robert looked at Mary Ann, though the question could surely have been answered by any one of them.

'A good few years,' Robert remarked at last, somewhat gruffly, and then turned his head away from her to study a small water-colour which hung on the wall; – which was strange since Robert never had much time for pictures.

Maria looked at it to see why it was of such interest. It was the sort of composition Richard might have painted to fill in a few long hours on a seaside holiday. It was certainly not remarkable enough to distract her from her present line of enquiry.

'Did he suffer much?' she persisted.

Robert continued to fix his gaze on the picture.

Maria cleared her throat and repeated her question more loudly.

Mary Ann looked up from her endless embroidery. 'Suffering?' she mused, and paused to tuck back a grey curl which had escaped the black cap which ill-suited her sallow complexion. 'What is suffering? It is an attitude of mind which can be entirely relieved by faith.' Her personal experience vouched for the efficacy of this statement, which she had used to effect during many a recent bilious attack.

'All pain,' I interposed, for I here thought back to my own experiences in child-bearing, 'can be borne if there is joy at the end of it.'

'But when there is only death?' asked Maria.

'If death,' replied Mary Ann, 'is seen but as the fruit of life, everything else assumes its proper place.'

'At forty-four?' queried Maria. 'I do not intend to die in five years' time. There is so much still to do, to see . . .'

'If God wills.' Mary Ann took out her gold thread, a treat which she relished above every other and so saved for the finishing touches to each stage of her work. As she spoke, she started on the letters IHS, which glimmered softly back at her. 'But if the anguish is one of the mind,' she continued, 'even there, there is the ultimate hope of reconciliation.'

Maria intercepted the look Robert gave her elder sister, and which made it obvious that she had given away too much.

'Was Stephen then much troubled in mind?' Maria burst out.

There was again the same momentary hesitation before Mary

Ann replied quite calmly, 'That is a matter between his soul and his Maker.'

Maria looked from face to face and I was forced to turn away, for I could not have denied her the truth had she then demanded it of me.

Fortunately, Stephen's widow here entered the conversation. 'Stephen was much changed, Mrs Phillip. Indeed I fear you would scarcely have recognised him by the end.'

'Oh no,' protested Maria, 'he was not changed at all. I'd have known him anywhere for my brother.'

At the grave-side, though that other funeral was so much in all our minds, it was never referred to directly. Stephen's interment passed, as it were, in the shadow of that previous event, and shades there were in plenty to drift across the landscape of our thoughts and cast their pall over the present.

Nor is this strange power confined to events. People too, living or dead, can in their absence make their presence strongly felt, and cast over quite ordinary proceedings their own grotesquely substantial shadows. In such manner did Robert Dadd senior rise ghastly from his grave and consign his son Stephen, even in death, to the obscurity in which he had lived all his life. So did Richard make himself more felt by his absence than he would have done by his presence in our midst.

But it is not merely in the imagination that this displacement occurs. How frequently does one person steal for themselves the leading role in the play! At Catherine's wedding reception, it was Richard who was the focus of all our concern. At my own, too, though absent in body, he monopolised the stage, – if stage it could be called, for the wedding was but a poor, hurried affair, at a time which afforded little occasion for joy or celebration.

Our silver wedding celebration later fared little better. We had planned, my husband and I, a modest party, consisting only of family and a few close friends from the neighbourhood. After a brief service of thanksgiving at our local church, in a rich Devon valley beset on all sides by windswept moors, we drove back to the hamlet in which we lived. Even as J. handed me down from the carriage, my daughter could contain herself no longer, and chose that moment during which I was receiving the congratulations of our small band of faithful servants, to announce her own engagement!

I do not tell you this out of pique. My joy almost matched hers at the announcement, as if a wheel had come full circle. Twenty-five years ago to the day, J. and I had pledged each other company for better or for worse. Now, that first fruit of our relationship was poised on the very threshold of that same mystery. It was with a heart overflowing with gratitude that I melted into the background. For the joy of an engagement is the celebration of youth and of that which is to come. For her it was a beginning; for us, almost an end. For J.'s health had begun, even then, to fail.

But to return to the year 1860, and the gathering in Manchester. If Stephen's obsequies were overshadowed by his father's death and the absence of Richard and George, it was Maria who stole the show. For who among you can see a childhood friend without those same feelings of love and companionship which once existed hovering again in the air between you? Like spectres, they so dazzle the sight that the stranger who now stands before you is quite lost in their glittering aura. For Reader, that is how I saw Maria that day – through the eyes of friendship and love. Perhaps there were other stars in the sky; if so, I saw them not.

Quite ordinary events graced the occasion. They are of little significance; they brushed past me like so much flotsam, and were gone. Yet all was not well. It was as if some unspoken dread was present among us. We ate and drank. We talked. We renewed old acquaintances and made new ones. The unease remained. And then, during a lull in the conversation, Maria finally voiced, – in tones which carried as clear as a bell, – that thought which weighed so heavily upon us all.

'The last time we were all gathered together,' she observed, 'was at Father's funeral.'

Her words fell among us like pebbles in deep water. In that moment of terrible silence, we might all have drowned, had not Marianne bustled among us with another plateful of sandwiches, chiding us for our failure to help ourselves.

148

Then suddenly everybody was talking again, twenty to the dozen, and the party proceeded by means of half-grasped conversations, – words and snippets snatched from here and there in a manner utterly fatiguing to the brain. So it was that I at last withdrew to the seclusion of a window seat, where, half-concealed by a thick blue velvet curtain, I thought to enjoy for a while the pleasure of my own thoughts and reflections.

From my vantage point, I could not help but notice, as the table was cleared for the desserts, that Sarah Dadd had manoeuvred herself into an adjacent corner, where she was now installed in a seat within the bay window alongside a total stranger.

Her new-found friend was of middle age, like herself, and spoke with a slight accent which was at once attractive and reassuring. It did not mark him out as too grand for a lady who was forced to earn a living, nor yet was it sufficiently broad to be classified as vulgar.

'It is your work which you have been describing to me,' he was saying. 'Now, tell me about your life.'

'My life!' Sarah's laugh was somewhat forced. The sound was strange to me. I had not heard Sarah laugh for so long. 'The simple answer is that a governess has no life.'

'My dear young lady!' protested the gentleman.

I could sense Sarah's pleasurable confusion at this terminology and sympathise with that brief fluttering of hope at the thought that she might still be described as young; and dear.

'A governess,' she continued, 'is a mere observer of life. Like a bird which sits on a branch studying its reflection in a deep, still pool, she sees the world quite clearly, but it remains inaccessible.'

'You exaggerate,' he objected.

'Did you then never have a governess?' Sarah inquired.

'Oh yes,' he replied laughing. 'A sad wearisome creature. We teased her unmercifully.'

'Exactly!' said Sarah.

'My dear,' he protested, 'I would not have described you as sad or wearisome.'

149

'That is because you see me now, as a fellow human being. In another context . . .' Sarah dismissed her own claim to humanity with a wave of the hand.

'Let us talk of more cheerful matters,' continued the gentleman. 'Since your life has such a depressing effect upon your spirits, let me tell you about my own.' The way in which he rested his hand on hers did not escape my notice, nor did the self-satisfied manner with which he then leant back comfortably and extracted a cigar from his pocket before he began.

He had proceeded no further than a few inane sentences about his early childhood, when Maria crossed in front of me and squeezed herself on to the window seat next to him.

I could see at once that this caused considerable annoyance to Sarah, but Maria was ever a creature who acted on impulse first, and reflected later.

'Sally,' she now said abruptly, without even considering the presence of the third party, 'was Stephen mad, and if so what did he die of? You don't die of being mad, do you, – I mean, look at Richard and George.'

'Of course he wasn't,' Sarah replied angrily. 'He was as sane as you are.'

'Won't you introduce me?' asked the gentleman, looking on this exotic bird who had come between himself and his companion who now seemed quite drab in comparison.

'My sister, Maria,' said Sarah reluctantly.

'I'm just another of the mad Dadds,' Maria continued recklessly.

'Maria!' poor Sarah reproved her.

'Oh I'm sure he will want to hear the whole sad history,' said Maria, becoming quite flushed and excited as she warmed to the subject.

'He will not!' I could see Sarah bite her lip with mortification.

'There is no point in hiding it,' said Maria, 'he's bound to have heard all about it.'

'I don't remember,' replied the gentleman.

'There you are!' retorted Sarah. 'So why rake it all up?'

'Why should it bother you?' Maria stretched her hands above her head and yawned.

'People don't like that sort of thing,' said Sarah sulkily.

'On the contrary, it is quite enthralling,' said the gentleman, looking more nervous by the minute.

150

'Oh you needn't worry,' Maria said to put him at his ease, 'it's only the men in our family who go mad. The women are quite delightful.'

Out of a certain delicacy of feeling in relation to my marriage vows, I felt under constraint not to inquire directly about Richard; but like the beggar at the rich man's table, how avidly did I devour those crumbs which came my way! It was ever Richard's contention, following Juvenal, that those at the top of the table received the best dishes. That may be so. But to those who have nothing, even the left-overs are a rich feast indeed, so that when Maria began speaking about Richard, I hung on every word.

'When Richard went to prison,' Maria next observed, at the top of her voice, and I do believe that she acted out of a certain devilry, being now committed to provoking them. In this she was successful, for loud was the outrage among her assembled relatives. 'Have I said something wrong?' she then asked innocently, in her usual melodious voice.

'Richard is in hospital,' Mary Ann pointed out quietly.

'I see no difference,' Maria protested. 'If to be confined against your will is not to be imprisoned, then what is it?'

'Richard is ill,' said Robert; 'he is not in a state to be held responsible for his actions.'

'Fiddlesticks,' said Maria. 'He is painting better than ever. His pictures now are quite wonderful.'

'They have no value,' said her brother as if that dismissed them from consideration.

'They have no value?' Maria was incensed. 'Can you look at them and not be moved? not see they are done by the hand of a master? Oh, Jock would soon put you right if he were here. He says Richard is incomparable.'

How I admired her for her bravery as she stood there quite alone against them all. Then unable at last to endure her isolation, I stepped forward and drew her arm through mine. And since she too professed herself weary of company, food and drink, we sought the solitude of the garden together.

'Did I say something wrong, Elizabeth?' she asked me.

'No,' I reassured her, laying a hand gently on her arm. 'They just don't like to be reminded.'

'How can they ever forget?' was her reply.

I tried to point out to her the difference between harbouring those memories and voicing them openly, for I was a past master of concealment.

'Have you been happy with J.?' Maria asked suddenly, as if she could read my very thoughts.

I hesitated a moment before replying. 'What is happiness?' I mused. 'J. is good and kind and patient. He loves me and I love him. I have my children. What more could I want?'

Maria remained silent, so that at last I was driven to prompt her. 'You are troubled, Maria? Is life with an artist not to your liking after all?'

'You are well free of that!' Maria spoke vehemently. 'For though there are times when I would not change my lot with anyone else in the world, there are others when I regret that I did not marry someone very like your own dear J.'

'Oh surely not,' I protested, trying to imagine my mercurial friend contained within the four walls of my tiny country home with such a down-to-earth being as my husband. 'You imagine such a picture as in a child's book,' I objected. 'You see only the whitewash and the roses round the door.'

'I see that it could be heaven,' she said wistfully.

'Heaven?' I replied impatiently. 'You would be more likely to find it hell.'

'Hell is loving someone who cares not a jot for you,' asserted my dear friend, turning on me such a look as rendered words superfluous.

Reader, I had been in that place myself; I knew what she meant, and for a moment I trembled once more on the brink of the abyss. I felt those fingers clawing at my skirts and struggling again to drag me down. I had escaped their clutches once by the grace of God and the strength of J.'s love, but I had not the strength to rescue my friend. J. had been able to save me because of his innocence, which burned before me like a beacon and guided me through the dark night of the soul. I could not boast of a similar strength. I was all too aware of the forces of the enemy and saw already their horrid entrenchments thrown up in every furrow of that dear, unhappy brow. And though I stretched out my hand to help her, I could feel her being slowly sucked away from me and engulfed in the darkness.

'Where is Jock?' I asked my friend, as we strolled between the neat urban rosebeds and lawns which were the complete antithesis of my own rural wilderness. Here, it was as if man reigned supreme; in Devon I was but the handmaiden of nature.

'Where is J.?' replied Maria, throwing the question back at me.

'At home of course. In Dartmouth,' I replied lightly. 'Where else would he be?'

'Jock is in Spain,' stated Maria flatly.

'How wonderful!' I was here inspired to click my fingers together and stamp my feet on the gravel path.

'Infidelity is no joking matter,' said Maria. Her face resumed its closed, troubled look.

'Infidelity? Surely not!' I simply could not believe it. For Jock had always worshipped Maria, and I could not imagine such passion ever turning sour. 'I mean,' I continued, 'look at me now, and yet J. swears he loves me as I am.'

'Does he?' Maria was sceptical.

'I don't doubt it. And you, Maria, you are still so young and beautiful.' I here took her hands and swung her round. 'Look at you!' I cried. 'How can he be unfaithful?'

'Oh not in body,' said Maria very seriously, as she suffered me to lead her to a bench out of the wind. 'There is a worse sort of unfaithfulness, – that of looking into your lover's eyes and seeing no reflection; as if you had ceased to exist.'

'I can't believe it,' I protested. 'Those letters!'

'Dear Elizabeth,' said Maria gently, 'just because in sleepy old Devon nothing has changed for centuries, and even J. ages like some old churchyard stone which, though retaining its essential nature, becomes ever more encrusted with moss and lichens, do not imagine that in other places life goes on in the same old way.'

I here protested mildly at hearing my husband compared to a stone, though in some ways the simile was apt, perhaps even more appropriate than my friend may have dreamt.

'He loved me, yes,' Maria now continued, 'but it was all a long time ago. Jock has changed in seventeen years, and so have I. He goes to Spain to get away from me.'

'He goes for his paintings,' I corrected her, 'and everybody says how fine they are in colour and execution.'

'He goes there to get away from me,' Maria insisted. 'He has been seduced, – oh not by a woman,' she continued when she saw my expression, 'it's not that, but by all women. By something which he can observe with an artist's passion; from which he can extract inspiration and then abandon with no regrets and no sense of responsibility. He behaves like the bee which extracts nectar from the choicest bloom with no thought for the flower at all. He has perfected the art of putting his hand into the flame and yet feeling no burn.'

I knew not how to comfort her, for such an experience was well outside the scope of my own sheltered childhood and even more sequestered married life.

'Jock,' she pursued at last, 'wants me to convert to the Roman Catholic faith.'

Her statement stunned me into silence.

'It is the Spanish influence, of course,' remarked Maria, quite calmly. 'He has absorbed it through the very air he breathes.'

What monster is this, I thought, that would lead the soul which has been entrusted to his care to the very brink of apostasy? I sat beside her until my limbs were as chill and dead as my heart, and then taking my friend by the hand, for words still failed me, I led her back towards the house.

We returned to find that the meal had at last been cleared away and those local guests who were in attendance were making ready to depart.

'Well,' said Mary Ann, rising to her feet as we were drawn into the mêlée. 'May I suggest that, as the senior member of the Dadd family and as the sole surviving full brother of the dear departed, Robert gives us a short eulogy of thanks and praise upon the life of our dear brother, Stephen Dadd?'

Maria was quicker off the mark than Robert, who as usual was hampered by a certain ponderousness of both character and physique.

'Why,' she demanded, 'do you refer to Robert as the sole survivor? Richard, and George, though unable to be present, are very much alive.'

154

'To all intents and purposes,' replied Robert, 'they must be thought of as dead to the world.'

'Rubbish!' commented Maria. 'You talk just like those ridiculous magazines which referred to Dicky as "The late Richard Dadd". But I saw him last month, I visited him and George, and I shall go again to tell him all about this . . . this travesty of a family gathering.'

Sarah and I, at either side of Maria, here tugged heartily at her skirt to encourage her to sit down. When she eventually did subside into her chair, it was as a result, not of our efforts, but of a crippling paroxysm of grief. Before the eulogy could proceed, Ellen was forced to lead her from the room and sit quietly next to her at the foot of the stairs while she sobbed out her affliction.

When Ellen returned to the company in the drawing room, – reassured that Maria had collected herself and wanted only an interval of peace and quiet, – Maria, instead of remaining in the cool, darkened atmosphere of the hall, hurried upstairs. She wanted to investigate a certain sinister, barred window which she had glimpsed as we returned from the garden.

Curiosity is only natural. If we did not possess that faculty, it is doubtful whether any of us would have advanced beyond the stage of infancy. Yet in infancy there is always that guiding hand, that sheltering spirit of loving parenthood which protects us from the shock of seeing too much until the intellect can make sense of what it sees.

Like the lamb that is born in Springtime and lifts its little face in complete trust towards the sun in heaven, each trembling new sensibility needs time to become strong before it can weather the autumn frosts. Reader, I have seen for myself the shock to those upon whom unwelcome knowledge is forced too soon. I have sat by the bedside of my own little ones who have been tormented by tales of witches and goblins related by older children, or who have glanced through a picture book which has been carelessly left lying around, and have afterwards found their dreams haunted by nightmare figures of spectres and ogres. But there is another danger which must be guarded against. Woe to the guardian who knowingly withholds information and lets his child go forth into the world unprepared for all that he may meet.

In this manner did Maria ascend those stairs. Though she was no child, – for as you well know she was a mother twice over by this date, – she sought to satisfy a childlike curiosity; childlike because uninformed and totally innocent. And in this Mary Ann and Robert must shoulder the blame, for they tried to keep her in a state of ignorance which was quite unsuited to her years.

Imagine, then, the shock which awaited a mind as delicately poised as a watch spring!

On reaching the upstairs landing, Maria saw before her an open door and in the room beyond, a bright fire burning in the grate. She hesitated, thinking that perhaps she had stumbled upon a sick room, but since all was quiet within, she summoned up the courage to enter. As she stepped over the threshold, she caught sight of a bed and ascertained with the merest glance that it was empty. Gathering her courage, she moved towards the comfortable fireside chair and was on the point of sinking into it when some instinct told her that the room was not after all deserted. Considerably upset by this realisation, she stammered her apologies.

'Go ahead, sit down if you want to.' The voice came from a large, powerfully built woman who sat in the window recess, almost completely obscured by the heavy folds of drapery. This person now indicated with a nod the one chair before the fire, which was covered with some heavy red material and had been plucked quite clean at the arm rests until the grey horsehair stuffing tumbled out in cloudy handfuls, like a fungus.

'He never could sit still,' observed the figure from the darkness.

'Who?' asked Maria, turning the chair slightly so that she could see the stranger.

'Your brother.'

'Stephen?' gasped Maria.

The woman nodded. Maria noticed that she had a garment made of some coarse material draped over her knee, at which she was stitching.

'How did you know Stephen was my brother?'

The woman laughed by way of reply, and pointed to the mirror over the mantelpiece. 'Take a look in there, dear,' she advised.

Maria got to her feet and stared at her reflection in the glass.

'I could tell you anywhere.' The woman paused in her sewing. 'Like as twins.'

'Oh, but Stephen never laughed,' objected Maria, smiling at herself with some satisfaction at this difference between them.

The smile froze on her face as she turned to confront her interlocutor and now noticed for the first time that the window embrasure in which she sat was heavily barred.

'Was this then,' she asked slowly, though she already knew the answer in her heart, 'my brother's room?'

'It was fitted out, special like.' The woman indicated the padding on the walls and the heavy bolt on the inside of the door.

'And you are . . .?' she inquired.

'His keeper,' replied the other with some pride. 'Widow Jones they call me.'

'Why are you still here?'

'Nowhere else to go,' sniffed the woman. 'Anyway, two weeks' notice is owing to me, so I'll bide my time until it's up. Might as well, mightn't I?' she asked aggressively.

'Yes, oh yes,' Maria agreed.

'I knew your other brother too,' the woman went on. 'George his name was.'

'Oh.' Maria's voice was quite faint. 'You were at Bedlam then?'

'This job's dead easy by comparison – only one, when you've been used to dealing with thirty.'

'Did you know my other brother, Richard?' Maria asked.

'No,' the woman sniffed again. 'I wouldn't have anything to do with them. Not the criminal element. That's not my speciality.'

'Was Stephen . . . very sick?'

'Oh dear me, yes. Mad as a hatter, – baying at the moon, all that sort of thing.'

Maria experienced a sense of growing relief as the woman went on to give examples of Stephen's distracted behaviour. There had been times recently when she had feared for her own sanity, but by comparison with Stephen, her own worries were but trivial and confined to inward, nagging doubts. 'My husband wants me to become a Catholic,' she said as the woman finished speaking.

'Dear me, miss.' She shook her head in sympathy.

'But I won't,' said Maria, 'indeed I won't.'

She looked at the strange garment which hung over the woman's lap. It seemed immensely complicated, all angles and straps. 'What are you making?' she asked.

'Mending,' replied the other. 'Tools of the trade, you know. This here, is your brother's straitjacket. A lovely fit it was, I made it myself and the mistress said as I could keep it.' She held it up for Maria to admire. 'I used to tie him in the chair, you see, dear, so's he couldn't hurl himself into the fire and do himself an injury. That way we both got a bit of peace.' She threaded her large needle with another length of coarse thread. 'Now, if you wouldn't mind, dear, just close the door, would you. There's a nasty draught.'

'I'd rather the door stayed open,' Maria protested shrilly.

'I'm in charge here,' said the other sharply. 'Like the Captain on the bridge of his ship. What I say, goes, Miss Dadd—'

'Mrs Phillip,' protested Maria weakly.

The woman shrugged. 'If you won't do it for me, I shall just have to do it myself. If I sit in a draught and make myself sick there's no rich relatives to hire a nurse for me, oh dear no . . .' Still speaking, she moved towards the door.

'No!' insisted Maria.

Widow Jones stopped, then looked more closely at Maria. 'Are you all right, dearie, you look a bit pale? Why don't you have a nice sit down by the fire? I miss the company.' She advanced slowly towards Maria as she spoke.

'No!' Maria backed away from her, closer and closer to the fire. 'No!'

There was a quick roar from the fire behind her, then suddenly flames were licking up her skirt. Instantly the woman was upon her, more frightening than any fire, enveloping her in immensely strong arms, and smothering the flames with her own skirts and flesh.

Downstairs as the dark, dreary afternoon drew to a close, the dark, dreary clothing of the assembled company blended into an amorphous dullness. Now and then an amoeba-like tentacle stretched and withdrew as a group oozed towards the tea tray before retreating and being re-absorbed into the pulsating mass which huddled in the darkest corner of the room where a fire had been lit, but had failed to flourish.

Against a gentle murmur of conversation as harmonious and hushed as organ chords in a church service, the remaining mourners picked at the delicate sweets and pastries, and exchanged recipes and opinions – on the subject of slavery specifically and foreign policy in general. The situation in America was giving particular cause for concern.

Indeed, Robert Dadd had gone so far as to express the opinion that his youngest brother John would be risking his neck to venture setting foot on the continent just now, when Maria appeared in the doorway.

Fortunately, she had suffered no ill effect from the fire. Nor had anyone downstairs been aware of the little drama which had taken place above. For the room which once contained Stephen smothered all sounds as effectively as its keeper, Mrs Jones, had smothered the flames. Thanks to her prompt action, the fire had been doused before it could cause any bodily harm, though the smell of singeing hair and scorched material was still strong in Maria's nostrils, like a reminder of the flames of Hell.

Her appearance caused considerable consternation, for she positively shimmered in the doorway, resplendent in a dress of brilliant satin which was at once suggestive of sunshine and wine and laughter and glowing eyes peeping from shaded casements – in short, and at a distance, she was the perfect replica of a Spanish beauty, from the carved ivory comb in her hair to the finely tooled shoes on her feet.

'Maria!' I clapped my hands with amazement and called out to her. 'Does Jock really not find you fine enough to paint?'

'It is not the outward trappings,' said Maria haughtily, 'it is a question of inner fire. He says I lack both soul and spirit.'

She made a majestic progress into the room, followed by the children, who ran up to finger the fine material and exclaim at the delicacy of her mantilla which cast patterns like blackened spiders' webs over their little hands.

Mary Ann, however, was at once on her feet. She detached herself from the group by the fireside and advanced coolly but purposefully.

'Maria, such a garment at a time like this!'

Maria felt rather than saw Robert closing in on her other side in a pincer-like movement. She darted nimbly forwards to the safety of the company assembled round the tea urn and coolly poured herself a cup.

'Why,' she asked icily, 'if my brother's death is cause for celebration, are we then pretending grief by wearing black? Should we not rather dress as for a celebration in all the colours of the rainbow, gaudy as butterflies about the summer blooms as if to say, hooray, here's another mad Dadd out of the way?'

The effect of such a declaration upon the assembled company may well be imagined. Certainly, it defied description. While admitting that Maria expressed herself neither wisely nor well, there was a certain truth in what she was saying. There was something tainted in the atmosphere of that day; a hypocrisy in which speech and action constantly belied thought and feeling.

I have often felt that Maria would have made a fine actress. In such a milieu her excesses would have passed quite unremarked, while her capacity for emotion could have been given full rein. A theatre audience would have adored her. They would have endured her revelations and swallowed those unpalatable truths in the comfortable knowledge that they applied only to others and never to themselves. For home consumption, her truths cut too near the bone.

Chapter Seven

I T was never our intention to burden Stephen's widow with our company for long. So it was, that having discharged the obligations of politeness and ascertained that all was well with her materially, we departed. Only Sarah remained behind, whether out of affection for her sister-in-law or because of a reluctance to return to her habitual employment, I cannot be sure. However, stay she did, and with their half-brother John departing thence to pursue his travels further north, it was a depleted and much subdued party which returned to London.

Reader, it was not merely the assiduity with which Stephen's keeper, Widow Jones, pressed herself upon each of us in turn, that so depressed our spirits. Her vociferous assertions of her professional abilities accompanied by the physical evidence of much thumbed and crumpled references, her scarcely veiled hints that she could see that the family would soon be requiring her services again and that she would therefore hold herself in readiness for the summons, – these could not depress as much as the evidence of our own eyes. Even her morbid and unwelcome presence was not as real to us as the nightmare spectre of Insanity which we could see looming ever larger over the frail figure of our poor dear friend and sister, Maria.

Our concern for her state, though unvoiced, was evident in the tender web of affection which we spun around her, in the indulgence with which we treated and made excuses for her numerous eccentricities of behaviour. We humoured, we petted and spoiled like fond parents. Affection made us weak where it should have made us strong. In short, we repeated exactly the same mistakes as her fated parent, just as if experience had taught us nothing. In this I, as much as the others, was to blame. We stood by, consoling both ourselves and her with conventional inanities. When the demon of madness mocked at us from her eyes, we

161

smiled and commended her high spirits; when she writhed under torments we could not conceive, we tried to divert her with books and plays, songs and baubles; when she voiced her preposterous notions we praised her vivid imagination and nodded like Chinese mandarins until our mouths were stiff with smiles and our heads bobbed up and down as if they had worked loose on their springs.

But London, yes. We returned to London. We crawled into the metropolis in a November fog such as I had never experienced before. Robert and Catherine, being anxious to return to their children in Poplar, took one cab. Mary Ann of course went with them. I offered to see Maria and Ellen and the children safely home – which also left me more conveniently placed in central London to make my return to Devon.

How I longed for the clear cold moorland air during that ride! For the crispness of a frosty night and the clear stars above the cold stark outline of tor and valley. Though still only midday, all around us was murk and gloom, as if the world had been plunged into perpetual twilight. The fog insinuated its ghoulish fingers into our very vehicle. It invaded the lungs and cloaked the city, reducing the few people who had ventured abroad to insubstantial phantoms, like figures in a nightmare. It swirled both outside in the streets and inside the cab, and deeper still in the fearful recesses of my mind.

Several times we thought that we might have been safer to have dismissed our conveyance and proceeded on foot. In such a manner we might have groped our way safely from one familiar landmark to the next. But we feared the cut-throats and pick-pockets who take advantage of such weather even more than the threat of collision. So we huddled fearfully together on the leather seats which seemed to perspire with a singular, ghastly clamminess while our driver conveyed us we knew not whither – it could have been into the very bowels of the earth.

Arriving at last at a long, high wall, our cab crawled along at a snail's pace until we happened upon an entrance, where the driver was forced to alight and inquire from the porter where we might be. A figure at once stepped forth from the portal, a grotesque subterranean creature bearing before him a small lantern which cast its dismal gleam upon a physiognomy so twisted and misshapen that its humanity could only be a matter for conjecture.

'Where are we, my good fellow?' shouted down our driver.

'Why, Bedlam, sir,' came the ringing answer. The voice of this Cerberus was indeed a strange contrast to the instrument which produced it.

'Bedlam!' said Maria, laughing hysterically.

Though I received the news with outward composure, my heart beat faster at the intelligence. I had never before ventured so close, and would never have done so knowingly. The walls were immense. They disappeared into the fog as if they went on for ever, to right and to left as massive as the walls of Jericho and as high as the very heavens themselves.

'Bedlam!' said Maria again. 'Shall we call in and take tea with Richard?' Before we could prevent her she was already hammering on the window and calling out to the cabbie to open the door.

Ellen and I did our best to calm her. We reminded her that such a place was unsuitable for the children, that visiting was only permitted at specified times, that the hour was growing late and we were still far from home, and at last reason prevailed. The cabbie remounted his box and we crawled on.

'I should have thought that you at least would have been glad to see him, Elizabeth,' Maria reproached me.

I was utterly confused and knew not how to answer her remark.

'I would never have thought,' she persisted in tormenting me, 'that you of all people would have turned your back on him.'

'The past is now dead and buried, Maria,' said I firmly, and was gratified to hear Ellen's grunt of approval.

'You're as bad as the rest,' Maria accused me, and how those words stung.

'I loved Richard as he was,' I said somewhat heatedly, and with a rashness which I afterwards regretted; 'for the Richard that now is, I can feel nothing stronger than pity.'

Still Maria would not let the matter rest.

'How do you know,' she asked slyly, 'how or what he now is, when you haven't seen him for twenty years?'

Reader, that question haunted me for another twenty years, for such was the period which elapsed before I allowed myself to see

163

him. At that moment, I only knew that I was not ready for such an encounter, in spite of the voice within me which urged me to gratify my curiosity. To have come so close! To be separated from him by a mere wall! I prided myself that Reason had come to my aid and conquered all temptation, until the carriage once more drew to a halt and Maria spoke again.

'There's no escape, Elizabeth,' she observed quietly as she lowered the window and leaned out to see where we were.

Looking over her shoulder, I realised that we had completed a full circle in the fog, and there was the same ominous gateway, the same lamps flickering dimly, and the same grotesque dwarf of a porter announcing that we had returned to Bedlam.

'No escape, indeed!' I retorted somewhat impatiently, though whether Maria's observation was made on her own account or on mine, I have never known. Certainly it could be said to have been, after a fashion, prophetic; for I was to visit Richard, – though neither then nor there. And as for Maria . . . but that comes later.

For now, finding ourselves once more in front of the main gates, perhaps this would be an apt place to give you some details of the history of the Institution, while I consider how best to proceed with my narrative. But Reader, be sure of one thing. I did not weaken. I stood by my judgement, and I am glad of it.

The Royal Bethlem Hospital was founded in 1246 as a leper-house for those sick in body, and some two hundred years later used to confine those outcasts whose hidden sores and deformities were equally unacceptable. Royal it was named, because Henry VIII donated as a free gift the lands on which the hospital was built, having discovered that he could no more find a purchaser for the site than he could find a satisfactory wife. After the Great Fire, the hospital was rebuilt. It teetered perilously on the shifting slopes of the City Ditch, which received the one hundred and fifty lunatics with the same enthusiasm as it had for centuries received the refuse of its citizens.

Then at the turn of our own century, came an age of enlightenment. A king was mad. Madness itself became all the rage; madness was respectable. From the pestilential airs of Moorgate, those sick in mind were offered new and elegant accommodation in St George's-in-the-Fields: eight hundred and ninety-seven feet long, and containing within its precincts eleven acres of gracious gardens and more of human misery than it is possible to imagine.

Gone are the days when, over the fifty-two Sundays of one year, 96,000 pleasure-seeking Londoners each paid one penny to view spectacles more thrilling than those of a zoological garden. To be a spectator at such scenes was to tremble on the very brink of civilisation and to feel the black abyss open beneath one's feet.

Those erstwhile visitors must now look elsewhere to experience such sensations of delicious terror. A new regime is in being. Gone are the iron bars, the manacles and chains, the straw beds as foul as cattle byres. This new understanding is echoed in the noble proportions of the building and the mighty central dome designed to recall the tortured mind to loftier thoughts. People come now not to gape and stare, but to visit family or friends, to sit awhile and exchange news and views as one would during any hospital visit. And if a certain *frisson* is felt as door after door clangs shut and is locked behind one, and if haunted, fevered eyes still follow one's every movement, people are now sufficiently broad-minded to evince no further terror than to huddle close together laughing and chattering, like schools of monkeys, to show how very broad-minded they are.

Reader, it must by now be obvious to you that I do not speak from hearsay alone, but also from the evidence of my own eyes. and for this, I must blame that same fog which delayed my departure from London. My kind friends would on no account hear of my undertaking the arduous journey into Devon while such conditions prevailed, and yielding at last to their entreaties, I found myself marooned at Maria's house for a period which saw, among other events, a visiting party to the hospital, which I was prevailed upon to join.

Let me state again that I did not visit Richard. Nor would I have done so for a queen's ransom. I would not insult him by going to 'view' him in those circumstances, for I had already been privy to the comments of his so-called friends. They had often greeted me in print, spitting out their salacious details to feed the clamorous appetite of a public which thrives on such fodder. I have seen worse. I have witnessed those who profess the deepest devotion and admiration for Richard, pore over his works as if they were the productions of some beast possessed of this one miraculous gift.

But I know that Richard and his painting were as inseparable as the caged linnet from her song. That little dull brown bird sings from the very depths of its soul. It sings because that is its nature, to give voice to those heavenly sounds which reverberate within its breast. But Reader, the caged bird no longer sings in response to the rising of the sun or the blueness of the sky or the feel of the wind from the ripe cornfield which ruffles its feathers; it sings because it must, because such is the ordinance of its Creator.

I would not visit Richard because I had no wish to number myself among the company of his detractors. And I entered that same Institution which contained him only after much persuasion, and then to accompany Ellen and Mary Ann on the blameless errand to minister to poor George, for they vowed that my presence would bring him some satisfaction. Out of concern for his feelings and for the sake of happy days gone by, I yielded to their entreaties. Consider the shameful display which I then witnessed and judge whether or not I acted rightly with regard to Richard.

I walked apprehensively beneath the copper dome among marble pillars as noble as those in an Egyptian temple. At the head of the throng of visitors was a conspicuous group which had halted at the foot of the splendid Italian staircase, before an unfinished painting clearly depicting the parable of 'The Good Samaritan'.

'That's Dicky's,' vowed one of the gentlemen loudly. His voice echoed strangely above the general hush as if someone had suddenly spoken out loud in the middle of a church service. 'I'd know his hand anywhere.'

The four middle-aged gentlemen, all of them apparently artists themselves, paused to observe and pass judgement, until a whisper circulated around the vast hall and people stopped in their tracks. 'That's Mr Frith!' was the delighted exclamation which passed from lip to lip. For Mr Frith had recently been favoured with commissions to paint not only the beloved queen and her consort, but various princes and princesses, – not to mention their dogs, cats, horses, and canaries.

I looked at Billy with some surprise, for I had once known him well and would now scarcely have recognised him. Gone was the slim and handsome youth, and in his place was a thick-set gentleman of middle years who would not have looked out of place at the horse races. Billy's friends I could also now make out as they stepped on to the staircase alongside their more distinguished friend. O'Neil and Egg also came in for hushed admiration, as gentlemen whose refinement of feeling made them candidates as unlikely for Bedlam as their friend Richard Dadd had been before them.

Indeed it was quite a lesson in painting that Billy Frith administered to us all, for none could now escape his instruction whether they would or no, the way forward being entirely blocked by him and his friends. I observed Mary Ann to shrink inside her hood for fear of being recognised, while Billy held forth on Richard's tone and colour, composition and brush-stroke, in a manner quite dazzling to the layman. Though he never mentioned his unfortunate friend by name, it was quite obvious that all present knew perfectly well to whom he referred, and that moreover they thrilled at the thought of finding themselves under the same roof, – albeit at a remove of several miles of corridor and many locked doors, – from a madman and a murderer. And although the topic of insanity was discreetly passed over and Richard's abilities received the highest acclaim, the murmurings of discontent gradually became louder. For it had to be admitted that if there was one thing that 'The Good Samaritan' most disappointingly lacked, it was any sign of madness. Among the many heavy oil paintings which grace our National Gallery, one could have passed by it any day without batting an eyelid.

I could not help observing among the crowd, and at no great distance from myself, Richard's one-time landlady, Mrs Jenkins, and her sister, Doris; nor fail to witness their loud-voiced chagrin at finding such a density of people between their own fair selves and the eminent gentlemen, which thus prevented them from openly claiming acquaintances of such distinction. How the estimable Mrs J. rued the lateness of her arrival! I do not intend any sarcasm in referring to her thus. She had proved herself to be a good and loyal friend to Richard. Were she a cur, one would have said of her that her bark was worse than her bite. Reader, she would rant and rave at those young artists as if they were the very devils of Hell come to torment her, and the next minute she would be dispensing tea and biscuits with a liberality far in excess of her slender means. But to return to the present; —

'I intended to be here a good half hour earlier at least, Doris,' she now stated, 'and not to arrive in such an ungodly crush.'

Doris looked round anxiously and clicked her tongue sympathetically. 'You're sure that these people really are all visitors?' she inquired of her sister. 'It's so difficult to tell sometimes.'

'If only,' Mrs Jenkins continued heedlessly, 'that wretched chicken had cooked itself sooner. I've never known a bird require so much boiling.'

'You should have got a younger one, Ethel,' was Doris's opinion.

'That would have cost another threepence halfpenny,' Mrs Jenkins observed sourly as she saw Billy Frith bow to the crowd and head off up the staircase. 'I do declare he's put on weight,' she muttered with some satisfaction.

'It's all this hobnobbing with monarchs and such-like. I expect the food's too rich,' Doris sniffed.

'He's heading for a nasty dose of gout, if you ask me.' The thought must have brought a certain consolation to Mrs Jenkins who at the age of sixty-five had become as gaunt as a spectre. 'He doesn't come here often, you know. He's not a regular, like me. He only comes,' she said as we all progressed up the stairs in a great tidal wave of humanity, 'when it suits him. I,' she added modestly, 'haven't missed a month for the past seventeen years, you know, Doris. I know this place like the back of me hand.' Mrs Jenkins halted suddenly as she came to a parting of the ways, a junction of corridors heading north and south, east and west, each one identical and stinking of the carbolic which was not quite strong enough to mask the underlying taint of human effluent.

'Like the back of your hand, eh?' asked Doris, a faint smile on her face as she witnessed the hesitation.

'Blow me down,' said the good Mrs Jenkins, — and despite the doubting Thomas at her side I do know that she was most regular in her attentions to her erstwhile lodger, — 'what with all this gossiping and lectures and I don't know what else, I haven't been concentrating. Do you know, I haven't a clue where we are.' And the two women stood there, like a pair of islands, about which the stream of visitors broke then re-formed in a swirl which presently hid them from our sight.

We could see George at the far end of the hundred foot gallery as soon as we entered the room. As we advanced, he inched his chair closer and closer to the large silver radiator. He was reading his precious volume of *The Old Curiosity Shop*. Even after all those years I would have recognised it anywhere, although it was now much battered and worn. He held the book on his knee with his left hand, while he rested his right upon the metal pipes. From time to time he raised his hand, studied the palm, which we could observe even from a considerable distance to have turned an unhealthy rose red. At this spectacle, he smiled with pleasure before returning his attention to the written word.

It was apparently only on occasions when work was expressly forbidden that George submitted to taking his ease. For under the new regime work was on hand for those who evinced the desire to apply themselves, and with George it had become an obsession. He toiled every available hour and in all weathers.

After seventeen years of striving to gratify the insatiable appetite of the enormous furnaces which worked the central heating system, he now presented an appearance which would no doubt have gratified Mr Darwin immensely. More anthropoid than human, with shoulders bowed, back bent and arms elongated from Herculean labour, he sat hunched over his book. In spite of the slicked hair which bore witness to a recent attempt to wash and tidy him up, his face remained as swarthy and as pitted with coal dust as that of any miner.

Poor George! His mind ran only on those narrow tracks from cellar to furnace and back again. The only peace he knew was that at the end of each weary travail, when a burst of flame and warmth exploded within the heart of the fires and enveloped him like a caress. Being physically at rest did not apparently contribute to a state of mental relaxation, for as I observed, he was ever restless, now touching those silver pipes again and

169

observing with grim satisfaction the blisters that appeared on his palm, now turning over the pages with a speed at which no human being could possibly read. Nor were the words necessary to him, for he muttered them openly by heart, seeming to latch at random on to a phrase here or the beginning of a chapter there.

Ellen bustled forward, muttering the while that he would burn himself up before she reached him. But her progress was hampered by her bulk and the heavy basket which she would entrust to nobody else.

George, having tired of the panorama of blisters which erupted on his palm, had now noticed that the room was unaccountably full of people in warm cloaks and hoods, gloves and mufflers and stout footwear. With a cry he leapt from his chair. Though the room still felt pleasantly warm to him, such garments betokened one thing only to his poor mind; that his furnace had gone out. With a cry that was pitiful to hear, he crouched by the radiator, and doubting this time the evidence of his hands, pressed his ear against its burning sides.

The blast of heat scorched the side of his face and he leapt back even as we dragged him away. But an expression of deep content had settled over his features. He had heard the deep-throated rumblings and gurglings of the central heating system which told him that his creature was still alive.

'Georgy?' said Ellen, smiling up into his face.

George looked blankly down at her.

'Georgy, aren't you going to say hello to Ellen?' Ellen placed her basket on the floor and untied her bonnet and cloak. 'Nice and warm you've got it today,' she said as she draped her cloak over the back of the chair. 'Really lovely!' She rubbed her hands briskly together in the heat above the radiator and her cheeks became as red as plums at the sudden change of temperature. 'It's bitter out,' she remarked.

'Bitter?' inquired George, with his head on one side, like a bird. 'Bitter?'

'Quite bitter,' Ellen repeated. 'It's been snowing. Snow, Georgy, snow!'

'Snow,' echoed George, remembering as if from a half-forgotten dream. Approaching his furnaces along the low dark corridors was like entering the very bowels of the earth and penetrating to the

170

fiery molten lava at its core. The heat was such that he worked in his shirt sleeves and its intensity remained with him throughout the journey across the white yards to the freezing coal sheds. 'I saw snow.' He laughed with delight.

'That's right, Georgy,' said Ellen. 'Clever boy, – snow.'

'The north wind doth blow,' cackled George.

'And we shall have snow,' continued Ellen, delighted with the conversation.

'What does the robin do then, poor thing?' George clasped his arms about him and shivered violently on behalf of the poor little ball of brown and scarlet feathers lying frozen in the snow.

'Have you forgotten, Georgy?' asked Ellen gently. *'He sits in the barn and keeps himself warm.'*

'Yes, yes,' said George eagerly.

Throughout this interchange, Mary Ann and I remained silent, Mary Ann out of the habit which allowed Ellen to attempt first to make contact with George, and I, because I was too overcome to do otherwise. Reader, I had last seen George Dadd as a robust teenager with big bright eyes and cheerfully curling hair, full of life and laughter, a skilled craftsman who took delight in his hands. What stood before me now brought tears to my eyes and a lump to my throat.

'George!' said Mary Ann, taking advantage of this lull in the conversation to greet her brother. She spoke not unkindly, but with her usual brusqueness.

George was plainly terrified. She stood before him, a tall, angular, black-clad figure with a face that seemed permanently set in a look of sorrow and resignation and a complexion apparently untouched by warmth or cold.

'Well, George,' she continued severely, 'how do you do, eh?' She did not extend her hand but kept it tightly tucked inside her sleeves.

George shrank behind Ellen and looked at his sister with terror. I doubt myself whether George derived any benefit whatsoever from the presence of anyone but Ellen. Certainly, he gave no indication of being aware of anybody else, though Mary Ann pressed him repeatedly to 'say good day to Elizabeth!'

'And hide his head under his wing, poor thing,' George responded, turning to Ellen.

171

'Who's my clever boy then?' Ellen took George in her arms and gave him a big kiss.

By way of reply, George closed his arms in a bear hug about his former nanny. During this rapturous embrace I feared very much that Ellen would be crushed alive, and indeed she turned a very unhealthy colour; whereupon Mary Ann was obliged to rap her brother smartly on the head with the Dickens and instruct him sharply to let go. 'Really, George,' she continued, 'nursery rhymes at your age!'

George hung his head in shame and I feared that at any moment great tears would well from beneath his eyelids and begin their mournful journey down those doughy cheeks.

By way of diversion, Ellen began at once to unpack her basket. During this process, George's eyes lit up with excitement. By the time she had removed the last snowy white tea towel they were positively smouldering.

'George!' said Mary Ann sharply, as a dribble escaped the side of his mouth. She sat very upright on her chair while denying herself the support of the back. It was one of those little mortifications of the flesh which it pleased her to impose upon herself.

George pinned his large hands firmly between his knees and sat there trembling all over like a dog. When Ellen removed a plateful of currant cakes, he could contain himself no longer, but was upon them like a vulture. They went into his mouth two or three at a time, in such quantities that, as he chewed, as much fell out as was retained by his overburdened lips.

Mary Ann's eyes glazed.

'Is that nice, my precious?' Ellen cooed. 'Do you still like your Ellen's cooking then?' She took out a small cloth and dabbed at the corners of George's mouth.

'Tiger, we calls him,' remarked an attendant, who had come over to make himself pleasant to the assembled party.

Mary Ann's look would have turned to stone anyone less used to dealing with the insane.

Blissfully immune to her Medusa's stare, the attendant continued, 'Because of the way he falls upon his food, – like a tiger on its prey!' and he chortled with admiration as the last little cake disappeared down George's gullet.

George leaned back and smiled blissfully.

172

Ellen next uncorked a bottle of ginger pop. The top flew off with a large bang which caused consternation throughout the ward until its harmless nature became apparent.

'Oh my Gawd,' said the attendant, his hand still clutched to his heart. 'If one of these got hold of a gun I fear we'd all be done for!'

'Now George, wait a minute,' said Ellen severely, for George had thrown himself on to the floor and lay underneath the bottle with upturned face and gaping mouth, trying to catch the cascade of fizzing ginger. 'It's the coach journey,' his nanny explained, 'it's become all shook up.' And she wiped George's sticky face tenderly.

'Why you have to spoil him so, I don't know,' said Mary Ann. 'The food here is excellent, and conversation would do so much more for him than all this pandering to the senses. I've brought several tracts here which we could discuss if only he would stop guzzling for a moment.'

But George was now on all fours, sucking at the bottle which Ellen held, as strongly and noisily as an orphan bull calf.

'It's the only pleasure he knows, Miss Dadd,' said Ellen stiffly. 'And conversation is quite beyond him. His mind's nearly gone.' She replaced the empty bottle in the basket and covered it up.

George let out an enormous, satisfied burp and sat looking at her with a smile as wide and innocent as that of a child.

'Now Georgy,' said Ellen, 'if you can guess what else I have in my basket, I will give it to you.'

'Give, give,' sang George happily.

'First guess,' said Ellen.

'Guess, guess,' sang George.

'Really, Ellen, you're wasting your time,' snapped Mary Ann.

'Georgy.' Ellen peeped under the cloth, and lifted up a corner. 'I spy a sugar plum.' And she took it out and popped it in his mouth.

George's eyes bulged as he gulped down the candied fruit without so much as a pause to chew it. Then he leaned forward greedily. 'More!' he ordered, clapping his hands together. 'More!'

While Ellen continued to feed him like a mother bird, George sat there with his head tilted back and his mouth wide open like some monstrous fledgling.

173

Mary Ann here abandoned any pretext of intercourse with her brother and moved instead to a table at the centre of the room, where some half dozen men passed their time industriously picking at the wood with tiny bits of mortar which the attendant informed us they had dislodged from the ward walls.

'Gentlemen,' said Mary Ann strongly, seating herself at the head of the table. 'Hear the word of the Lord.' She was ever of the opinion that God alone could drive out the demon of insanity.

'Hallelujah!' yelled one of the men by way of response. 'Glory to God.'

'Amen,' observed the sallow-faced spinster fervently. 'Shall we pray together?'.

'Hallelujah!' bellowed the man again and again. 'Hal–ley–loo–yah.'

I leant over and popped a sugared almond into George's wide open mouth. His breath made me quite faint, as if I hovered over the sulphurous discharge of a volcano.

The almond, having slithered straight down George's throat unchewed, now lodged there and caused a violent choking spasm. He gagged and heaved, and tears streamed from his eyes.

'Lay your burden upon the Lord,' intoned Mary Ann, raising her voice loud over the ensuing uproar; for Ellen was at once out of her chair and patting George heartily on the back, just out of the reach of his wildly flailing arms.

'Hallelujah,' roared the lunatic at Mary Ann's table, rising up to stand on his chair as if that would bring him closer to heaven. 'Glory be to God.'

Still George continued in the wildest of fits. His cheeks burned redder than any of his furnaces. His eyes poured forth whole oceans of salt water. To no avail, – the almond stuck fast. He began to turn a ghastly shade of purple; his hands clutched despairingly at the air, and his lungs pumped like the bellows of a demon blacksmith.

The attendants looked down on him in some wonder, and discussed whether or not the doctor should be sent for, while Mary Ann implored them for the love of God to act quickly and save her brother.

What they would have done next is not clear, for Nature now undertook the remedy in her own way. George's stomach

174

contracted violently and the offending article was ejected like a ball from a cannon, followed by an irruption of biscuits, plum cake, sweetmeats, and candied fruit which issued forth, half chewed and still less digested, in a scarcely to be credited profusion.

George now presented a truly nauseating spectacle, – on observing which, two attendants closed in on the poor unfortunate. Seeing them coming, George backed off in terror, putting a chair between himself and them and gibbering with fear.

Ellen firmly intervened. 'That's quite enough,' she said sternly, as if this was her own nursery in days of yore. 'I myself will clean up Master George.' And ignoring the overpowering stench, she coaxed George into the washroom and firmly bolted the door in the faces of the astonished attendants.

I could hear her as I passed by, tunelessly and monotonously crooning 'Oranges and Lemons' over and over again, while George gurgled with pleasure. For by this stage it was apparent to me that my presence was entirely superfluous, and besides I had not the stomach to extend my stay. I therefore announced to Mary Ann that I would await them in the foyer, and took my leave of that dismal place.

As I descended the vast, uncarpeted stairway, a figure hurried by me at such speed, and with a face so contorted by anger, that it took me some seconds to realise that this was Mr Frith. By the time it occurred to me that I might call out and renew our acquaintance, he had clattered across the marble foyer and departed into the November twilight. I was not too much put out by this incident, for in truth I was still much disturbed by what had gone before.

I had been a while reflecting in front of Richard's painting of 'The Good Samaritan', which I finally conceded was both conventional and dull, when another series of footsteps burst upon my ear. They came from the rest of Richard's companions, and by now, utterly composed, I stood with my back to the banisters, in anticipation of their greeting.

175

Reader, they passed me by without a second look! And I laughed to see myself standing there, so dejected. Admit the truth, I reproved myself; for if Billy Frith was middle-aged, why so was I. If his paunch bore witness to years of good living, my own stature was a tribute to maternity and an equally comfortable life. If his greying hairs were but the inevitable dusting of Time, then so were mine. I was still meditating on my own presumption, when a more discerning figure descended the staircase, – Mrs Jenkins in person.

Never has friendly face appeared more welcome! To me, at that moment, she seemed like an oasis, a small, still pool from whose depths Sanity stared calmly back at me in spite of the veritable *khamseen* of madness which raged within the confines of that place. It was not then within my power to speak to her myself, but she paused on the stair alongside me. She turned, looking behind her for her sister Doris whom she had unaccountably mislaid, and then catching sight of my person, she addressed me directly.

'Miss Carter?'

'Now Mrs L.,' I replied, and seized her hand eagerly.

'You have come to see him?' she inquired, searching my face.

I disengaged my hand. 'How is he?'

'In my opinion,' she stated forthrightly as we descended that vast staircase side by side, 'there's a good few people as should have been put inside before they laid hands on him!' She nodded significantly in the direction of Richard's remaining friends who, catching her knife-edged glance, now fled through that front door as if it would at any moment lodge in their breasts. 'Friends!' she said scornfully.

'I saw Mr Frith,' said I.

'He's the worst,' she stated flatly. 'They none of them help him,' and she proceeded to tell me what had happened within the ward.

Completed only fifteen years earlier, the men's criminal wing was the glory of the Institution. In the central gallery, elegantly white-washed and patriotically highlighted in red and blue, the twittering of birds from the aviary was as loud as the babbling of a summer brook and squirrels chased one another through the boughs of artificial trees.

Into this Elysium burst the visitors, to find Richard engaged on a picture which was nearing completion. Mrs Jenkins told me that Richard had been working on it for six years, and that two attendants hovered at the express orders of the Medical Superintendent, lest any harm should come to this masterpiece. And danger lurked everywhere; – not from Richard, who even in his wildest excesses had never been known to damage one of his brain children, but from the other inmates who, though at times emulating the dainty yet charged steps of pet greyhounds and expending a restless energy pacing up and down the hundred foot gallery, were also capable of aping the less desirable characteristics of the canine species: a snarling, snapping violence which reduced the original models to a state of quivering terror.

Mrs Jenkins and her sister had hung back at the far end of the ward, anxious not to disturb the visiting gentry. They diverted themselves by feeding the caged birds and animals with those stale crumbs which they reserved for such occasions, together with a few of Pieces' precious nuts and seeds for the squirrels. Thus lurking amid these artificial groves, they were afforded ample opportunity for observing what subsequently befell.

'What! Painting?' Billy Frith had approached with a certain arrogant bonhomie and clapped a hand familiarly on Richard's shoulder.

Mrs Jenkins' scorn at this comment may well be imagined. It was shared by Richard, who looked at the easel, the unfinished picture, his brushes, mahl stick and palette, and spared himself the trouble of a reply.

'Nice bit of work, Dicky!' Billy persevered. 'A new one?'

'If you haven't seen it before, it means that it is six years since you last came to see me,' said Richard, continuing quietly with his work.

'Yes, well . . .' Billy here stammered a few words by way of excuse, – how busy he was, how heavy his family commitments, – 'but I'm here now!' he said, rounding off his explanations cheerfully.

'So I see.' Richard carefully wiped his brush.

'Egg and O'Neil are here too,' continued the eminent artist since Richard hadn't seemed to notice them. 'In fact, it's just like the good old days, isn't it?'

'Is it?' asked Richard drily.

His friends looked from one to another uneasily.

'Six years, eh?' commented Egg at last. 'That's a long time to spend on one painting. I couldn't do it; they'd have to shut me up first.' He realised what he had said and fell into an embarrassed silence. 'I mean,' he continued at last, somewhat red in the face, 'so that I wasn't continually distracted.'

'You could still study your precious moonlight streaming through the bars,' retorted Richard, referring to one of Egg's pictures, which had been unmercifully criticised by Mr Ruskin. (For this information I am indebted to Mrs Jenkins and her encyclopedic knowledge of Art.)

'You keep abreast of things in the art world then, Richard?' the conversation went on.

'We do have a library,' he replied, 'and I note everything that Ruskin has to say about you. My word, Frithy, I bet you didn't spend six years on "At the Opera".'

Billy here went into a sulky silence.

'It is not the kind of painting which will ever bring great fame or deserve it,' quoted Richard, determined not to let him off the hook, while Mrs Jenkins and Doris dived behind a goldfish tank to hide their mirth.

'I've done better since,' said Billy.

'His "Derby Day",' commented O'Neil, 'was a runaway success, – wasn't it, Billy?'

Billy modestly demurred.

'They had to put bars all around it because of the crush at the Academy.' Egg was quite overcome at the thought of this incontrovertible evidence of success. 'You're in it too, Dicky, did you know? In a red fez, – quite unmistakable.'

'The popular manner of painting,' recited Richard, drawing his brush tip delicately over a butterfly's wing, *'is necessarily, because popular, stooping and restricted.'*

'You seem quite determined to be disagreeable today, Richard,' snapped Billy. 'I don't know why we bothered to come.'

'I certainly never invited you,' answered Richard.

Billy had by this time endured more than his wounded vanity could bear. He turned on his heel and stalked off down the ward, totally ignoring those others who clamoured for a word from him.

'I saw him!' I here interrupted Mrs Jenkins. 'He strode right past me quite puffed up with passion, as if I didn't exist.'

Mrs J. said that his departure did not seem to trouble Richard one jot. He had calmly proceeded with his painting, merely remarking after some time, 'Is he gone?'

'Dicky,' Egg rebuked him, 'that was hardly fair. Was it out of pique?'

'What else, dear boy? It is hardly easy to sit here and be overtaken in reputation by such a philistine.'

'He is your friend.'

'Friends!' Richard shifted his chair even closer to the easel.

'He defended you when all the world was against you,' persisted O'Neil.

'He buried me alive,' said Richard bitterly. 'He consigned me to the grave. "The late Richard Dadd", indeed! He killed me as an artist in the eyes of the public as truly as if he had plunged a dagger into my heart.'

'We none of us thought you would ever paint again.'

'Well, you were wrong, weren't you? I'm painting better than ever. I have outstripped the lot of you.'

'Come on now, sir.' Sam Smith, Richard's keeper, here appeared quietly at his elbow. 'Let's have a care for your masterpiece, eh? We wouldn't want anything to happen to that, would we now?'

Richard allowed Sam to take away the canvas and lock it in his room. Then he began cleaning his brush, plucking at the bristles so savagely that it was completely bald by the time Sam returned. Egg and O'Neil looked on in silence, not knowing what to say or do next.

'Best be cutting along, sirs, if you don't mind my suggesting it,' Sam advised them. 'It's nasty weather, you'd best be safe at home before dark.' He ushered them gently towards the door. 'He's just a bit upset,' he apologised for Richard, 'he'll be sorry tomorrow for the way he's treated you.'

Egg and O'Neil stalked off down the gallery. Though they looked back when they reached the door, Richard did not spare them so much as a glance.

179

'Is he much changed, Mrs Jenkins?' I could no longer forbear from asking.

'We're none of us getting any younger, are we, Mrs L.?' was her reply. 'He is somewhat stouter and his hair shows signs of greying. He is . . .' she searched about for the right word, 'untidy. What was once carelessness in his attention to dress, is now become slovenly. In my opinion,' she here looked at me closely, 'he requires a woman's touch.'

I here affected a professional rather than a personal interest.

'All those men looking after other men,' she went on, whether mindful or not of my feelings, I could not tell. 'I don't question that it might not be sensible in this place, but it shows. There is not the same attention to detail. His linen is not as well cared for as when I looked after it. His hair is not as neatly trimmed. And I would certainly have turned his jacket cuffs before they started to fray.'

My heart ached at these little signs of neglect.

'But he is well fed,' Mrs Jenkins continued thoughtfully. 'He is warm. He is as comfortable as they can make him.'

We stood for a moment in silence, united by a womanly concern for the object of our affection.

'Anyway,' she continued her narrative, 'when the coast was clear . . .' Mrs Jenkins had allowed a margin of time to elapse, for she could see that the previous visitors had upset Richard deeply; and then she stepped forward.

'Coo-ey, Mr Dadd,' she sang as she crept up behind him and placed her hands over his eyes. 'Guess who?'

'I couldn't, Mrs J., I really couldn't,' protested the artist. 'Not in a month of Sundays!'

'It's me!' said the good lady, now placing both hands on his shoulders and peeping round into his face.

'Have you got,' inquired he, 'the necessary?'

She placed her fingers on her lips and pointed dramatically to her bag which, it had not previously escaped my notice, sagged somewhat heavily. At the same time, she exchanged a wink with Richard's attendant, Sam Smith, who ostentatiously looked the other way.

'You're a treasure, Mrs J.,' observed my friend and the good lady almost purred as she repeated these words of praise.

180

Sam Smith here drew forward a chair, on to which Mrs Jenkins lowered her bony self with an exclamation of dismay as she came in contact with the hard wood.

'More padding, that's what you need, dear lady,' cried Richard gaily, and he patted his own ample behind by way of example. 'We don't have padded chairs here,' he explained; 'some would rip 'em to pieces and others have no more control over their bladders than a babe in arms.'

'Mr Dadd!' the good lady protested, stifling her giggles behind a frilly handkerchief. Then she remembered her sister Doris and, her threadbare arms spinning like windmills, she beckoned her over to join the party.

And quite a party it was, apparently. Doris approached, tripping lightly, with a delicate blush to her cheek. She was arrayed in her prettiest dress, which elicited gasps of admiration from Richard's fellow patients, as did her bonnet with a brim as wide as a garden path and as abundantly trimmed with flowers, beneath which protruded the luxuriant curls of a blonde wig.

'Madame!' Sam gallantly bowed her to a chair.

'Well, dear boy, and what have you been up to since I saw you last?' Mrs Jenkins asked Richard as she drew off her gloves. 'Don't tell me you have been sitting here idly? And Pieces will ask, you know, – he will want to hear all about you.'

'How is dear Pieces?' inquired Richard, and I could well imagine the kind tone in which he had asked after a mere creature who was nonetheless the apple of his landlady's eye.

'Now, Mr Dadd.' Mrs J. leant forward and playfully tapped Richard on the knee with her gloves. 'There's no evading the question, you know, oh deary me, no.'

'Sam,' ordered Richard. 'Bring on the picture.'

While Sam was acting on his orders, and at the same time slipping the bottle of brandy into Richard's bedroom, Richard produced from his pockets a sheaf of papers. He was in the habit of copying by hand as many disparaging remarks about his friends' artistic abilities as he could glean from the publications at his disposal, and passing them on to Mrs J.

'Pieces will be ever so grateful, Mr Dadd.' Mrs Jenkins slid them into her copious bag. 'He enjoyed the last lot so much, you've no idea. The memory of that bird! That bit about your friend Mr

Frith. *"It is not a kind of painting which will bring great fame or indeed deserve it."* How we laugh over that one, don't we, Doris?' Mrs Jenkins here nudged her sister violently with her elbow, causing the overweighted bonnet to tip a barrowload of blooms over her eyes.

But the painting was at last returned to the easel. Sam whisked off the cloth and then withdrew to one side, from which position he eyed the picture as critically as the two good ladies.

'I tell you, Mrs L.,' said Mrs Jenkins, here clapping her hand to her mouth to stifle her shrieks of laughter. 'I just roared! "Oh my word, Mr Dadd," I gasped. "What a tease you are!"'

Richard looked at her in amazement. 'I call it "Contradiction",' he said. 'It's Oberon and Titania from Shakespeare.'

'Shakespeare, my foot,' roared our critic between gusts of laughter. 'They're no more fairies than you are!' And she poked at Richard's plump thighs. 'And you'd never get off the ground now, would you?'

Reader, Mrs Jenkins' temerity quite amazed me. But since she did not volunteer any further information as to how Richard had taken such comments when he had previously showed himself to be so sensitive to the remarks made by his friends, I was driven at last to ask her outright.

The dear lady merely replied, 'Oh, he doesn't mind what I say. He knows I always give an honest answer.'

She then continued her story. 'When I looked at the picture again,' she went on, 'I knew straight out who it was. And I told him so. "You can't deny it," I said to him.'

I held my breath at this further audacity, but Richard had apparently leaned back in his chair with a pleasant smile on his face and said, 'Very well, my noble patroness, go on then, tell!'

Mrs Jenkins had been forced to wipe her eyes before she could proceed. Even then the identities were too terrible to be revealed out loud. Instead, she whispered the names in Richard's ear; Richard in turn whispered in Sam's ear, before Sam murmured the same into Doris's teasing mop of ringlets.

Doris, it appeared, then spoilt the whole game by sitting up with a puzzled expression on her face which accentuated all those little lines and wrinkles which she took such pains to conceal. Then she shook her head until the ringlets danced out around it, and said loudly,

'Victoria and Albert?'

'Sssh, Doris,' chorused the others.

The two figures at the centre of the picture stared back unamused.

'Mere figments of the imagination,' said Richard. 'Fairies.'

'Mr Dadd,' remonstrated Mrs Jenkins when they had all recovered from their laughter. 'Fairies don't age.'

'I fear they do,' said Richard, suddenly serious.

Sensing his change of mood, Sam hastily removed the picture.

'Not that I can see, Mrs L., why the Super should get to keep it, any more than Sam Smith should himself,' Mrs Jenkins commented, – with which sentiment I agreed entirely.

'But if,' Mrs Jenkins continued in my ear, now thoroughly possessed by her role as art critic and with no notion where to stop, 'if those *were* mere, well nearly mere, middle-aged mortals, why were there all those giant butterflies and snails creeping around the borders?'

It was a question which I too was unable to answer. 'We will have to leave that to the experts, I fear,' I replied.

We must have presented a strange sight, the two of us standing there beneath that vast cupola in the fast fading light, engaged in earnest conversation.

'Like a pair of tourists in St Paul's,' was Doris's version when she finally caught us up.

After the appropriate introductions were made, we began our goodbyes. But just as I turned to go, Mrs Jenkins said as a parting shot, 'Those others couldn't hold a candle to him. He did a lovely picture of you a few years back.'

'Did he?' I asked in confusion.

'Don't worry, dear, I never let on that I knew, not to anyone else, – though he knew that I knew,' she said enigmatically. 'He called it "Columbine" after the flowers in your hair.'

'Flowers,' I exclaimed. 'Oh dear, you must be mistaken. Flowers at my age indeed!'

'How could he paint you as you are now?' she asked scornfully. 'But sure as eggs is eggs, it's you as you was. I would have known you anywhere.'

'Would you indeed?' I replied laughing. 'And if that is so, why wouldn't everyone else recognise me, who had known me then?'

'There are portraits and portraits,' she replied sagely. 'And there's looks and looks, if you take my meaning.'

'Not entirely,' I confessed.

'There's some looks,' she persevered in the face of my incomprehension, 'that are not generally shown in public by a lady such as yourself . . .'

Reader, I here lost track of her discourse. My senses, which had been so mercilessly bombarded with conflicting impressions ever since I entered that terrible place, withdrew from active engagement as if to say, 'Enough! No more!'

It was not the evidence of madness that was unnerving as we stood beneath that chilly dome, which towered over us beyond the reach of lamplight like a night sky devoid of stars; it was rather its absence: an overwhelming sense of complete and icy containment within that grave marble hall which seemed to deny its very existence. It was this that made me shiver and draw my cloak firmly about me so that at length even Mrs Jenkins paused in her monologue to inquire whether I had not caught a fever.

It was no bodily fever that made my eyes glitter so brightly. It was more as if a frost had settled upon my brow, touching my mind with a dreadful numbness which froze logical thought. Beneath this glacial surface, thoughts and emotions now tumbled freely, like creatures in the slime at the bottom of a pool. I could by no means control them without the overriding hand of reason, and in that moment I longed for my rock, my J. That epithet which once seemed to me the grossest insult now appeared the highest accolade. Had he been there, I would have clung to him though the whole world had rocked about me in the grip of some mighty earthquake.

Mrs Jenkins continued her narrative undeterred by my strange looks, while I chased my errant thoughts like some hill farmer who, without his dogs, tries in vain to round up his silly, recalcitrant sheep. These thoughts, more fluff than flesh, led me over hill and dale, plunging dangerously down into every ravine and clambering thence only with the greatest difficulty. Neither gentleness nor sternness had any effect. They seemed heedless of habit and custom. Freed from the fold in which they had long been penned and now deprived of all that was familiar and comfortable, they bolted in every direction.

Madness was engraved on the walls of that place, as ineradicable as the words carved on a tombstone. Insanity screamed in the terrible silence broken only by the occasional clatter of footsteps and the passing by of a heavily muffled figure. It assumed many guises, rearing its head now as the perpetual nursery world of silly gentle George, now with the shrieks of one who is roasted alive on a spit. In the course of my visit I had witnessed those who lived in the happy world of delusion. I had seen emperors and queens, gods and beasts, – and artists whose acts were so professional that they came and went as free as air. And now I was hearing from Mrs Jenkins' own lips the evidence that there was contained within these walls, one whose bearing and demeanour bore no trace whatsoever of insanity; one whose humour, gentleness and skill remained unimpaired by these frightful surroundings.

'A real gentleman through and through is Mr Dadd,' was how she summed him up as we parted. 'Not like some of them as visits him!'

Reader, how could I connect this same person with the brutal slayer of his father? I could not and yet I knew that this one dear body housed those two irreconcilables, that there was a point at which the rational and the irrational met in whirling confusion.

So ended my one and only visit to Bedlam.

Chapter Eight

READER, I should have gone home at once, but I put off my departure from day to day. I did not return to my family, even though such a course would have been advisable, – even though I yearned heart and soul for my Devon valleys, for the clear, cold outline of the moor and the crisp air which clears and invigorates mind and body; even though my own hearth and family called me and I pined with every breath for the happy bustle and good cheer of ordinary family life. For I could under no circumstances describe the household in which I was then living as 'ordinary'. There was no thoughtless babble of children's voices, rarely a sound to disturb the silence unless it was my friend's terrible laughter or her frequent, heart-rending outbursts of grief. Under that roof reigned no conventual calm such as characterises the presence of God, but rather an ominous absence of sound which proclaimed the presence of his adversary. Where there should have been every virtue characterised by that familiar term 'home', there was only fear. Fear of Maria? Ah, no. You misunderstand me. We feared her no more than we had once feared Richard. We cherished her as we had once cherished him, as a dear, loved and loving creature. It was not her presence which clamped the icy grip of terror about our hearts, but that Fiend which stalked her and from whom we endeavoured to defend her with every Christian weapon at our disposal, – with love and understanding, with peace and prayer.

Indeed, I could not leave her in her extremity. My own household would, I knew, function very well without me, though I trusted selfishly that my absence would not go entirely unnoticed. I wrote to J. explaining the reasons for my remaining in London and he replied most kindly. Though they missed me, he said, life carried on much as usual and they quite understood if for the time being my duties lay elsewhere. This sensible response upset me unreasonably, and indeed my hand was on the bell to summon a servant to bring me my trunk for immediate departure. I could have withstood a passionate plea for my return (though to be sure to the luxurious accompaniment of many tears and sighs), but to feel myself entirely dispensable was a blow indeed!

Like a poor timid rabbit who fears to find his burrow closed against him, I was ready to bolt for home. But at that precise moment occurred one of Maria's many crises with which Ellen was no longer able to cope, though they had given her little trouble in her younger days. I found myself at once distracted from my own cares and wholly immersed in my roles of nurse, nanny and housekeeper. And later, when I found myself at leisure to peruse the letter again, I was able to view it more dispassionately and accept that from such a reasonable being as my husband, I could have expected no more, and no less. J. was my rock, and a rock cannot provide at the same time complete security and those volcanic outbursts of passionate feeling which I so craved.

In such terms I reasoned with myself as the days grew ever more cold and dreary and we were drawn towards what seemed to be the perpetual night of mid-December. But not all the leaping flames of that alien fireside, no amount of coal, no heap of pine-scented logs could thaw the deadly chill that entered and possessed me as I watched my dear friend locked in mortal combat with that pitiless foe.

I sat with Maria, to all appearances calmly enough, with my sewing box ever to hand, and a pile of books by my side with which to provide distraction for her and her poor, bewildered children (for she liked to see them so occupied and to hear for herself the tales which delighted them). I held her hand by the hour and listened to the tortured outpourings of her soul, – but though I took her in my arms to comfort her and drive away the terrors which assailed her, though I pressed her to me until every muscle in my arms ached, though I disputed every inch of ground lost, I felt her slipping away from me inch by inch. Like the mother in the sickroom of a beloved child who fights long and hard and implores her beloved with every glance, every gesture, not to give up the struggle, it was as if a stronger presence than mine had invaded her body. Slowly and inexorably, he claimed her soul. His shadow crept across her eyes, extinguishing their gentle softness and replacing it with that cold, hard lustre which was a reflection of himself.

And yet these harrowing moments which remain so powerfully in the memory were but isolated incidents, – ugly, craggy islands set in an otherwise tranquil sea. For this record I have but to refer to my letters to J.; I wrote home every day and my letters thus form a diary for this period. For the sake of economy I did not despatch each one individually, but sent them in bundles of four or five at a time. Of course, any events relating to this biography were interspersed with expressions of homesickness and those domestic concerns which inevitably haunt the absent wife and mother. I enclosed new recipes and remedies which I learned in the metropolis for the treatment of colds and chilblains. I gave my dear ones minute instructions on their dress and reminded them to wear extra vests as the frosts increased in severity. I advised J. to purchase stout new boots for the children before the first snowfall and to see that they were well oiled before their first wearing. And I always concluded with a string of questions respecting insignificant matters which were to me, at the time, of the utmost importance.

My husband replied once a week, regular as clockwork. The children were well. The weather was average. The housekeeper was competent. His work was proceeding normally. He trusted I was comfortable. My instructions were duly noted. He signed himself off with an assurance of his continuing affection, of which I in any case entertained no doubt whatsoever, and I would then compose myself to await the following Monday's identical epistle.

But these affairs are of little relevance to the subject of this biography. I am ever mindful of the stricture to rise above my own personal feelings so that the truth may be set free to speak for itself. Maria's health was, as I have said, variable, although there were days when she could be the most delightful companion, a loving mother to her children, and a housekeeper whose zeal and energy knew no bounds. As Christmas approached, however, I could not but be aware of a general lowering of her spirits.

'Do you think that Jock will come?' she asked many times a day, vowing that the festival would not be complete if all the family were not gathered together.

I confess that kindness forbade me to express too bluntly the feelings these questions aroused in my own breast, for she would not hear of my departing to remedy that omission in my own family circle. She had never met my husband and children, and continued to behave as if they did not exist, as if I were still that solitary and giddy creature that I had been twenty years before, which was a curious omission in an otherwise generous and loving spirit. However, I curbed my own thoughts on the subject sufficiently to inquire dispassionately whether she hoped her husband would return in time for the festive season.

'Return, or write, at least to let me know whether he is alive or dead,' she responded, looking covetously at the letter which I even then held on my knee, though Heaven knows, the contents were little to be envied.

'If it were the latter,' I replied with some asperity, 'you are likely enough to have heard.'

'What is the matter with you, Elizabeth?' she was prompt to ask. 'You seem so out of sorts these days!' And she pouted like a spoilt child.

'If you must know,' I was driven to reply, 'I miss my husband as much as you do yours.' I hoped perhaps to receive from her some sympathy, perhaps even an acknowledgement of my own sacrifice. I received none.

'What fun!' cried she, clapping her hands and becoming quite animated. 'Let us be bereaved together! Let us console one another!' And she snatched the letter from my grasp before I could prevent her. 'Do you remember,' she cried as she opened it, 'that night— ' She stopped abruptly. There could be no more hilarity at the memory of that terrible night when we lay quoting from our girlish *billets-doux* at the moment when dear Mr Dadd was fighting for his life.

She handed me back the letter, unread. Then she smiled wryly. At that moment I think we both remembered not merely the accompanying horrors of that time, but also the contrasting style of the authors of our letters, – my J. and her Jock.

189

'He hasn't changed,' I said, thinking back to those neat, stilted expressions of my own suitor compared with the passionate and almost illegible outbursts from Jock. 'You can see if you like,' I said holding out the letter again. 'There is nothing here to make me blush.'

'Poor Elizabeth!' said she, scorning to take the envelope and seating herself on the settle by my side.

I could say nothing further, for as she put her arms around me I gave way to all those years of pent-up grief, while at the same time I chided myself for such indulgence. At the age of forty, I should have known better.

'Things might have been so different,' she said softly.

Indeed they might, I thought, though such speculation is dangerous. What is done is fixed and unalterable, and not all the twistings and turnings of the imagination can escape that truth. We can only accept and make the best of it, according to the inclinations which God has seen fit to grant us. But Maria was not susceptible to such reasoning. She was ever a creature of dreams, and on she went to torture both her own spirit and mine with endless, fanciful imaginings, although I begged her often enough to desist. Strangely, it was these same extravagant fantasies which served to bind me ever more closely to her and forced me to turn my back on the present, if not with joy then at least with resolution, and to apply myself to her care at the expense of my own better judgement and duties.

So we crept unwillingly towards Christmas: Maria grieving painfully at the thought of the family circle being incomplete; and myself, tortured cruelly by my divided loyalties. But there were Maria's children to consider, and Colin and Amy counted the days with a bright-eyed eagerness and excitement that would not be suppressed. For their sake we were forced to make some attempt at celebration.

As matters turned out, Maria was doomed to less disappointment than I. I was to remain solitary, while it seemed that her every wish was to be granted; – for one morning, her husband did return.

Totally disregarding the coldness of the air, Jock Phillip wedged his tam o'shanter over his ears and, clutching it firmly with one hand for good measure, thrust his head out of the window of the carriage which was bearing him home.

'Faster!' Jock called to the driver, as he later told me, ever more impatient as each familiar landmark came into view, – the small park where the children used to play, the butcher's shop, the old neighbourhood pub, – all of which only served to increase his desire to arrive. For that same mercurial temperament which drove him to seek his freedom abroad, compelled him now with equal urgency to seek the company of his wife and children at home.

'Faster!' he called again and the driver cracked his whip and the lash crackled against the ground so that the horse started and put every last ounce of energy into the final sprint.

Jock had by now wound his scarf about his face until he had quite taken on the appearance of a brigand. But how delightful was this sting in the weather to one who had for the past year experienced the torment of eternal sunshine and warmth.

On the opposite seat, – for in spite of the driver's fears for his upholstery, Jock had refused to entrust all of his luggage to the roof, – sat a large black, metal box. That it was valuable to its owner, was attested by those glances which he cast in its direction, which were as tender and anxious as those a mother might cast over a new-born babe.

The contents of the trunk could not of course be diamonds, for such would fit comfortably into the purchaser's pocket; nor gold since the container betrayed its lack of weight by almost flying off the narrow seat at every jolt. Indeed, the cab driver himself had looked suspiciously at this particular receptacle, which the curious, brown-skinned fellow had protected so jealously from the hustle and bustle of the docks. The offer of a sovereign by way of a bonus had, however, conquered his initial scruples, and he had thereafter driven like a devil out of hell so as to be rid of his strange passenger at the very first opportunity.

Jock was in fact quite sane. After passing one full year among the orange groves of Seville, he was simply anxious to get home. If his appearance was alarming, it was because he now looked more Spanish than British. But these changes were not confined to outward characteristics alone. Along with the country of his birth, he had shaken off its puritanical shackles, and experienced at first hand the exuberance of the Latin temperament. Together with the red wine and the sunshine, he had imbibed the full splendour and glory of the Catholic Church. It was as if he had been born anew to a different, more vibrant self.

Jock leant precariously out of the carriage window, his vision obscured by the thick folds of the muffler which he had wrapped around his head to keep out the unaccustomed cold, while he drank in the sights, sounds and smells of early morning London. So distracted was he by these re-discovered delights that he only realised how far and fast his driver had transported him, when he saw his own green front door and the familiar wrought iron railings racing towards him.

'Stop!' he yelled, hammering with his fist upon the roof at the same time, for his voice was snatched away by the wind.

The driver, unable to halt his horses at such short notice on the icy cobblestones, simply took this instruction as further evidence of his passenger's lack of judgement and drove on by.

Jock saw his home, as in a nightmare, recede into the distance, and swearing at his conductor in a mixture of Spanish and Scottish, he bellowed at him to go round the block again.

Seated as we were by the drawing room fire, it was thus that we received the first intimation of Jock's return.

'See, Mama,' observed Colin, who was standing at the window as the rattling contraption thundered by. 'A runaway coach!' The boy breathed heavily on the frosted pane and rubbed at it with his finger tip until he had cleared a peephole into the street.

Both Maria and I paled at the thought of the danger both to the occupants of the carriage and to any pedestrians who might find themselves in its path. Why, only half an hour later Amy, Colin and Ellen would have been crossing that very road on their way to the park! So run the narrow thoughts of mothers vigilant for the well-being of their offspring.

'Is your Latin exercise finished?' Maria asked the boy, anxiety adding an unusual severity to her tone.

Colin returned to his seat at the table.

Amy, a year younger, looked up at her mother and smiled angelically; not even runaway horses could distract her from her careful copying of a French poem about Père Noel.

'How many days until Christmas?' sighed her brother.

'Three,' his mother responded. She was quite calm this morning and engaged in making a kissing bunch to hang in the hall. 'Could you not have got any fresher holly, Ellen?' she asked. Tears stung her eyes as the fierce spikes drew blood from her fingers.

'Let me do it, Miss Maria. You do the bow instead.' Ellen leant across from her chair on the other side of the hearth, and the two women exchanged their handiwork.

'Who will you kiss this year, Mama?' asked Amy thoughtfully.

'A tall dark handsome stranger!' Maria twined the shiny scarlet satin in and out of her fingers.

'Will that be Papa?' persisted the child.

'Is your Papa, then, a stranger?' Maria's eyebrows contracted, so that the deep lines which had become etched on her forehead over the past year, deepened into furrows. 'Who knows?' She looped the ribbon carefully in the span of her hand, tied the bow, then trimmed the end in a neat v-shape.

Colin had only just taken up his pen again when the wild pounding of hooves was heard once more thundering down the street. 'He's going in circles!' cried the child with delight, hurrying to the window again. 'It's like the races, isn't it, Mama?'

This time Amy joined him, and their two little mouths breathed clear twin circles in the frosted fantasy of flowers and ferns.

'Oh!' they cried, as the carriage this time slithered to a halt at their own front door, with the steel rim of the wheels striking sparks from the stones as the brakes locked. Even before the horse had fully stopped, the carriage door was flung open and a figure leapt out on to the pavement.

'It's a foreigner, Mama,' observed Amy. 'Like the knife-grinder. He looks very dark and coarse.'

'Silly!' sneered Colin, springing for the door. 'Don't you know who that is? It's Papa!' and he was off like lightning across the hall and out into the street, leaving all the doors wide open to admit a trail of frosty air.

193

Maria shivered as the icy fingers crept about her shoulders. 'Aren't you going to go and say hello to Papa?' she asked her daughter as she set aside the ribbon. Though her voice was calm, her hands were far from steady.

The little girl came nervously to her side, and shrank behind her mother's skirts as they proceeded to the front steps together.

Jock stood there on the pavement, angrily motioning to his son to be still while the luggage was taken down.

'Papa, Papa!' The little boy danced up and down on the pavement in a frenzy of impatience. But before greetings could be exchanged, the precious paintings had to be removed from the carriage and brought safely into the hall. Then at last, Jock was free to turn to his family with his arms extended in welcome. But somehow the moment had passed. Colin's enthusiasm had been much diminished by the delay; all spontaneity was fled. Though he now submitted with passable grace to the hugs and kisses which his fond father showered upon him, he had to be coaxed to show any fondness in return.

'Is this all your Papa gets when he has missed you so much?' Jock asked, looking at both children with a hurt expression. For Colin now sat stiffly on his lap by the fire while Amy continued to regard him with suspicion from the safety of her mother's embrace. I would gladly have withdrawn and allowed the family reunion to take place unhindered by my presence. But Maria would have me stay.

'Go and kiss your father,' Maria then said sharply, pushing her daughter forward to the arm of her father's chair.

Amy bobbed a little curtsey and suffered her father to run his fingers fondly through her hair.

'Is this your doing, Maria?' asked Jock bitterly. 'Is it you who has turned my own children against me?'

The unjustness of the accusation stung Maria keenly. 'It is your own doing,' she replied. 'You could think only of your precious paintings. You have hurt their feelings.'

Jock stared angrily into the fire. All the excitement of the last few weeks evaporated in a moment; all the longing to be with his family which was so strong that it amounted almost to a sickness, had turned sour within a few minutes of his arrival. Already he was wondering why he had bothered to come, why the lure of hearth and home, so strong in the abstract, failed to materialise in reality.

'Have you been keeping well?' he asked his wife.

'Quite well, thank you,' she replied as if addressing a total stranger. 'The doctor is much pleased with my progress.'

'I shall have to speak to him myself.' Jock's statement evinced more of threat than of concern.

Maria picked up the holly bunch, which Ellen had abandoned on the hearth, and began to wrestle with the reluctant sprigs. A spiked leaf drove up under her nail, but though I observed her to wince, she did not cry out. 'I have looked forward to your coming, Jock,' was all she said timidly, as she sucked her finger.

Jock kicked at a smouldering log so that sparks flew and Colin jumped off his father's lap and scampered about the hearth rug stamping out the glowing embers.

'Papa,' said Amy, who had gathered up her courage during this diversion. 'Have you brought me a present?' She had long entertained dreams of the wonderful store of treasures her father would have amassed for her.

'Of course,' he said fondly, pinching her cheek. 'There are tangerines and nuts for Christmas. And a Spanish doll for you, and silks and mantillas and ivory combs.'

Amy's eyes grew wide at the thought. 'Will I be able to dress up just like Mama?'

Her father's eyes clouded over and he did not answer.

'When can we see them?' asked Colin. 'I want to see them now.'

'Why not wait for Christmas?' suggested Maria.

'Now, now!' cried both children together, quite unable to tolerate any delay and, seizing their father's hands, they dragged him towards the pile of luggage in the hall.

Jock hampered their progress by swinging them wildly round and round by the arms until they were dizzy and Maria's eyes softened at the sight.

'Now, let me see,' said Jock, reeling down the hall. 'Where did I put your presents?' and he made to look among the boxes and cases while the children squealed with excitement.

'Hurry,' they called, 'hurry, Papa!'

His delaying tactics were almost too convincing to be true.

'That's funny,' he said, 'I can't find it anywhere.'

The children clapped their hands and danced up and down, scarcely able to contain themselves.

'That's *very* funny,' said Jock shaking his head ever more sadly. The joke began to pall. The children had had enough of it.

'I think,' said Maria, 'that Papa's joke should be over now.'

Jock turned on her angrily. 'Who said it was a joke?'

'Where are they, Papa, where?' Amy's eyes filled with tears.

'The box,' said her father. 'I can't understand it. It was on the roof.'

Maria looked at him reproachfully.

'It's all your fault,' he said, as if aware of her thoughts. 'You rushed me. You all came piling out of the house, shouting and distracting me until I couldn't think straight.'

Then, unable to bear the disappointment in his children's eyes, he hoisted the trunk of paintings on to his shoulder and went into his studio, where he locked the door firmly behind him.

In those days leading up to Christmas, – days which should have been so joyful, – this scene, alas, was but one of many. So frequently was I witness to the ill effects of one sensitive nature upon another that I was constrained to bless God for providing me with J.; I could see him then as the perfect foil and antidote to my own restless being. Before me, I now beheld at close quarters creatures of such similar natures and tastes that they seemed to be forever locked either in perfect harmony or utter discord. There were indeed moments when the evidence of their mutual adoration and happiness brought home to me my present solitary state. But there was, even about such idyllic interludes, an unhealthy warmth, a closeness in the air like that which precedes a thunderstorm. And sure enough the pressure in the atmosphere would gather to a point where it would break in a veritable outburst of cosmic grumblings and forked lightning such as seemed bent on destroying not just their own two selves, but everybody in the vicinity.

These episodes left my dear friend Maria depleted of all life

and energy. I could leave her neither during those periods of un-
earthly happiness to which no mortal should aspire, nor when the
jealous gods finally struck. I remained to provide what levelling
influence I could, and when my presence could be spared, I took
the opportunity to renew former acquaintances in and about the
city.

One such expedition to which I had taken a particular fancy
ever since my visit to the Royal Bethlem Hospital, was to call
upon Richard's former landlady, Mrs Jenkins, who, – despite her
careful preservation of every appearance to the contrary, – had,
as I learnt from Ellen, now fallen upon hard times. So it was that,
in those last days before Christmas, I took advantage of one of
the honeymoon phases of my hosts to pack a small hamper and
betake myself to Newman Street.

Strange it was to traverse that very road which had once been
familiar to me, and to see again that front door and those windows
which had once caused my heart to beat so fast. The same two
tubs stood on the doorstep now much overgrown and run to
weed. But the brass bell gleamed as brightly as ever in the wintry
sunshine, and having pressed it, I found myself in no time at all
seated in Mrs Jenkins' front parlour with a cup of tea thrust into
my unwilling hand. It has never been my custom to partake
excessively of that beverage, which I find excites the nerves to
a state of quite painful elation, – which fear was subsequently
borne out on this occasion.

You will, I am sure, not have forgotten Pieces, who was so
overjoyed by the presence of a visitor (especially one bearing a
little treasure chest of his favourite nuts and seeds), that Mrs
Jenkins and I found it well nigh impossible to carry on a sensible
conversation through his interminable interruptions.

'. . . sorry to see . . .' he chattered, '. . . fair little child . . .'
He here paused to crack open a sunflower seed. '. . . too kind
friends . . .' The glossy black and white striped casing fell away.
'. . . toasted and toyed . . .' he muttered as he gulped the seed
down, '. . . into selfishness and misery!' Pieces concluded his
speech with a burst of laughter, followed by a brisk clacking of
his tongue against the roof of his mouth to simulate applause.

'Really, Pieces,' said his adoring mistress, joining in both the
laughter and the clapping, 'you are a caution. It is Mr Ruskin's

criticism of Mr Frith's portrait of his daughter,' she added for my benefit, having rightly surmised that I was not in a position to understand the allusion. 'Not that I think Mr Ruskin is always correct, dear boy,' she reproved her pet.

The parrot howled like a dog at the blasphemy.

'Now, Pieces, remember the principle of free speech.' Mrs Jenkins here popped a large peanut into the parrot's mouth to preserve that right for herself. 'You forget, my lad,' she continued, 'that I have been in Mr Frith's house . . .'

The parrot gulped down the nut and uttered a squawk which echoed my own astonishment.

'Say what you like, Pieces,' Mrs J. here waggled a fearsome feather duster before those eagle eyes, 'I, your humble servant,' and she coughed deprecatingly, 'have trod on the self-same sacred floorboards and rugs as our gracious monarch. And,' she continued sternly, 'whatever Mr Ruskin may say, I have seen that little cherub of a child . . .'

I would have been interested to hear more, having learnt much upon the same subject myself from my unfortunate sister-in-law, Sarah Dadd, who had suffered at that same child's hands. But anything further which Mrs Jenkins might have said was entirely drowned out by the heavy peal of the door bell.

'You will excuse me, Mrs L., won't you?' said my hostess and without waiting for a reply, she was off into the hall.

'Yes?' Mrs Jenkins opened her front door no more than a hair's breadth, while expressing the opinion that these days you couldn't trust anyone, not after everything you read in the papers.

'Is this the house,' I heard a gentleman's voice inquire, 'which was once the home of Mr Richard Dadd, the artist?'

At this my heart quite missed a beat.

'I wonder,' continued the gentleman, 'whether it might be possible to view the room in which the unfortunate artist once worked?'

Reader, though my prime purpose on this visit was avowedly charitable, I must confess that the same thought had been uppermost in my mind ever since I crossed that threshold, though I knew not how to broach the subject. However, Mrs Jenkins seemed reluctant to admit this stranger, and I could well understand the delicacy which prompted her hesitation. I feared for a moment that he would be rebuffed, until I heard the chink of coins and observed their effect. Instantly the door was flung open to a most gracious welcome.

It was at this stage that I realised the gentleman was not alone. Judging from the scuffling of feet on the hall mat, the nervous clearings of throats and the hushed whispers, he seemed to be accompanied by a sizeable party. As Mrs Jenkins led the way upstairs, I seized the opportunity to follow them.

'It's all just as it was. You're the first people to go in since the police, twenty years ago,' she lied. She and Doris had even contrived to make the lock squeak most convincingly, so that the lady visitors in front of me shuddered with apprehension.

The only alteration that Mrs Jenkins had to make, as she told me on another occasion, was to the eggs.

'It was more than flesh and blood could bear, Mrs L.,' she confided to me. 'There are limits,' she added, 'and young Mr Dadd would be the first to admit in his line of business, it is not what is true that matters, but what appears to be true. Artistic verisimilitude we call it,' she concluded convincingly.

Seeing my puzzled look, she continued: 'It was the smell really, dear. I only know that I couldn't live with the smell. It would have killed me!'

So each month, it appears, while other housewives baked their shortbread fingers and oat-cakes, Mrs Jenkins baked a fresh batch of the vinegar-scoured egg shells (followed by egg custards *ad nauseam* to use up the contents) which I now observed to crackle so convincingly under the feet of her horrified guests.

'Curious sketches,' observed one of the party, approaching the row of heads on the mantelpiece.

'I daresay you'd look quite curious with your throat cut,' retorted Mrs Jenkins.

'Who are they?' asked one of the ladies faintly.

'Well,' said Mrs J. 'From left to right, Prince Albert, the Pope, Mr Dadd, the artist's father, Mr Frith the eminent painter, the Emperor of Austria, or is it the Archduke . . .?' I realised at the same instant as she did herself, that somehow the pictures had become jumbled up, perhaps during the dusting, so that Mr Frith sported whiskers like Santa Claus while Prince Albert was clean-shaven.

'I would have expected better likenesses from one of his talent,' commented one of the gentlemen. 'These look as though a child drew them.'

Mrs Jenkins drew in her breath sharply at this. I knew perfectly well that Richard could not have drawn these monstrosities. He was incapable of anything so clumsy and indelicate. As I discovered later, they were the works of Mrs Jenkins and her sister Doris who had spent hours at the kitchen table trying to reproduce the originals which the police had refused to return.

'Of course, he was mad,' Mrs Jenkins said loudly above the ensuing debate, after which reminder it seemed unnecessary even to consider the pictures' artistic merit.

She next led the way through to the bedroom, where the freshly laundered sheets had been arranged in a pleasant, lavender-scented confusion, to which the bloodstains from some Sunday joint, carefully dripped across the windowledge and over the floorboards (avoiding the precious Turkey rug) were the crowning glory.

Reader, you may wonder that I was not outraged by this travesty of the truth, by this pandering to the sensational by which Mrs Jenkins now earned her living. But I knew the true feelings of affectionate regard which she harboured for her former lodger, which were borne out by those wearisome trips to the hospital month after month, when most of his friends and family alike had fallen by the wayside. Besides, Richard was himself blessed with a rich sense of humour, and I could well imagine that this little charade, coupled with the fact of Mrs Jenkins' own drawings being passed off as his own, would have afforded him the greatest amusement.

'I thought,' drawled the leader of the party above those exclamations of horror which are always evoked by the sight of blood, 'that the murder was committed down in Kent.'

By this time, I was so completely on Mrs Jenkins' side, that I too was ready to curse the man inwardly for being such a know-all.

'Self-mutilation,' muttered my hostess darkly, with considerable presence of mind, while the ladies looked faint and expressions of revulsion crept across those well-bred faces.

'I bet you could tell us some tales,' urged one of them, clinking some coins discreetly in his pockets as he spoke.

Mrs Jenkins passed one liver-spotted hand over her brow in a gesture which would have convinced any theatre audience of her reluctance to divulge any secrets, before she sank comfortably into the easy chair beside which she had conveniently placed herself. And after a decently observed pause, during which she draped one hand artistically over the arm of her chair with the palm turned unobtrusively upwards, she began . . .

Reader, do not judge Mrs Jenkins too harshly for her fabrications. Admire, rather, the resourcefulness of a widow who was forced to earn her own living. Consider that she had made of Richard's studio a work of art, her fund of tales a theatrical performance. Mr Dickens' melodramatic exhibitions in Cobham Park had not even the excuse of financial necessity to atone for their lack of taste.

For my part, standing that day in Richard's studio, I was glad to have our ghosts exorcised by a crowd of trippers; to have seen his exquisite sketches replaced by clumsy caricatures; to have smelt only furniture polish and vinegar, and to have seen the aspidistra unadorned by stray socks and rogue handkerchiefs and cravats. Those rooms held nothing for me, and I never ventured into them again.

But if poignant reminders of his presence were lacking in Richard's lodgings, they were omnipresent in Maria's house, as it had become since Jock's return. Not that Richard was ever mentioned, nor was his physical presence missed in a house in which he had never set foot. It was something about the atmosphere that suggested itself to me; in the smell of paint, thinner and cleaning fluid on Jock's paint-speckled smocks, which lay about the house until someone thought to gather them up; in the irregularity which now became part of our life. For meals waited until Jock was ready. His friends called quite unannounced, at all hours of the day and night. The difference between this way of living and my own quietly regulated existence in Devon would have to be experienced to be believed.

And of course, I met Richard's old friends, who now flocked to see Jock. My name aroused no more than a faint flicker of recognition which was quickly extinguished when they learned that I had not been in touch with Richard for almost two decades. They saw me only as a middle-aged housewife and mother, and I professed to be no more. Of course, had they seen me at my own hearthside, I would have said that I professed to be 'no less', but here, values were different and I no longer knew whether I stood on my feet or on my head.

Christmas Day dawned. Since Jock was home, Maria was determined that the family celebrations would take place at their house, and Jock further compounded the numbers by inviting all of his artistic acquaintance. Ellen and I relieved Maria of the practical cares of organisation, but allowed her the full glory of presiding over her family on the great day.

Sarah, who had been given the day off from her duties as governess to little Lizzie Frith, arrived early, almost before the breakfast was cleared away. Then came Robert and his family, including of course my own sister Catherine and his sister, Mary Ann.

'Where is Jock?' was the question on everybody's lips, for there we were, all assembled by the fireside, and his absence was keenly felt, especially by Robert, who was the only male member of the party.

'Painting,' said Maria. 'Morning, noon and night. Spanish ladies, sun-baked mud walls and wine skins. We scarcely see him.' She sat down and took up her embroidery which she had been advised would have as steadying an effect on the nerves as it did on the hands. After several failed attempts to thread her needle, she handed it to Sarah.

'I am not sure what is wrong with good, solid, English subjects,' said Robert, drumming on the mantelpiece with his fingers.

'I think,' said Maria, 'that he likes to paint ladies as different from me as possible.'

'Surely not.' Robert stifled a yawn.

'I am fair, so they must be dark.' Maria accepted the threaded needle from her sister. 'My skin is that of an English rose, therefore theirs must be as dark as roasted coffee.'

'You must not give rein to these wild fancies, Maria,' observed Mary Ann. 'They are unworthy of you.'

'If I wear pastel colours, pinks and peaches and delicate yellows, theirs must be all ablaze with violent colours. He makes me feel as insubstantial as a ghost,' she continued.

'Perhaps,' ventured Sarah, 'you are imputing the wrong motive to his work. Perhaps he paints them not with admiration and love, but with a sense of revulsion and loathing.'

'Revulsion and loathing,' said Jock in his broad Aberdeenshire accent, here bounding jovially into the room. He was a small, slight man, but the bounce and spring in his step served the purpose of adding at least two inches to his height. He was never still, but darted here and there like some india-rubber ball rebounding off this person then that in a manner quite bewildering to the senses.

'Revulsion and loathing,' he repeated. 'On Christmas Day?'

Sarah blushed and declined to expound her meaning any further. Jock kissed her heartily and asked how Billy Frith's work was progressing. Without waiting for an answer he added that he had invited him to call in later.

Sarah stiffened perceptibly. At the prospect of her employers' arrival, I saw that her day was quite ruined. Though kindness itself to her, their kindness did not extend to protecting her from the spiteful little monster in her charge. I watched her startle at every footstep in the street and every horse's hoofbeat.

Jock paused for long enough in passing his wife to observe of her embroidery, 'That colour won't do, y'know. It quite clashes with the rest.'

Maria bit her lip and patiently unpicked the stitches already worked in that shade.

'Robert,' said Jock, 'not drinking? Good God . . .'

Mary Ann shrank at the blasphemy. Jock's flirtation with Roman Catholicism had, in her opinion, rendered him quite coarse.

Jock now bustled about with porter and a hot poker and called for the spices and mugs which his wife had been plaguing him to prepare since yesterday.

'Will this colour suit, do you think, Jock?' She held up a brilliant scarlet thread, quite at variance with the delicate tones she had so far employed.

'Why do you ask me?' he said sharply, as he plunged the sizzling poker into the mug of ale. 'It's your work, not mine.'

The morning merged somewhat heavily into lunchtime and lunchtime somehow fell over itself into the afternoon, in the course of which the other guests arrived. By this time, the children had reached that quarrelling and fractious state caused by an overdose of excitement, and most of the adults wanted nothing more than to be left in peace for a quiet doze. However, into that dreary gathering strode Mr and Mrs Frith, all bright-eyed energy and enthusiasm (for they had not yet dined). Tripping delicately between them came their little daughter Lizzie, who persisted in seeking out Sarah and tormenting her with displays of apparent devotion which brought forth cries of 'What a little darling!' from those near by.

Oh how strange is this world of art and artists where interests and petty jealousies are rife, and pride vies with a false modesty seeking ever to impose itself upon our notice. For soon after the arrival of Mr Frith, Richard's old friend Augustus Egg entered, bearing a large canvas under his arm, which he at once vowed he would not show us. Why then, wondered I, has he brought it along so conspicuously if not thereby to attract attention? At last an easel was brought, on which Jock had carelessly, or so he made it appear, left a canvas of his own, and after that had been duly admired, Billy Frith, putting a hand into his pocket, – in search, so he said, of a cigar, – unwittingly pulled out a small sketch book. We yawned our way through the endless sketches of Lizzie on her summer holiday, and then at last poor Augustus, who in the intervening period had been quite relegated to obscurity, was prevailed upon to display his treasure.

'"The Temptation",' he said proudly, setting it on the easel.

The scene depicted a young mother being tempted to leave her home for the arms of her lover. On the floor, oblivious of the drama, two small children were playing with bricks. I at once recognised the ringleted mop of the one, and as if anybody else in the room could have been left in doubt as to that pampered creature's identity, a little voice at once cried out, 'That's me!' and Lizzie Frith seized her father by the hand to drag him closer. 'Look, Papa, there I am again.'

Sarah's expression told me quite clearly that in her opinion the mother would be well advised to follow her inclinations.

'Sarah! I am surprised at you!' Mary Ann's voice caused me to look more closely at the other figures. And I at once recognised Sarah in the person of the tempted wife.

'I didn't know, Mary Ann, indeed, I was quite unaware . . .' Poor Sarah seemed mortified at the slant which the picture cast upon her virtue. 'He did not tell me . . .'

For Sarah had been pressed into service as a model entirely in ignorance of the finished subject. In vain had she protested that her job left her not a minute to call her own, and when that failed to persuade, that her features were too plain, – a plea which Augustus so charmingly denied.

'It's not the first time I've painted you, Sally,' he had reminded her as he arranged her in front of the piano in the Friths' parlour, staring into the eyes of an imaginary lover, for the present represented by a music stand. 'Fact is,' he continued as he took up his pencil, 'you're just the person I need. Obviously a lady. Virtuous without being startlingly beautiful' – how Sarah's poor heart bled as he thus categorised her virtues as a model, – 'and well trained by your brother in the art of standing still for hours on end.'

However, as the finished picture was exposed, it was left to Mary Ann to express the opinion that 'any woman with a home and children should be down on her knees thanking God for the privilege instead of wasting a moment's thought over some philanderer'. She then closed her lips with a finality which indicated that, for her part, there was no more to be said.

'Sarah?' Augustus prompted his model. 'Have you nothing to say?'

Sarah blushed at the attention thus drawn to her and, – quite missing the point of the question, which was, I assumed, related to the virtues of composition rather than subject, – confessed quite out of turn, 'I can see that she might be tempted.'

'Surely,' said Robert stiffly, 'no woman of virtue would even entertain the thought.' In the utter confidence of this sentiment, he closed his eyes and resumed his after-dinner nap.

'How can you say that?' Maria now burst out, quite startling us all. 'Do you not think that women have the same feelings, the same emotions as men?'

'My dear,' said her brother, opening one eye again. 'I do not deny it. I would also trust that no gentleman in his right senses

205

would thus put temptation in the path of a woman who was bound by the holy sacrament of matrimony.'

'The scene, then, strikes you as implausible, sir?' cried Egg, much put out by this reception of his masterpiece.

'In my experience, yes,' admitted Robert complacently.

'Then allow me to open your eyes,' said the artist quietly.

'You hear that, Jock,' inquired Maria, in a voice designed to carry to her husband on the far side of the room. 'Shall we not also admit it to be a failing on the part of the husband if a wife is driven to seek for love and approval from an illicit source?'

'The case is purely hypothetical,' retorted the Scotchman scornfully.

Reader, it was a strange topic for family discussion on a Christmas afternoon, when I could well imagine that at home my own family would now be indulging in the traditional games of Oranges and Lemons and Blind Man's Buff, with all the carefree jollity usually associated with this time of year. But it was ever so in that household, where emotions were so thinly veiled and every encouragement was given to their expression. Small wonder then that the party broke up, not on a note of happy contentment and peace and goodwill to all men, but rather with uncomfortable feelings of doubt and dissatisfaction. Nor is it surprising that Maria took all these things to her heart and that they returned to torment her in the darkness of night.

As the first fingers of dawn crept through the bedroom curtains and sought her out where she lay, still sleepless and fearful, Maria arose and slipped into the Spanish costume which Jock had given her after his first visit to Spain. It had then fitted her like a glove, so that the stretched satin caught the light and she seemed to move with all the flickering brilliance of a tongue of fire. Now it hung about her in so many folds and creases, almost as if there were no one inside it.

'A coat hanger,' she said out loud to her image. 'You're nothing but a coat hanger!' To stifle the incipient peals of laughter she crammed a lace mantilla into her mouth as a gag. Jock must not be disturbed. Oh no! Jock's art was sacred. Jock and his Spanish lovelies . . .

The thought was enough to restore her at once to perfect sobriety. She began to extract the yards of lace from her mouth again. Ectoplasm! The muscles of her face contracted in a horrible grimace, which she realised from the accompanying gurgles in her throat must be laughter. Still gagging, she saw in the mirror a strange pale figure standing behind her. Ghosts! The world was peopled by ghosts! And still the ectoplasm came forth from her body. She looked at it doubtfully.

'You're up early, my love,' came Ellen's voice.

'Ellen?' said Maria, when at last her mouth was clear. 'I thought you were a ghost.'

'Not me, dearie. I'm far too solid for that.'

Maria poked her finger into Ellen's side. The flesh had a comforting spongy feel to it. She poked her own spare middle and discovered only bone. She was a mere skeleton. She must eat. She had been neglecting herself lately. Upon this thought, she hustled Ellen downstairs and into the kitchen.

'More,' cried Maria, 'more!' after she had devoured a plateful of kidneys, bacon, tomatoes, mushrooms, and fried bread.

Sweat was trickling down Ellen's face as she stood over the roaring stove, despite the fact that she wore only her nightdress and a shawl. 'More, Miss Maria?' she queried, but she went into the pantry and looked inside the meat safe. 'Nice to see you with such a good appetite, dear,' she said as she returned into the inferno of the kitchen with a plate of kippers. 'You're quite sure now?'

'Quite sure, Ellen. I am building myself up.' Maria sat at the table quite composed, with her knife and fork poised for the next course. 'I have become dreadfully thin.'

'Why not have a nice piece of bread to mop up your plate?' Ellen suggested as she returned the frying pan to the stove.

Maria cut herself a chunk of bread and rubbed it in the bacon grease and congealed egg yolk. Then she looked down and observed herself closely to see whether this gargantuan meal was making any observable difference to her figure. She remained disappointingly flat-chested and scraggy. On a sudden inspiration, she stuffed the whole loaf down inside the bodice of her dress and there at last was a shelf of a bosom to be envied.

'Fried bread?' asked Ellen, turning round again. 'That's funny. Where did it go?'

'Just kippers will do very nicely, thank you, Ellen dear.'

At last bloated almost beyond endurance, her dress stretched pleasingly tight around a waist she could no longer see beyond the overhang of her enormous bosom, Maria struggled to her feet and waddled off in search of her husband.

I caught sight of her as she crossed the hall, where she paused to pluck two roses from the vase on the table. She set one between her teeth and tucked the other into her hair just over her right ear. Before she knocked at the door of Jock's studio, she listened at the key-hole, and what she heard brought a delighted smile to her face. Jock was not yet at work. His constant pacing denoted that impatient search for inspiration which preceded every new composition.

In spite of a rose thorn which pierced her upper lip, Maria was at that moment quite transfigured with happiness. She would herself be the subject of his next picture. She would be his inspiration and his model. She could already picture her voluptuous form filling the whole vast canvas. And with this conviction in her mind, she flung open the door and stood provocatively before him.

Mrs Jones was sent for at once. Since she had been unable to find alternative employment and Stephen's widow had been unwilling to enforce her departure into certain penury, Mrs Jones had remained in residence and had taken on the role of housekeeper, which she performed with an efficiency that had rendered her quite indispensable. Sarah at once volunteered herself to supply that deficiency, and, pleased to escape from the Frith household, she headed north for Manchester with all possible speed while Mrs Jones sped towards our troubled abode in the opposite direction.

This final episode, which had prompted us at last to seek out that professional help which we had so long avoided, was not the only calamity to beset us at this time. For even as we awaited Mrs Jones' arrival, a letter was received advising us of a sudden deterioration in the condition of George. No sooner was his illness made known to Ellen, than she had a basket packed and was off to the hospital with all the haste that could be expected of her seventy-odd years. In her opinion, there was no one who could so effectively nurse her darling in his final sickness, for no one else had known and loved him as she had, since his birth.

She found George in the infirmary, unusually clean and tucked in with a stiff starched sheet which imprisoned him there as efficiently as any strait-jacket.

At once, her apron was on and she was bustling about the sick room as though she owned the place. Never in the whole history of Bedlam had been seen such a cleaning and a scrubbing as now took place.

'Hospital?' she remarked scathingly. 'I wouldn't keep a pig in here.'

George, though scarcely conscious, floated on a cushion of dreams whose fabric was woven from a medley of household sounds which were once as dear to him and as familiar as a mother's heartbeat is to the child in the womb.

'Ellen,' he murmured from time to time, when roused by the ring of a broom handle against the metal bed frame or the slamming of a window after a duster was shaken.

'Ellen's here, dear heart, Ellen's here.' And she hovered momentarily to wipe his face with a cool flannel or to straighten the bedclothes if a wrinkle displeased her eye.

And when a coughing fit seized his giant frame, it was Ellen who waved aside offers of help, and who supported him alone as he spewed up globules of fresh blood into an enamel bowl.

'There Georgy, there,' she soothed him as he sank back exhausted by the attack, and sang him into a sleep in which the haunting worry about his furnaces and his own failing strength dissolved in pleasanter dreams.

As for me, I awaited only Mrs Jones' arrival before departing myself. It was becoming increasingly clear that there was little I could do to help my friend now. Colin and Amy were despatched to live with their cousins in Poplar until affairs should be sorted out, and it was a quiet and sorry household in which I now found myself. Maria spent much of this time in a drugged stupor, and Jock tiptoed about the house in an agony of fear lest anything should disturb his wife's repose. He was even known at this time to rush out into the street and soundly berate street vendors who were crying their wares, or a cab driver whose horse's shoes rang particularly loudly in his ears.

'This is,' the doctor was forced to remind him, however unpleasant the notion, 'but an interim measure. Other arrangements will have to be made.' For the medical expert was, on this occasion, not sanguine about Maria's chances of recovery.

Jock, however, would not suffer the word 'Asylum' to be uttered in his presence.

'My wife,' he said with a shudder, 'in one of those places? You can have no idea of the sensitivity of her nature if you can even consider the possibility for one moment. It would kill her. And me in consequence.'

So he refused to look any further than the arrival of Mrs Jones, who now appeared to him in the light of a ministering angel. He expected a miracle of her. And Maria did seem to settle, but into a state of what seemed to me unnatural calm. Though my coach was booked, the day for my departure came and went, for I did not like to leave this poor careworn creature to the none too tender mercies of Widow Jones. The very thought filled me with abhorrence.

But at last, as is often the case, Fate or Nature stepped in to have the last word and to force action upon us when we least wished it.

One cold, grey January day, when Maria was convalescent, she managed to evade her guard for long enough to make her way to Jock's studio. I saw this, Reader, and I did not alert the dragon, for Maria placed her finger in mute appeal upon her lips and, – for friendship's sake, – I merely followed her quietly.

'May I come in, Jock?' Maria was quiet today, filled with opiates and weary to the core.

I could see Jock look at her for a moment and wonder, as I myself had done recently, whether even a manic wife was not preferable to this dispirited drudge.

'Come in, come in,' he remarked heartily, flinging open the door and ushering her into his studio.

210

Once inside, Maria stood uncertainly on the threshold, un-decided where to place herself.

'There's a lovely fire.' Her husband drew up a chair by the hearth and Maria obediently sank into it. 'Such a bitter day!' His voice took on that unnaturally loud quality in which people so often address small children or idiots.

'There is nothing wrong with my hearing,' said Maria with a quiet dignity. And she took out her sewing while Jock resumed his stance at the easel. For a short time, nothing disturbed the serenity of the scene. It was a picture of domestic bliss sadly ruptured by the entry of Widow Jones with her sleeves rolled back over her enormous biceps and her face flushed with anxiety.

'Mrs Phillip,' she protested, 'I've been looking for you all over.' And without further ado, she seized Maria by the arm.

'Jock says I may rest here,' the poor woman protested dully as she was hauled to her feet and her sewing tumbled in disarray about her feet.

'Come along now, do as you're told!' Mrs Jones stooped to retrieve Maria's work while she stood by utterly helpless with tears coursing down her thin cheeks.

'Mrs Jones,' objected Jock, barely able to endure the sight. 'I gave my wife permission to sit with me.'

Mrs Jones' face tightened with displeasure, but she seated herself quietly by the fire, opposite her charge. Jock once more settled to his work, and had just taken up his brush when Maria suddenly got to her feet, and moved across to perch on the windowledge.

Her husband looked up impatiently, but said nothing beyond asking her gruffly to move out of his light.

Maria scuttled to the other end of the window, placing Jock and his easel directly between herself and her keeper. Then she took up her needle and spread the embroidery carefully over her knee. She was working a Spanish fantasy designed for her by her husband during the period that she had been confined to bed. The colours were hectic and the swirling patterns made my head spin, but it pleased Jock to see Maria profitably employed on one of his own compositions, and his pleasure in this respect must have afforded her some satisfaction.

211

In spite of the snow piled on the outside sill, Jock's studio was roasting hot for he always painted in his shirt sleeves. In consequence, Maria, who had been as warmly dressed by Mrs Jones as an infant in its crib, soon began to perspire. The needle slithered between her fingers as she passed it back and forth, and before long it began uttering tiny shrieks of protest at each stitch.

By the fire, Widow Jones, comfortably ensconced in one of the best armchairs, began to snore.

I was aware of the tension in the room as if a barometer before my eyes were measuring the pressure. Yet I knew not what to do, how to act.

Maria's needle groaned like a fog-horn.

Jock stabbed blindly at his canvas piling colour upon colour indiscriminately until at last he stepped back and saw that the whole composition was quite ruined. He uttered a bellow of rage, at which Maria looked up in surprise.

'How can I work?' he roared at her. 'How can I get anything done in this madhouse?'

Mrs Jones' head jerked up off her chest and she smiled with a quiet satisfaction. Mr Phillip would perhaps learn to rely on her professional judgement from now on, she remarked loudly. After all, she knew what she was talking about.

Poor Maria, whose spirits were so delicate that they could be ruffled by the mere dropping of a pin, was unable to bear such an outburst. She retreated instead into a world in which persecution was to be her lot. Expecting constant rebuke, she hoped for no better. Even the slightest act of kindness now seemed to her a rebuke for some deeper omission. None of my ministrations could bring her any comfort, and Jock's presence or absence alike were equally intolerable to her.

When matters came to this pass, I left. I returned to the bosom of my family and took up the threads of my own life like one who walks in her sleep. I saw and felt the love and kindness of my dear ones all about me. Thus was I spared the final scene in the drama of Maria's madness.

When the news came that all was over, it was as if I had already been witness to that event in the grey shadowplay of my imagination. For Maria was committed to the asylum of her husband's choice. And for this, he returned her to that grim, grey granite city of his childhood, as far from family and friends as it was possible for her to be. He consigned her to spend the rest of her days in a country that was as foreign to her body as the landscape of madness was to her tortured mind. I have often asked myself, why?

Chapter Nine

IT was twenty years before I saw Maria again. Repeatedly, I asked myself what prompted Jock to send her so far away from all that she knew and loved. It was a cruel act, to subject that body already stretched upon the rack of a tormented spirit to the harsh exigencies of a northern climate. To the mind that is already wandering without anchor, how then shall it find its way when the very landscape is harsh and unyielding and even the constellations cannot be our guides? Perhaps Jock already knew that he was not destined to live long and transported his wife to his own homeland where his family might care for her after his demise.

As for me, over two decades elapsed before I was able to consider a journey of such length. I undertook my pilgrimage in 1883, the year which encompassed both my husband's last illness and his death. Both these events heralded for me a new freedom. I found myself released from those sickroom duties which had occupied the previous five years of my life, and though I would not like to imply that my husband's death was a cause for anything but grief to those of us who knew and loved him, for me the emergence into the world that lay beyond those four walls was, once the initial pangs of disabling grief were past, like a rebirth. I also discovered myself to be the possessor, if not of untold riches, of more than enough for my own modest needs and quite sufficient to guarantee my independence for as long as my health allowed.

My children being by then all comfortably settled, for the first time in my life I had only my own wishes to consult. Consult them I did, and thereafter followed their directives. My family, however, had quite different expectations. They greeted my newfound release with attempts to impose shackles of a different kind. They expected me to devote myself entirely to their concerns, and especially to my several grandchildren. That same covey of little people has ever been a source of immense joy to me, – and how often during those sleepless nights and days spent in attempting to alleviate J.'s many physical discomforts had I regretted that I could not devote more time to them! But to my mind, one of the privileges of being a grandparent is to indulge and enjoy without that responsibility which so plagues parenthood. I thus resisted every effort to divide my time equally between the households of my children, and insisted on maintaining a separate household in the cottage which had been my home for the best part of four decades.

I fear that I then further scandalised them by announcing that I had decided to spend some months in travelling and renewing such old acquaintances as had been spared by the scythe of Time.

Age is a sad and tedious thing; longevity no boon when, one by one, friends and relatives fall away until one is left, as it were, the sole craggy oak on the skyline, gnarled and battered by wind and storm and with none to share the memories of happier times. Those few who remain become infinitely more precious, and for this reason I was not to be shaken in my resolve to renew acquaintance with those two dear childhood friends, Maria and Richard Dadd.

From Devon, I first proceeded to London, there to visit my sister Catherine. She professed herself to be scandalised both by my refusal to wear widow's weeds (she herself had spent the last seven years costumed in a dreary habiliment of black bombazine), and by my, as she put it, 'gadding about' with such unwidow-like frivolity.

'Frivolity?' said I. 'Is it then frivolous to make the best use of one's remaining years in attempting to draw together the various strands of one's life, and ultimately to find some pattern and significance to it all?'

She merely laughed at my presumption. 'Pattern?' she echoed. 'Significance! I am content to live from day to day and leave such things to the Almighty.'

I was well used to my sister's fatalistic observations and merely continued with my knitting.

'All for a madwoman!' remarked she, scornfully.

'No,' I was goaded to reply. 'Not unless the madwoman you refer to is myself. I go entirely for my own satisfaction.'

Reader, this was not entirely true. There was deep within me the hope born of pride that perhaps I could, even now, help my friend where all other hands had failed; that somewhere way in our shared past lay the key to her present misery, and that I alone guarded that secret. There was no one else to help her, if I could not. Robert, Stephen, George and Arthur were dead. Mary Ann lived with John in Milwaukee. And though Sarah was alive and remained as companion to Stephen's widow in Manchester, her relationship with Maria had never been close, and as far as I knew, there had been no contact between them for many years.

I had already gathered that I was the sole recipient of those painful epistles which tumbled through my letter box at regular intervals. I did not keep them, for they contained little of interest, being simply the outpourings of a tormented soul. They were repetitive and often incoherent, raging against the Pope and against her nurses with equal venom.

My own less frequent replies contained light-hearted attempts at diversion, together with such items as I considered might have the effect of focusing her mind on the more practical aspects of daily living. I remarked on which vegetables were ripe for harvesting in the garden and described my consequent labours in the kitchen. I tried to interest her in those minutiae which I observed during my moorland rambles, whether the tracks of a fox in the snow or the first flowering of the violet in spring. She never commented upon my epistles, and I observed a similar reticence with respect to her own.

I booked a place on a packet steamer for the voyage north. My family recommended that I should travel at least part of the way by train. I persisted in my plan. Ship building has been in the blood for generations. I was myself born but a stone's throw from the Royal Dockyards, and I grew up hearing all about me the details of the trade. The high points in our family calendar were the dates of launchings, to which the lesser events of anniversaries and festivals took second place. It was a great delight to my father that my husband, his son-in-law, should have been of like mind, and it was indeed to J.'s unfaltering perseverance in that respect that I owed my present affluence.

'What is good enough for our Queen, is good enough for me,' I asserted, referring to our beloved monarch's attachment to her most northerly dominions, and her mode of transport when visiting the same. Let them say what they like about railways being the transport of the future, my resolve to travel by sea was unshakeable, and one day in early September I boarded my chosen vessel in the Port of London.

All went well until we were nearing the Firth of Forth, when a fearful squall blew up from the north east. It was if Nature conspired either to blow us back to our port of departure or, if that failed, to consign us to the bottom of the sea with all possible haste. Then I discovered that not all the technical knowledge in the world, not a life-time's familiarity with the intricacies of ship-building could preserve me from that scourge of sea-borne travellers of which I had previously made light. Sea-sickness attacked me with such violence that I feared to find myself turned quite inside out before we reached our destination.

But arrive we did, eventually, though even that first sight of the harbour and town of Aberdeen was far from reassuring, since it echoed the very greyness of the steely depths of the North Sea. Wave upon wave of granite buildings massed themselves in sombre array about the little harbour above which the seagulls wheeled and shrieked like the lace-whipped froth on the top of mountainous seas.

It was several days before the effects of excessive turbulence subsided sufficiently for me to undertake the short walk from my hotel to the private wing of the hospital which held my childhood confidante. It was an especial cause of wonder to me that though I had left the capital enjoying the balmy days of a glorious late summer richness, here Autumn already held full sway. I at once regretted the fact that no one had seen fit to advise me to include some good warm clothing among my luggage, and was forced to the extravagance of purchasing a woollen overcoat to remedy the deficiency. I had, you see, reached the age where one tries to avoid such expenditure on the grounds that one's remaining years do not warrant such purchases. It may be, however, that since the quality of the tweed is quite exceptional, some relative will have the benefit therefrom, after my departure.

Though the wind off the sea seemed to seek out relentlessly every thoroughfare down which I passed, I now discovered the city to be less daunting than I had at first imagined. And even if nothing could soften that austere climate, there was a pleasant feeling of openness about the wide streets and their handsome houses which was pleasing to the eye. The inhabitants, though grim-looking (which was not to be wondered at), were courteous and helpful.

The hospital itself was a fine building, set among its own acres of farmland and gardens. A further cry from Bedlam could scarcely be imagined, and from this point of view, I approved Jock's choice. The private wing which housed Maria was set apart from the charity blocks, and was a pleasant, mellow building, finely proportioned, and set among delightful parkland.

Inside the mansion there were, of course, the usual locks and bolts to remind one that one was not after all in some luxury hotel, but all was discreetly managed, and the atmosphere, to a visitor at least, was not oppressive. Even so, I was glad that Mrs Phillip was reported to be at that moment out for her afternoon walk, and I was advised to seek her in the garden among her favourite trees and flowerbeds.

Thither bending my steps, I at length came upon her.

She was standing among a grove of beech trees just inside the high granite wall which marked the perimeter of the garden. Within the garden it was sheltered, but the leaves of those great boughs which had been exposed to the cutting edge of the very gale which had caused me such misery at sea, had prematurely died. Even today's light sea breeze now sufficed to shake them free in a capricious downward flight which seemed to say 'Beware! Autumn is here!'

It was a harsh sentence when the flowerbeds beneath were still in their full autumn glory. Heavy-headed dahlias and shaggy-toothed chrysanthemums still flaunted their splendours and impatiently shrugged off those few early harbingers of doom with every confidence in their own immortality. Others may fall, but we? – ah no! And they seemed to shake and preen themselves in the sunshine.

I watched my erstwhile companion threading her way between the massive grey green beech trunks. A poor, withered creature, with more affinity to those prematurely aged leaves than to these

218

flowers still confident in their own passing glory. For though she was younger than myself, Autumn sat like a dead weight upon her shoulders and her face was as criss-crossed with crisp lines as the veins of a dying leaf. She moved stiffly, her walking stick held out before her, not as if she were feeling her way like a blind man, but using it like an extension to her finger tips. Sensitive as a dog's snout, she moved it constantly from side to side through the grass, sniffing and snuffling, burrowing and turning over, searching continuously for I knew not what.

All at once she was distracted. A leaf fluttered down and settled on her head. She batted it off impatiently, but it crumbled beneath her hand and became embedded in her hair. She looked up then, and caught sight of its partners which still drifted in the air like little golden butterflies against the day's cloudless blue sky, and as she saw them the old woman smiled. The smile was like an eraser. It swept away those lines of care like a flat iron passing over ruffled damask. Maria became almost beautiful for that fleeting moment and I hesitated to approach and disturb the thoughts which produced such an expression.

What was she seeing in her mind's eye? Surely not that cold alien garden. Perhaps another lawn, in another place, in another time; perhaps a sun-filled, leafy garden in distant Kent? Oh that garden! Why do so many childhood memories seem to take place out of doors? And why in every scene was there sunlight and warmth and happiness?

Imagine the happiness of a small group of children assembled in a garden in sight of the gateway, waiting for the return home of a beloved parent. Mr Dadd had never left his children for so long before, not since their Mama had died a year ago. And now he had been gone for a whole twenty-four, – no, twenty-six hours. We all, Dadds and Carters alike, whiled away the time by chasing after the falling leaves. For each leaf caught before it reached the ground was a wish that would be granted. And today of all days, those wishes would come true, for Mr Dadd had promised us a surprise on his return.

At the age of six, I was already in those long skirts which betokened a certain degree of childish maturity while Maria still wore the loose gown and cap which marked her out for the nursery. She quickly tired of the exercise and joined instead her youngest brother, George, who was far more interested in cramming his pockets with treasures – feathers, broken egg shell from a blackbird's nest, coloured stones and pieces of moss.

Richard stayed with the others, even though, as he informed me, his wishes kept changing and he knew that they could not all come true. At the age of nine there was so much in the world to wish for – a donkey or a puppy or a fishing rod, a sailing boat or a new spinning top. He chased after the leaves until he was quite dizzy with excitement and elated with a sense of success. For at that moment, the whole universe was ours for the asking. Everything was possible. King Midas could have aspired no higher.

But at last the clatter of hooves broke the Sunday afternoon silence of the sleepy Chatham street. Catherine, my brothers and I hung back shyly, but Mr Dadd's children ran out to meet him. They raced down the driveway and then stopped suddenly. For as the gig turned in through the gate, they saw not one person, but two seated up there above them. And they shrank together, forming a small, suspicious, silent group.

'Well,' said Mr Dadd as he leapt out and his feet crunched on the gravel. 'Here's a fine welcome!' He held out his arms but no one moved, except little George, who threw himself into his embrace. But then George was too young to know any better.

'Come and meet your new Mama,' instructed their father quietly. He reached out with his free hand towards the others and at last Robert, blushing furiously, moved forward with his own hand extended.

Catherine and I, sensing by now that we were intruding upon a family occasion, faded away into the shrubbery. Meanwhile, the poor discomfited stranger, her face hidden behind a small veil, sat all alone on the front seat of the vehicle. Maria considered her for a moment then made an uncertain movement forward, but Richard grabbed her arm and hissed in her ear, 'She's probably a witch! Behind that veil she's got a hare-lip and warts!' And that was indeed how he would have wished anyone to be who dared to take the place of his beloved Mama.

My sister and I hurried home, anxious to break this momentous news to our parents. 'Mr Dadd has got a new wife,' we shrieked even as we entered the hall, unable to contain our excitement any longer. This was, of course, a fact already familiar to the adults, but one which, for reasons known only to themselves, they had seen fit to conceal from us children. I did not think then, nor am I of the opinion now, that it was right of Mr Dadd to keep his children in ignorance of such a major change in their lives. I have ever found with my own family that discussion and the frank interchange of views, painful though they may be at times, lead to a greater harmony in the long run. When it comes to dealing with such sensitive creatures as Richard and Maria, I believe that the effect of the feelings excited by this sudden appearance of a new mother was of major importance to their subsequent development. Certainly, everyone who knew the family as well as we did at the time, noted the sudden change in their behaviour.

'And Richard's run away,' we then added, which did cause some surprise. For Richard had been off, shinning over the wall and then hurtling down the narrow street towards the harbour. 'He's run away to sea,' we told our astonished parents.

But as it turned out, he was sent back by one of the sentries at the Royal Dockyard gates. Not that he returned home even then; – he climbed back into the garden by means of the kitchen wall and hid himself in one of the apple trees, from where he had the satisfaction of hearing his father call for him by the hour.

It was the smell of apple pie which brought about his capitulation. However much he loved his mother, his stomach screamed for a piece of pie as he lay there cold and hungry, breathing in the smells from the nearby kitchen window; and just as Ellen was carrying the pie across the hall to the dining room, he sneaked up behind her so suddenly that she let out a little scream.

'Please, Ellen,' he whispered, 'just a little piece.'

'And take in Cook's beautiful creation with a slice missing?' she asked indignantly.

In the end, Ellen persuaded Richard to follow the pie into the dining room and to join his family at the table.

She poked him hard in the back as he sat down. 'What do you say?' she prompted.

'I'm sorry I am late, Father,' the boy mumbled.

'I think, Richard,' said his father, laying down his napkin, 'that if it is your wish to deprive us of your presence, then we would not like to detain you here.'

Richard pushed back his chair. Ellen slid a knife through the pie crust releasing the smell of cinnamon and apples. Richard's eyes began to water as much as his mouth, as he rose to his feet.

'No, Robert,' came a quiet but confident voice from the opposite end of the table. 'At my first meal in your house, I would like to have all my children about me.'

Ellen put a helping of pie in front of the new Mrs Dadd, who added a spoonful of cream so large that the children looked towards their Papa with fearful eyes. Then she calmly stood up and walked round the table until she stood behind Richard's chair, and put her own plate in front of him.

'We are glad to have you with us, Richard,' she said.

But Richard at once got up, and with tears streaming down his face, fled to the safety of his bedroom.

After that episode, he took to tormenting all of us younger children. 'Mama's ghost will come and haunt you,' he warned us, if ever we showed more affection towards his step-mother than was strictly necessary for politeness' sake. He even dragged us into the bedroom where his mother had died to impress upon us the truth of what he said.

At that stage, the second Mrs Dadd had not ventured to put away his Mama's hairbrushes and jewel box, which still lay on the dressing table, together with a broken string of pearls coiled in a glass jar. But there was still something about the air in that room which spoke of death. In spite of his step-mother's powders and perfumes and the scattering of her belongings about the chairs and on every conceivable surface, some indefinable taint remained.

'Can you smell it too?' asked Richard.

An unsavoury scent at once clotted at the back of our nostrils. 'What is it?' we asked with rising panic.

'Death!' he replied with all the authority of his nine years.

The situation was not helped by the behaviour of the elderly Dadd relatives who descended upon the house to inspect the new mistress, but who persisted in observing in full the period of mourning which extended until after the unfortunate bride's honeymoon was over.

The relatives were mainly of the female variety. They filled the sofa and overflowed the chairs with their huge dresses of black crape which made the whole room dark, and we children, such a crowd of us, hid behind the sofas in the hope of getting a few of the leftovers from the party.

'Well, at least she's out of her misery,' observed Aunt Smith, of her niece, the first Mrs Dadd, looking closely around the room for any signs of incompetence in her successor. 'In my opinion,' she continued, 'seven children in nine years is little short of murder.'

'Not one easy birth among them, poor soul! I'm surprised she survived so many.'

'She should have had the sense to say no, if you ask me.'

'Men are animals.'

'Monsters!'

'Separate beds. That's the only answer.'

'Separate rooms if you ask me. And a big lock on the door!'

'My niece was very religious,' observed Aunt Smith hotly, defending her niece's character. 'But she would never shrink from her duty.'

'I've heard,' said another, 'that the new Mrs Dadd is very attractive.'

'And how old is she, pray?'

'Eighteen.'

'Poor girl!'

'For the children, of course, it must be wonderful.'

'If he'd been thinking of the children, he would have found someone a bit more motherly.' Aunt Smith spotted a thin film of dust on top of the clock and closed her mouth firmly upon the pronouncement with a certain triumph.

'You mark my words, he's married her for one thing only . . .'

But though we strained our ears for this final revelation, what that one thing was, we never discovered. But by the time the relatives left, all the old dears were calling her Sophia dear and Sophia darling, and offering her help whenever she needed, – which would surely not be before too long, they hinted.

But first of all came Christmas, only four months after her marriage, and she worked hard to make it a success. The decorations were a triumph. Paper flowers and stars, some dainty, others more clumsy and obviously proceeding from the scissors of little George, hung everywhere. She discovered in Richard a talent for drawing and he produced a whole host of Christmas figures, — toys and angels and Santa Clauses in happy profusion.

On Christmas Eve the last tangerine was bound up in red ribbon and hung upon the tree, and we were all gathered together at the Dadds' house, it being slightly larger than our own and better able to accommodate such a party. Beneath the tree was a stack of brightly coloured parcels on which the children's eyes feasted.

How each heart beat as Mr Dadd adjusted his spectacles and read the labels! Maria's package was gratifyingly large. She took off the paper carefully and folded it neatly away before removing the lid of the box. Inside lay a china doll so breathtakingly beautiful that she replaced the lid as quickly as she could, as if afraid that her eyes were deceiving her.

'Don't you like it, Maria?' asked her step-mother, fearful that she had failed to please her, for the little girl's eyes were filled with tears. I knew that they were tears of wonder and disbelief.

I watched poor Richard's face as his father worked his way up through the branches, past the yachts and toy cannons and packets of lead soldiers. And there, just beneath the star, was the smallest, lightest parcel and the one which bore his name.

'Open it, Richard! Show us what you've got!' I tried to encourage him. I had opened my own present at once and now held out the lace shawl for him to see. He watched with eyes glazed with misery as I swung it over my shoulders, then fastened the corners together at the front with a brooch.

Richard shrugged and blinked to keep back the tears. 'At least it's too small to be anything as stupid as a shawl,' he remarked.

'Aren't you going to open it, silly?' I whispered to him. Mr Dadd and his new young wife were watching him anxiously. Richard then managed to fix his face in a hideous grin of enthusiasm before tearing at the red and green paper.

Inside was a magnifying glass. He laid it on his knee and bit his lip to keep back the tears.

'Well?' said his father. 'What do you say to your Mama?'

'Thank you,' said the boy huskily. He wandered over to the window and crept behind the velvet curtains so that none should see his disappointment. I followed him, and there in that little alcove we stood, watching the snowflakes land silently against the window pane. If the fall continued, tomorrow there would be tobogganing. That at least was something to look forward to. Richard idly raised his magnifying glass and suddenly saw a thing of such wonder, that it took his breath away. 'Look, Elizabeth,' he breathed. 'Look!' It was a white seven-pointed star finer and more fragile than any lace shawl, clinging there brightly against the darkness outside. The miracle was repeated as each flake fluttered gently against the pane.

When he tired of the snowflakes, Richard moved the lens on to the wooden window frame and discovered the narrow gap between the planks, where the woodlice lay curled in their winter nests and a silken purse of spider eggs hung suspended precariously behind the shutters, waiting for Spring.

Back in the room, the party began with Oranges and Lemons. But we sat in the window, cocooned in the darkness, – two children filled with an infinite content, happy in the silence of one another's company. It was a moment of happiness which I have never forgotten.

But if Sophia had sought to win over her stepson's affections by the gift, she was disappointed. For though Richard was not to be parted from his magnifying lens, he retreated more and more into the little world which it encircled and enlarged, and he drew Maria after him.

With the arrival of Summer, they wandered about the garden hand in hand, peering at this and that. Whole microcosms appeared like magic before their eyes. And just looking was not enough. They wanted to enter that miniature world and become part of it.

Sophia, from her bedroom window, where she sat feeling hot and cumbersome in the late stages of pregnancy, watched the children on their hands and knees as they scoured the lawn for that magic pass into fairyland, the four-leafed clover.

Oh the birth of Arthur! Fifty years ago, there was not that happy anticipation which heralds the arrival of a baby nowadays.

Then, every confinement carried within it the threat of death; every pregnancy was a pilgrimage of the soul, a preparation for that eternal sleep from which there is no awakening. I do not think it was mere prudishness that kept children in ignorance of the prospect of a new brother or sister, it was rather the wish to spare them anxiety, – as if we could not but be aware of the darkening of Mr Dadd's expression in proportion as Sophia's time neared.

Even the birth of my own beloved children was not without its attendant dangers, nor without that pain to which Eve's transgression predestined us, and for which there was no relief. How things have changed! My daughter presents me with grand-children with as little discomfort as the drawing of a tooth. She emerges from childbed as radiant as a bride. Chloroform is the answer, apparently. She swears by it. It is but another thing for which we women owe a debt of thanks to our beloved Queen.

But in the 'thirties, it was different. And besides sharing the common apprehension of the mortal danger in which Sophia stood, our own recent experience stood powerfully before our eyes in the person of the first Mrs Dadd. So it was that, at the first intimations of the birth of the child, we children were all despatched into the countryside, under the pretext of having a picnic.

'Come follow, follow, follow . . .'

We all raced up the hill which overlooked the town, shouting and singing. We girls hitched up our skirts as we ran, the boys had their jackets undone and the buttons of their shirts unfastened. It was one of those rare summer days when the air sparkles and the sun picks out every detail of the landscape with a fine clarity. Our progress was marked by a heaven-borne trail of skylarks which had risen in alarm from the sheep-cropped turf to trill in our wake.

As we reached the crest of the downs, we fell silent, dazed for a moment by the enormous expanse of quivering, shimmering sea and the specks which were sailing-ships way out in the distance. Then we were off again, hurtling down towards the cliff top. 'Whither shall I follow, follow, follow . . .' until we reached the very brink of the cliff itself with the seagulls whirling and swooping directly below us.

At a spot safely removed from the precipice, we spread our skirts and sat down in a circle, like the petals of a multi-coloured flower, – Mary Ann, Sarah, Catherine and myself, with the picnic baskets at the centre of the ring. Together we plied little George with ginger ale and biscuits to keep him with us, while Maria jostled for a place on her elder sister's knee. The older boys had disappeared.

'Do you think she will die?' whispered Catherine in horrified tones.

'She might,' Mary Ann mouthed. 'After all, Mother did.'

'How long do we have to stay here?' I asked. I enjoyed a picnic as much as anybody, but didn't like the feeling of having been sent out of the way.

'Having a baby can take a long time.' Mary Ann looked worried.

'Will you miss her, Mary Ann?' I asked.

'Of course. But she's not really like a mother— '

'Who?' Sarah came up with her apron full of daisies.

'Big ears!' said my sister Catherine, slicing up the rabbit pie and passing it around. 'Anyway, who says she's going to die?'

'Who?' Maria quite lost interest in the food and stamped her foot.

'Ask no questions, tell no lies,' said Mary Ann.

'Someone dying?' The boys miraculously reappeared the second the pie was served.

'No, Richard. No one is dying,' said Mary Ann firmly. 'Who could possibly die on a day like this?'

But the answer was of course their step-mother; as a year earlier it had been their mother.

On that occasion, I had found Maria in the garden, burying her beautiful porcelain doll under a rhododendron bush.

'If babies kill their mothers, then they have no right to be born!' she said, slamming the earth mound down with the flat of the spade. She was wearing her new black silk to greet Richard on his return home from boarding school.

Maria threw down her spade and paced restlessly up and down the lawn. I kept her company, idly kicking at the spiked cases of fallen conkers. Then at last a carriage drew up and out stepped a young man who paid Maria not the slightest attention, but turned instead to help his parent down.

'Richard?' she said shyly.

'Sarah,' he said, his face lighting up.

'No,' Maria laughed shrilly. 'It's Maria. I'm Maria.' And side by side, but as distant as strangers, they left me and walked together up the steps into the house.

How many thoughts can be aroused by something as insignificant as a falling leaf! I don't know if Maria's thoughts were in any way the same as mine, for I did not disturb her in that moment of inward serenity. I waited quietly on the garden path until the peaceful expression left her face and she resumed that same anxious, muttering search for I knew not what.

'Are you looking for something?' I then ventured, stepping forward to her side.

'New here, are you?' she replied suspiciously.

Reader, she did not know me! Though I explained who I was, and further racked my brain for little incidents that might recall me to her memory, all was in vain. I could have been the Queen, as she indeed suggested I was, moved perhaps by my increasing plumpness of figure and similarity of age to Her Majesty. Nor did she seem the least disconcerted by the presence of such an august personage, since she reproved me for delaying so long in answering her summons.

After following her obsessive ramblings, and searching in vain for other more coherent paths which we might take, we retired at last to her room, for after sunset, a deadly chill pervades that northern town. There was a bright fire burning in her grate, but we were denied too close a proximity to its warmth by a large fireguard. Her attendant, who never withdrew from earshot, but strove always to maintain a most modest and inconspicuous presence, whispered that it was because they feared that Mrs Phillip might harm herself.

'*Auto da fé!*' said Maria with a wicked glint in her eyes. As she took off her gloves, her hands were revealed to be covered in bandages. 'I have endeavoured,' she informed me, 'to get used to the agony, so that when I am at last consigned to the flames I shall at least know what to expect.' And she settled herself on

228

the opposite side of the fire, whence she darted continual strange looks at her attendant.

There ensued the oddest and most wearisome conversation which it has ever been my lot to engage in. Maria bent her face close to mine, indicating with various grimaces that such subterfuge was necessary to evade the vigilance of her keeper. She then proceeded to pour a stream of troublesome nonsense into my ear. She vowed that all those about here were merely paid spies, puppets of the Cardinals, there to catch her out. She swore that I was failing in my duty as Monarch to tolerate such treatment of my subjects in my own realm. She was therefore, she affirmed, thrust back upon her only defence, – the defence that since she was herself a mother, she was therefore the Mother Mary, and as such, immune from their profane touch. And yet, if she was Mary, where was her baby, her son?

'You have a son, Maria,' I pointed out gently, trying in this manner to draw her back to reality. 'His name is Colin.'

'Colin?' she asked.

'Jock's son. Your husband's,' I added since the name seemed to mean nothing to her.

'I have no husband, therefore I am a virgin,' she stated. 'The Virgin Mary.'

'You had a husband,' I insisted, 'Jock Phillip.'

'Jock Phillip.' She meditated on the name a while. 'He married my brother, Richard,' she stated at last.

I laughed at the preposterous notion. 'He married you,' I insisted.

Maria shook her head and laughed raucously as if my statement was some sort of joke.

'And you had two children,' I persevered, for I had brought photographs to show her. 'First, Colin' – I here drew out the appropriate picture.

She looked at the handsome face with its profusion of side-burns and whiskers which were the height of contemporary fashion, and then looked back at me suspiciously, as if I was trying to trick her. 'That isn't a child,' she asserted at last.

Reader, the look in her eyes as she said this nearly broke my heart. 'He is a big boy now, Maria,' I explained. 'He is grown up and a father himself.'

Maria cradled an imaginary baby in her arms and rocked it to and fro, singing the while.

'Rock-a-bye baby,' she sang.

'Maria,' I said sharply, trying to bring her back to me. 'There is no baby in your arms. There is nothing!'

'Nothing?' she echoed with a frightened look. 'If there is nothing, then they will burn me at the stake. But they cannot for I am with child.'

I reproved her. 'You are rising seventy, Maria, that is simply not possible.'

'The Immaculate Conception,' said she. 'Have you not heard of the Immaculate Conception?'

'A popish doctrine,' I said sharply.

'A miracle,' said she. 'Look!'

I was here forced to call for help, since she began to divest herself of her garments, vowing immodestly that she would show me the ultimate proof; for though the hair on her head was snow-white, she vowed that other tresses were as golden brown and eternally youthful as ever.

At this point, I saw the folly of my visit and made my escape. However, I tarried several days longer in the city, having left my name and address with Maria's physician, in the hope that during some lucid spell she might ask for me. For two whole weeks I waited on her summons, but it never came. During that period I indulged myself as a tourist, and sought to make the most of my stay by acquainting myself with the history and geography of Aberdeen. But never a day passed which did not see me pacing along the foot of that same wall under which I had met her. I bent all my thoughts to her as I imagined her perhaps six feet away, strolling among those same flowerbeds, as if through my own willpower I could alert her to my presence.

After the fortnight had passed, I notified the hospital that I was leaving the following day by the morning tide. Fortunately, my voyage was this time blessed with calm seas and a strong following wind which seemed to share my own desire to put as many miles between myself and my poor, dear friend as possible.

But though the gale had long since subsided, that tempest which raged in my mind continued unabated. I cursed myself for my arrogance in coming here, in persevering in my own misconceptions against all odds and all advice, just as I had done so many years ago. For then also, I had remained in London under the conviction that there was still something which I could do for my unfortunate friend. To have reached such an age and still to have acquired no more wisdom than this!

But the sea itself exerted a calming effect upon the turmoil in my breast. No one could look, day after day, upon that serene blue without drawing some benefit therefrom. Day after day, I saw about me the vast sweep of the horizon. Day after day, despite the currents which still stirred in the depths of my soul, they were gradually overlaid by that same surface smoothness that surrounded our vessel. I concentrated on that lustre which is but a mirror image of the heavens above, and felt the gentle slap of water against the ship's hull soothe my soul like a lullaby.

I disembarked in the Port of London quite restored to my usual sanguine and cheerful self and vowed that even my experiences in Aberdeen would not deflect me from the other purpose of my tour. Having visited one of my surviving friends, I was now determined, with all possible speed, to renew acquaintance with the other. Thus, without informing my family of my intention, I merely wrote a card acquainting them with my safe return to the capital and after one night spent at an inn in the neighbourhood of Waterloo Station, I betook myself from there by train to Berkshire.

I approached this interview with Richard with more caution, and did my best to detach myself from that state of starry-eyed idealism in which I had called upon his sister. But though unreal expectations can to a certain extent be conquered by reason, I found it impossible to suppress a sense of tremulous excitement as the high brick walls and those terrible gates flanked by twin watchtowers reared up out of the Berkshire greenery. My trepidation increased all the more after I had rung that dismal bell, and found myself seated in a small, locked hallway, where my letter of introduction was perused by various officials and the small bag which I carried was emptied out on the table in front of me and its contents inspected.

I at once regretted my speed in hastening hither as this strange jumble gave evidence of my magpie-like disposition. I have never been a good packer of suitcases, and my handbag was in consequence crammed with all those objects I had discovered about my hotel room that morning after I had already closed my valise and despatched it to the waiting carriage.

It therefore contained, – beside those embarrassing oddments and articles of an extremely personal nature which bore witness to an old woman's vanity, – a miniature Bible in the Presbyterian version which I had purchased in Aberdeen to have by me during the voyage home lest that venture proved yet more perilous than my journey thither; a crumpled and stained handkerchief whose condition caused me the utmost mortification; various hairpins and odd buttons which had detached themselves from my person over several years and which I had deposited in my bag for safe keeping and promptly forgotten; there was also a score of old letters once neatly packaged, whose ribbon had long since come untied; a black rimmed card announcing my husband's death which they perused with no more feeling than if it had been a shopping list, and finally my embroidery, from whose folds they extracted a packet of needles and a small pair of gold scissors which were returned to me only on my departure.

I have never since been able to look upon my sewing implements with the same equanimity as before. What were once mere tools of trade have now taken on a more sinister meaning, and whereas I once left my sewing lying about with the utmost carelessness, I now find myself carefully shutting it away out of sight. Since my visit to that Institution, I have developed a similar horror of cutlery, – and even the stones upon my garden path have taken on a new and threatening aspect since I learned that the former Superintendent of Broadmoor Hospital was mortally wounded in the chapel by an inmate who had constructed a cosh made of a woollen sock laden with pieces of gravel.

All this attention put me in a state of considerable apprehension, as did my guide's asseveration that 'You need eyes in the back of your head for this job!' as he led me through locked door after locked door, each of which was fastened again behind us. I have never cultivated an attitude of suspicion and watchfulness and I fear that at my advanced age, it was too late for me to begin to do so. My life had, you see, required no such defensive measures; I had never felt myself to be under physical threat before. I therefore remained close to my guide, who towered over me with his vast bunch of keys, and thus in his shadow proceeded door by door and lock by lock until we at last met with the intelligence that, the weather being so fine, Mr Dadd was not to be found indoors after all, but outside taking the air on the terraces.

We emerged from the bowels of that terrible building to a breathtaking view. For the whole acreage of buildings and gardens was set on a south-facing hillside so that from the front of the building at least, the impression was one of openness and freedom.

How welcome was that rush of free air to my lungs! How wonderful the open sweep of the countryside after those endless corridors! And as we descended step after step, the grim buildings fell away behind us, and at last my conductor introduced me to a Mr Samuel Smith, who was responsible, he informed me, for Mr Dadd's supervision.

'I am an old friend,' I explained, 'old in every sense of the word. I have not seen Mr Dadd these past forty years.'

The man responded most civilly. 'And I,' he informed me with the greatest courtesy though in a broad Cockney accent, 'have known him almost as long. Indeed,' he added with a wry smile, 'we have, you might say, grown old together. If it weren't that I knew him like the back of my hand, I would have been drawing my pension long since – but I applied to accompany him here from Bedlam, having become attached to him as you might say over the years, and I plan to continue here for as long as he does.'

'God bless you for your kindness,' I cried out, and seizing one of his hands in mine, I shook it most warmly.

His loyalty put me to shame, for it had become apparent from the surprise which my visit aroused, that Richard had received neither visitors nor letters for many years. Perhaps most of his friends either fancied him dead or were dead themselves by then. Or it may be that he had simply been abstracted from the world for too long to figure any more in their thoughts.

When my vision had cleared sufficiently for me to look around, – and during this interval, Mr Smith remained discreetly absorbed in the view, – I next inquired where my friend was to be found. Leading me round a small shrubbery, he brought me to him.

'Your name, madam?' inquired Mr Smith.

'Mrs L.,' I answered, following close at his heels.

'Mrs L. to see you, sir.' Mr Smith spoke the words very gently, having discovered Richard to be fast asleep in the somnolent warmth of the early afternoon sun. And as he spoke, he gently shook him by the shoulder.

Richard looked up startled. 'God bless my soul, eh? What's up, Sam?'

'Mrs L. to see you, sir.'

Richard's eyes flickered over me once, without interest, and then closed again.

'He might know me better as Elizabeth. Elizabeth Carter,' said I, stepping forward more boldly. For even his first words had assured me that here was a creature capable of rational thought.

'Elizabeth,' said Mr Smith more loudly into Richard's ear, 'Elizabeth Carter come to see you, sir.'

For some minutes Richard did not respond. Then his eyes opened with a look of curiosity that brought a laugh to my lips. I could not help it. There we were, two old people, each inspecting the other for some lingering sign of those youthful bodies that had once been so drawn, each to the other. And what did we see? I saw a corpulent figure in cord trousers, with somewhat lank white hair and heavy features. But when those blue eyes met mine, I knew him at once.

'Lizzie?' he said in astonishment. 'Little Lizzie Carter!'

'Dicky,' I admonished him, casting an eye at his large paunch.

'Elizabeth,' he reproved me sternly, for I was no sylph myself.

He took my hands in his; my poor, liver-spotted arthritic hands, which I would have liked to have hidden from his sight, – only I saw then that his were no better.

'Still painting, Richard?' I inquired for I doubted whether those poor hands retained the facility for the fineness of detail which characterised his works.

'Fire buckets,' said he.

'Fire buckets?' We laughed over the fact together. 'For the Royal Academy?' I ventured as I wiped my eyes.

'Of a sort,' replied he. 'Those which pass the approval of the Board are exhibited along every corridor. I am surprised you did not notice them. I am become quite famous in these parts for my works of art: fire buckets, chair backs, murals, Christmas decorations all made to order. You could probably do as well yourself.'

'Age,' responded I, 'the great leveller!'

'Ever the philosopher, Elizabeth?' he inquired.

'Ever,' I replied, 'openly conservative and submissive, but inwardly rebellious and cowardly.'

'It is a deception which I too have learnt to my advantage.'

'Maria has not learnt that,' I told him, and with great sadness related the full history of my visit to her.

'Maria would never compromise,' Richard agreed. 'She was too honest.'

'And you are not?'

'I have acquired the art of dissimulation.' This appeared to cause Richard no pain at all, for he here laughed again and closed his eyes to enjoy the full radiance of the sun.

His answer surprised me. 'In your art?' I was driven to inquire, – and here I must confess that the 'Columbine' was uppermost in my mind, for to learn that that was mere artifice would have caused me the utmost pain.

'In my art, never,' he avowed. 'I was ever true to that mistress. It is life to which I refer.'

'When we were children, Richard . . .' I began, for I wished to return the conversation to a more personal level.

He rebuked me, mildly to be sure, but I still felt the admonition acutely. 'The past is over, Elizabeth,' he said gently: 'it does not do to dwell upon it.'

I inwardly cursed my tactlessness, for how could he, of all people, look back to the past after what had happened, how could such a sensitive nature bear the reality of what he had done?

'I married J.,' I said somewhat lamely. The statement was at once a confession and an appeal for forgiveness.

'Did that make you happy?' he inquired, turning on me those same eyes.

'Happy?' I laughed. 'Over the years I achieved a degree of contentment, which is perhaps more to be valued. I cannot tell.'

For in that moment, I truly doubted the philosophy which had sustained me over a lifetime and which now seemed to me no more than a defence to keep at bay a greater sorrow.

'But were you true to yourself, Elizabeth?' Richard now asked, determined, it seemed, to make me query the very roots of my existence.

'How could I be?' I asked angrily. 'You took that option away from me.'

'I did?' he asked in surprise.

'Yes, you!' I said, now thoroughly heated. For when I lost him, I was deprived of all freedom of choice, and became a mere creature of chance, to be pushed hither and thither by circumstance.

This accusation seemed to give him cause for reflection and it was a while before he spoke again. 'Elizabeth,' he reproved me, taking both my hands firmly in his and looking at me until I felt my anger draining out of my very finger tips. 'You misunderstand me.' Here, I tried to pull myself free, but he would not release me. 'To follow the truth, without compromise, one is always alone.'

Tears of pity for his solitary state here sprang to my eyes.

'Dear me!' he said, handing me his handkerchief. 'You misunderstand me again. I am speaking in a spiritual sense . . .'

He waited for me to recover myself.

'It smells of turpentine, Richard,' I said as I handed the handkerchief back. 'And it still has as many colours as Joseph's coat.'

'Some things,' he said, 'don't change. But aah, feel how God is pleased with us tonight!' And he stretched out his hands palm upwards to the sun.

'Do you really think He cares?'

'The proof is all about me.'

For a few minutes we sat in silence, and the sun was so pleasant that we might have nodded off together, the pair of us, an aged couple sitting on a public bench.

'There are other times, of course,' Richard then said, 'when He gives me proof to the contrary.'

Reader, he went on to give me an explanation for this observation which only made sense to me after several years of investigation. At the time, he spoke of his experiences with a certain chill logic, and his argument had a strange but undeniably sound construction. I told you earlier that it was his belief that he had died in Egypt. Everything that had happened to him since, he had then interpreted in the light of his conviction that he was in the Duat, the Egyptian Underworld, where it was his duty to earn his soul's salvation.

He quoted to me many instances by way of proof. Those locked doors, which were to me hideous reminders of captivity, he saw as separating one stage of spiritual progress from another. He welcomed the opening of the one just as much as the closing of another behind him. And if confirmation were required that he was no longer in the land of the living, he came across that in plenty. As if the title of one particular article in an art magazine was not sufficient, – 'The Late Richard Dadd', – it continued with the words, *'for though the grave has not actually closed over him he must be classed among the dead.'* And all about him there were the excesses of the other inmates who comported themselves in a manner which was further evidence that he was in fact in Hell.

For all this evidence, Richard was extremely grateful. A soul has, he told me, only a certain time in which to work towards its own salvation, a period determined by the continued existence of the physical body. It was this that caused him the greatest anxiety, and had always led him, he vowed, to strive towards the highest possible standards of cleanliness and hygiene.

In his search for salvation, Richard had found two events of particular significance and hope. The first was his removal from Bethlem to the comparative ease of Broadmoor. The second had occurred more recently and he took it as a sign that the gods had not forgotten him. He told me that a new Superintendent had recently been appointed, who had at once set about reviewing all the patients. Only he, he insisted, had been aware of the true nature of this man.

Richard failed at the time to catch his name, but that was irrelevant. He knew at once, – as he drew an enormous ledger towards him and took up his pen, – that the man was Thoth, scribe to the gods as they sat in judgement over the souls of the dead. And as if the pen and ledger were not in themselves sufficient clues to his identity, Thoth had besides a nose as sharp as the beak of an ibis.

'It is my duty,' continued this celestial being, 'to assess your case for . . .'

As he listened, all Richard's fears about the dissolution of his flesh were quite forgotten.

'Name?' Thoth opened up his vast tome, took up the feather of Truth, dipped it in the inkwell and began his questions.

Richard knew better than to speak the words out loud. Knowledge of a person's name conferred power. It was one thing for Thoth to know who he was, quite another matter for his keeper, who sat just behind him, to overhear the same. Therefore, taking a scrap of paper and a pencil from his pocket, he inscribed *Richard Dadd* in his best copperplate, folded the paper carefully and handed it across the table. The scribe made notes all the time.

'Father's name?'

This did put Richard in a quandary. Which father did he mean? He pondered the question at length, under the pretence of being preoccupied with pushing back the cuticles of his left hand with the pencil tip. Thoth meanwhile laid down his pen and waited courteously. The clock ticked loudly. A pale gleam of sunshine crept between the clouds and across the table top towards Richard, and the answer at once came to him.

'Dad.'

The sun seemed to gain in strength at the cleverness of this answer. The scribe wrote in his celestial ledger.

'Dadd what?'

Richard was startled. He looked up at the sun in bewilderment.

'Christian name,' explained the scribe.

Richard had laughed then. A Christian name for Osiris, when he had preceded Christianity by millennia?

'A–*pop*–is,' he replied, stressing the middle syllable so that only that was audible. 'We used to call him Pop sometimes,' he added, for the scribe looked at him curiously. He would not mention that earthly father, for that man was evil, – the serpent of darkness with whom he had battled and won.

'Well, Richard,' Thoth said, when he had carefully blotted all that he had written so far. 'Do you know why you are here?'

Richard nodded vigorously but said nothing. Thoth knew and he knew, but they both knew that no one else should know.

'Well?'

After a lengthy pause, Richard leaned forward and whispered intently, 'To work for the salvation of my soul.'

He could tell at once that his answer was a good one, for Thoth nodded vehemently and his pen set off again at the speed of light.

The God then shifted his chair slightly, so that the legs grated on the floor, and asked, 'What is your opinion of the First Commandment, Mr Dadd?'

Richard had learnt by heart the Forty-Two Negative Confessions of the Dead, and prayed in that moment that his memory would not fail him. He used the ritual response: 'I have not sinned.'

'May I refresh your memory, Mr Dadd,' said his interrogator. 'The First Commandment is, "Thou shalt not kill."'

Richard then realised how naïve he had been. Of course Thoth could not refer to the Negative Confessions so openly. He had then to take them obliquely by an elaborate system of cross-reference: the first of the Ten Commandments became the fifth of the Negative Confessions, and so on. Richard began to sweat.

'I have not sinned, your Honour.'

On that occasion, the doctor, as Thoth, wanted to know every detail of what had happened to Richard in realms spiritual and material over the last decades. On other occasions, such as when he visited the galleries, he appeared in his other form as the cosmic ordering principle, issuing edicts for the smooth running of the hospital. Richard used on such occasions to refer to the man as COP.

'Harmony and equilibrium is what we must strive for,' said the COP one day, standing over the easel while Richard worked.

Under the warm glow of this encouragement, Richard felt compositions flow from his finger tips. He painted as never before, aspiring to heights of which he had not believed himself capable. He became the true slave of art. Having nothing to lose, he could risk all. It was at this time, he told me, that he began to put on weight, for he ate prodigiously out of fear that his soul might otherwise go hungry, and his inspiration fail.

Reader, I was at a loss how to understand him. It took many years of enquiry before I came anywhere near to seeing what he meant and by then he was dead and I could not share my discoveries with him. But we passed a pleasant hour together, two old people reminiscing in the autumn sunshine, until at last the supper bell recalled us to our present surroundings.

Then Richard and Mr Smith accompanied me to the main gate, not through those dismal corridors, but around the outside of the building, where we took our leave in the manner of old friends parting at a railway station. Richard begged me to call again the next day, but out of a strange perversity I did not. Had our hour together passed less companionably and pleasantly, I might have been tempted to return in the hope of some more fruitful contact. As it was, we parted the best of friends, and I feared that to attempt another meeting might have been to tempt Fate to introduce some element of discord into our reunion. It was sweeter by far to me to part on this happy note of regret.

It was only during the long journey back to Devon and over the subsequent years that a sense of dissatisfaction about our meeting gradually took hold of me. I was reminded again of my childhood visits to the Dadd family, where every day passed in a haze of pleasantries and brilliant theorizing which ultimately denied the expression of true feeling. And there grew in my mind the suspicion that he had once more been evading me. I had been hypnotised by his wayward philosophy while he had once again denied me that personal response which I so earnestly desired. I was forced back again on to my recollections of his 'Columbine'. It is the only picture of his that I remember seeing, in which he portrays any emotion. It depicts a young girl wreathed in flowers and ribbons and is painted with an inexpressible delicacy of longing and tenderness. Here at last was not me as I saw myself, but me as I might have wished to be seen by him; – and yet such knowledge brings only a bleak satisfaction.

Did I ever tell you that on a rare visit to London in the company of my husband, to celebrate the christening of Robert and Catherine's fifth child, I discovered the picture in a shop window quite by chance. I returned there later with my husband, hoping that he would have been sufficiently impressed to purchase it.

'Come,' I said, 'I have found something that will interest you.'

240

He took my arm and trailed along as mildly as was his wont, and after some few minutes' walk, we stood before the little water-colour. He observed it at length, both from a distance and close up, turning his spectacles round and using them like a spy glass for he was increasingly troubled by long sight. At length he remarked, 'Quite pretty.'

'It is by Richard,' I pointed out. 'He calls it "Columbine".'

'Oh,' was his only comment before turning away. I did not point out that the subject was myself, for I was struck then by a terrible sense of guilt. If my own husband failed to recognise me, it was because I had never shown him that same look. I did not suggest, as I had planned, that we should enter to inquire the price. I did not want the evidence of my own wifely shortcomings eternally before my eyes.

So after a final, regretful look at the picture, I hurried after my husband, and with my arm tucked securely through his, we returned to our lodgings.

Chapter Ten

ODAY, my birthday, sees also the christening of my first great-grandchild — my daughter's daughter's daughter. I begin to feel quite like our own dear Queen, with an apparently endless line of progeny to my name. My great-granddaughter will wear the same dress and bonnet made by my grandmother in which Catherine and I were christened, and which yesterday, newly bleached and gleaming in a fitful sunshine, graced my washing line. It now lies over the back of J.'s empty chair on the other side of the fireplace. The maid ironed it for me, since my sight and fingers are no longer to be trusted with such fine ribbons and frills, gophers and gathers. I was surprised that the old-fashioned garment was requested at all, since my granddaughter, the infant's mother, is such a thoroughly modern young person, but she assures me that the antique is all the rage.

The antique! Even the terminology conspires to make of this fragile dress something from history, something dead. Yet though my grandmother stitched this particular garment some years before my birth, I can remember her well into this century, bent over her lacemaking with those countless bobbins and spindles flying this way and that with dizzying speed and accuracy. Nowadays, machinery achieves within minutes more yards of lace than she created over a lifetime. Yet, that memory of her stooped over the cushion lends to those few lengths of intricate design more value than a year's output of all the Nottingham factories combined. That lace lives in my mind.

Now, even more than ten years ago, do the memories of my childhood seem consigned to the dust of oblivion. My grandchildren question me and laugh over little incidents which are no more to them than the stories in some ancient chronicle. I almost feel myself to be ready for consignment to the glass show-case of a museum, – dried, stuffed and labelled like a fossil, and of no more than scientific interest to the rest of humanity.

I have, you see, become something of a connoisseur of museums and antiquities, since I returned from having seen Richard with the firm resolve that I would at least try to understand something of what he had been saying to me. For someone not blessed with a scholarly education, the task which I now set myself was heavy indeed. I spurned my usual reading in favour of weightier fare. Nor was my new-found appetite to be slaked by all that the public library in our neighbouring town had to offer. The subject of Egypt, which had so seduced Richard, now gripped my heart with equal passion. Books had to be ordered from far afield to gratify my curiosity. Some of these tomes were so large and weighty that an assistant would be obliged to follow me right to my carriage door, and to hand them in after me.

'Another book on Egypt?' the librarian would say to me with a scornful stare. 'But you have read so many already.'

'Yes, if you please,' I answered with a humility which veiled my determination not to gratify his curiosity.

'Planning to travel, are you, Mrs L.?' he continued, eyeing the brace of walking sticks which were now my constant companions with a look that comprised both sarcasm and humour.

'Travel does indeed broaden the mind,' I remarked sweetly.

He acknowledged my remark with a nod and a superior little smile.

'It wants only sufficient imagination to make those same excursions without leaving the comfort of one's own fireside,' said I, and while he was searching for a suitable reply, I turned and hobbled painfully towards the door.

No amount of scorn, no amount of teasing, could deflect me from my goal. I read and made copious notes, for my memory was become much impaired with age. Where I could not comprehend, I did not hesitate to seek enlightenment from experts, and my correspondents at the time included archaeologists, historians, theologians and even the Keeper of Antiquities at the British Museum. My temerity was equalled only by my passionate desire to understand. In short, I became something of an expert in the field myself.

Even my family were forced at last to take my exploits seriously when I was invited one day to lecture upon the subject of Egyptian mythology to a local literary institution. I fear that these worthy people did not take kindly to my thesis that this ancient religion which preceded both the Greek and Roman was the fountainhead for many of our Christian beliefs. First Darwin, and now my own little theories displacing both man and Christianity from the centre of the universe! It was too much for a sleepy Devon village, which had been lost for centuries in the narrow maze of winding lanes which afforded no views beyond their own narrow perspective of the sky above.

On this account also, I almost found myself ostracised, and revelled in the experience of being, at long last, an out and out rebel. For one can be a rebel, you know, at rising eighty; indeed, one's views are received with far more tolerance than at the dangerous stage of youth, – a tolerance which can be mortifying when one is treated like a child again, meeting with amused indulgence where one seeks, perhaps, to shock!

I became in much demand as a speaker, something from which I would have shrunk in my younger days. It was now extremely pleasant to find my views sought on a whole host of matters, and my outspokenness on such subjects as Votes for Women were greeted with rapture by my granddaughters. However, none of this is strictly relevant to the subject of my biography. For initially, my excursion into Egyptology had been intended to throw light on the mystifying process by which Richard had been 'converted', – for this was how he viewed his seduction to the cause of Osiris. It was a stance he maintained to his dying day: I do not think he ever wavered in his faith. I hope not. For that was what gave meaning to his life and sustained him. Through his belief, he transcended the narrow confines of his existence.

I picture him often, – an old man on a wooden bench in the shelter of a red brick wall, his breathing indistinguishable from the humming of the bees among the last of the summer roses. The roses too are worthy of attention. They have absorbed the sunshine until they are quite bloated, until each heavy petal can scarcely support its own weight. The mere brush of a butterfly's wing would reduce all to ruins, to a crumpled heap of yellow or peach or crimson satin releasing an avalanche of fragrance as it falls.

An old person is but a fragile thing, — a cluster of memories about a stem of bone. The merest whisper, a caressing fragrance, the touch of a colour, any of these is sufficient to release the accumulated experiences of a lifetime like the cloud of spores from a puff ball.

So what does he see as he sits there? Surely not the silver trail of a river which meanders through the sun-soaked valley below the hospital, nor yet the gleam of the gentle Medway as it wanders slowly through the rich Kentish valleys echoing with the cries and splashings of children and the rainbow thrash of a captive trout on the end of a line. Does he not see both these and more, that mightier waterway whose silent progression marks the division between life and death? For each river flows into the sea and the seas merge into oceans and the oceans encompass the earth. And all becomes one in the end.

So he waits patiently, just as I do, for the boat in which he will make his final crossing. Life began cushioned by water and so shall it end. There is a pleasing symmetry to the equation.

Having confided in you the extent of my research in the realms of Egyptology, for more information upon this subject I can do no better than to draw to your attention the excellent displays at the newly refurbished British Museum. There, with some exercise of imagination, one can experience the echoing vastness of those temples until the grey London sky falls away and you feel yourself transported to those sunnier climes where you may hear not the awed murmur of other visitors, but the mysterious chants of priests about their daily sacrifice.

Unfortunately, it seems that the main attraction of this exhibition lies not in its spiritual significance but in the profane indulgence of a morbid curiosity. Those desiccated figures in various, and to my mind scandalous, states of exposure were not treated in accordance with the sacred rites of mummification merely to gratify the baser instincts of idle spectators many thousands of years later. They were preserved that the souls of the departed might retain a mortal resting place while they went about their business of earning eternal salvation in the Underworld.

I must here relate to you a strange incident which occurred on my last visit to that charnel house. The year must have been 1890, that of my own dear sister's death, and the breaking of yet another tie with the past. Dear Catherine! How I used to envy her association with that brilliant family! And yet such proximity was not without its burdens. She could not withdraw as I could, when the pressures became too great. Hers was an involvement which admitted of no relief, and she suffered cruelly, – not so much on her own behalf, as on that of her children. That is ever where a mother is most vulnerable, and Catherine was tortured by fears, as she watched over her own little brood, lest that same tainted blood might be fermenting in their tiny veins, and waiting only the appropriate moment to break out. I am happy to report that she went to her grave some years after her spouse, secure in the knowledge that her children and grandchildren, nephews and nieces, had been spared the family curse.

In view of my years and general debility, my daughter and her husband insisted on accompanying me to the metropolis, and it was only with the greatest difficulty that I evaded their vigilance for long enough to pay a quick visit to the Museum. Having completed my tour at speed, for I did not wish to cause my relatives too much concern, I emerged from the main gates to find myself accosted by a beggar, – a sailor with one leg, who swore he had lost the other in the bombardment of Alexandria some eight years before.

Whether he was telling the truth or not I cannot say, but a more worthless old reprobate I never saw, for even at that hour of the morning (it was scarcely eleven o'clock), he was as drunk as a lord. Two things still inclined me in his favour and led me to search out my purse; one, that he was after all a sailor; two, that he had visited Alexandria. It was while I was questioning him upon the latter, about which he seemed singularly ill-informed that, – fearing perhaps that I might depart without leaving him any gratuity at all, – he swatted the parrot upon his shoulder so violently that the poor half-starved creature almost fell. Then, even before it had recovered its balance, he instructed it harshly to 'Show the kind lady your tricks!'

'Damned if I will!' replied the bird, and continued with a string of imprecations that would have driven me away upon the instant, had I not felt it my duty to pause for long enough to remark, 'Shame upon you, sir, for corrupting a poor, innocent bird with your own filth and iniquity.'

The bird was indeed a poor, mangy creature, dull of feather and bleary of eye, in a manner not much different from his master, – one whom it seemed that the first frost (for the sailor vowed that those steps upon which we stood were parlour, kitchen and bedroom to him) would mercifully finish off.

I was struggling with the strings of my reticule, having resolved to return my coins to its safe-keeping and give nothing whatsoever to this unsavoury pair, when the bird suddenly spoke in more intellectual vein. 'Mr Dadd is emphatically the poet among painters,' he said, and for a moment I fancied that his eye gleamed with that same malevolence which I remembered of old.

'Pieces!' I cried, and it seemed to me that the poor thing cocked his head in response. 'Pieces of Eight!'

'Know him?' asked his degraded owner, and he spat in the dust at my feet.

'Certainly I do,' I replied. 'I have known him for half a century,' and I searched in my bag for something to give the starving parrot. I discovered only some stray mint humbugs which he gulped down gratefully, though they made his eyes nearly pop out of his head.

Unfortunately, Pieces had retained none of those graceful manners taught him by his adoring mother, Mrs Jenkins, for I was rewarded by a string of curses which attracted a considerable crowd of onlookers.

'Pieces,' said I sternly, 'I am ashamed of you!'

The old sailor here administered the parrot another hefty clout by way of reproof, so that he toppled to the ground and lay there momentarily stunned.

Reader, how could I leave him in those ungentle hands? Even the crowd which had gathered was thoroughly incensed on the creature's behalf, and I was thus able to purchase him at a price which was considerably less than his value.

My family thought at first that I had become quite senile when I returned home to my nephew's house bearing a bedraggled parrot on my shoulder. However, after a week of warmth and good food and company, Pieces' feathers had quite recovered their sheen, and his manner had become as impertinent as ever I remembered.

We returned to Devon by coach. During the journey I subjected him to the indignity of a cage which I kept covered, for besides a tendency to snap, his language could be distressingly coarse. I am happy to say that he settled down in his new surroundings, though I sometimes wonder whether he does not find the countryside a little dull. To me, he is not only a reminder of happier times but a veritable encyclopaedia of art, and I have learned a lot under his instruction. In return I have been teaching him something of Egyptian mythology. On the whole, he has proved a delightful companion, though he suffers from periods of moroseness during which his manner becomes increasingly solemn until he calls for beer and spirits in language which is quite unrepeatable.

Banishment is the only punishment which he comprehends, and I leave him alone in a darkened room until the fit has burned itself out and he becomes his usual self again. I have recently discussed with him whether he would not like to be preserved after his death; – not, alas, in the manner of the ancients, although such courtesy was extended to the ibis, but according to our own secular procedures of taxidermy.

As for his former master, I arranged for him to be admitted to a home for disabled and retired mariners in south-east London, but he did not remain there for long. In his own inimitable way, he consigned everyone there to the devil and vowed he would be free. If freedom be the freedom to suffer hunger and cold and discomfort, I wish him well of his decision.

I can scarcely imagine the Museum now without his foul-mouthed presence at the gate. It almost obliterates for me the thought of those treasures which lie within. Perhaps that, too, is as it should be: the living should take precedence over the dead, – or should they, if those same spirits still haunt the world, seeking their own salvation?

Richard died on the eighth of January 1886. I received a letter from the Superintendent of the hospital, who knew of no other living relatives. I hope that I did not fail him. I assented to his burial in grave number 337 within the hospital compound, because I did not see how I could do otherwise. Heaven grant that, having completed his purgatory here on earth, his spirit departed in peace. I would not like to think of him nailed to the rack for further millennia of torment.

It is to you, Richard, and to all those other ghosts of my past that I dedicate this, my anniversary, and that of our beloved Queen. Yet no one else will know that to me you will be more present than all those who gather to celebrate both that occasion and my great-granddaughter's christening. I cannot help wondering what will lie in store for this helpless, gurgling little creature that is my descendant. Young people today seem to have their lives entirely planned out. They are quite frighteningly methodical. So strong! I wonder whether anything could ever take this child by surprise. Certainly I can imagine nothing to which her mother would prove unequal.

'How do you like her, Granny?' she asked me when I first made the acquaintance of our newest family member who lay tucked up at her mother's side.

'It's a start, anyway,' I acknowledged somewhat severely, partly to hide my emotion at finding her so well; so alive.

'A start?' she exclaimed indignantly. 'And the finish too!' It seems that there will be no house full of brothers and sisters as was once considered normal. My granddaughter vows that she has her own life to lead and that one child is quite enough. How times have changed! – for this seems to be no idle threat: she has apparently at her disposal the means to carry it out. My generation were by contrast so utterly accepting, so foolishly eager for self-sacrifice.

Reader, I feel as if my whole life has been one long, slow suffocation. When I look back over it, what have I done? I have had a husband, now dead, for whose companionship I was profoundly grateful. I have created a home for my children, who like any fledglings have long ago stretched their wings and left the nest. In due season, I have made jams and jellies, pickles, preserves, chutneys, cakes, pastries and puddings, which have all been devoured and vanished without trace. My whole life will leave less of a mark upon the face of the earth than a ploughman's furrow.

Yet I must count my blessings; – among them, a robust and cheerful disposition which has withstood the ups and downs of daily living. I have participated in the joys of all those little festivals which make up our existence: the weddings and christenings, the birthdays and Christmases, the welcoming of the spring and the gathering of the harvest. I have felt anger at injustice and suffered the thoughtlessness of others. I have endured cruel pain, but never more than I could bear. I have buried child, parents and husband and known the grief of eternal separation.

Why, then, my regrets?

It was the discovery of Maria's letter which prompted these reminiscences, and stirred again the embers of a passion which I had thought to have died. I therefore set myself to write about Richard, hoping to offer a view of his life which was unprejudiced and impartial. I have tried to present the truth, but though I have searched long and hard, I fear that it may have eluded me. I am no better than the rest.

Perhaps I do him an even greater injustice than they did; for, though my motives were different, I see now how I have sought to blame him for all that has happened and has not happened in my life. Perhaps I even sought to make you pity me. Reader, if this has been the result, I beg you to put such misplaced sympathy out of your mind once and for all.

Consider again that picture; – Richard's 'Columbine'. When I first saw it a quarter of a century ago, I read in it the story of myself as I might have been. I was at first flattered. I saw no further than the romantic image of a beautiful girl wreathed in flowers. Richard had loved me after all. I could have been his future, – his saviour even. But if I could have been his saviour, then a certain guilt was mine – by default perhaps, but guilt all the same, that I had taken no active part to help him. I had let myself be swept away on the flood-tide of life like a mere piece of driftwood, inert and lifeless.

Look again more closely! What are those purple flowers twined so enchantingly through her hair? Reader, they are the fragile blooms of convolvulus, those limpid exotics which draw the eye like some will-o'-the-wisp. 'Morning Glory' is their common name. It is most apt. They enjoy but a brief allure before they wither, and even that is only in response to the call of the sunlight. Richard, you were the sunlight that evoked such a transient flowering of ecstasy within my breast. That call was both too little and too much, – too little to satisfy but sufficient to awake a tumult of emotions that would never lie quiet again!

For twenty years and more, the image of myself, wreathed in those short-lived flowers, has obsessed me. Day and night, I have racked my brains to pinpoint the exact moment of that awakening. Could I have lived through it unaware of what was happening to me? The time, the place, must surely be imprinted on my mind if only I could find the page.

But though my memory of those distant years is otherwise excellent, this occasion escapes me. I have never posed in such wanton disguise, never given such a look to any man. Finally the answer has come to me. Whether or not such intercourse occurred was irrelevant. The truth was that those sensations were real for both of us; they were real.

But even then, the matter is not so easily settled; there was more – the strange twinings are not those of flowers alone. The symbolism has defied the critics for years, as has the identity of the central figure. It is fishing tackle with which the maiden's hair is so generously laced; hooks, lines and lead weights instead of ribbons and bows. For all these years I have pushed the unwelcome images to the back of my mind, preferring instead to dwell upon the brief radiance of the flowers.

I shall be ever grateful for the tenderness and accuracy with which he recalled my features. The emotion which elicited such a response remains with me like a warm glow within the darkness of my soul. But he saw clearly then what I am only now beginning to grasp, that I was the snare that would have lured him away from that independence of mind which was so necessary to his whole existence.

Reader, he misjudged my powers! It almost makes me laugh

251

to think of it. For while he had the strength to avoid that brief, exotic passion, I, in my weakness and dependancy, have suffered in its hold for nigh on seventy years. Ah Richard! How should I then have painted you, if it had been my skill to do so? Would I have shown you like Hephaestus, beating out the red hot links with ringing hammer blows and then plunging them through clouds of steam into a trough of water?

That would be unjust. You would never knowingly have chained another to you. See rather my own self in a coarse canvas apron working blindly amid the noise and the steam to forge those fetters with which to bind myself in the hopeless slavery which has been my life. For right or wrong, you trusted your imagination and followed it where it led. I lacked the courage to make such a choice. I held out my wrists and let them bind me. I have only myself to blame.

What comfort is left to me now? Can I say to them when they come to collect me for the christening, 'No more! Let me go at last!' And where could I go, now, frail as I am? Yet for the sake of my soul, I must be free even now. Let me not fade and dwindle by my own fireside! Take me rather to the topmost tor and set me down on its granite peaks, and there let me lie and see the stars revolve above my head, millions upon millions receding into infinity. Leave me there until my bones are picked clean and the frost sparkles in the sockets of my eyes and the wind sings in my rib cage. Only do not bury me; I have been buried for too long.

Nor do I seek heaven. No restful ease for me! I could not face an eternity of that. Let such a reward be for those who have suffered here on earth. Let Richard enjoy his Elysian fields, – God knows, he has earned them. I have earned nothing – not even my own self-respect. Therefore grant me merciful oblivion. Let me be one with the rocks and the stars and hear at last within my empty skull the music of the spheres.

But Reader, I am weak. I know that I shall say nothing. I shall go to the christening and afterwards take a glass of wine and eat a piece of cake and smile and nod and receive compliments on a longevity which is burdensome to me. And afterwards I shall return to my own fireside and Pieces' company to enjoy the reality of my dreams. That is all that is left to me. It is all that I ever had.

Forgive me, I digress. I ramble through the perilous landscape of the mind giving evidence of nothing more than my own frailty. For this was Richard's story, and not mine. My life would fill but a fraction of these pages; — and be of little interest.

E. L.   Devon. 1897.